Classics in Lesbian Studies

Classics
in Lesbian Studies

Esther D. Rothblum, PhD
Editor

Classics in Lesbian Studies, edited by Esther D. Rothblum, was simultaneously issued by The Haworth Press, Inc., under the same title, as a special issue of *Journal of Lesbian Studies.* Volume 1, Numbers 1 and 2 1997.

Routledge
Taylor & Francis Group
New York   London

ISBN 1-56023-093-2

First published by
The Haworth Press, Inc., 10 Alice Street, Binghamton, NY 13904-1580 USA

This edition published 2013 by Routledge
711 Third Avenue, New York, NY 10017
2 Park Square, Milton Park, Abingdon, Oxon OX14 4RN

Routledge is an imprint of the Taylor & Francis Group, an informa business

Classics in Lesbian Studies has also been published as *Journal of Lesbian Studies*, Volume 1, Numbers 1 and 2 1997.

The development, preparation, and publication of this work has been undertaken with great care. However, the publisher, employees, editors, and agents of The Haworth Press and all imprints of The Haworth Press, Inc., including The Haworth Medical Press and Pharmaceutical Products Press, are not responsible for any errors contained herein or for consequences that may ensue from use of materials or information contained in this work. Opinions expressed by the author(s) are not necessarily those of The Haworth Press, Inc.

Library of Congress Cataloging-in-Publication Data

Classics in lesbian studies / Esther D. Rothblum, editor.
    p. cm.
    "Also published as 'Journal of lesbian studies,' vol. 1, numbers 1 and 2, 1997"–verso t.p.
    Includes bibliographical references.
    ISBN 0-7890-0014-8 (THP : alk. paper).–ISBN 1-56023-093-2 (HPP : alk. paper)
    1. Lesbianism. 2. Lesbians. 3. Gay and lesbian studies. I. Rothblum, Esther D. II. Journal of lesbian studies.
HQ75.5.C53 1996
306.76'63–dc20
                                                      96-38180
                                                       CIP

CONTENTS

HISTORY AND LITERATURE

PHYSICAL AND SOCIAL SCIENCES

BACK TO POLITICS

ABOUT THE EDITOR

Esther D. Rothblum, PhD, is Professor in the Department of Psychology at the University of Vermont. Her research and writing have focused on lesbian mental health, and she is former Chair of the Committee on Lesbian and Gay Concerns of the American Psychological Association. She received the Distinguished Scientific Contribution Award from the Society for the Psychological Study of Lesbian and Gay Issues in 1991. Dr. Rothblum has edited 20 books, including *Lesbian Friendships* (New York University Press, 1996), *Boston Marriages: Romantic but Asexual Relationships Among Contemporary Lesbians* (University of Massachusetts Press, 1993), and *Loving Boldly: Issues Facing Lesbians* (The Haworth Press, Inc., 1989).

Introduction:
What Are "Classics" in Lesbian Studies?

Esther D. Rothblum

On June 21, 1993, the cover story of *Newsweek* was entitled "Lesbians: Coming out strong; what are the limits of tolerance?" and depicted two young, white lesbians embracing. The first paragraph stated:

> "Two, four, six, eight, how do you know your grandma's straight?" the women chanted, many thousands strong, on the eve of the recent gay- and lesbian-rights march in Washington. There were, in fact, lots of grandmotherly types proceeding down Connecticut Avenue that spring evening, along with bare-breasted teenagers in overalls, aging baby boomers in Birkenstocks and bald biker dykes in from the Coast. Advertising execs strode arm in arm with electricians, architects with politicians. As onlookers pondered the stereotype-defying scene, the demonstrators reveled in their sheer numbers. It was, for once, an unabashed display of lesbian clout.

As the twentieth century nears its end, lesbians are coming out in increasing numbers. Over 40% of the U.S. population reports having a gay/lesbian friend or acquaintance–almost double that of a few years ago (Rothblum, Mintz, Cowan & Haller, 1995). By the mid-1980s, over two-thirds of the lesbians in the National Lesbian Health Care Survey lived in a community that had lesbian support groups, lesbian cultural events, lesbian sports teams, lesbian therapists, a lesbian bar, lesbian or gay religious groups, and a lesbian or feminist bookstore (Bradford, Ryan & Rothblum,

[Haworth co-indexing entry note]: "Introduction: What Are 'Classics' in Lesbian Studies?" Rothblum, Esther D. Co-published simultaneously in *Journal of Lesbian Studies* (The Haworth Press, Inc.) Vol. 1, No. 1, 1997, pp. 1-7; and: *Classics in Lesbian Studies* (ed: Esther D. Rothblum) The Haworth Press, Inc., 1997, pp. 1-7; and: *Classics in Lesbian Studies* (ed: Esther D. Rothblum) Harrington Park Press, an imprint of The Haworth Press, Inc., 1997, pp. 1-7. Single or multiple copies of this article are available from The Haworth Document Delivery Service [1-800-342-9678, 9:00 a.m. - 5:00 p.m. (EST). E-mail address: getinfo@ haworth.com].

1994). Only 18% of lesbians lived in communities where there were no lesbian activities, but 50% of these lesbians lived within 50 miles and 22% lived within 100 miles of communities with lesbian activities. And these communities are increasingly diverse demographically. There are organizations, religious groups, and newsletters for lesbians with disabilities; for African-American, Latina, Asian-American, and Native American lesbians; for lesbian teens and old lesbians; for fat lesbians; for lesbian athletes. On the other hand, lesbians who live in rural, politically conservative, or traditionally religious areas may be isolated and closeted.

Where once lesbian scholarship was combined with scholarship about gay men (and, increasingly, with bisexual and transgender women and men), the focus here is on lesbians. At a time when the term "queer" is used to combine individuals of minority sexual orientations, my interest is on women who identify as lesbians. In journals, books, and gay studies programs at universities, lesbians are still in the minority; the purpose here is to highlight the lesbian experience.

I asked leading lesbian scholars to suggest articles and book chapters that they considered to be "classics," and was flooded with suggestions. Some of the "classics" have been reprinted so often–like Adrienne Rich's "Compulsory Heterosexuality and Lesbian Existence" and Carroll Smith-Rosenberg's "The Female World of Love and Ritual"–that I decided to leave them out. By the late 1990s there is a considerable scholarship about lesbians across academic disciplines, and I wanted to organize this volume by discipline. The pieces that follow are in four categories: (1) identity, (2) history and literature, (3) physical and social sciences, and (4) back to lesbian politics. Most lesbian scholars today are affected by their own discipline and this is reflected in the scholarship that follows. Theory and methods of lesbian literature, for example, are quite different from lesbian psychology.

As I began preparing this collection, the editor of a queer theory journal asked me quite seriously whether there was a future for lesbian studies. I decided to begin this volume with a poem by Paula Gunn Allen. A Native American poet, she compares lesbians to Indians:

> ". . . like Indians dykes
> are supposed to die out
> or forget . . .
> or go away
> to nowhere . . ."

The purpose of this edition is to ensure that lesbian scholarship increases rather than fades away, so that theory, research, and new writing about lesbianism continues while "classic" pieces are reprinted and not forgotten by the new generation of lesbian students and scholars.

Identity. What does it mean to be a lesbian? In the first article, Gloria Wekker describes two ways in which Black women in the Diaspora have constructed and named their sexual and romantic feelings for other women. One group has sexual relationships with women while maintaining relationships with men. This group has a more Afrocentric and working class identity, and typically does not identify with the term "lesbian." The second group more often uses the term "Black lesbians" and comes from a middle class background. To illustrate the differences between these expressions of erotic and sexual relationships among women, Gloria Wekker provides excerpts from interviews with two eminent Black poets, Audre Lorde and Astrid Roemer.

How do we become lesbians? Most lesbians have a coming out story, and several books of coming out stories have been published. Several theories have been developed to describe stages in the coming out process, but more recently these "stage theories" have been criticized as too simplistic. Paula Rust is one of the leading theorists in the field of identity development, and has surveyed hundreds of lesbians and bisexual women about the factors that led to their identity. She describes lesbian and bisexual identity formation in a changing social environment, and presents a flow-chart of identity changes. Not surprisingly, she has found that many women switch back and forth in their sexual identity, feel ambivalence at various times, and live in environments that themselves redefine sexual identity.

Regardless of self-identity, lesbians learn to function in two cultures: the lesbian community and the heterosexual macrosociety. In contrast to members of ethnic minority groups, who first become acculturated within their own group and then later are socialized (by schools, the media, the church) within the dominant culture, lesbians and gay men are first socialized by the dominant culture and later identify with the minority culture. Joyce Albro and Carol Tully surveyed lesbians about the ways in which they negotiate both cultures and function within both the micro- and macro-culture.

In contrast to lesbians who come out in early, middle, or late adulthood, lesbian adolescents rarely have access to the lesbian and gay communities, since most communities are adult-oriented. In past decades, lesbian community groups and publications limited membership to those over age 18 or 21, to avoid charges of seducing minors. This deprived adolescent lesbians of resources and contacts. Margaret Schneider explores the experiences of lesbian adolescents. Based on interviews with Canadian lesbians, she describes identity formation from a developmental perspective–"coming out and growing up."

Lesbian aging has been virtually ignored. Lesbians in surveys tend to be young, and lesbians who are currently old or even middle-aged have lived through oppressive times when it was important to be closeted in order to keep their jobs, custody of their children, and relations with friends and family. Mary Riege Laner compared the experience of growing older between lesbians and heterosexual women. She used an intriguing methodology–that of studying the content of "personal ads" placed in newspapers for their description of age and age-related attributes.

There has been little research attention paid to the lesbian in prison. Yet there is a common stereotype that the experience of being in an all-female environment will "cause" women to become lesbians. Alice Propper administered questionnaires to nearly 500 adolescent inmates of four all-female and three coeducational correctional institutions in the U.S. There were no differences between the all-female and coeducational prisons in rates of sexual and romantic activities with other women. Adolescent females who engaged in sex or passionate kissing, or who described themselves as "going with or being married" to another adolescent female, tended to have been lesbian before imprisonment.

Most lesbian scholarship has virtually ignored ethnic minority women who are lesbians. Judy Grahn (1986) has written about the eradication of the history of lesbianism in Native American tribes. She states (page 43): "Out of 99 tribes who kept written records, 88 made reference to homosexuality, with 20 including specific references to lesbianism. The latter references are more remarkable considering how little information has been recorded about anything concerning women." Nevertheless, her research found that the tribes that were exposed early to white Christian culture were most likely to deny evidence of homosexuality. Thus, ethnic minority groups may not be aware of lesbians and gays in the history of their own culture.

Beverly Greene has referred to lesbians of color as being exposed to a "triple jeopardy"–being female, lesbian, and members of ethnic minority groups. In her article, she describes African American lesbians, Native American lesbians, Asian American lesbians, Indian and South Asian American lesbians, and Latina lesbians as distinct populations.

History and literature. In a recent book about lesbian fiction in the nineteenth century, Susan Koppelman (1994) stated, "With the publication of *Surpassing the Love of Men: Romantic Friendship and Love between women from the Renaissance to the Present* (1977), Lillian Faderman established as a fact that women loving each other has a history and a culture" (p. 9). Lillian Faderman is a leading scholar of women's friendships and romantic relationships in the past and present century. Included in this volume is her piece entitled "Who hid lesbian history?" She describes how lesbians are invisible because writers had to omit or disguise accounts of women loving women. When the lover relationship is obvious, biographers have avoided or distorted such accounts, or reassured the reader that the author must have really loved a man. She argues that women's lives in past eras need to be reexamined and reinterpreted in light of lesbian-feminist scholarship.

Leila Rupp has critiqued the tendency of historians to assume that women couldn't have been sexual in past centuries or, conversely, of lesbians to assume that all women who loved women in the past must have been genitally sexual. She argues that we cannot use simple categorizations for the complexity of women's relationships, but instead need to specify in detail the nature of the relationship between women and how they described it.

Lesbianism has been linked with deviancy so pervasively, argues Catharine Stimpson, that lesbians are either depicted as tormented souls or, more recently in fiction by heterosexual writers, represent "a sexual interlude or caper." Few, if any, texts have "zero degree deviancy," and that is the title and purpose of her article.

Sarah Hoagland has conceptualized a scholarship of lesbian ethics. In traditional phallocentric ethics, she writes, those who are considered virtuous are subservient and obedient. Lesbians question social norms and women's oppression, and her article describes lesbian ethics and female creation.

Physical and social sciences. For decades, lesbians were looked at, mostly by heterosexual male scientists and social scientists, and the focus was on pathologizing an already stigmatized group. Even today, scholars in the physical sciences wonder what science has to do with lesbian studies. The lead article in this section is by H. Patricia Hynes, who in 1979 submitted an article to a lesbian feminist newsletter describing the formation of a group of lesbians in science. Her article describes how women study science and how lesbians can discuss the ideas that first "fired our mental passion."

The social sciences fared no better in their stigmatization of lesbians, often limiting their sample to lesbians in prison or in therapy, when studies of heterosexual women were not focused exclusively on these groups. Several years ago, a prominent U.S. university was promised an endowed chair in lesbian and gay studies. The donor stipulated that the recipient of this endowment should not be from the discipline of psychology, because of the very recent past of the role of psychology in pathologizing homosexuality.

In the mid-1980s, Judith Bradford and Caitlin Ryan conducted the largest survey of lesbian health and mental health. At a time when most studies of lesbians based their results on a few dozen women, this survey included 1,925 lesbians. Entitled the National Lesbian Health Care Survey, it yielded data on level of outness and participation in lesbian community events, as well as on depression, anxiety, suicide, physical and sexual abuse, anti-lesbian discrimination, substance abuse, eating disorders, and use of counseling.

There is a common stereotype that women become lesbians as the result of negative experiences with men. JoAnn Brannock and Beata Chapman examined the validity of this stereotype by surveying lesbians and heterosexual women about traumatic experiences with men. The results showed no differences between traumatic experiences of lesbians and heterosexual women, negating this stereotype.

In the 1960s and 1970s, lesbians were reluctant to use counseling and psychotherapy services. Mental health professionals viewed "homosexuality" as a mental illness and lesbians were sometimes subjected to "reorientation therapy" to become heterosexual. By the 1980s, most communities had lesbian or lesbian-affirmative therapists, and, interestingly, lesbians began to seek therapy in higher numbers than did heterosexual women. Rachel Perkins has criticized this phenomenon, arguing that psychological terminology has replaced political activism in the lives of lesbians.

Back to politics. Lesbian activists who first wrote and spoke out about lesbian politics have argued that the lesbian experience is increasingly de-politicized. This collection ends with Janice Raymond's piece "Putting the politics back into lesbianism." As her article states:

> We used to talk a lot about lesbianism as a political movement–back in the old days when lesbianism and feminism went together, and one heard the phrase, lesbian feminism. Today, we hear more about lesbian sadomasochism, lesbians having babies, and everything lesbians need to know about sex–what has fashionably come to be called the "politics of desire." In this article, I want to talk about *lesbianism as a political movement,* but before doing that it is necessary to address *lesbianism as a lifestyle*–what has for many come to be a sexual preference without a feminist politics.

As the field of lesbian scholarship becomes part of the mainstream academy and scholars are sought out for jobs *because* they are lesbian, it is vital that the field of lesbian studies maintains its connections to grassroots activism.

REFERENCES

Bradford, J., Ryan, C., & Rothblum, E.D. (1994). National Lesbian Health Care Survey: Implications for mental health. *Journal of Consulting and Clinical Psychology, 62,* 228-242.

Grahn, J. (1986). Strange country this: Lesbianism and North American Indian tribes. *Journal of Homosexuality, 12,* 43-57.

Koppelman, S. (1994). *Two friends and other nineteenth-century lesbian stories by American women writers.* NY: Penguin Books.

Rich, A. (1980). Compulsory heterosexuality and lesbian existence. *Signs: A Journal of Women in Culture and Society, 5,* 631-660.

Rothblum, E.D., Mintz, B., Cowan, B., & Haller, C. (1995). Lesbian baby boomers at midlife. In K. Jay (Ed.) *Dyke life: From growing up to growing old,* (pp. 61-76). NY: Basic Books.

Smith-Rosenberg, C. (1975). The female world of love and ritual: Relations between women in nineteenth-century America. *Signs: A Journal of Women in Culture and Society, 1,* 1-29.

Some Like Indians Endure

dykes remind me of Indians
like Indians dykes
are supposed to die out
or forget
or drink all the time
or shatter
or go away
to nowhere
to remember
what will happen
if they don't

they don't
anyway
even though it
happens
and they remember
they don't

because the moon remembers
because so does the sun
because so do the stars
remember
and the persistent stubborn
grass
of the earth

Paula Gunn Allen

"Some Like Indians Endure" from *Living the Spirit* (co-ordinated by W. Roscoe) pp. 9-13, St. Martin's Press, 1988. All rights revert to the author upon publication. Reprinted by permission of the author.

[Haworth co-indexing entry note]: "Some Like Indians Endure." Allen, Paula Gunn. Co-published simultaneously in *Journal of Lesbian Studies* (The Haworth Press, Inc.) Vol. 1, No. 1, 1997, p. 9; and: *Classics in Lesbian Studies* (ed: Esther D. Rothblum) The Haworth Press, Inc., 1997, p. 9; and: *Classics in Lesbian Studies* (ed: Esther D. Rothblum) Harrington Park Press, an imprint of The Haworth Press, Inc., 1997, p. 9.

IDENTITY

Mati-ism and Black Lesbianism: Two Idealtypical Expressions of Female Homosexuality in Black Communities of the Diaspora

Gloria Wekker, PhD

SUMMARY. There are different ways in which black women in the Diaspora have given expression to their erotic fascination with other women. In this article two idealtypical expressions of black female homosexuality and the outlines of their underlying cosmologies are sketched: *mati-ism* and *black lesbianism.* Mati (or matisma) is the Sranan Tongo word for women who have sexual relations with other women, but who typically also will have had or still have relationships with men, simultaneously. More often than not they will also have children.

While both types can only be understood via a constructionist view of homosexuality, the institution of *mati-ism* will be shown to

Gloria Wekker, *Journal of Homosexuality*, Volume 24, Numbers 3/4. © 1993 by The Haworth Press, Inc.

[Haworth co-indexing entry note]: "Mati-ism and Black Lesbianism: Two Idealtypical Expressions of Female Homosexuality in Black Communities of the Diaspora." Wekker, Gloria. Co-published simultaneously in *Journal of Lesbian Studies* (The Haworth Press, Inc.) Vol. 1, No. 1, 1997, pp. 11-24; and: *Classics in Lesbian Studies* (ed: Esther D. Rothblum) The Haworth Press, Inc., 1997, pp. 11-24; and: *Classics in Lesbian Studies* (ed: Esther D. Rothblum) Harrington Park Press, an imprint of The Haworth Press, Inc., 1997, pp. 11-24. Single or multiple copies of this article are available from The Haworth Document Delivery Service [1-800-342-9678, 9:00 a.m. - 5:00 p.m. (EST). E-mail address: getinfo@haworth.com].

have retained more Afrocentric, working class elements, while black lesbianism has more middle class, Eurocentric features. *[Article copies available from The Haworth Document Delivery Service: 1-800-342-9678. E-mail address: getinfo@haworth.com]*

INTRODUCTION

In this article I want to focus on the experience of black women and the ways their erotic interest in those of their own gender have taken shape. I shall begin by giving a resume of the historical and social factors which enable us to think of the black female experience in the Diaspora as a unitary, though multifaceted, process. I shall then indicate that ideas about female homosexuality in black communities in the Diaspora are anything but uniform. By presenting a large excerpt from a public discussion with two black women poets, I hope to elucidate the contours of two idealtypical cosmologies as far as female homosexuality is concerned. I am assuming that their views are representative of those held by larger groups of women in black communities in the USA, Suriname and the Netherlands. These cosmologies may be indicated as *mati-ism* and *black lesbianism.*[1] My argument will make clear that both types can only be understood via a constructionist view of homosexuality.

YOU ARE THE OFFSPRING OF SLAVES

Black women of the Diaspora share a terrible history involving the slave trade based on Africa, a history of being transported like cattle across the Atlantic Ocean, of rootlessness in the "New" World, of centuries of living under a system of slavery, of various degrees of retention in their communities of African elements and after Abolition (Suriname 1863; USA 1865) of living in sexist and racist societies, based on class.[2]

Originating from West Africa, an area which stretches from Senegal to Angola and extending far into the interior, the slaves belonged to various tribes with hundreds of different languages and dialects, different systems of family relationships and many habits and customs. For centuries, slaves of both sexes in the Americas were forbidden to learn how to read and write and hardly had opportunities to develop their creative and artistic gifts. The list of prohibitions to which they were subjected was extensive: no marriages were permitted without the consent of their masters nor other relations among themselves, no control over children born to such relationships–the children were the property of the mother's owner, no right to own property or to wear shoes, and no protection against cruel and unreasonable treatment by the master-class.

For both the North American and the Surinamese slaves, one of the things which enabled them to maintain themselves in the new environment was their African culture, which they endeavored to keep intact in the given circumstances and which, in the unspeakable misery of their existence, gave them a sense of having something to which they belonged and which afforded them some foothold. In the days of slavery and later on, the role women played in preserving, communicating and developing elements of African culture was of inestimable importance. Recent scholarship indicates that the principal residue of the African cultural heritage in the Diaspora should be explored in the realm of social values and orientations to reality rather than in more or less concrete sociocultural forms (Mintz and Price 1976).

Important differences between the history of black women in the USA and that of black women in Suriname can be pointed to. Some of these differences had their effect on the degree to which retentions–especially orientations to reality–were able to continue almost unharmed. One of these differences concerns the ratio of blacks to whites that existed during a great part of the 18th and 19th centuries in the (former) British and Dutch colonies. In North America there was always a considerable numerical preponderance of whites over blacks. The ratio in 1780 was, for example, 15 to 1 (Price 1976). On the estates of the Surinamese colony, on the other hand, a handful of whites endeavored to exert control over an immense number of slaves. The ratio there ranged from 1 to 25 in the urban area, to 1 to 65 in the plantation districts further removed from the capitol (van Lier 1949).

It was partly due to this numerical relationship that a different cultural policy towards the slaves took shape in the two colonies. The British colonists succeeded in forbidding their slaves to speak their original African languages. As a result, black English with a grammar, a syntax and a lexicon of its own developed. In Suriname, on the other hand, slaves were left free to develop their own tongue, a creole called Negro English (now Sranan Tongo), for centuries. They were also allowed to elaborate and work out their own cultures. Government policy in the colony until Abolition and after, until 1876, was aimed at creating as wide as possible a geographical, cultural and psychological gap between the colonists and the slaves. The ban on speaking Dutch was only one of an endless series of ordinances designed with this view in end.

Generally speaking, the Surinamese slaves had more freedom than their

North American partners in misfortune and for a longer period of time they were able to cultivate their languages and their ways of life and thought, as long as these did not conflict with the interests of the planter class. That the African constituent in the Surinamese orientation to reality must have been considerable for many centuries is emphasized by the fact that the importation of so-called "saltwater negroes" (i.e., slaves newly transported from Africa) was a continuing necessity until the official ban on the slave trade in 1808. In contrast to the situation in North America, where the capacity of female slaves to produce children was encouraged and in certain periods even subjected to coercion, the Surinamese planters preferred to force as much labor from the slaves as possible in the space of a few years. The maltreatment, undernourishment and murder of slaves repeatedly saw to it that within a few years the entire body of slaves could be "written off." Surinamese female slaves hardly reproduced. Whereas at the end of the U.S. Civil War there were 4 million blacks, the Surinamese census only counted 50,000 ex-slaves at the time of Abolition, while roughly the same number of slaves (350,000 to 400,000) had been imported over the course of the past two and a half centuries (van Lier 1949). The world the slave owners created in Suriname was one which one left as soon as one could, with one's pockets loaded with money.

Despite the differences between North American and Surinamese history, the correspondences are so marked that one can speak of a unitary, though multi-faceted, experience of black women in the Diaspora.

CONSIDERING THE ROOTS, SURINAMESE STYLE

In describing the history of black women in the Diaspora I have made no distinction between the history of black women in general and "lesbian" women in particular. There are various reasons for this. First, black "lesbian" women have for the greater part of the time they have been in the Diaspora been an integral part of their communities; they were subject to the same orders and prohibitions as other women in these communities. Secondly–this is important as regards their position in their own circles– they often had simultaneous relationships with men and had children.

The earliest information about *mati-ism* in Suriname dates from the beginning of this century, 1912, and refers precisely to its being embedded in the culture of the ordinary Creole population. A.J. Schimmelpenninck van den Oye, a high ranking Dutch government official, remarks in a memorandum on the physical condition of the "underprivileged":

Speaking about the physically weak condition of so many young women, in addition another reason should be mentioned. I am referring to the sexual communion between women themselves ("mati play"), which immorality has, as I gather, augmented much in the past decades, and, alas!, penetrated deeply into popular customs.(–). It is not only that young girls and unattached women of various classes make themselves guilty of this, the poorest often going and living together in pairs to reduce the cost of house rent and food for each of them, but women who live with men, and even schoolgirls, do the same, following the example of others. (Ambacht 1912: 98-99)

Somewhat later, in the 1930s, mati culture had taken on such proportions that another reporter, Th. Comvalius, expressed his disturbance about:

the unusual relationships among women in Suriname, which were not dependent on social rank, intellectual development, race or country of origin. Love(?) brought women and young girls of very different walks of life together as intimate friends.(–)While this in itself(–)could be called a "sociological misconception," there is another, dark side to it, the discussion of which is no concern of ours. Probably it was blown over here from the French West Indies. (Comvalius n.d.: 11)

With hindsight, it is possible to state that the institution of mati relationships did not just fall down out of the blue sky. Linguistically, two explanations for the word "mati" are offered: one would trace it to old Dutch "maatje," meaning buddy, mate; the other one is more convincing and links it to Hausa "mata" or "mace": woman, wife. It is now known that in a number of West African regions from which slaves were taken, for example, Ashanti and Dahomey, that female homosexuality occurred in times long past and that it was not burdened with negative sanctions prohibiting it. The anthropologists Herskovits reported that in Dahomey a woman could formally marry another woman and that offspring born to the one woman were regarded as the children of the other woman (Herskovits, M. and F. Herskovits 1938/I). The women slaves who were carried off to the "New" World were therefore familiar with the phenomenon. Elsewhere it is stated about the Saramaka Maroons, the descendants of the runaway slaves who formed viable societies in the rainforests of Suriname from the 17th century on, that in Saramaka society:

Mati is a highly charged volitional relationship, usually between two men, that dates back to the Middle Passage—matis were originally "shipmates," those who had survived the journey out from Africa together; (–)*Sibi* is a relationship of special friendship between two women. As with the mati relationship, the reciprocal term of address derives from the Middle Passage itself: sibi referred to shipmates, those who had experienced the trauma of enslavement and transport together. (Price, R. and S. Price 1991: 396, 407)

The word "sibi" does not occur with this meaning in Sranan Tongo, the coastal creole; here the term "mati" covers all modalities. It may very well be that, encapsulated in Sranan Tongo "mati," there may at one time also have been the notion of shipmates who had survived together, but at present that connotation is not there anymore.

Features of mati culture that are mentioned in older sources, have been preserved to this day. There were, for example, female couples who wore "parweri": the same dress, women who embroidered handkerchiefs with loving texts in silk for each other: "lobi kon" (love has come) and "lobi n'e prati" (love does not go away), women who courted each other by means of special ways of folding and wearing their *anyisa,* headcloths, and finally the widespread institution of "lobi singi" (love songs). In these songs women sing the praises of their mati, in metaphorical language, and enlarge the faults of their rivals (Comvalius n.d.; Herskovits 1936). One such text is sung as follows:

Roos e flauw	The rose is weak
A de fadon	It has fallen down
Roos e flauw	The rose is weak
A de fadon	It has fallen down
Ma stanvaste	But "steadfast"[3]
Dat e tan sidon	That stays upright.

Mati relationships in 1990 are a very visible feature of Afro-Surinamese working class culture. Spokespersons speak of "one big family," where everyone knows each other and older women clearly predominate. But women and men of younger age-groups also are present. Many female couples have a marked role division, where one partner will play a "male" role, and the other a "female" role. It is, furthermore, important to note that a mati career, for most women, is not a unidirectional path: thus it is very possible that a woman takes a man for a lover, after having had several relationships with women. It also is not unusual for a woman to have a female and a male lover at the same time. Nor does mati life necessarily imply restriction to one partner. As one 35 year old informant told me:

> I never have just one lover, at the same time. I have my "tru visiti" ("steady girlfriend") and then two or three other lovers. If my "steady" is a Creole woman, I take care that the others are of different ethnic origin or just over here on vacation from Holland, because Creoles aren't likely to take this arrangement easily. I handpick my lovers, I don't take just anybody. Because it takes a lot of time to find a "Ms. Right," I can't afford to begin looking, after me and my steady have broken up. So I keep them in reserve.[4]

AN AFRO-AMERICAN ANGLE

The literature of black North American women writers, which began to appear in a rich variety of forms from the beginning of the 1970s, makes it clear that the societies they describe would have been unthinkable failing the strong ties of love and eroticism among women. The literature also reveals a certain tolerance of homosexuality in the working classes, as long as it does not bear a name, and this corresponds with the situation in Suriname. I want to illustrate this by a single fragment from the bio-mythographical novel *Zami, A New Spelling Of My Name* by Audre Lorde. In this fragment the North American black communities of the 1950s are discussed and Lorde describes the attitude of Cora, a factory worker and mother of Zami's first woman lover, Ginger:

> With her typical aplomb, Cora welcomed my increased presence around the house with the rough familiarity and browbeating humor due another one of her daughters. If she recognized the sounds emanating from the sunporch on the nights I slept over, or our haggard eyes the next day, she ignored them. But she made it very clear that she expected Ginger to get married again. "Friends are nice, but marriage is marriage," she said to me one night as she helped me make a skirt on her machine. . . . "And when she gets home don't be thumping that bed all night, neither, because it's late already and you girls have work tomorrow." (Lorde 1982: 142)

LESBIANISM, SAY WHAT?

In addition to the established custom of women having relationships with other women and the degree of tolerance for this in black communities, there is another reason for my choosing not to make a sharp distinction between the history of black women in general and "lesbian" women in particular. There are strong indications that the western categories of "homo," "bi," and "hetero" have insufficient justification in some black situations. The concept of "homosexuality" introduces an etic category that is alien to the indigenous, emic system which exists in some sections of black communities.

Sexuality cannot be considered independently from the social order in which it exists. Ross and Rapp state rightly that the biological basis of sexuality is always experienced and interpreted according to cultural values. The simple biological facts of sexuality are not self-explanatory, they require social expression. The image they employ for the universal rootedness of sexuality in larger social units such as family relationships, communities, national and world systems, is that of the union. One may have the illusion that by peeling off one layer after another one comes nearer to the core of sexuality, after which one realizes that all the different layers together form its essence (Ross and Rapp 1983).

How societies precisely give form to sexuality remains relatively obscure. I am not claiming to describe all the different layers of the emic system of sexuality to which mati-ism belongs. I would, however, like to sketch the outlines of two idealtypical socio-historical structures, situating two differing cosmologies, as far as female homosexuality in black communities is concerned.

In the summer of 1986, black women in Amsterdam had the good fortune to be witnesses to and participants in a public discussion between two eminent women poets, true children of the black Diaspora, Audre Lorde and Astrid Roemer.[5] While many subjects were addressed during this discussion, the burning question, which also aroused a passionate interest among the audience, proved to be the matter of namegiving/nomenclature: how important is it that black women who love other women should call themselves "black lesbians"?

TWO IDEALTYPICAL EXPRESSIONS

ASTRID ROEMER: "I do not call myself 'lesbian' and I do not want to be called 'lesbian' either. Life is too complex for us to give names not derived from us, dirty, conditioned words, to the deepest feelings within me. If I were to call myself a lesbian, it would mean that I should be allowing myself–on the most banal, biological level–to be classed as one who chooses persons who also have female genitals. If I love a woman, I love that one woman and one swallow does not make a summer.

People have a masculine and a feminine component in them and these two components constantly seek to come into equilibrium with each other and with the rest of the world. Who is to say whether I shall not love a man in my later life? The result of that search for equilibrium is not a constant. I should be terribly ashamed as a human being were I to know in advance that for the rest of my life I should love only women. It would, moreover, conflict with feminism, for feminism also insists that men can change."

AUDRE LORDE: "First of all, I want to make clear what I understand by a 'lesbian'. It is not having genital intercourse with a woman that is the criterion. There are lesbian women who have never had genital or any other form of sexual contact with another woman, while there are also women who have had sex with other women but who are not lesbian. A lesbian is a woman who identifies fundamentally with women and her first field of strength, of vulnerability, of comfort lies in a network of women. If I call myself a black, feminist lesbian, I am acknowledging by that that the roots of my strength, and of my vulnerability, lie in myself as a woman. What I am trying to achieve in the first place is changes in my awareness and that of other women. My priority does not lie with men.

There are two reasons only why I call myself a black lesbian. It makes me aware of my own strength and shows my vulnerability too. In the sixties we could do anything we wanted to as long as we did not talk about it. If you speak your name, you represent a threat to the powers that be, the patriarchate. That's what I want to be too. The price I pay for that and the vulnerability it makes me aware of are no greater than what I feel if I keep it a secret and let others decide what they want to call me. That also perpetuates the positions of inferiority we occupy in society.

The other reason I consider it important is that there may be a woman in my audience who, through this, may see that it is possible to speak your name and to go on living. If we, who are in a relatively more secure position enabling us to come out for what we are, if we fail to do so that will only perpetuate the vicious circle of inferiority."

ASTRID: "I think your definition of a lesbian is interesting. In that sense, all Surinamese women are lesbian, because they draw their strength to carry on from women. All the same, I do not see why it is necessary to declare oneself a lesbian. In the community from which I come, there is not so much talk about the phenomenon of women having relations with other women. There are, after all, things which aren't to be given names— giving them names kills them. But we do have age-old rituals originating from Africa by which women can make quite clear that special relations exist between them. For instance, birthday rituals can be recognized by anyone and are quite obvious. Also, when two women are at a party and one hands the other a glass or a plate of food, from which she has first tasted herself, it is clear to everybody and their mother what that means. Why then is it necessary to declare oneself a lesbian? It *is* usual there. Surinamese women claim the right to do what they want to do. They can love women, go to bed with men, have children. We distinguish between the various levels of feeling and experiencing which life has to offer and allow ourselves the opportunity to enjoy these things in a creative manner. This is different from the situation in the Netherlands, where you are shoved into a pigeon-hole and find your opportunities restricted. My not wanting to declare myself a lesbian is certainly not prompted by fear. I also want to remain loyal to the ways in which expression has been given from of old in my community to special relationships between women. Simply doing things, without giving them a name, and preserving rituals and secrets between women are important to me. Deeds are more obvious and more durable than all the women who say they are lesbian and contribute nothing to women's energy."

AUDRE: "I respect your position and I recognize the need and the strength that lie behind it. It is not my position. I think it necessary for every woman to decide for herself what she calls herself, and when and where. Of course, there have always been rituals and secrets between women and they must continue. But it is important to make a distinction between the secrets from which we draw strength and the secrecy which comes from anxiety and is meant to protect us. If we want to have power for ourselves this secrecy and this silence must be broken. I want to encourage more and more women to identify themselves, to speak their name, where and when they can, and to survive. I repeat: and to survive.

Finally, I think it important to state my essential position as follows: it is not my behavior that determines whether I am lesbian, but the very core of my being."

TOWER OF BABEL

So much for the burning discussion among the black poets. The positions taken up here are shared by large groups of women in the black communities of the Diaspora and are typical of two idealtypical cosmologies, where female homosexuality is concerned. The position defended by Audre Lorde is a prototype of that held by groups of black lesbians within the USA, Suriname and the Netherlands. In the attitudes adopted by Astrid Roemer, features can be discerned of the mati paradigm, whose protagonists are also to be found everywhere in the Diaspora yet who, almost by definition, attract less attention.

Perhaps it is unnecessary to say that in practice numerous intermediate positions and hybrid forms exist. Without wishing to force people into one camp or the other, or to question the legitimacy or "political correctness" of either position, I seek to throw light on the outlines of these two ideal-types. Exchanges around the theme of namegiving often give rise to heated discussions, that aren't particularly fruitful, because as in a true tower of Babel people speak in mutually unintelligible tongues.

Central to my thinking on the matter is the fact that orientation to reality—which includes the meaning given to and the form taken by homosexuality in black communities in the Diaspora—is more or less colored by the cultural heritage from Africa. In the cosmology of *mati-ism* more African elements have been preserved, while the black lesbian groups have drawn more inspiration from Western influences. *Mati-ism* is characterized by a *centripetal*, a comprehensive and inclusive movement, whereas in the black lesbian world a *centrifugal*, exclusive spirit seems to be present. This is reflected in the attitudes in various circles to relationships with men. While in the lives of many mati-women men play a role, among the black lesbians this must generally be regarded as excluded. Children in the lives of black lesbians are either a residue from a former lifestyle or a conscious choice within a lesbian relationship. Neither circumstance necessarily asks for continued emotional and/or financial commitment from the father to the child or the mother. The part played by men in the life of mati-women, apart from possible economical support for children, is underscored by the fact that motherhood is regarded as a rite of initiation into adulthood and by many as a sign of being a woman.

Besides displaying a differential level of African elements, *mati-ism* and *black lesbianism* are exponents of two different *class cultures*. Mati typically are working class women, whose claims to social status lie in their capability to mobilize and manipulate kin networks. Indeed, according to Janssens and van Wetering, matisma can be seen as entrepreneurs, who through their extensive kin networks with women and men, try to build up social and real capital (Janssens and van Wetering 1985). While in Suriname, middle and higher class black lesbians are largely invisible, obviously not having found appropriate models to style their behavior, in the USA and in the Netherlands, they have increasingly come out of the closet. Through their education, income and often professional status they are insulated against some of the survival hazards of working class black lesbians.

A further difference distinguishing mati relationships from black lesbian connections is the often wide *age gap* between mati partners, while in the latter circles "equality" along many dimensions, including age, seems to be an aspiration. It is not at all unusual, in the mati world, to find a 20 year old ("yong' doifi," young dove) having a relationship with a 60 year old woman. For the young woman, the emotional and financial security of the older woman, who will typically have raised her children and will get financial support from them, is an important consideration. The older woman, for her part, now as almost sixty years ago when it was first recorded (Herskovits, M. and F. Herskovits, 1936), will demand unconditional loyalty and faithfulness from her "young dove," in return for indulging and spoiling her with presents, notably gold and silver jewellery. Ideally, she teaches her young dove "a mati wroko" (the mati work) and she "trains" her the way she wants the young woman to be.

A further differentiation would seem to lie in the *underlying self* that organizes all life's experiences, sifts through them and integrates them into manageable material. Though this issue awaits further elaboration,[6] the self of matisma would seem to be a *sociocentric* phenomenon, while the self of black lesbians could be characterized as an *egocentric, individualistic* entity. Among matisma, sociocentrism is evident not only in the zeal with which human capital is constantly being mobilized, but also in the perceptions of what a person is. Linked with the folk religion "Winti," persons are perceived to be built up out of several components: kra (= jeje), djodjo and several "winti" or Gods, who each have their specific characteristics.[7] "Kra" with its male and female component can be understood as the "I"; "djodjo," also male and female, are like "guardian angels," gotten at birth. The different "winti" or Gods are divided into four pantheons: those of the Sky, the Earth, the Bush and the Water. Male homosexuals are often believed to have a female "Aisa," the (upper-) goddess of the Earth, who is said to be frightfully jealous of real women the man would get involved with. Female homosexuals are perceived to be "carried" by a male Bushgod, Apuku, who cannot bear to see the woman connected, on a longterm basis, with a flesh-and-blood male.

Black lesbians' personhood, on the other hand, seems more aptly characterized by Western notions of individuality, persons as self-contained "islands," with their own motivations and accountabilities.

An additional distinction between matisma and black lesbians is that concentration on women for the latter is a *political issue,* aimed at male dominated society. In their own communities they often wage war on sexism and homophobia. While they experience their sexual choice as a matter of politics, matisma tend to see their behavior as a *personal issue.* A typical response is: "Mi na wan bigi uma f' mi eygi oso. No wan sma e gi mi njan," (I am a big woman in my own house. Nobody gives me food), meaning it's nobody's business but my own with whom I sleep. In a small scale society like Suriname (400,000 inhabitants), this can be seen as a rather defiant survival posture.

Lastly, one could posit that matisma display *lesbian behavior,* while black lesbians have a *lesbian identity.* I assume that matisma unwillingness to declare oneself can, functionally, be explained with reference to this point. In a society where the avenues to status for working class women are limited, it would not seem wise to declare oneself openly and thereby alienate potential personnel, men and women, from one's network.

EPILOGUE

Within black communities there are many different ways of giving expression to erotic relationships between women. The biological basis of sexual desire takes form in various socio-historical structures, underpinned by differing cosmologies. Mati-ism and black lesbianism are two of these structures. Lesbians have not always existed in black communities. In some sectors, today, they still do not exist. But this statement is not a complaint about the lack of sexuality between those of the same gender in the black communities of the Diaspora. Rather it is a statement which tells us more about the socio-historical structure of the concept "lesbian."

NOTES

1. Mati is the Sranan Tongo word for "friend," used both in a heterosexual and a homosexual context. It is used by and for men and women. The word *matisma* (literally "mati people") specifically connotes women who have sexual relations with other women. By *mati-ism* I mean the institution of those who are mati, in this case women. In Dutch I would use the term "matischap."

2. "For Each Of You," Lorde 1982: 42, 43.

3. This text was recorded at a lobi singi in Paramaribo, November 1990. Stanvaste/"steadfast" is the name of another flower.

4. See my dissertation, "'I am Gold Money' (I Pass Through All Hands, But I Do Not Lose My Value): The Construction of Selves, Gender and Sexualities in a Female, Working Class, Afro-Surinamese Setting," University of California, Los Angeles, July 1992.

5. This public discussion, organized by the black lesbian group Sister Outsider, took place on June 21, 1986, in the black and migrant women's center Flamboyant in Amsterdam. Astrid Roemer (born in Paramaribo in 1947), is an Afro-Surinamese poet/novelist, living in the Netherlands, while Afro-American Audre Lorde (Harlem, NYC, 1934) now resides on St. Croix, U.S. Virgin Islands.

6. See note 4.

7. See Wooding, C., 1988.

REFERENCES

Ambacht. (1912). *Rapport van de commissie benoemd bij Gouvernementsresolutie van 13 januari 1910.* Suriname: Gouvernement.

Comvalius, Th. (n.d.). *Krioro: Een bijdrage tot de kennis van het lied, de dans en de folklore van Suriname.* Deel I. Paramaribo.

Herskovits, M. and F. Herskovits. (1936). *Suriname folklore.* New York: Columbia University Press.

Herskovits, M. (1938). *Dahomey: An ancient West-African kingdom.* New York.

Janssens, M. en W. van Wetering. (1985). Mati en Lesbiennes. Homosexualiteit en Ethnische Identiteit bij Creools- Surinaamse Vrouwen in Nederland. *Sociologische Gids,* 5/6. Meppel: Boom.

van Lier, R. (1949). *Samenleving in een Grensgebied.* Een sociaal-historische Studie van Suriname. Amsterdam: Emmering.

van Lier, R. (1986). *Tropische Tribaden.* Een Verhandeling over Homosexualiteit en Homosexuele Vrouwen in Suriname. Dordrecht/Providence: Foris Publications.

Lorde, A. (1982). *Chosen Poems, Old and New.* New York: W. W. Norton & Co., Inc.

Lorde, A. (1982). *Zami. A New Spelling of my Name.* New York: The Crossing Press.

Mintz, S. and R. Price (1976). *An Anthropological Approach to the Afro-American Past.* Philadelphia: Ishi.

Price, R. (1976). *The Guiana Maroons.* A Historical and Bibliographical Introduction. Baltimore: The Johns Hopkins University Press.

Price, R. and S. Price (1991). *Two Evenings in Saramaka.* Chicago/London: The University of Chicago Press.

Ross, E. and R. Rapp (1983). Sex and Society: A Research Note from Social History and Anthropology. In: Snitow, A. et al. eds. *Desire, The Politics of Sexuality.* London.

Wooding, C. (1988). *Winti.* Een Afro-Amerikaanse Godsdienst. Rijswijk: Eigen Beheer.

"Coming Out"
in the Age of Social Constructionism:
Sexual Identity Formation
Among Lesbian and Bisexual Women

Paula C. Rust

SUMMARY. This article examines sexual identity formation among 346 lesbian-identified and 60 bisexual-identified women. On average, bisexuals come out at later ages and exhibit less "stable" identity histories. However, variations in identity history among lesbians and bisexuals overshadow the differences between them and demonstrate that coming out is not a linear, goal-oriented, developmental process. Sexual identity formation must be reconceptualized as a process of describing one's social location within a changing social context. Changes in sexual identity are, therefore, expected of mature individuals as they maintain an accurate description of their position vis-à-vis other individuals, groups, and institutions.

Social sexologists became interested in homosexual identity development in the 1970s. This interest arose as attempts to discover the etiology of homosexuality gave way to efforts to understand the lives of lesbians and gay men, a shift that occurred in response to social and political

Author's Note: This research was supported in part by a grant from the Horace H. Rackham School of Graduate Studies of the University of Michigan, Ann Arbor, Michigan.

Paula C. Rust, *Gender & Society*, Volume 7, Number 1, pp. 50-77, copyright © 1993 by Sociologists for Women in Society. Reprinted by permission of Sage Publications, Inc.

[Haworth co-indexing entry note]: " 'Coming Out' in the Age of Social Constructionism: Sexual Identity Formation Among Lesbian and Bisexual Women." Rust, Paula C. Co-published simultaneously in *Journal of Lesbian Studies* (The Haworth Press, Inc.) Vol. 1, No. 1, 1997, pp. 25-54; and: *Classics in Lesbian Studies* (ed: Esther D. Rothblum) The Haworth Press, Inc., 1997, pp. 25-54; and: *Classics in Lesbian Studies* (ed: Esther D. Rothblum) Harrington Park Press, an imprint of The Haworth Press, Inc., 1997, pp. 25-54.

changes in society at large. Social and political circumstances continued to change, and, during the 1980s, researchers once again shifted their attention toward more contemporary topics such as acquired immune deficiency syndrome (AIDS).

Meanwhile, sexological theory progressed as social constructionists carefully exposed and challenged essentialist assumptions. This scrutiny changed scientific understandings of sexuality, sexual identity, sexual politics, and the history of sexuality. But sexologists have not yet fully reexamined the process of sexual identity formation. The result is a disjunction between contemporary concepts of sexual identity and available models for describing sexual identity formation. This disjunction magnifies some of the conceptual problems in the existing literature on sexual identity formation and highlights the need to reconceptualize the process.

One problem is the linearity of most available models. Homosexual identity formation is not orderly and predictable; individuals often skip steps in the process, temporarily return to earlier stages of the process, and sometimes abort the process altogether by returning to a heterosexual identity. Recognizing this shortcoming, earlier theorists modified linear models by introducing feedback loops, alternate routes, and dead ends. These efforts produced linear models with ample room for deviation rather than models that effectively describe the formation of sexual identity. What is needed is a completely new model.

Earlier work on the coming out process also neglects bisexual identity. Despite ample evidence of prevalent bisexual behavior and frequent theoretical admonishments for ignoring this evidence (e.g., MacDonald 1981, 1983; Paul 1985), few researchers in the 1970s and 1980s gave bisexuality more than a passing nod. Because prevailing models of sexuality were either dichotomous (Paul 1985; Ross 1984) or scalar (e.g., Bell and Weinberg 1978; Kinsey, Pomeroy, and Martin 1948; Kinsey, Pomeroy, Martin, and Gebhard 1953; Shively and DeCecco 1977), bisexuality was either considered nonexistent or conceptualized as an intermediate state between heterosexuality and homosexuality. Bisexual identity, therefore, might be adopted as a steppingstone on the way to homosexual identity (e.g., Chapman and Brannock 1987) but was not considered an end in itself.

Recent constructionist criticism of the dichotomous and scalar models of sexuality has paved the way for the recognition of bisexuality as an authentic form of sexuality. Coincidentally, the AIDS epidemic and the increasing politicization of bisexual people have called attention to the practical and theoretical importance of bisexuality. A few recent studies explicitly and intentionally include bisexuals. Many of these studies explore AIDS-related issues within samples of gay and bisexual men (e.g.,

Lyter et al. 1987; McCusker et al. 1989; Siegel et al. 1988; Winkelstein et al. 1987). But AIDS researchers are not concerned about bisexuality per se and rarely distinguish between gay and bisexual subjects. Other studies focus on clinical issues raised by heterosexually married bisexual, lesbian, and gay psychotherapy clients or compare bisexuals to heterosexuals, gays, and lesbians on a variety of health, personality, attitudinal, and behavioral variables (e.g., Daniel, Abernethy, and Oliver 1984; Engel and Saracino 1986; LaTorre and Wendenburg 1983; Nurius 1983; Smith, Johnson, and Guenther 1985; Stokes, Kilmann, and Wanlass 1983). Despite the increased interest in bisexuality, research that focuses on bisexuality identity remains scarce.

The present research renews empirical investigation into the coming out process in an effort to develop a nonlinear model of identity formation that treats bisexual identity and homosexual identity as equally valid alternatives to heterosexual identity. The inquiry begins by recognizing that women who are raised to assume heterosexual identities nevertheless adopt both lesbian and bisexual identities. The identity history patterns of women who currently possess lesbian and bisexual identities are compared to each other, and then individual variations in identity histories are examined. Observations about individual differences serve as a springboard for a constructionist critique of existing models of identity formation and a reconceptualization of the process.

PREVIOUS LITERATURE

In scientific literature and popular lesbian and gay literature, the term *coming out* refers to processes as well as particular events within these processes. Early researchers typically defined coming out as a single event, usually first identification of oneself as homosexual (e.g., Cronin 1974; Dank 1971; Hooker 1967). More recent theorists conceptualize coming out as a process, and many have proposed developmental models of this process. Working within the developmental paradigm, some researchers document the order and nature of milestone events in individuals' lives (e.g., Coleman 1982; Hencken and O'Dowd 1977; Lee 1977; McDonald 1982; Schäfer 1976; Troiden and Goode 1980), whereas others discuss the psychological changes that occur during and between these events (e.g., Cass 1979, 1990; Fein and Nuehring 1982). Each author chooses a particular point as the beginning of the process and a particular point as its termination. Some discuss the assumptions that underlie these choices (e.g., Cass 1984), but few question the assumptions that underlie the developmental paradigm itself.

These assumptions are numerous. First, a developmental process is linear and unidirectional, with a positive value assigned to later stages in the process. The process has a beginning stage and an end stage, connected to each other by a series of intermediate and sequential steps. Persons are expected to move from each step to the next in the sequence, with progress defined as movement from earlier steps, to later steps and maturity defined as achievement of the end stage. Movement in the other direction is defined as regression. The end stage becomes the goal of the process, and all activity taking place prior to achievement of this stage is presumably directed toward this goal. This activity is expected to cease upon achievement of the end stage, and continued activity is taken as a sign of immaturity.

As applied to homosexual identity formation, the developmental model defines progress as the replacement of a heterosexual identity with a homosexual identity. The privileged status given homosexual identity as the goal of this process is justified by the assumption that this identity is an accurate reflection of the essence of the individual.[1] In other words, coming out is a process of discovery in which the individual sheds a false heterosexual identity and comes to correctly identify and label her own true essence, which is homosexual.

The assumptions of linearity and stage-sequentiality are evident in the writings of early coming out theorists. For example, Troiden and Goode (1980) assert that their 150 gay male respondents "did embrace the components of the gay experience in a specific sequence" (p. 387) and describe this process as a series of five milestone events. The sequence starts when one first suspects that one might be homosexual and ends with one's first homosexual relationship. Coleman (1982) also identified five steps, beginning with childhood feelings of being different and ending with the integration of public and private identity, whereas McDonald (1982) prefers an expanded series of nine milestone events. De Monteflores and Schultz (1978) argue that individuals first recognize their homosexuality and then integrate this knowledge into their lives, implying a stepwise progression toward greater personal integrity.

Several theorists acknowledge that the linear processes they describe do not accurately reflect the experiences of some subjects. McDonald (1982) observes that some of his subjects did not "move predictably" (p. 40) through the five steps he outlines, and Coleman (1982) acknowledges that not all individuals follow the stages of coming out in sequential order. Cass (1979, 1990) asserts that each stage of coming out might be followed by "foreclosure," or termination of the process, instead of the next step in the process. Nevertheless, these theorists present linear, stage-sequential models of coming out, revealing their assumption that coming out is fundamentally a linear and orderly process. Normal and expected though they are, complexities like sequential disorder and foreclosure are understood as deviations from the underlying linear process of coming out.

Research conducted under the developmental model provides information about the average ages at which lesbians and gay men experience the stages of coming out. Despite the fact that this research spans a decade during which the relaxation of social attitudes toward homosexuality should have eased the coming out process, different researchers report remarkably similar findings. Most lesbians who have ever experienced homosexual arousal recall having such feelings around the age of 12 or 13, but they typically did not become aware of their sexual feelings toward other women until ages 14 through 19. Women begin suspecting that they are lesbian at an average age of 18, but they do not define themselves as lesbian until a few years later at an average age of 21 to 23, with 77 percent having done so by age 23. Research on gay men indicates that they experience these events at younger ages and more rapidly than lesbians (Bell, Weinberg, and Hammersmith 1981; Califia 1979; Cronin 1974; de Monteflores and Schultz 1978; Jay and Young 1979; Kooden et al. 1979; McDonald 1982; Riddle and Morin 1977; Schäfer 1976; Troiden 1988).

Bisexual women experience each milestone at older ages than lesbians. On average, bisexual women become aware of homosexual feelings at age 16 and define themselves as homosexual at age 28 (Kooden et al. 1979). Bisexual women also exhibit more discrepancy between adolescent and adult sexuality than homosexual women, suggesting that the preferences of bisexual women might become established later in life (Bell, Weinberg, and Hammersmith 1981).

The developmental paradigm has been challenged by symbolic interactionists who view sexual identity formation as a process of creating an identity through social interaction rather than a process of discovering identity through introspection. Interactionists vary in the degree to which they discuss the effect of contextual factors on this interactive process; some describe particular social situations that are conducive to the creation of gay identity (e.g., Dank 1971), whereas others examine the constraints imposed on the process by socially constructed conceptions of sexuality.

Plummer's (1975) description of the process of "becoming homosexual" is one of the earliest interactionist analyses of sexual identity formation. His four-stage model begins with the "sensitization" stage, during which one has experiences that later acquire sexual meaning. These experiences, for example, same-sex childhood fantasies or close friendships, become part of the coming out process only after one comes out and retrospectively reinterprets them as early evidence of homosexuality. Thus the sensitization stage is not a particular prehomosexual state of being, and homosexuality is not an essential characteristic awaiting discovery. Rather, homosexual identity is socially created, and the coming out process itself is retrospectively constructed. Despite these insights, Plummer nevertheless describes coming out as a goal-oriented process that culminates with the acquisition and stabilization of homosexual identity.

In a series of publications on bisexual behavior and identity, Blumstein and Schwartz (1974, 1976, 1977, 1990) emphasize the mutability of human sexuality and sexual identity as well as the normalcy of incongruence between an individual's sexual identity and sexual behavior. They describe subjects who exhibit various combinations of identity and behavior, for example, women who identify themselves as lesbians but engage in bisexual behavior. In so doing, Blumstein and Schwartz treat these combinations as phenomena worthy of explanation in their own right rather than as temporary transitional states or unstable deviations from a hypothetical normal state in which identity accurately reflects essence. They explain these phenomena by asserting that identity formation is a process of creation (1990) that is influenced by social factors such as dichotomous thinking about sexuality, antagonism toward bisexuality (especially among lesbians), political ideologies, and gender role expectations (1974, 1977). For example, dichotomous thinking about sexuality inhibits bisexual identification by encouraging individuals to emphasize either their homosexual or their heterosexual experience and to produce a consistent account of either homosexual or heterosexual identity by reinterpreting past events (1977). Such assertions extend the interactionist insights of Plummer (1975) into a recognition of the impact of social constructs on self-identity.

Since the publication of Blumstein and Schwartz's work in the late 1970s, several researchers have confirmed the finding that incongruities between sexual identity and sexual experience are commonplace (e.g., Klein, Sepekoff, and Wolf 1985; LaTorre and Wendenburg 1983; Loewenstein 1985; Nichols 1988). The work of Blumstein and Schwartz remains pivotal, however, because the investigation of incongruities between identity and behavior is not the central research question in most of these recent studies, and few of these authors discuss the social and political factors that influence sexual identity.

Richardson and Hart (1981) argue that any sexual identity is the product of an ongoing process of dynamic social interaction. An individual's sexual identity may therefore change at any stage of the life cycle, and the meaning of a given sexual identity may differ among individuals and over time. Moreover, identity stability is no less a dynamic product than identity change. By applying interactionist principles to identity stability as well as identity change, Richardson and Hart finalize the divorce between sexual identity and sexual essence, reconceptualize identity as a process rather than a goal, and produce a fully interactionist account of sexual identity. Richardson and Hart agree with Blumstein and Schwartz that the lack of social validation for bisexual identity makes the maintenance of bisexual identity difficult, and they argue that a woman who has adopted a lesbian identity on the basis of her sexual experiences with other women might not have done so if she lived in a society in which sex of partner was not considered an indication of essential sexual orientation. These ideas have not been fully developed into a social constructionist account of sexual identity formation.

METHODS AND MEASURES

The difficulties inherent in collecting a sample of an undocumented, invisible, and stigmatized population are well known. The sample-selection and data-collection methods used in the current study were designed to maximize coverage of the target population. In order to reach secretive lesbian-identified and bisexual-identified women, data were collected via self-administered questionnaires and postage-paid return envelopes, thus guaranteeing complete anonymity for respondents. Questionnaires were distributed by several methods, including booths at lesbian, gay, and women's conferences and through lesbian, gay, and bisexual social and political organizations, friendship networks, and newsletter advertisements.

The cover of the questionnaire presents the survey as a study of "women who consider themselves to be lesbian or bisexual, or who choose not to label their sexual orientation, or who are not sure what their sexual orientation is," thus defining the sample population as all women who have questioned or rejected heterosexual identity. The majority of the respondents are currently self-identified lesbians, dykes, gay, or homosexual women (N = 346 or 81 percent),[2] and a minority are self-identified bisexuals or "straights with bisexual tendencies" (N = 60 or 14 percent). In the interest of brevity, these two groups of respondents will henceforth be called *lesbians* and *bisexuals,* respectively; these terms refer to current self-identity only and imply neither that self-identity reflects essence nor that it is static. The findings will show that many individuals, especially those who currently identify themselves as bisexual, frequently switch back and forth between identities. Bearing this in mind, the current sample is a "snapshot" of respondents' sexual identities at a particular point in time.

Twenty-one respondents indicated that they do not know their sexual orientation, that they are still wondering, or that they prefer not to label themselves. These women, who might possess sexual self-representations that are not organized into sexual identities, will be called *not sexually identified.* Because an understanding of women who have not created sexual identities is relevant to the larger question of sexual identity formation, some data about the identity histories of these 21 women are presented.

The sample is predominantly young, white, well educated, and employed, but with low income. Respondents range in age from 16 to 78, with the majority in their 20s (45 percent), 30s (38 percent), or 40s (12 percent). Two-thirds are involved in serious or marital relationships with either women or men, and 15 percent have children. Four percent of the sample is African-American, and 2 percent is Arab, Asian, Indian, Native American, or Latina/Hispanic. The remaining 94 percent are white. Thirty-four percent of respondents have 18 or more years of formal education, 25 percent have completed college, and only 7 percent have no schooling beyond high school. Despite this high level of education, the median household income is $20,000. Eighty-nine percent are employed, one-quarter of whom are also students. An additional 7 percent are nonemployed students, and 4 percent are unemployed or retired. Most (84 percent) currently reside in a single midwestern state, although 24 states are represented in the sample.

Respondents answered a series of questions about their sexual identity histories. These questions asked whether each of several psychological events had taken place in their lives and, if so, at what age. Some of the events are milestones that were reported in previous research on coming out as a developmental process, whereas others are events that have not been previously studied, such as changes in identity that occur subsequent to initial identification as either lesbian or bisexual. The former include a respondent's first awareness of homosexual attraction, first questioning of heterosexual identity, and first self-identification as lesbian. The latter include first self-identification as bisexual, the last time a self-identified lesbian wondered whether she was bisexual or identified herself as bisexual, the last time a self-identified bisexual wondered whether she was lesbian or identified herself as lesbian, and whether a respondent has switched between lesbian and bisexual self-identities zero, one, or more times.[3] Respondents who do not currently identify themselves as either lesbian or bisexual were asked whether they had ever wondered if they were lesbian or bisexual or identified themselves as lesbian or bisexual and, if so, at what age they last did so. Whenever the word *lesbian* appeared in a question, it was accompanied by the alternative terms *gay, homosexual,* and *dyke.* Respondents were instructed to read the question using the word with which they felt most comfortable.

FINDINGS

The average lesbian and the average bisexual woman experienced the psychological events in almost identical order although the average bisexual experienced each event at an older age than did the average lesbian (see Table 1). Lesbians first felt sexually attracted to women at an average age of 15, whereas bisexual women did not experience these feelings until an average age of 18. Slightly less than two years after this experience, respondents in both subsamples began questioning their heterosexual identities. It then took another five years for the average lesbian or bisexual woman to first adopt the identity she now has; the average lesbian was nearly 22 years old at this time, and the average bisexual was age 25. Among those who also at some point adopted the other identity, both lesbian and bisexual respondents did so slightly prior to adopting their current identity. The average lesbian first called herself a bisexual shortly before her 21st birthday, and the average bisexual first called herself a lesbian as she approached her 25th.

Within each subsample, the average respondent continued to wonder about her identity even after adopting her current identity. Those lesbians who ever wondered if they were bisexual did so for an average of almost four years after adopting a lesbian identity, and those who ever thought of themselves as bisexual gave up this bisexual identity for the last time at the average age of 25. Those bisexuals who ever wondered or identified themselves as lesbians continued to do so for a similar period of time following their adoption of bisexual identity, until an average age of almost 30.

The difference between the ages at which lesbian and bisexual respondents experienced each milestone increases steadily with each successive milestone. The average bisexual was 2.7 years older than the average lesbian when she first felt attracted to a woman, 3.0 years older when she realized that she might not be heterosexual, 3.3 years older when she first adopted the identity she currently possesses, and 4.2 years older when she stopped wondering whether she should have chosen the other identity. Thus the process not only occurred at an older age for the average bisexual than for the average lesbian but also happened more slowly.

TABLE 1. Average Ages at Which Events in Respondents' Identity Histories Occurred

Milestone	Average Age		
	Lesbian Identified	Bisexual Identified	Not Sexually Identified
Current age	31.2 (N = 342)	32.5 (N = 60)	29.9 (N = 20)
First homosexual attraction	15.4 (N = 329)	18.1 (N = 56)	20.2*** (N = 21)
First questioning of heterosexual identity	17.0 (N = 339)	20.0 (N = 60)	20.9** (N = 20)
First lesbian identification	21.7 (N = 331)	24.5* (N = 44)	-
First bisexual identification	20.9 (N = 133)	25.0*** (N = 55)	-
First identification as either lesbian or bisexual, whichever came first	20.9 (N = 331)	23.4* (N = 55)	-
Last wondered about bisexual identity	25.4 (N = 208)	-	27.2 (N = 16)
Last bisexual identification	25.1 (N = 125)	-	26.2 (N = 11)
Last wondered about lesbian identity	-	29.6 (N = 45)	27.2 (N = 18)
Last lesbian identification	-	28.8 (N = 33)	25.5 (N = 13)

*$p \leq .01$; **$p \leq .005$; ***$p \leq .001$.

But these figures conceal much variation in the coming out process among lesbian and bisexual women. For example, not all lesbians have ever identified themselves as bisexual, not all bisexuals have ever identified themselves as lesbian, and not all individuals experience the events in the same order or at the same ages. Some respondents change identities frequently, whereas others, after questioning their original heterosexual identity, adopted the identity they now have and maintained it ever since.

Figure 1 is a flowchart of the patterns of identity change reported by lesbian and bisexual respondents. Fewer than one-half of lesbian-identified respondents have ever identified themselves as bisexual, although nearly two-thirds have wondered if they were bisexual. In contrast, most

FIGURE 1. Flowchart of Lesbian and Bisexual Respondents' Identity Histories

a. Cases with missing data are deleted stepwise. Therefore, the total number of respondents at each level of the flowchart may be smaller than the total number of respondents at higher levels.

b. Percentages given in each cell of the flowchart represent the percentage of the total lesbian or bisexual subsample that falls in that cell. Percentages are calculated based on the total number of respondents for whom relevant data are nonmissing.

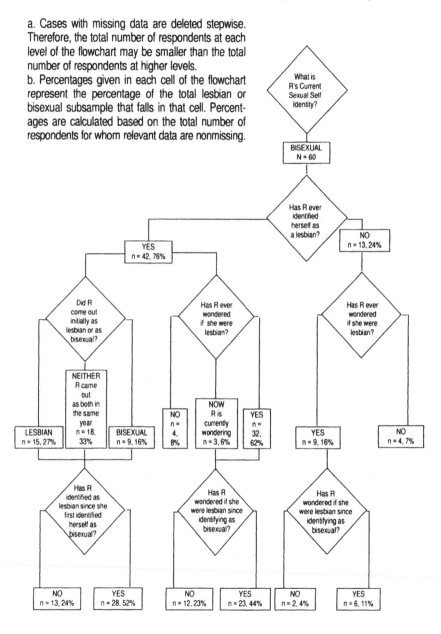

FIGURE 1 (continued)

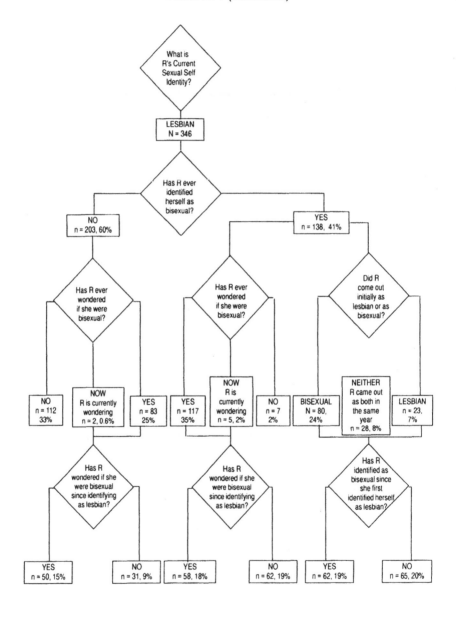

bisexuals have not only wondered if they were lesbian but have identified themselves as lesbians in the past. Bisexuals are no more likely than lesbians to be wondering about their sexual identity at the current time, however. Most respondents who report no current sexual identity (not shown in Figure 1) have identified as both lesbian and bisexual in the past (80 percent and 74 percent, respectively); in fact, most are currently wondering whether or not they are lesbian or bisexual (74 percent and 70 percent, respectively). Bisexual women report switching between lesbian and bisexual identities more frequently than lesbian women; 58 percent of bisexual women and 14 percent of lesbian women report switching identities two or more times.

The order in which respondents adopted lesbian and bisexual identities also varies among both lesbians and bisexual women, although certain patterns are prevalent within each subsample. Bisexuals were much less likely than lesbians to come out initially as lesbians; 27 percent of bisexuals compared to 66 percent of lesbians initially identified themselves as lesbians. The difference is not accounted for by a complementary tendency among bisexuals to come out initially as bisexual; fewer than one-half of the respondents who now consider themselves bisexual adopted this identity in the first place. Twenty-four percent of lesbians came out as bisexual at least one year prior to adopting a lesbian identity, a finding that might account for the role of bisexual identity as a transitional identity in developmental theories of lesbian identity development, as well as the lesbian cultural belief that bisexuality is a phase in the process of coming out as a lesbian.

Even after adopting the identities they possess today, many respondents continued to undergo periods of alternative identification or uncertainty about their sexual identities. One of five lesbians has experienced a period of bisexual identification since first adopting a lesbian identity, and one of three has wondered if she were bisexual since identifying herself as a lesbian. In fact, most of the lesbian-identified women who report ever wondering if they were bisexual have done so since adopting a lesbian identity. The figures are higher for bisexual women; one of two has identified herself as a lesbian, and one of two has wondered is she were a lesbian since she first identified herself as a bisexual.

Table 2 presents distributions of the ages at which each event occurred in respondents' lives. The first events in most respondents' lives were becoming aware of homosexual feelings and questioning their heterosexual identities. Two of three women experienced these events during their teenage years or early 20s, but many other women had these experiences prior to puberty, and several did not have them until their 30s or 40s.

TABLE 2. Incidence of Milestone Events and the Ages at Which They Occurred (Percentages)

Age	First Homosexual Attraction	First Questioning of Heterosexual Identity	First Self-Identification as Either Lesbian or Bisexual	Last Bisexual Identification (Excludes Bisexual Rs)	Last Lesbian Identification (Excludes Lesbian Rs)	Last Wondered if Bisexual (Excludes Bisexual Rs)	Last Wondered if Lesbian (Excludes Lesbian Rs)
Preschool, 0-4	2.5 (N=10)	2.6 (N=11)	0.5 (N=2)	0.0 (N=0)	2.2 (N=1)	0.4 (N=1)	0.0 (N=0)
Child, 5-9	9.6 (N=39)	6.7 (N=28)	0.3 (N=1)	0.0 (N=0)	0.0 (N=0)	0.0 (N=0)	0.0 (N=0)
Preteen, 10-12	15.5 (N=63)	13.1 (N=55)	5.2 (N=20)	0.0 (N=0)	2.2 (N=1)	0.4 (N=1)	1.6 (N=1)
Young teen, 13-15	23.6 (N=96)	16.0 (N=67)	9.6 (N=37)	2.2 (N=3)	0.0 (N=0)	1.3 (N=3)	0.0 (N=0)
Old teen, 16-19	28.3 (N=115)	29.4 (N=123)	31.3 (N=121)	14.0 (N=19)	4.3 (N=2)	15.2 (N=34)	4.8 (N=3)
Young adult							
20-24	11.3 (N=46)	17.7 (N=74)	28.2 (N=109)	41.9 (N=57)	30.4 (N=14)	37.1 (N=83)	27.0 (N=17)
25-29	4.7 (N=19)	7.4 (N=31)	13.7 (N=53)	19.1 (N=26)	23.9 (N=11)	20.5 (N=46)	25.4 (N=16)

Adult

30-34	1.7 (N=7)	4.1 (N=17)	4.4 (N=17)	11.8 (N=16)	10.9 (N=5)	12.9 (N=29)	19.0 (N=12)
35-39	1.5 (N=6)	1.9 (N=8)	3.9 (N=15)	3.7 (N=5)	19.6 (N=9)	5.8 (N=13)	11.1 (N=7)
40-44	1.0 (N=4)	1.2 (N=5)	2.3 (N=9)	6.6 (N=9)	4.3 (N=2)	4.0 (N=9)	6.3 (N=4)
45+	0.3 (N=1)	0.0 (N=0)	0.6 (N=2)	0.7 (N=1)	2.2 (N=1)	2.2 (N=5)	4.8 (N=3)
Range (Total)	0-46 (N=406)	0-42 (N=419)	4-50 (N=386)	14-45 (N=136)	3-45 (N=46)	4-50 (N=224)	11-50 (N=63)

For most respondents, awareness of homosexual feelings preceded or coincided with questioning heterosexual identity, but a substantial minority of each subsample reported that they began to question their heterosexuality before experiencing attraction to other women (see Figure 2). This latter pattern is more common among lesbians than among bisexuals; one in four lesbians began to question her heterosexuality before experiencing homosexual feelings, whereas only one in seven bisexual women did so ($p < .05$). The number of years that passed between these two events also varies considerably among individuals. Some respondents did not question their heterosexual identities until as many as 26 years after first experiencing homosexual feelings, whereas others experienced homosexual feelings a many as 15 years after questioning their heterosexual identity. Such lengthy periods are rare, however, especially among bisexual women; 52 percent of bisexual women, 31 percent of lesbians, and 40 percent of sexually unidentified women reported that these events occurred within a single year of each other. The difference between bisexual women and lesbians is statistically significant ($p = .03$).

These findings contrast sharply with the finding in Table 1 that the average bisexual woman experiences the coming out process more slowly than the average lesbian. Figure 2 shows, on the contrary, that, once bisexual women become aware of their homosexual feelings, they begin to question their heterosexuality more quickly than lesbians. The former finding is an artifact of the fact that bisexual women become aware of their homosexual feelings at older ages than lesbians and the fact that lesbians are more likely than bisexual women to question their heterosexuality prior to experiencing feelings of sexual attraction to other women.

After experiencing feelings of homosexual attraction and questioning their prescribed heterosexual identities, most respondents eventually adopted either a lesbian or a bisexual identity. Approximately one in four women did so immediately, and another one in four did so within 5 years, although others took up to 35 years to do so. There is no significant difference between lesbian and bisexual women in the time lag between these two events. For most respondents, these events occurred in their late teens or early 20s (see Table 2).

Among those respondents who have changed identities since first adopting a lesbian or bisexual identity, bisexuals typically did so more quickly than lesbians (see Figure 3). Two-fifths of bisexual women changed identities within the first year of coming out, but only one-fifth of lesbians did so. A substantial number of lesbians who came out initially as bisexual took up to 10 years to adopt a lesbian identity.

As reported above, many lesbian and bisexual respondents continued to

FIGURE 2. Time Lapse Between First Awareness of Attraction to Women and First Realization that One Might Not Be Heterosexual

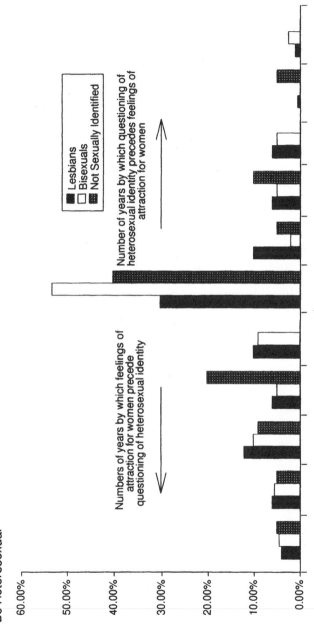

FIGURE 3. Time Lapse Between Initial Lesbian or Bisexual Identification and Subsequent Change in Sexual Identification

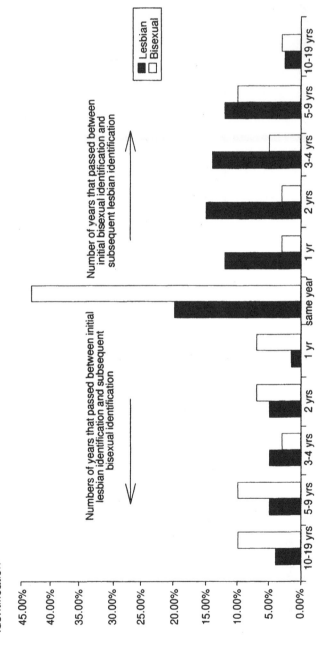

42

consider alternative identities even after adopting their current identities. There are no striking differences between lesbians and bisexual women in the length of time that passed before they ceased to question their sexual identities; periods of up to a decade are not uncommon within either subsample. There is a difference in the ages at which lesbian and bisexual women ceased considering alternative identities, however; most lesbians gave up their bisexual identity by age 25, whereas bisexuals last identified themselves as lesbians at older and more varied ages (see Table 2).

The variation in ages at which bisexuals last identified themselves as lesbians is explained by the fact that most (54 percent) bisexuals last identified themselves as lesbians within the past year. Respondents who are not currently sexually identified are even more likely than bisexuals to have recently possessed a different sexual identity; 73 percent have identified as lesbian and 92 percent have identified as bisexual within the past year. In contrast, only 18 percent of lesbians have identified themselves as bisexual within the past year; the modal lesbian has not identified herself as bisexual for over five years.

In summary, there is considerable variation among lesbian-identified, bisexual-identified, and sexually unidentified women, and this variety overshadows the average differences between women with different sexual identities that are presented in Table 1. There is, however, one consistent difference between the patterns found among bisexual women and those found among lesbians; on almost every measure, bisexual women describe less "stable" identity histories than lesbians. Most lesbians initially adopted a lesbian identity and have maintained it ever since. Bisexual women, on the other hand, are more likely to wonder about or change their sexual identities, and they change identities more rapidly and more frequently than lesbians.

DISCUSSION

Previous authors' descriptions of sexual identity formation as a developmental process were based on the calculated average ages at which various milestone events occurred in subjects' lives. When presented in this form, the current findings also suggest that coming out is an orderly, stage-sequential process. The average ages at which lesbians in the current study first experienced homosexual attraction, first questioned their heterosexual identities, and first identified themselves as lesbians are consistent with the findings of previous research. Also consistent with previous research, bisexuals in the current study apparently came out more slowly and at older ages than lesbians.

But the statistical distributions behind these averages tell a different story. Most individuals do not progress through stages in an orderly sequence. On the contrary, as first noted by Blumstein and Schwartz (1976, 1977), individuals often switch back and forth between sexual identities. Women in the current study also experience periods of ambivalence during which they wonder about their sexual identities and periods during which they have no particular sexual identity. Different individuals experience different events in different orders; in fact, with the exception of questioning heterosexual identity and the near exception of experiencing homosexual feelings, none of the assessed events was experienced by all of the women in the current study. Although some women do progress from awareness of homosexual feelings to questioning heterosexual identity and then to ultimate and permanent identification as a lesbian, this pattern is by no means universal. Variations on this experience are too common to be considered deviations from the norm. The developmental model must be replaced by a social constructionist model of sexual identity formation in which variation and change are the norm.

Social constructionism teaches that self-identity is the result of the interpretation of personal experience in terms of available social constructs. Identity is therefore a reflection of sociopolitical organization rather than a reflection of essential organization, and coming out is the process of describing oneself in terms of social constructs rather than a process of discovering one's essence. By describing oneself in terms provided by one's social context, one locates oneself within this social context and defines one's relations to other individuals, groups, and sociopolitical institutions in this context. For example, a woman may adopt lesbian identity as a representation of her relationship to her woman lover and the differential romantic potential of her relationships with women and men in general, as well as her structural location vis-à-vis sociopolitical institutions such as the lesbian movement, legal marriage, Judeo-Christian religions, and the tax and social welfare structures. Heterosexual identity would imply a very different set of structural relations to these individuals, groups, and institutions.

Unlike individual essences, social contexts are constantly changing. Within the developmental model of coming out, changes in self-identity are considered indicative of immaturity, that is, signs that one is still in the process of development. The achievement of homosexual identity signals the achievement of maturity, and, once achieved, this identity is expected to be permanent. In contrast, within the social constructionist model of identity formation, changes in self-identity may in fact be necessary in order to maintain an accurate description of one's social location within a changing social context; hence changes in self-identity are to be expected of psychologically and socially mature individuals.

There are many types of changes in social context that may lead to changes in one's sexual self-identity. First, the social constructs that provide a language for the description of social location change over time. Historical changes in the conceptualization of sexuality change the meaning of existing constructs and generate new constructs. As an example of the former, although the homosexual construct has existed since the late 1800s, it has changed from a descriptive clinical category to a pejorative psychoanalytic category to a category imbued with myriad positive social and political meanings. Such changes in meaning are often symbolized by changes in terminology. For example, Ulrichs's urnings became yesterday's homophiles and today's gay men, and yesterday's gay girls are today's lesbian feminists. Changes in meaning are not always symbolized by changes in terminology, however; for example, a lesbian feminist identity represented a very different relationship to the feminist movement in 1972 than it did in the late 1970s. In response to changes in the meanings of constructs and the terminology used to represent them, individuals must sometimes update the language they use to describe their own social locations or risk misrepresenting themselves to others.

As an example of the latter, contemporary academic and political discourse on sexuality is constructing bisexuality. As this discourse continues, the bisexual construct will take shape and become increasingly available as a category for the description of social location. As it does, the homosexual and heterosexual constructs must also change to accommodate it, and some individuals will modify their language of self-description. For example, a woman who was heterosexually married prior to her current union with another woman could comfortably call herself a lesbian during the late 1970s and 1980s, when the lesbian construct did not imply the absence of previous heterosexual relations. During the 1990s, however, it will become increasingly difficult for her to maintain this lesbian identity as the bisexual construct becomes the accepted descriptor for a mix of homosexual and heterosexual relations. At some point, she might find that the term *lesbian* no longer accurately describes her social location because it denies the fact that she has an ex-husband.

Second, social constructs vary cross-(sub)culturally. Some of this variation reflects the fact that historical changes occur more quickly in some cultural pockets than others, and some reflects racial-ethnic, class, generational, geographic, and political differences in the social construction of sexuality. An individual might use different constructs to accurately describe her social location within different cultural contexts. For example, a woman who occupies a progressive position vis-à-vis lesbian and gay political institutions might call herself a lesbian when speaking to her parents but call herself a queer when she attends a planning meeting for a Lesbian and Gay Pride March. Her parents have never heard of Queer Nation and would not understand the reference to this branch of sexual politics, whereas her co-planners would underestimate her affinity for other sexual and gender minorities if she identified herself as a lesbian to them. Even though this woman presents herself differently within these different contexts, she probably does not feel that she is misrepresenting herself to either audience. On the contrary, she is merely using the language that most accurately describes herself within each context.

Third, the sociopolitical landscape upon which one locates oneself can change. As new political movements emerge, develop, and change, new social and political institutions are built, and new social and political positions are created. In other words, old landmarks disappear and new ones appear. Language that locates oneself in relation to old landmarks becomes meaningless as these landmarks fade; eventually, such language locates one within a historical context but cannot accurately describe one's location within the contemporary sociopolitical context.

Finally, one's own location within a sociopolitical context can change. As one develops new relationships with other individuals, groups, and sociopolitical institutions, new self-descriptions become necessary. For example, when a woman who identified herself as a homosexual because she read the word *homosexual* in a book from the HQ section of her local library discovers and joins the lesbian community, she may begin to call herself lesbian instead of homosexual. Her new lesbian identity represents her membership in this community. Then, when she falls in love with a man, she may begin to call herself a bisexual in order to acknowledge this relationship. When she is told by other lesbians that it is OK for her to sleep with a man, but that she should still call herself a lesbian in order to protest heterosexism, she may begin to call herself a lesbian again. Her renewed lesbian identity represents a commitment to the lesbian political movement.

But individuals themselves generally do not experience their sexual identities as socially constructed and variable descriptions of their social locations. They experience their own sexuality as stable (Blumstein and Schwartz 1977; Richardson and Hart 1981) and essential (Hart 1984; Ponse 1978, 1980; Richardson 1981; Warren 1974, 1980), and they retrospectively perceive changes in their sexual identities as part of a goal-oriented process of discovering and accepting this essential sexuality. Popular essentialism is an integral part of the social context within which individuals seek to locate themselves. If a social constructionist model of sexual identity formation is to be useful, it must account for the fact that the process is understood as a goal-oriented process of essential discovery by those who experience it (cf. Epstein 1987). This is accomplished by recognizing that goals themselves are constructed. In short, the social constructionist must avoid incorporating essentialist goals into theories of sexual identity formation but allow for the possibility that individuals who are creating their own identities will introduce their own goals.

Individuals choose their goals from the options they perceive, and these options arc defined by the available social constructs. As a result, most individuals who are searching for sexual identity perceive heterosexual identity and homosexual identity as the two possible options. Because bisexuality is still not considered an authentic form of sexuality in popular discourse, few perceive bisexual identity as a valid, permanent option. The goal introduced into the coming out process by the identity-seeking individual, then, is to discover whether her essence is really heterosexual or homosexual. This determination is made through the observation of evidence that is believed to reflect essence—her own sexual thoughts, feelings, and behaviors. The catch is that, for many individuals, this evidence is neither consistently heterosexual nor consistently homosexual. The result is that people whose experience of sexuality is highly varied try to fit themselves into a dichotomous model of sexuality.

Heterosexual and homosexual constructs are not equally matched players in this game, however. Because individuals are raised to assume heterosexual identities, the development of nonheterosexual identity requires the perception of a contradiction between one's initial heterosexual identity and one's own psychosexual experience. Much experience goes unacknowledged and uncodified, particularly experience that does not fit into an existing perceptual schema or that is socially disapproved (Plummer 1984). Heterosexual identity serves as a perceptual schema that filters and guides the interpretation of experience; experiences are given meanings that are consistent with heterosexual identity. Same-sex attractions and intimate relationships that might otherwise be viewed as homosexual can be interpreted as platonic or transitory or attributed to nonessential causes, such as drunkenness or situational constraints, whereas comparable other sex attractions and relationships are interpreted as reflections of heterosexual essence.

It follows that the likelihood that one will perceive a contradiction depends on the capacity of the heterosexual construct to provide credible meanings for same-sex experiences, the degree to which one's same-sex experiences challenge this capacity, and the availability of nonheterosexual constructs. Generally speaking, the heterosexual construct provides meanings for a wide range of psychosocial experiences and owes its persistence to this ability to "co-opt" potentially challenging experiences. There is, however, no monolithic heterosexual construct; the construct varies in breadth and rigidity across social contexts. A heterosexual identity that is grounded in a rigid and narrow concept of heterosexuality is more easily broken than one that is more flexible. Because male heterosexuality is more rigidly defined and more exclusive of intimate same-sex interaction than female heterosexuality, men tend to come out at earlier ages and more rapidly than women.

Even female heterosexuality is incapable of providing meanings for all same-sex experience, however. Although much same-sex hugging and kissing and even sexual contact can be reconciled with heterosexual identity under the rubric of "practice for the real thing," ongoing homosexual relationships and postadolescent experiences present a greater challenge. Women whose experiences are more challenging to the heterosexual construct are more likely to search for alternative sources of meaning for these experiences, and to do so with less delay than women whose experiences are readily interpretable within the heterosexual construct. Moreover, because constructs capable of accounting for both heterosexual and homosexual experience are largely unavailable, experiences cannot be given homosexual meaning without calling into question the heterosexual meanings that have already been given to other experiences. Thus women whose histories are heavily invested with heterosexual meaning or whose other sexual experiences have no credible interpretation within the homosexual construct are less likely to attribute homosexual meanings to same-sex experiences. Furthermore, if and when these women begin to reinterpret these experiences, they will do so more gradually if only because of the sheer volume of heterosexual meaning that must be reexamined. Some of these women may eventually hit on the bisexual construct as a suitable framework for the interpretation of their experience, but this process will also be delayed by the relative unavailability of the bisexual construct.

Therefore, women with more heterosexual and less homosexual experience are expected to retain heterosexual identity more effectively and for longer periods of time than women with less heterosexual and more homosexual experience. The finding that bisexual-identified women became aware of their homosexual feelings and questioned their heterosexual identities at older ages than lesbian-identified women supports this argument; if those who now call themselves bisexual experience higher ratios of heterosexual:homosexual experience,[4] then they were able to maintain heterosexual identities for longer periods of time.

One might expect that individuals who come out at older ages would continue to exhibit greater "inertia" once they did come out. In fact, however, the current findings indicate that, once bisexual-identified women begin to come out, they do so more quickly than lesbians and subsequently exhibit less, not more, identity stability that lesbian-identified women. Social interactionists have argued that the greater instability of bisexual identity is attributable to dichotomous thinking about sexuality and the lack of social support for bisexual identity–the same factors that delay the coming out process among bisexuals. They suggest that bisexuals change identities and wonder if they have adopted the right identity frequently because they are trying to fit themselves into a typology that does not describe their experience of themselves. Lesbians, on the other hand, exhibit more stable identity histories because the dichotomous typology provides a more adequate fit for their experience.

But this argument rests on the questionable assumption that the bisexual construct remains unavailable to an individual even after she has adopted a bisexual identity and implies that bisexual women are engaged in a constant search for a satisfying sexual identity. It is quite possible that, at any given moment, women who switch back and forth between different sexual identities feel that the identity they currently possess is entirely satisfactory. Although the bisexual women in the current study are more likely than lesbians to have ever wondered about their identities and very likely to have done so within the past year, they are no more likely than lesbians to be wondering about their sexual identity at the current time. Presumably, therefore, they are momentarily satisfied with the bisexual identity they currently possess. What changes cause these women to become dissatisfied with a previously satisfactory identity more frequently than currently lesbian-identified women do?

One's self-identity is a description of one's social location. Changes in identity are to be expected of mature individuals and reflect changes in these individuals' social locations or in the language used to describe social location. But change is as socially constructed as the constructs that are being exchanged. One cannot cross a fence that has not been built no matter how many times one walks across the field; similarly, one cannot "change" if categories of meaning have not been constructed on the experiential space one traverses. Conversely, the construction of categories creates the possibility of change. In particular, the construction of sexual categories based on partner gender creates a boundary that bifurcates sexual experiential space. A woman who repeatedly crosses this boundary as she accumulates psychosexual experience, that is, a "*bi*sexual," gives the appearance of sexual mutability and inconsistency. In contrast, a woman whose sexual experience consistently lies on one side of this boundary gives the appearance of greater sexual constancy–unless and until she, too, crosses the boundary. The former woman may adopt bisexual, lesbian, or heterosexual identities at different points in time, depending on the particular constellations of relationships represented by her sexual identity at these different times, whereas the latter woman will probably maintain a consistent lesbian or a consistent heterosexual identity.

Both lay and scientific authors frequently confuse the concepts of bisexuality and sexual mutability because of a failure to recognize the constructed nature of change. Bisexuality is perceived as sexual mutability only because the observer perceives sexuality in terms of the dichotomous constructs, heterosexuality and homosexuality. Perceived without benefit of this dichotomous framework, the bisexual is a person who is consistently open to having lovers of either gender, or to whom gender is as irrelevant as eye color. The bisexual is not more essentially or socially mutable than is the lesbian or the heterosexual; the appearance of greater change is a product of the socially constructed context within which the bisexual is beheld.

Descriptions of bisexuality as sexual mutability are often associated with an idealized conception of bisexuality as the most open form of sexuality. In this view, bisexuals are seen as individuals who have overcome repressive sexual scripts to enable themselves to experience the whole range of their human sexual emotions or as individuals who are uniquely nondiscriminatory in their lovemaking. These appealing images of bisexuality are merely euphemistic variations on earlier stereotypes of bisexuals as indecisive, promiscuous, and fickle. Both conceptions of bisexuality ulitmately rest on an outdated dichotomous conception of sexuality that reifies the importance of gender as a criterion in the choice of sexual partners.

Changes in the conceptualization of sexuality must be accompanied by parallel changes in models of sexual identity formation. Outdated developmental models can be replaced by an understanding of sexual identity formation as an ongoing dynamic process of describing one's social location within a changing social context. Identity change should no longer be understood as a sign of immaturity but as a normal outcome of the dynamic process of identity formation that occurs as mature individuals respond to changes in the available social constructs, the sociopolitical landscape, and their own positions on that landscape.

NOTES

1. The positive value assigned to homosexual identity by developmental theorists was at least in part a reaction to the negative value assigned to homosexuality by the illness model of homosexuality (Coleman 1982). Whereas the illness model presented heterosexual identity as the desirable goal of a process of treat-

ment for homosexuality, developmental theorists presented homosexual identity as the desirable goal of a process of essential self-discovery.

Ironically, the assumption of homosexual essence is based on the privileged status accorded heterosexuality in society. Because homosexuality is suppressed in a heterosexually dominated society, an individual who displays any evidence of homosexuality is suspected of being homosexual despite concurrent evidence of heterosexuality. Evidence of heterosexuality is easily dismissed as an attempt to conceal one's homosexuality, whereas evidence of homosexuality can only be explained as a reflection of the essence of the individual (Zinik 1985, 10).

2. Sexual self-identity was assessed with the question, "When you think about your sexual orientation, what word do you use most often to describe yourself?" a question designed to elicit expressions of self-identity rather than presented or perceived identity. Respondents chose from among the following responses: lesbian, gay, dyke, homosexual, bisexual, mainly straight or heterosexual but with some bisexual tendencies, unsure (don't know, undecided, or still wondering), and "I prefer not to label myself."

3. Respondents were not asked whether they had ever returned to a heterosexual identity. Future research in this area should include this question as well as other more detailed questions about the sequence and circumstances surrounding identity changes.

4. The psychosocial experiences of the lesbian-identified and bisexual-identified women in this study have been described elsewhere (Rust-Rodríguez 1989; Rust 1992) and are consistent with this argument. Bisexual respondents have higher ratios of heterosexual:homosexual feelings of sexual attraction and report having more recent and more serious heterosexual relationships than do lesbian respondents. Some of this difference may be due to differential interpretation of experience in retrospect. The fact of marriage, however, is not subject to interpretation; bisexual respondents are more likely to have been married than lesbian respondents.

REFERENCES

Bell, Alan P., and Martin S. Weinberg. 1978. *Homosexualities: A study of diversity among men and women.* New York: Simon & Schuster.

Bell, Alan P., Martin S. Weinberg, and Sue Kiefer Hammersmith. 1981. *Sexual preference: Its development in men and women.* Bloomington: Indiana University Press.

Blumstein, Philip, and Pepper Schwartz, 1974. Lesbianism and bisexuality. In *Sexual deviance and sexual deviants,* edited by Erich Goode. New York: Morrow.

_____. 1976. Bisexuality in men. *Urban Life* 5:339-58.

_____. 1977. Bisexuality: Some social psychological issues. *Journal of Social Issues* 33:30-45.

_____. 1990. Intimate relationships and the creation of sexuality. In *Homosexuality/heterosexuality: Concepts of sexual orientation,* edited by David P.

McWhirter, Stephanie A. Sanders, and June Machover Reinisch. New York: Oxford University Press.

Califia, Pat. 1979. Lesbian sexuality. *Journal of Homosexuality* 4:255-66.

Cass, Vivienne C. 1979. Homosexual identity formation: A theoretical model. *Journal of Homosexuality* 4:219-35.

_____. 1984. Homosexual identity: A concept in need of definition. *Journal of Homosexuality* 9:105-25.

_____. 1990. The implications of homosexual identity formation for the Kinsey Model and Scale of Sexual Preference. In *Homosexuality/heterosexuality: Concepts of sexual orientation,* edited by David P. McWhirter, Stephanie A. Sanders, and June Machover Reinisch. New York: Oxford University Press.

Chapman, Beata E., and JoAnn C. Brannock. 1987. Proposed model of lesbian identity development: An empirical examination. *Journal of Homosexuality* 14:69-80.

Coleman, Eli. 1982. Developmental stages of the coming out process. *Journal of Homosexuality* 7:31-43.

Cronin, Denise M. 1974. Coming out among lesbians. In *Sexual deviance and sexual deviants,* edited by Erich Goode and Richard R. Troiden. New York: Morrow.

Daniel, David G., Virginia Abernethy, and William R. Oliver. 1984. Correlations between female sex roles and attitudes toward male sexual dysfunction in thirty women. *Journal of Sex & Marital Therapy* 10:160-69.

Dank, Barry M. 1971. Coming out in the gay world. *Psychiatry* 34:180-97.

de Monteflores, Carmen, and Stephen J. Schultz. 1978. Coming out: Similarities and differences for lesbians and gay men. *Journal of Homosexuality* 34:59-72.

Engle, John W., and Marie Saracino. 1986. Love preferences and ideals: A comparison of homosexual, bisexual, and heterosexual groups. *Contemporary Family Therapy* 8:241-50.

Epstein, Steven. 1987. Gay politics, ethnic identity: The limits of social constructionism. *Socialist Review* 17:9-53.

Fein, Sara Beck, and Elane M. Nuehring. 1982. Intrapsychic effects of stigma: A process of breakdown and reconstruction of social reality. *Journal of Homosexuality* 7:3-13.

Hart, John. 1984. Therapuetic implications of viewing sexual identity in terms of essentialist and constructionist theories. *Journal of Homosexuality* 9:39-51.

Hencken, Joel D., and William T. O'Dowd. 1977. Coming out as an aspect of identity formation. *Gai Saber* 1:18-22.

Hooker, Evelyn. 1967. The homosexual community. In *Sexual deviance,* edited by John H. Gagnon and William Simon. New York: Harper & Row.

Jay, K., and A. Young, eds. 1979. *The gay report: Lesbians and gay men speak out about sexual experiences and lifestyles.* New York: Simon & Schuster.

Kinsey, Alfred Charles, W. B. Pomeroy, and C. E. Martin. 1948. *Sexual behavior in the human male.* Philadelphia: W. B. Saunders.

Kinsey, Alfred Charles, W. B. Pomeroy, C. E. Martin, and Paul H. Gebhard. 1953. *Sexual behavior in the human female.* Philadelphia: W. B. Saunders.

Klein, Fritz, Barry Sepekoff, and Timothy J. Wolf. 1985. Sexual orientation: A multi-variable dynamic process. In *Two lives to lead: Bisexuality in men and women,* edited by Fritz Klein and Timothy Wolf. New York: Harrington Park Press.

Kooden, H. D., S. F. Morin, D. I. Riddle, M. Rogers, B. E. Sang, and F. Strass-burger. 1979. *Removing the stigma: Final report of the board of social and ethical responsibility for psychology's Task Force on the Status of Lesbian and Gay Male Psychologists.* Washington, DC: American Psychological Association.

LaTorre, Ronald A., and Kristina Wendenburg. 1983. Psychological characteristics of bisexual, heterosexual and homosexual women. *Journal of Homosexuality* 9:87-97.

Loewenstein, Sophie Freud. 1985. On the diversity of love object orientations among women. *Journal of Social Work and Human Sexuality* 3:7-24.

Lee, John Alan. 1977. Going public: A study in the sociology of homosexual liberation. *Journal of Homosexuality* 3:49-79.

Lyter, David W., Ronald O. Valdiserri, Lawrence A. Kingsley, William P. Amoro-so, and Charles R. Rinaldo. 1987. The HIV antibody test: Why gay and bisexual men want or do not want to know their results. *Public Health Reports* 102:468-74.

MacDonald, A. P., Jr. 1981. Bisexuality: Some comments on research and theory. *Journal of Homosexuality* 6:21-35.

_____. 1983. A little bit of lavender goes a long way: A critique of research on sexual orientation. *Journal of Sex Research* 19:94-100.

McCusker, Jane, Jane G. Zapka, Anne M. Stoddard, and Kenneth H. Mayer. 1989. Responses to the AIDS epidemic among homosexually active men: Factors associated with preventive behavior. *Patient Education and Counseling* 13:15-30.

McDonald, Gary J. 1982. Individual differences in the coming out process for gay men: Implications for theoretical models. *Journal of Homosexuality* 8:47-60.

Nichols, Margaret. 1988. Bisexuality in women: Myths, realities, and implications for therapy. *Women and Therapy* 7:235-52.

Nurius, Paula S. 1983. Mental health implications of sexual orientation. *Journal of Sex Research* 19:119-36.

Paul, Jay P. 1985. Bisexuality: Reassessing our paradigms of sexuality. In *Two lives to lead: Bisexuality in men and women,* edited by Fritz Klein and Timothy Wolf. New York: Harrington Park Press.

Plummer, Kenneth. 1975. *Sexual stigma: An interactionist account.* London: Routledge & Kegan Paul.

_____. 1984. Sexual diversity: A sociological perspective. In *The psychology of sexual diversity,* edited by Kevin Howells. New York: Blackwell.

Ponse, Barbara. 1978. *Identities in the lesbian world: The social construction of self.* Westport, CT: Greenwood.

_____. 1980. Lesbians and their world. In *Homosexual behavior: A modern reappraisal,* edited by Judd Marmor. New York: Basic Books.

Richardson, Diane. 1981. Lesbian identities. In *The theory and practice of homosexuality,* edited by John Hart and Diane Richardson. London: Routledge & Kegan Paul.

Richardson, Diane, and John Hart. 1981. The development and maintenance of a homosexual identity. In *The theory and practice of homosexuality,* edited by John Hart and Diane Richardson. London: Routledge & Kegan Paul.

Riddle, D., and S. Morin. 1977. Removing the stigma: Data from institutions. *APA Monitor,* November, 16-28.

Ross, Michael W. 1984. Beyond the biological model: New directions in bisexual and homosexual research. *Journal of Homosexuality* 10:63-70.

Rust, Paula C. 1992. The politics of sexual identity: Sexual attraction and behavior among lesbian and bisexual women. *Social Problems* 39:366-86.

Rust-Rodríguez, Paula C. 1989. When does the unity of "common oppression" break down: Reciprocal attitudes between lesbian and bisexual women. Ph.D. diss., University of Michigan, Ann Arbor.

Schäfer, Siegrid. 1976. Sexual and social problems of lesbians. *Journal of Sex Research* 12:50-69.

Shivley, Michael G., and John P. DeCecco. 1977. Components of sexual identity. *Journal of Homosexuality* 3:41-48.

Siegel, Karolynn, Laurie J. Bauman, Grace H. Christ, and Susan Krown. 1988. Patterns of change in sexual behavior among gay men in New York City. *Archives of Sexual Behavior* 17:481-97.

Smith, Elaine M., Susan R. Johnson, and Susan M. Guenther. 1985. Health care attitudes and experiences during gynecologic care among lesbians and bisexuals. *American Journal of Public Health* 75:1085-87.

Stokes, Kirk, Peter R. Kilmann, and Richard L. Wanlass. 1983. Sexual orientation and sex role conformity. *Archives of Sexual Behavior* 12:427-33.

Troiden, Richard R. 1988. *Gay and lesbian identity: A sociological analysis.* Dix Hills, NY: General Hall.

Troiden, Richard R., and Erich Goode. 1980. Variables related to the acquisition of a gay identity. *Journal of Homosexuality* 5:383-92.

Warren, Carol A. B. 1974. *Identity and community in the gay world.* New York: Wiley.

———. 1980. Homosexuality and stigma. In *Homosexual behavior: A modern reappraisal,* edited by Judd Marmor. New York: Basic Books.

Windelstein, Warren, David M. Lyman, Nancy Padian, Robert Grant, Michael Samuel, James A. Wiley, Robert E. Anderson, William Lang, John Riggs, and Jay A. Levy. 1987. Sexual practices and risk of infection by the human immunodeficiency virus. *Journal of the American Medical Association* 257:321-25.

Zinik, Gary. 1985. Identity conflict or adaptive flexibility? Bisexuality reconsidered. In *Two lives to lead: Bisexuality in men and women,* edited by Fritz Klein and Timothy Wolf. New York: Harrington Park Press.

A Study of Lesbian Lifestyles
in the Homosexual Micro-Culture
and the Heterosexual Macro-Culture

Joyce C. Albro, MSW
Carol Tully, MSW

SUMMARY. Ninety-one lesbians were surveyed in an effort to determine how homosexual women function within the heterosexual macro-culture and the homosexual micro-culture. Those sampled tended to be young, white, urban, and well-educated professionals. By exploring four major categories (demographics, lesbian lifestyles/homosexual culture, social relationships, and participation in the heterosexual culture) it was found that respondents felt isolated from the heterosexual macro-culture and turn to the homosexual micro-culture for friends, emotional support, and social interaction. It was also discovered that while lesbians do feel isolated from the majority of society, they function productively in a dual role within their general environment. *[Article copies available from The Haworth Document Delivery Service: 1-800-342-9678. E-mail address: getinfo@ haworth.com]*

This article is based on the master's thesis submitted in 1977 by the authors and Bonnie L. Kessler to the School of Social Work, Virginia Commonwealth University, Richmond, Virginia.

Joyce C. Albro and Carol Tully, *Journal of Homosexuality,* Volume 4, Number 4. © 1979 by The Haworth Press, Inc.

It has been estimated that there are several million homosexual men and women now living in the United States (Livingood, 1972, p. 2); however, there are no known statistics on how many of this group are lesbians. Due to the general societal proscriptions against homosexuality, the lesbian remains hidden, a member of an invisible minority within the dominantly heterosexual society. In order to cope with society's condemnations, lesbians generally tend to unite with each other in lesbian subcultures which co-exist with the larger society. While most lesbians function in both the larger society and their own subculture, heterosexual society tends to ignore any difficulties the homosexual female might have because of this dual existence.

With the beginning acceptance of lesbianism as a viable alternative lifestyle, it is imperative that we know how the lesbian operates in society. Unfortunately, few researchers have sought to discover how lesbians function, either within their own subculture or within the total society. Those researchers who have studied lesbians have been hampered by lesbians' invisibility to society and the consequent general inaccessibility of lesbian samples.

One type of research that has been done has concentrated on in-depth studies of lesbian samples focusing on their lifestyles and present functioning. *The Ladder* (1960) conducted a survey of its readership and found that the lesbians who responded (N = 100) had a high educational level, a high professional status, and a stable, responsible mode of living. In a later study also using readers of *The Ladder* as a sample, Gundlach (1967) found that many lesbians were employed in well-paying jobs, often at the administrative level of organizations. These data accord with the findings of Saghir and Robins (1969, 1970, 1973) who concluded that being a homosexual female or male was compatible with functional and interpersonal productivity.

A study by Chafetz, Sampson, Beck, and West (1974) examined the sources of support and of strain on lesbians by conducting extensive interviews with lesbians. The results showed lesbians felt strain when dealing with heterosexual people. Economic institutions were seen as not being supportive of lesbians' lifestyles. Most of the women interviewed felt constrained to "act" like heterosexual women on the job, with their families, or at social events. Support systems seemed to come from the homosexual subculture and friendship circles, not from the larger society. How lesbians actually do function within society is a significant gap in the body of research literature.

PURPOSE AND METHODOLOGY

This study included both exploratory and descriptive elements and examined the functioning of homosexual women within their homosexual micro-culture and the heterosexual macro-culture. While Chafetz et al. (1974, 1976) researched some aspects of lesbians' societal functioning and noted sources of support and strain for lesbians in the macro-culture, the present study sought to determine if their findings were supported and to gather data about lesbians that previous researchers had neglected.

The sample population was requested to complete a questionnaire designed by the researchers. The initial question was adapted from Kinsey's Scale for determining sexual orientation, and only participants rating themselves as 4 ("predominantly homosexual, but with more than incidental heterosexual contact"), 5 ("predominantly homosexual, with incidental heterosexual contact"), or 6 ("exclusively homosexual") were included in the study. The other questions fell into four major categories: demographics, lesbian lifestyles/homosexual culture, social relationships and participation in the heterosexual culture. Most of the questions required the respondent to select a coded response; some questions were open-ended.

No restriction on the sample was set other than the participants' voluntary disclosure of homosexuality. The sample of 91 lesbians was drawn from 17 east coast cities, 11 in Virginia. Respondents lived in areas as far north as Massachusetts and as far south as Georgia. Over 50% of the sample lived in Richmond, Virginia.

In order to secure voluntary participation, the researchers contacted a lesbian organization (Lesbian Feminists of Richmond, Virginia) as well as persons already known to the researchers to be lesbians. All volunteers were asked to distribute questionnaires to other lesbians. In this way, participants who were not members of any homosexual organization were obtained, and the sample was expanded beyond Richmond, Virginia. A cover letter indicated the purpose of the project, general directions, confidentiality of information, use of results, and a target date for return of the questionnaires. One-hundred and sixty questionnaires were mailed; 96 (60% of the total) were returned. Five questionnaires in the sample were unable to be used because the respondents' sexual orientations on the modified Kinsey Scale were heterosexual or bisexual (0-3).

RESULTS AND DISCUSSION

Demographic Information

The first item on the questionnaire was the adapted Kinsey sexual orientation rating scale. Most respondents (N = 62 or 68.1%) rated themselves as 6 or "exclusively homosexual." A 5 rating ("predominantly homosexual, with incidental heterosexual contact") was indicated by 23 respondents (25.3%). Six respondents (6.6%) rated themselves as 4 or "predominantly homosexual, but with more than incidental heterosexual contact." It is evident that there exists a minority of lesbians who do not consider themselves exclusively homosexual.

All respondents were white, and their ages ranged from the late teens to over 60. Approximately 75% of the women were age 30 or younger; the median and mode age of the respondents was 27. This age distribution is similar to that obtained by Chafetz et al. (1976), in which 67% of the respondents were age 30 or under.

The present sample was well-educated, with 55.7% having a college degree and an additional 20.4% having some type of graduate degree. Although most major educational fields were represented in the sample, the social sciences and helping professions predominated. For example, 42.6% listed major fields of psychology, social work, nursing, sociology, anthropology, or criminal justice. This finding reflects the traditional socialized role model of women, whether homosexual or heterosexual.

The sample was biased toward professionals (43.3%). The student category (26.7%) was the second largest occupational classification. Of the students, 27.3% were seeking baccalaureate degrees and 66.7% were seeking a variety of graduate degrees. A wide range of occupations was included in the sample, e.g., chemist, journalist, speech therapist, lawyer, printer, mechanic, and welder.

The largest number of the respondents earned annually between $5,000 and $9,999 (34.1%). The median salary for the sample is similar to the median salary for all women employed full-time in 1973: $6,488 (U.S. Department of Labor, 1975). Approximately 33 1/3% of the sample earned over $10,000 annually, and 22% had purchased their own homes. Most of the women (56.5%) had been at their present employment for 2-5 years, while 37.1% had held their present jobs for one year or less. As 75% of the respondents were age 30 or younger, it is understandable that only 5.8% had been at their present employment for 6-10 years.

The present findings concerning occupation, income, and length of time at employment agree with the conclusions of *The Ladder* survey (1960) and of Gundlach (1967) that lesbians tend to have a high level of education, a high professional status, and a stable and responsible mode of living. These findings, however, are apt not to be representative of all lesbians but only of those lesbians who are educated enough to understand a study's usefulness and who are consequently willing to participate in research.

Most of the respondents were single (81.7%), while 11% were divorced, 4.9% were separated, and 2.4% were married. Seven of the women (8.3%) had altogether a total of 11 children, but only two women had custody of their children. (Since lesbians are often viewed as unfit mothers, the custody statistic was no surprise.)

The majority of respondents indicated no religious preference. This is possibly related to basic religious proscriptions of homosexuality. The finding is supported by Gagnon and Simon (1973).

A demographic composite of the typical respondent in this study is a lesbian who: is exclusively homosexual, 27 years old, white, single; rents in a metropolitan east coast city; is college educated; professionally employed; earns $5,000-9,999; has held her present job for 2-5 years; and is not affiliated with an organized religion.

Lesbian Lifestyles and Interaction in the Homosexual Subculture

Another section of the questionnaire dealt with lesbians' lifestyles and their interaction with the gay subculture. General topics in this section included respondents' present and past sexual relationships, the experiences of lesbian couples, and the individual lesbian's current involvement in the homosexual micro-culture.

While a majority (83.5%) of the sample was involved in a lover relationship with a woman at the time of the study, slightly more than half (52.7%) actually lived with a female lover. Only 11% lived alone, while 12.1% lived with lesbian nonlovers and 4.4% with heterosexual female friends. Generally, these findings tend to support the studies by Chafetz et al. (1976) and by Gundlach (1967), who reported that most of their respondents lived with female lovers. Two percent were married and lived with their husbands, 4.4% lived with parents or with close relatives, and 13.2% lived in other types of situations. The tendency was for lesbians to live in households without men (80.2%). More than half (66.7%) hoped to maintain their present living situation, while 33.3% hoped their situation would change.

There was a significant correlation (p < .00001) between a respondent's present living situation and whether or not she wished to maintain that living situation indefinitely. Those who lived alone or with persons not their spouses or lovers tended to want to change their living arrangements; but of the 48 women who were currently living with a female lover and of the two who were living with their husbands, all 50 (100%) hoped to maintain their living situations indefinitely.

Of those who wished to maintain their present living situations, most reasoned that they were satisfied, in love, happy, secure, and willing to build a life together with their partner. The two major reasons why women did not wish to maintain their present living situations were loneliness and lack of independence.

It was anticipated that the older the respondent, the longer she would have been involved in her present lover relationship. When correlated, the relationship between these two variables was significant at the $p < .0001$ level. For those who had been involved in their present relationship for two to four years, the mean age was 27.6. The mean age was 39.7 for those who had been involved in their present relationship for more than 11 years.

Respondents who were involved in a lover relationship with other women were asked to describe their relationships by responding to several descriptive adjectives. Table 1 shows that most women saw their present lover relationships as stable, happy, a source of support, and satisfying. An overwhelming percent of these women did not see their relationships as turbulent, unhappy, a source of strain, guilt producing, or frustrating.

Data collected showed that less than half (45.4%) of the lesbians who were involved in a lover relationship with a woman engaged in sexual experiences with others during the relationship. If sexual experiences did occur, they tended to be with only one other person, who was usually a female. This supports Cotten's (1975) findings that lesbians have few sexual partners and that exclusivity is usually practiced to a high degree when a woman is involved in a lover relationship.

Of the total sample, 91.2% had been sexually involved, prior to their present relationship, with a total of between zero to four women; over half (52.2%) of all previous ongoing relationships had endured from two to seven years, while the remainder had lasted from less than six months to one year. The most common reason relationships ended was because the respondent's lover terminated the relationship to become involved with another woman. Often, though, the respondent said she herself had terminated the relationship because her own needs and values differed substantially from those of her lover.

One woman's response seems typical:

I have been involved with three women in what I would consider an ongoing lover relationship. Why each ended varies. One woman left me for another woman, I ended one relationship because our philosophies were not at all congruent and, finally, my first relationship ended because my lover's father discovered our "secret" and insured there were several hundred miles between us.

It seems that, for me, it was hard to find other lesbians which meant that I had little choice in partners. I was also quite young, idealistic, and too eager to enter into a "permanent" relationship. Had society accepted my situation with the same ease as it does heterosexual dating, my options would have been greater, and I could have enjoyed "dating" without the urgency that I felt to find a permanent partner.

TABLE 1. Adjectives Describing Present Relationships

N = 76

Positive Adjectives

	Stable	Happy	Source of Support	Satisfying
Percentage reporting these characteristics as not representative of any of their present relationships	10.5	3.9	18.4	3.9
Percentage reporting these characteristics as representative of one relationship, one of two relationships or both of their present relationships	89.5	96.1	81.6	96.1
Total	100.0	100.0	100.0	100.0

Negative Adjectives

	Turbulent	Unhappy	Source of Strain	Frustrating	Guilt Producing
Percentage reporting these characteristics as not representative of any of their present relationships	90.8	96.0	81.6	81.1	96.1
Percentage reporting these characteristics as representative of one relationship, one of two relationships or both of their present relationships	9.2	4.0	18.4	18.9	3.9
Total	100.0	100.0	100.0	100.0	100.0

While Chafetz et al. (1976) found that most of their sample had been involved with an average of 12.5 female partners, 75% of the present sample had been involved with between 1 to 6 females. These findings more closely relate to those of Loney (1972) who reported an average of 3.7 partners. The typical lesbian in this study reported approximately 4 partners and infrequently or never (93.4%) engaged in one-night-stands. Gagnon and Simon's (1973) and Chafetz et al.'s (1976) findings on one-night-stands are supported by the present study.

Since few data have been gathered on lesbian couples, part of the questionnaire was designed for women who regarded themselves as involved in a lesbian couple relationship. Of the 59 women who considered themselves in this couple category, 51% had lived together for more than two years. Their mean age was 34.1. Over 26% of the women had lived with their partners for more than five years. These women (89.8%) did most or all of their socializing together and saw their relationship as being a permanent commitment (93.2%). In addition, 52% said they would marry if homosexual marriages were legal while 6% said they would "perhaps" marry, were it possible. Lesbians who wished to marry cited similar reasons as heterosexual persons: romance, financial and legal advantages, security, and the desire to make a public commitment. Of the minority (42%) who did not wish to marry, most stated marriage was unnecessary because they already felt secure in their relationships or because they objected to the institution of marriage. Most heterosexual women want to marry, and their subsequent marriages embody societal rewards for procreation and child-rearing. Evidently because lesbians are rejected by society, many tend to reject society's institution of marriage. The lesbians who do want to marry may be seeking acceptance and the same societal benefits bestowed on heterosexual females.

Data collected indicate that, although some sexual involvement with other women occurs outside the primary relationship (22 out of 59 had been so involved), those involved do not attempt to keep it a secret from their partners even though the impact of such sexual activity on the couples' relationships was reported as negative (66%). Also, 82.6% of the respondents tended to have negative or ambivalent feelings about their lovers' sexual involvement with others. It seems that regardless of the absence of a legal commitment, the reactions of lesbians to sexual relations outside the primary relationship are similar to the reactions of heterosexually married individuals.

Most couples (93.2%) characterized their relationship as a permanent commitment. Half (50.8%) had no jointly held property, bank accounts, loans, stocks, bonds, or motor vehicles. Knowing that women continue to be discriminated against in various commercial transactions, lesbians, because of their minority status, may be reluctant to pursue joint transactions. Such transactions could be viewed as nontraditional by commercial establishments and, hence, as bad risks. Although couples had few jointly owned items, 67.2% stated they would indefinitely support their partner if necessary. The present study suggests that if a lesbian is involved in what she considers a permanent relationship, she is willing to support her partner financially (p < .0156). These findings differ from Cotten's (1975) findings, where only 16% (N = 30) of the sample said they would support their partners financially.

Respondents were asked to indicate the three most frequent ways they met other lesbians. The most frequent way was through homosexual friends; the second most frequent way women met was through women's group meetings; the third method was by going to gay bars. Interestingly, this finding is consistent with the social activities our sample engaged in most frequently: (1) dining with friends, (2) entertaining at home, (3) participating in activities sponsored by lesbian organizations, and (4) going to gay bars. Evidently, lesbians enjoy socializing away from the heterosexual culture. While lesbians seem to go to gay bars regularly, most (86.5%) go less than once a month. Of those who do frequent gay bars, all said they went for social reasons. A typical response was: "I get a feeling of uplift from seeing so many healthy, happy gays and it makes me feel less alone and different."

Of the sample, 48.2% claimed membership in a gay organization while 51.8% stated they did not belong to any kind of gay organization. Of those who did belong, most paid dues and attended meetings regularly. In the Chafetz et al. (1976) study only 34% (N = 65) belonged to gay organizations, but the number of such organizations has increased since the Chafetz data were gathered in 1973.

The two principal reasons lesbians gave for belonging to gay organizations were: (1) to sense the feeling of support they got from other homosexual persons and (2) to further gay rights. These reasons seem typical of the motives of any minority member who joins a group and agree with Chafetz et al.'s (1976) finding that lesbians join gay organizations primarily for moral support or to effect social change.

A majority (86.9%) of our respondents stated they did attend functions sponsored solely by gay organizations, indicating some amount of personal openness within the gay subculture, but only 23.5% reported having participated in a gay rights campaign by writing letters that supported homosexuality. Only 24% had ever publically demonstrated for homosexuality. However, 58.3% stated they had donated money to further gay rights issues.

In summary, present data and Gagnon and Simon's (1973) data show that since lesbians do not feel accepted by the heterosexual macro-culture, they turn to the homosexual micro-culture for their social life and support systems. The lesbians in our sample seemed well-integrated within this subculture. Their access to the subculture was through homosexual friends.

Disclosure of Sexual Orientation

Participants were asked to rate themselves on an openness scale in which a score of 1 indicated a hidden sexual orientation and a score of 7 indicated complete openness and honesty about sexual orientation. (See Table 2.) The responses to this question approximated a normal distribution curve, indicating that the sample represented lesbians who ranged from being totally hidden to being totally open about their sexual orientation.

A woman's openness about her sexuality was positively correlated (p < .009) with whether or not she was a member of a gay organization. For those women who did belong to organizations, the mean rating on the openness scale (see Table 2) was 4.44. The mean score on the same scale for those who did not belong to organizations was 3.52.

A negative correlation existed (p < .106) between age and the openness rating scale; the older a respondent, the more she tended to keep her sexual orientation hidden. As previously mentioned, the sample for this study was quite young. It is difficult to obtain a representative sample of a stigmatized group such as lesbians. Younger homosexual women seem to be more open about their sexual orientation and, therefore, easier to locate for research purposes.

Eighteen questions dealt with familial and general social relationships. Only 28.4% reported having told their mothers of their lesbianism, and even fewer (19.3%) chose to tell their fathers. A much greater percentage (42.9%) had told their siblings. Both Chafetz et al. (1976) and Gagnon and

TABLE 2. Responses to Openness Scale

N = 91

Sexual Orientation Hidden with Few Exceptions	1 6.6%	2 16.5%	3 16.5%	4 20.9%	5 18.7%	6 18.7%	7 2.2%	Complete Openness and Honesty about Sexual Orientation

Simon (1973) reported that a large proportion of lesbians have been willing to look to family members—especially to parents—for support, it is possible that the family is indeed a potential source of support for the lesbian.

Many lesbians remembered feelings of uniqueness and of complete isolation upon first discovering their lesbianism and stated they had not believed that they had the option of exclusive homosexuality until many years later. Some women had married because they had not believed they would ever become acquainted with other lesbians who could become friends or lovers.

The Lesbian in the Heterosexual Macro-Culture

When asked whether they felt constrained to present themselves as heterosexual in a number of settings, the respondents answered that they felt most constrained with their families (67.9%), an indication that they dreaded rejection by their families more than rejection by others.

Approximately one-half of the respondents (51.8%) reported attempting to present themselves as heterosexual at work and in public. At the same time, many respondents commented that they preferred to present themselves authentically, without regard to how their behavior might be interpreted by others. Most respondents generally did not try to appear either heterosexual or homosexual.

Many respondents (54.2%) fear losing their jobs if their lesbianism were to become known to their employer. Others stated that, minimally, their jobs would be made more difficult if their sexual orientation were discovered. Some individuals believed that they had lost jobs due to their sexual orientation. Similar findings were reported by Chafetz et al. (1974, 1976).

We were interested in exploring how lesbian clients characterized their professional counselors and therapists. At some point in their lives, approximately 80% of the participants in this study had sought counseling from various professionals. Most reported that their counselors had been accepting of their lesbianism, although some did report that the counselor had attempted to "cure" them of their homosexuality or had been generally unaccepting of it. This finding of acceptance by counselors is striking in light of previous research and could indicate that most helping professionals no longer automatically regard homosexuality as an illness to be cured. It is also interesting to note that ministers were the least accepting counselors (29% not accepting), which is consistent with traditional religious dogma regarding homosexuality.

Participants were asked whether they knew of resources in the community where they could comfortably seek various types of services, even if this involved revealing their sexual orientation. Approximately one-half felt they could locate such health, legal, and counseling services, but only 13.5% felt they could locate suitable financial services through banks and loan companies.

Several questions explored respondents' feelings about their relationship with society and about society's views concerning homosexuality. Over 72% of the respondents were at least somewhat concerned about the criminality of their sexual activities. One respondent stated: "The laws bother me because they are wrong and oppressive, but they don't bother me in the sense of influencing my behavior." Almost an equal number (over 73%) of the respondents felt very much or somewhat isolated from society as a result of their sexual orientation. One respondent wrote in response to the question about isolation: "What bothers me most is I feel constrained from forming meaningful friendships with straight people I like. It's not possible to have a real friendship if I hold back information on such an important part of my life–my lesbianism. Yet there are too many risks in telling."

Even more of the respondents (over 82%) considered society's acceptance of them as lesbians to be somewhat or very important. There was a positive relationship ($p < .02$) between the desire for acceptance and the respondents' expression of a need to present themselves as heterosexual in public. This relationship might be explained by the concern expressed by many respondents regarding the criminality of their sexual activities. Although they wish to be accepted as lesbians, they do not believe this is possible as long as homosexual acts are illegal; so they sometimes feel constrained to appear heterosexual.

In regard to isolation from society and the need for acceptance by society, some researchers have questioned whether society rejects the lesbian, or the lesbian rejects society, or both. Siegelman (1974) raised this question of rejection in reference to lesbians' attitudes toward their parents. Some comments on acceptance or rejection of society were made by respondents in this study:

I see so much wrong with heterosexual society that I am not pained to be separate from it.

. . . many of my friends are very defensive about that subject and seem to feel that it is not a question of whether heterosexual society accepts them but whether they accept a heterosexual society.

My circle of friends are lesbians or accepting straights, therefore I've isolated myself from the (typical) straight world.

The question that remains unanswered is whether the lesbian rejects society spontaneously or whether she rejects it as a result of its rejection of her.

In terms of participation in traditional social activities, lesbians in this study were more likely to involve themselves in professional organizations than in other types of activities, such as volunteer work, community activities, women's organizations, or church related programs. The overall findings illustrated further the lesbian's isolation from society and showed the lesbian as involving herself more in gay organizations or in professional organizations and as staying removed from the more traditional types of community activities.

The most striking information obtained in this study with regard to the lesbians' participation in society is on how they present themselves. It seems that although lesbians do feel isolated, are concerned about the criminality of their sexual activities, and desire social acceptance, they are unwilling to make an active effort to appear heterosexual in order to enhance their acceptance. Many, however, reported feeling obliged to present themselves as heterosexual in some situations, especially when with relatives, at work, or in public.

CONCLUSIONS

It was found that lesbians in this study do feel isolated from the heterosexual macro-culture and turn to the homosexual micro-culture for friends, for emotional support, and for the majority of their social interactions. Generally, Chafetz et al.'s (1974, 1976) findings were supported by this study, as the lesbian sample perceived society as nonaccepting and found it difficult to interact with it.

The sample in the present study is biased toward the young, white, urban, well-educated, professional, "middle class" lesbian. The results might not be particularly relevant for the older lesbian, the economically impoverished lesbian, the nonwhite lesbian, the incarcerated lesbian, the mentally ill lesbian, the lesbian mother, or the rural lesbian. Obtaining reliable statistics on these groups and on others will create a challenge for future researchers, who must now start to fill the gaps in the data collected previously.

REFERENCES

Chafetz, J., Sampson, P., Beck, P., & West, J. A study of homosexual women. *Social Work,* 1974, *19,* 714-723.

Chafetz, J., Sampson. P., Beck, P., West. J., & Jones, B. *Who's Queer? A Study of Homo- and Heterosexual Women.* Florida: Omni-Press, Inc., 1976.

Cotten, W. L. Social and sexual relationships of lesbians. *Journal of Sex Research,* 1975, 11, 139-148.

Gagnon, J. H., & Simon, W. *Sexual Conduct.* Chicago: Aldine Publishing Co., 1973.

Gundlach, R. Research project report. *The Ladder,* 1967, 11, 2-9.

The Ladder, 1960, 4, 4-25.

Livingood, J., ed. *National Institute of Mental Health: Task Force on Homosexuality.* Washington: U.S. Government Printing Office, 1972.

Loney, J. Background factors, sexual experiences and attitudes toward treatment. *Journal of Clinical Psychology,* 1972, 38, 57-65.

Saghir, M. F., & Robins, E. Sexual behavior of the female homosexual. *Archives of General Psychiatry,* 1969, 20(2), 192-201.

Saghir, M. F., & Robins, E. *Male and Female Homosexuality.* Baltimore: The Williams and Wilkins Company, 1973.

Saghir, M. F., Robins, E., Walbran, B., & Gentry, K. Psychiatric disorders and disability in female homosexuals. *American Journal of Psychiatry,* 1970, 127(2), 147-154.

Siegelman, M. Parental background of homosexual and heterosexual women. *The British Journal of Psychiatry,* 1974, 124, 14-21.

U.S. Department of Labor: Employment Standards Administration. *Highlights of women's employment and education* (brochure). Washington: Women's Bureau, May 1975.

Sappho Was a Right-On Adolescent:
Growing Up Lesbian

Margaret Schneider, PhD, C Psych

SUMMARY. Beginning with the interaction between the coming-out process and adolescent development, this paper explores the young lesbian experience. The words and perceptions of over 20 young lesbians are used to depict the experience from their own points of view. *[Article copies available from The Haworth Document Delivery Service: 1-800-342-9678. E-mail address: getinfo@haworth.com]*

As Adrienne Rich (1980) once wrote, "The lesbian experience [is] a profoundly *female* experience" (p. 650). Indeed, research indicates that lesbians have more in common with their heterosexual counterparts than with gay men in matters that include expectations of relationships, equality, and the development of sexual awareness (Dailey, 1979; Peplau, Cochran, Rook, & Padesky, 1978; Simon & Gagnon, 1967). Yet, in the study of homosexuality, as is often the case in social sciences research, the male experience is frequently taken as the norm. In recognition of the underrepresentation of the lesbian experience in current research, this paper focusses on the lives of young lesbians, as females and as adolescents.

Research on lesbian and gay identity formation describes the coming-

The author would like to thank David Kelley and Bob Tremble for their contributions in collecting the data for this paper, and Lesbian and Gay Youth Toronto for helping to contact research participants.

Margaret Schneider, *Journal of Homosexuality*, Volume 17, Numbers 1/2. © 1989 by The Haworth Press, Inc.

out process beginning with first awareness and delineating the stages that culminate in identity consolidation. The psychological and situational factors that facilitate movement through these stages are identified (Cass, 1979; Coleman, 1982; Cronin, 1974; Ponse, 1978; Schäfer, 1976). The present research differs in that it examines coming out in the context of the developmental process and describes experiences once lesbian identity has been established, during the stages that Cass labeled Identity Acceptance, Identity Pride, and Identity Synthesis.

TORONTO AND THE GAY AND LESBIAN COMMUNITY

Toronto, a city of over 2,000,000, resembles many large, North American cities. The downtown core offers a rich mixture of business, stores, and entertainment, including performing and visual arts, museums, galleries, sporting events, and a variety of restaurants. The main streets are dotted with buskers and vendors selling crafts, food, and souvenirs. Although the surrounding suburban areas have developed self-sufficiency in many respects, downtown Toronto remains where the action is, particularly for youth.

Toronto is unique due to its ethnic diversity. A variety of ethnic groups are represented, each having its own self-contained local neighborhood, which includes commerce, entertainment, and shopping. The city is also unique because of the mixed-use characteristic of most neighborhoods. Most areas combine commercial and residential use, with businesses along the main streets and residential buildings along the side streets. Types of residences include high-rise and low-rise apartment buildings, Victorian mansions converted into flats and apartments as well as single family dwellings. Even the downtown core constitutes a neighborhood, resulting in lots of people on the streets at all times. Thus, the city is relatively safe because it is populated at most times of day and night. Toronto is also remarkably clean.

The putative gay area is located in the northeast corner of the downtown area with focal points on two parallel streets, Church and Parliament. The latter marks the boundary of Cabbagetown, a neighborhood once inhabited by poor Irish and Scottish immigrants. It has undergone extensive gentrification during the past ten years. It is now one of the preferred residential areas for well-to-do gay men, and is very expensive. The area looks much like the trendy, upscale part of any city; however, many subtle signals identify it as the center of gay community life.

The gay and lesbian community consists of over 100 organizations that include recreational, political, and social service organizations. Among these are: peer support groups; counselling services; organized sports leagues; political action groups; theatre companies; a number of gay, lesbian, and feminist publications; and a youth group, Lesbian and Gay Youth Toronto (LGYT). Many of these organizations meet at a local community center on Church Street.

LGYT is the only niche for youth in the homosexual community. It is a peer support group which meets once a week at the community center. It is organized by a steering committee and has a changing membership of over 200 young men and women at any given time. Apart from this group, the only alternatives for socializing are the bars.

Like many identifiable gay and lesbian communities, Toronto's visible community represents only the tip of the iceberg of the city's gay and lesbian population. This visible element is white, middleclass, youthful, and generally male dominated. The composition of the remainder of the population and the networks through which individuals socialize is anyone's guess. Its existence is only surmised by extrapolating from the statistics that estimate the percentage of gays and lesbians in the general population. This scenario is much the same throughout urban North America.

METHOD

Participants

The research participants were 25 self-identified lesbians, ages 15 to 20. They were contacted through friendship networks, word-of-mouth, a coming-out group, and through LGYT. Only two of the women were black, from the West Indies. The rest were Caucasian. The majority came from the middle socioeconomic bracket, and were raised in suburban Toronto, although three had moved to Toronto from rural communities. Some of these women had rarely or never gone downtown until their first LGYT meeting.

About one-third lived with their parents. The remainder lived on their own, downtown, sharing accommodation with friends. Of the latter, some have moved to be closer to the community, others were kicked out when their parents found out they were lesbians, and a few left in order to avoid lying to their parents. A portion of these young women moved frequently, crashed with friends, or had friends crashing with them. One of the support functions of LGYT is to make sure, in an informal way, that everyone has a place to sleep.

Some of the youngsters work full-time at unskilled jobs. Those who go to high school or community college work part-time. They are a mixed group, preppy, punk, ordinary, unusual. They are generally articulate.

They have found lesbian peers and a niche in the lesbian community. They are at least fairly comfortable with their sexual orientation. They are not necessarily representative; they speak for themselves, but through their words we may come to a better understanding of the young lesbian.

Procedures

The data reported here were gathered over a period of two years, beginning in the summer of 1984, as part of a larger study of coming out among male and female adolescents. Particular attention was paid to stresses and coping mechanisms.

Participants were asked to take part in a study of coming out. They were paid $10.00; although most, if not all, would have participated without remuneration.

A relatively unstructured interview was used, lasting from 1 to 3 hours, averaging about 1 1/2 hours. Participants were asked to describe (a) how they realized they were lesbians, (b) what they did about it, and (c) how they felt about it at different points in the process. Interviews were conducted by the author or a male research assistant, usually in the author's office at a children's mental health center, or at the local community center. The choice of interviewer was determined by whomever made the initial contact with a particular youngster.

Rapport was established by attending LGYT and other meetings to talk about the research. This enabled potential participants to get to know us before they consented to the interview. Participants consented enthusiastically once they knew a friend had participated. They seemed to enjoy talking about their coming-out experiences, and some utilized the opportunity to talk to an adult about things that were troubling them. In anticipation of this, we were prepared to refer young people to appropriate professional services, if necessary.

The data presented here represent a preliminary and qualitative examination of the interviews with young lesbians. Themes that became conspicuous through repetition in a number of interviews are reported here, and the quotations are those which, in the opinion of the author, illustrate the themes articulately and often poignantly. Emerging from the data is an indication that adolescent development is atypical for young lesbians (as well as for gay males). By focussing on the subjective experiences of these young women we can identify major issues in coming out and growing up.

ADOLESCENT DEVELOPMENT
AND THE COMING-OUT PROCESS

Being both lesbian and adolescent means that two interrelated processes are taking place simultaneously, coming out and growing up. These processes provide a framework for conceptualizing the experiences of young lesbians as well as gay males.

Coming out is defined as "the developmental process through which gay people recognize their sexual preferences and choose to integrate this knowledge into their personal and social lives" (De Monteflores & Schultz, 1978, p. 59). It involves at least five interrelated areas of development: (a) the growing awareness of homosexual feelings and identity, (b) developing a positive evaluation of homosexuality, (c) developing intimate same-sex romantic/erotic relationships, (d) establishing social ties with gay and lesbian peers or community, and (e) self-disclosure. Disclosure is reached once labelling takes place, a gay-positive feeling develops, sexual orientation is appropriately placed in perspective relative to the individual's entire identity, and friendships and intimate relationships are established with gay and lesbian peers. These tasks take place in the larger context of general life issues. For example, developing social ties with gay or lesbian peers is part of establishing a community of friends (gay or straight), at work, at leisure, and in the neighborhood. Self-disclosure is one aspect of delineating boundaries between the private and public aspects of life.

To some extent, the tasks of coming out parallel major developmental tasks of adolescence that include: (a) establishing a sense of identity, (b) developing self-esteem, and (c) socialization, including learning how to form and maintain friendships and, in the context of a growing sexual awareness, finding meaning and a place in life for intimacy. Coming out adds a new dimension to these tasks. How do the two processes interact?

Adolescence is a time for identity consolidation (Erikson, 1963), for asking the question, "Who am I?" The lesbian adolescent must also ask, "What does it mean to be a lesbian?" She may also wonder about her place among both heterosexual women and gay men. These are complex issues. Beyond same-sex attraction, being lesbian holds diverse meaning for different individuals (Eisner, 1982; Golden, 1985), and the experiences shared with gay men are accompanied by profound differences. Furthermore, lesbians have much in common with heterosexual women (Cronin, 1974; Rich, 1980). There are pitfalls in arriving at answers. The young person may feel compelled to act out the ubiquitous myths and stereotypes. The characteristic "lesbian" may be allowed to obscure all the other important attributes that comprise the individual. The task for the young lesbian is to put sexual orientation into an appropriate perspective, which is exemplified by Cass' (1979) description of Identity Synthesis, "With the developmental process completed, homosexual identity is integrated with all other aspects of self. Instead of being seen as *the* identity, it is now given the status of being merely one aspect of self" (p. 235).

In a world which tells lesbian youngsters that they are criminals, sinners, or mentally ill, self-esteem becomes a major issue. Until gay-positive feelings emerge, lesbian youngsters have difficulty feeling good about anything they do in school, at home, or in social situations. With gay-positive feelings come self-esteem in other areas of life. Conversely, successes in other parts of life form a foundation on which to build gay-positive feelings.

Socialization for young lesbians is atypical in many respects. They may "date" heterosexually in response to peer pressure and in an attempt to fit in. Confused, conflicted youngsters may engage in promiscuous heterosexual behavior to try to make themselves straight, or to make absolutely sure that they really are lesbians (Schneider & Tremble, 1985). Pregnancy among teenage lesbians is becoming a conspicuous phenomenon (J. Hunter, personal communication November 18, 1986).[1] Those who are involved in an intimate same-sex relationship must keep it a secret. Thus, lesbian adolescents have little opportunity to date, develop intimate same-sex relationships, or experiment sexually in the safe, socially sanctioned context in which heterosexual youngsters develop their social awareness. "At a time when heterosexual adolescents are learning how to socialize, young gay people are learning how to hide" (Hetrick & Martin, 1984, p. 6).

The following discussion will examine the interaction between these two simultaneous processes from the perspective of these young lesbians. How do their experiences compare to those of older lesbians or their young gay male counterparts? What are the pitfalls and what are the strengths to be drawn upon? What are the responsibilities of adults in the lesbian community and in the larger community to respond to the needs of these growing young people?

Identity

In spite of the increased visibility of gays and lesbians, the myths and stereotypes of homosexuals are extant. These images are a source of confusion for gay and lesbian youngsters who erroneously believe that they must adhere to the stereotypes (Schneider & Tremble, 1985). Eventu-

---

1. Joyce Hunter is Director of Social Services at the Hetrick-Martin Institute in New York.

ally, as part of the coming-out process, they realize that life-style and personal style involve options and choices.

Is the lesbian stereotype relevant to the lives of these young women? A few felt pressured to conform to standards that reject traditional femininity. A particularly attractive 19-year-old remembered:

> I was criticized for looking politically incorrect. I dressed the way I wanted to and the way I felt most comfortable, and in the way that would attract other women, and it certainly did! I didn't want to have to live by anybody else's standards. I heard so many times, "You look straight." I thought that was stupid. Looking straight! What's looking straight, what's looking gay? Give me a break. I told them that they were trying to get rid of stereotypes and then creating their own.

A few went through a phase of acting out a stereotype:

> I don't dress butch anymore because I decided that's not what I wanted. But I used to walk down the street with "Women are Powerful" on my leather jacket. That jacket for the past couple months has just been hanging in my closet. It's not that I'm going through a femme phase now. It's that I'm wearing things that are more comfortable. I realized that I don't have to make a statement about what I am. Straight people don't have to go up to people and say, "Hey, I'm straight." (Beth, 16 years old)

Generally, the stereotypical masculine image of the lesbian is perceived as a thing of the past.

> I guess the older people are so used to the stereotype because that's all they had to go on, whereas now we have ourselves to go on. There are some people who look butch all the time. But that's them. They don't do it to look butch. (Emma, 18 years old)

These young women were more interested in being comfortable and having fun with the way they looked. For lack of a better term, they referred to this style as femme. A 19-year-old art student explained:

> Being butch you've got one leather jacket, one pair of jeans, one pair of cowboy boots. That would bore me out of my mind. But being femme you've got a great closet and you can go through all your stuff. Look at it that way and it just seems more interesting.

Ann, age 17 explained, "I don't think I have to change in order to look like a lesbian. If there is a lesbian look, it's comfortable casual clothes and short hair. It's preppy. And lesbians don't wear heels!"

Some noted that the young gay males are the ones more likely to act out a stereotype by being effeminate. Some young women hypothesized that this was a way for males to advertise their sexual availability when they first come out. Others believed it to be a backlash to the heterosexual demands to fit a masculine, macho image. It may also indicate a greater confusion among males between sexual orientation and gender role. In addition, playing the stereotype might serve as a distancing technique for males who, in spite of their sexual orientation, are like heterosexual males in that they are not used to expressing affection for other males. For whatever reason, the salience of the stereotype is one major difference that exists between the contemporary experience for gay males and lesbians.

Adolescents are coming out now at a time when some pop culture figures are openly identifying themselves as gay or lesbian, and when rock songs occasionally refer to same-sex eroticism. Sometimes this is the youth's first indication that she is not alone:

> When you first become aware of your feelings, you think you're the only person in the world. And when Carol Pope sang in "High School Confidential" that she was in love with a woman, at least I knew there was someone on the same planet that felt like me. (Maria, age 18)

Furthermore, unlike the gay males, young women are coming out in a subculture of lesbian and feminist music, art, humor, and political thought. For example, women's music has emerged as a major component of the subculture over the past decade. Exemplified by the work of performers such as Cris Williamson, Holly Near, and Meg Christian, the music began as a reflection of the lesbian and feminist experience and as a celebration of womanhood. Although much of woman's music has transcended these boundaries by appealing to a wider audience, it still remains woman-identified.

To what extent is women's culture relevant to these young people? It depends on personal interests. As one art student pointed out, "People pursue lesbian culture in their own way. I identify with the art, and it helped me to come out, seeing my feelings on canvas. The art I do is lesbian. It focusses on women." Women's music is not especially youth-oriented. It is not their sound. Concerts and records tend to be expensive and not particularly accessible. Nonetheless, the fact of its existence is important. A punk rocker (age 15) comments, "The music is too mellow. I'm not into mellow. I'm into anger. But I think it's great that women have their own music and can do it on their own."

To some, the feminist movement itself is passé. From the perspective of young women who have not experienced the full impact of being a woman in society today, the movement seems to have fulfilled its purpose and it seems to them time to move on the other issues. For others, the feminist movement is still alive; although it poses some conflict for the more politically involved young women. Carrie, a radical lesbian feminist at age 16 explained:

> The feminist movement has helped lesbians a lot, but leading feminists never mention the work of lesbians. We don't belong in the gay movement because we're women, and we don't belong in the feminist movement because we're gay. These feminists, who are supposed to have the best interests of women in mind, don't like lesbians because they don't want anyone to think they're lesbians.

In spite of some ambivalence and occasional indifference to women's culture, it is a source of pride. It may be something that these adolescents grow into. At the very least it provides older lesbian role models for young lesbians, something that is missing from their day-to-day lives. They need to see adults who are happy and productive. Without role models, lives and relationships are difficult to imagine:

> I can't imagine being 65 and still with the same person, but I could imagine being with a man for that long. Long term relationships is a concept that straights have. I just can't get hold of it. I can't imagine being older and being with a woman. (Maria, age 18)

> I worry about being alone ten years down the road. I see a lot of young lesbians out there. What happens when you get old? What happens to old lesbians? I don't know. I mean, do they live together and move out to the suburbs or something? (Naomi, age 18)

In summary, identity issues for these young lesbians are somewhat different than issues for their female predecessors or their gay male peers. They seem less influenced by the prevailing stereotypes. They have the advantage of a women-identified subculture, which may become increasingly relevant as they get older and the subculture evolves. However they are lacking appropriate adult lesbian role models, an important component of identity development for young lesbians.

Self-Esteem

The young lesbians in this study had all developed a positive lesbian identity. This was accomplished through a combination of personal resources and external supports.

Some brought to the coming-out process a trust in their own feelings, which shielded them from society's proscriptions:

I never really thought there was anything wrong with appreciating a poster of a woman instead of a man. I just accepted that that was what I thought. I never put a label to it. I never said, "Hey, I'm a lesbian." It was just what I was doing. (Maria, age 18)

I knew enough of the negative beliefs to know not to talk about it. But this feeling was so natural, I guess I trusted my own feelings enough not to believe anybody else's negative ones. Because I felt that if what I'm doing is what they're saying is sick and bad, well, they must be sick and bad. Because I felt so good about it. (Naomi, age 18)

Most youngsters, lesbian or straight, grow up with a sense of being different. That sense is accentuated for the young lesbian. How she feels about being different will influence her self-esteem. Some can make peace with feeling different:

There are people at school who don't like me and my girlfriend because we're gay. But they wouldn't like us anyway. They can just put a name to it now. I don't care, but I just don't like people who are scum feeling like they have something on us. Like guys come up to me and say, "I'd ask you out, but I know you're not into guys," as if I'd go out with them if I was. (Punk rocker)

I was always different. I read a lot more than most kids. I played sports more than my girlfriends. All the things that made me feel different were also the things that made me feel good. When I started thinking I was gay it was just one more difference. (Brenda, age 17)

More youngsters than we realize had serious difficulty:

There was a total rejection of the idea of being a lesbian. Just a total and utter rejection of it. There was absolutely no way that I wanted to feel different and I felt very different from everyone and I didn't want that. So I didn't feel normal unless I had alcohol or drugs in me. (Sarah, age 20)

External support had to complement internal resources. When it was forthcoming the path was easier. When it was absent, life was painful:

It's painful, but if you have a positive image about yourself, you pick the right friends and your family's really supportive, and even if your family's not, you'll generally find friends who will be, if they're good friends. Just keep your chin up. (Adrienne, age 16)

Connecting with people my own age who were lesbians would have made my life a lot easier, or being told that it was okay. I didn't know where to go to find them. I didn't know if I wanted to find them on my own, alone. I needed someone to say, "It's okay. It's okay to feel confused or to be a lesbian." And all around me were girls my own age who were dating guys, who seemed to be enjoying that, and my parents who are heterosexual. I was surrounded by all that. So I felt like there was a part of me that wasn't being acknowledged. That it didn't exist, and it made me feel alone and depressed. (Theresa, age 19)

Thus, contact with other lesbians was frequently a milestone:

I hadn't met any lesbians up until then. I knew they were some-where, but I felt isolated. Then I got involved with this lesbian group at the community center and I realized that these women were feel-ing the same things that I felt and what I'd been reading about lesbians was, in fact, what I am. That's when I started feeling really good. (Brenda, age 17)

When you find friends who are supportive, not only supportive, but in the same boat as you, and you can see for yourself that their life isn't hell and that a lot of things you hear about gay lifestyle and gay people isn't true, and you find there's nothing really different about them. Then you think, "Gee, it's okay." (Sarah, age 20)

Like any life crisis, coming out provides the context for developing and honing coping skills and personal strengths that in turn contributed to self-esteem. A 20-year-old business student explained:

I feel that I am the terrific person I am today because I'm a lesbian. I decided that I was gay when I was very young. After making that decision, which was the hardest thing I could ever face, I feel like I can do anything.

For lesbians, coping competency becomes a feminist as well as a per-sonal issue, as young women prepare for life outside of a traditional heterosexual relationship without a male provider to depend upon. Patty, who spent some time as a street kid, observes:

You have to protect yourself. Straight women think, "I have a man to protect me," but for me, it's just me. You've got to stick up for yourself and survive every day–just having the strength and using it. (Patty, age 17)

> You can't turn to men for typical things. You have to depend on yourself, and on other women. Men tell you that you can't do things on your own, that you need a man. I don't need a man to help me with anything because I can do it myself. I may depend on other women, but it's not being dependent. (Jackie, age 18)

Assaults on self-esteem can be managed with a combination of personal resources and external support. The struggle often results in increased coping competency. In this the young lesbian differs little from her male counterpart. However, her struggle takes place within the larger context of feminist issues. Her strength and independence as a lesbian is merely part of being a strong and independent female at a time when all women are divesting themselves of their traditional dependent posture.

Socialization: Friendship, Intimacy, and Community

Making friends, working in groups, or earning a living are among those aspects of socialization that can be fulfilled for the young lesbian in a heterosexual context: in the home, at school, and in the community. However, coping in a largely rejecting society requires lesbian peers and role models who provide a forum for problem-solving and comparing experiences. The young lesbian also requires a safe context for exploring intimacy and relationships. The visible lesbian community provides that milieu; although, in many respects, it is an atypical environment for young people.

The young women in this study, including the 15-year-old, consider themselves lucky that they can pass for 19, the legal drinking age in Ontario. A fake I.D. and some makeup gains them access to "the hot meeting places," but not necessarily to the adult world. Older lesbians seem reluctant to have much to do with under-aged lesbians, primarily out of fear of being accused of recruitment or seduction of minors, a charge that all gays and lesbians are particularly vulnerable to. What seems self-preservation to some adults is often interpreted by youth as rejection, ageism, and envy:

> When my teacher discovered I was gay, I was thrown out of the closet. I was 15. I had had a lover for six months and I had no interest in the lesbian community. But when I was forced out and what happened became public, then I had to start finding the community and the support. I'm lucky, because I look 19 and I can talk my way out of anything. So getting to know people wasn't easy, but it was easier than it could have been. But I swear to God, people will support you if they think you're 19. They'll sleep with you. They'll do anything with you. They hear you're 16, and nothing. (Kathy, age 16)

The older people are so tight together because they had to work so hard together. Young people are coming out now in a society that is more accepting of being gay and they're a bit jealous and angry, in a way, that they never had that. (Jan, age 17)

The impropriety of the bar scene for adolescents is evident to the youths themselves:

We need some sort of hang-out-in-the-mall atmosphere, like, you go from hanging out in the mall with your boyfriend to going out to a bar with your girlfriend. Like overnight. It's such a change. What you need . . . is somewhere that the casual comfortableness is still there. (Brenda, age 17)

The bar scene was good because it was my first chance to really meet other lesbians; although most people were just interested in one night stands. But once you meet people at the beginning and make the connections, you don't need the bars as much. But you do at first. (Angie, age 19)

Carrie, age 16, explained, "Let's face it. It's loud, it's smoky, and you drink a lot. It's not healthy. And it's expensive. I'm a student and so are my friends. We don't have that kind of money." And Beth, who is 16, told us, "In the straight world you don't have to go to a bar to meet people. In the gay world you sort of have to. . . . It's the only way you know that people are gay."
Still others said:

They [the adult gay and lesbian community] don't realize how many 15- and 16-year-olds they have in the bars. If they really cared, if they truly cared, they would find other ways for kids to socialize away from the bars. (Susan, age 18)

I'd spend Friday after school at my lover's house. We'd make love and then go out to the bar. I'd ride my bike home to Rosedale and have breakfast on Saturday morning with my family, who had no idea where I'd been. I'd look around the table and feel like screaming. (Mary-Anne, age 17)

I spent most weekends with these women, most of whom were a lot older than me. I'd play hockey and go to the bars even though I was only 16. Then I'd go back to school on Monday. What could I say when people talked about their weekends? I felt like I was two different people during the week and then on the weekends. (Wendy, age 18)

These words reflect an ambivalence to the bar scene. It is where the action is. It is a place to meet people, but going special places just to meet lesbians seems artificial. The alcohol-focussed, sexually loaded environment is, admittedly, not appropriate for young people, and they themselves know it. The experience is akin to culture shock, suddenly moving from a straight, adolescent world to the fast lane in the adult lesbian scene. Little wonder that many describe a schizophrenic sense of living in two separate worlds. It creates problems at home, as well. As Damien Martin, Executive Director of the Hetrick-Martin Institute (formerly the Institute for the Protection of Lesbian and Gay Youth), points out, even parents who accept their gay or lesbian youngster will become understandably concerned when their teenager starts going to bars and coming home late at night.

Yet, these youngsters continue to frequent the bars, which are, after all, places to dance, meet friends, and are springboards to the rest of the lesbian community. They are drawn downtown from the suburbs and bedroom communities by the noise and excitement of the downtown core and the need for a lesbian community. To youth, the bars exemplify that community.

Alternatives to the bar scene include organized sports, political groups, and outdoors groups. To varying degrees, these activities are open to young lesbians, but they are largely populated by adults. Twenty-five-year-old lesbians and 16-year-old lesbians have about as much in common as their heterosexual counterparts. While socializing among teenagers and adults can be rewarding for both groups, it leaves much to be desired if it is the sole option for adolescents. At the end of the day, when the team goes out for a beer, is the 16-year-old permitted to join in? The young lesbian is in a double bind. She is out of place with her heterosexual friends at times, and there are few comfortable places for her in the lesbian community.

What alternatives do these young women envision? They "want somewhere to go to be normal and gay. I would like to do regular, normal things with other lesbians." They want to go on short trips, go dancing, camping, or simply hang out in casual surroundings with their lesbian friends. Their recreational needs are much the same as those of heterosexual youngsters, with the additional need to spend a portion of time in a completely lesbian environment. Unlike their heterosexual counterparts, their friendship networks are not large enough to support some of these activities, and their geographical dispersion over a large area mitigates against spontaneous get-togethers. Yet, outside of the weekly LGYT meeting there are no places for young lesbians to go to gather and socialize openly among themselves.

As adolescents in an adult environment, these young lesbians are out of place. Their abrupt introduction to an alcohol-focussed and sexually loaded environment bypasses the gradual and safe ways in which most heterosexual youngsters learn to deal with alcohol and sexual intimacy. Yet, they need lesbian adults in their lives, not as peers, but as role models. They are not surrounded, as are heterosexual youngsters, by an adult presence which reassures them that life ahead can be happy and productive. Role models of stable lesbian relationships are conspicuously absent in their lives.

Older lesbians, for their part, remain largely unaware, not uncaring, of the dilemma for youth. The social service providers and community developers in the lesbian community are often stymied in outreach to youth by legalities, limited funds, and manpower. Young lesbians, like most youth in an adult-oriented society, feel that adults are largely unresponsive to their needs. "They don't listen to us," is a common theme for all adolescents, but in the microcosm of the lesbian community it is magnified to far greater proportions.

CONCLUSION

These youth share some common experiences of growing up and coming out. Yet, the meaning of the experiences is different for each of them. What does it mean to them to be a lesbian?

You have to drop a lot of options. Like economic security. Women don't usually have a lot of money. (Wendy, age 18)

It's a real love and trust of women, and respect. It's something inside me that I can't explain. (Brenda, age 17)

I have the same goals and dreams. Those don't change because of your sexuality. You don't have different goals just because you're gay. (Shannon, age 17)

It's just realizing something about yourself that's different. You're not going to get married and live the way your parents want you to. (Beth, age 16)

It's not that important. Like, it's the most important unimportant issue. It's not a way of life. It's just a part of my life. You have to sneak around. It's difficult that way. (Ann, age 17)

I don't want it to be a central part of my life. But it keeps coming up. Like when someone asks how come you don't have a boyfriend yet. It means a lot of lying. (Patty, age 19)

My soul feels more comfortable. It feels right. (Shannon, age 17)

It means a certain amount of independence and dependence on women. . . . a sense of democracy, and strength and power in women. (Carrie, age 16)

Being a lesbian means being strong, secretive, nonconforming. It is full of contradictions. It means being different and simultaneously being the same. "The most important unimportant issue," captures the ultimate contradiction in coming out: that the characteristic "lesbian" is a private, personal issue, far from being the mainstay of identity; yet it becomes a central focus for organizing identity and life-style as the result of the need to hide, lie, and to be accepted. In the end, these young women almost unanimously wanted me to express their need and desire for acceptance. I will let them express it for themselves:

> For the straights who are reading it, just to accept us. I don't consider myself different from the average 16-year-old. Except instead of talking about guys I talk about women, or I don't talk about it at all, (Beth, age 16)

> We aren't asking for the world. We're asking to be accepted for what we are as human beings. You don't have to care about our privacy, our sexual pleasures. We're human. (Sandy, age 18)

> We've been through a lot to accept what we are. I'd like them to respect the choice and to appreciate people for what they are, not to judge them by what they do sexually. (Deb, age 17)

> Let them realize how hard it is and just to give us a chance to be who we are. Just to give a human being a chance. I mean, that's who we are. And to other gay kids: don't give up! (Emma, age 18)

REFERENCES

Cass, V.C. (1979). Homosexual identity formation: A theoretical model. *Journal of Homosexuality, 4*(3), 219-235.

Coleman, E. (1982). Developmental stages in the coming-out process. *Journal of Homosexuality, 7,* 31-43.

Cronin, C.S. (1974). Coming out among lesbians. In E. Goode & R.R. Troiden (Eds.), *Sexual deviance and sexual deviants.* New York: Morrow.

Dailey, D.M. (1979). Adjustment of heterosexual and homosexual couples in pairing relationships: An exploratory study. *Journal of Sex Research, 15,* 143-157.

De Monteflores, C., & Schultz, S.J. (1978). Coming out: Similarities and differences for lesbians and gay men. *Journal of Social Issues, 34,* 59-72.

Eisner, M. (1982). *An investigation of the coming-out process, lifestyle, and sex-role orientation of lesbians.* Unpublished doctoral dissertation. York University, Downsview, Ontario.

Erikson, E. (1963). *Childhood and society.* New York: Norton.

Golden, C. (1985, April). Diversity and variability in lesbian identities. In J. Russotto (Chair), *Developmental milestones in the lives of gay men and lesbians.* Symposium conducted at the Annual Meeting of the American Orthopsychiatric Association, New York.

Hetrick, E., & Martin, D. (1984). Ego dystonic homosexuality: A developmental view. In E. Hetrick & T. Stein (Eds.), *Innovations in psychotherapy with homosexuals.* Washington: American Psychiatric Press.

Peplau, L.A., Cochran, S., Rook, K., & Padesky, C. (1978). Loving women: Attachment and autonomy in lesbian relationships. *Journal of Social Issues, 34,* 7-27.

Ponse, B. (1978). *Identities in the lesbian world: The social construction of the self.* Westport, CT: Greenwood Press.

Rich, A. (1980). Compulsory heterosexuality and lesbian existence. *Signs: Journal of Women in Culture and Society, 5,* 631-660.

Schäfer, S. (1976). Sexual and social problems of lesbians. *Journal of Sex Research, 12,* 50-69.

Schneider, M., & Tremble, B. (1985). Gay or straight? Working with the confused adolescent. *Journal of Social Work & Human Sexuality, 4,* 631-660.

Simon, W., & Gagnon, J. (1967). The lesbians: A preliminary overview. In W. Simon & J. Gagnon (Eds.), *Sexual deviance.* New York: Harper & Row.

Growing Older Female:
Heterosexual and Homosexual

Mary Riege Laner, PhD

SUMMARY. An analysis of the age-related content of "Personals" ads placed by heterosexual and homosexual women was undertaken to test hypotheses derived from theoretical notions about differences and similarities between lesbian and nonlesbian aging. No support was found for a hypothesized overrepresentation of older advertisers of either sexual orientation. Contrary to popular notions, lesbians were not found to be seeking young partners. However, age differences between groups did indicate support for "accelerated aging" among heterosexual women. Possible advantages of lesbian over nonlesbian women in their experience of aging are presented. *[Article copies available from The Haworth Document Delivery Service: 1-800-342-9678. E-mail address: getinfo@haworth.com]*

Although recent empirical studies have compared aging processes in heterosexual and homosexual men (Kelley, 1977; Laner, 1978(b); Minnigerode, 1976), little interest has been shown in comparisons between lesbian and nonlesbian aging. The imbalance probably reflects the general tendency of social researchers to study men more often than women, even though significant differences between the sexes have been reported in a

This paper was prepared for presentation at the annual meetings of the Society for the Study of Social Problems, San Francisco, 1978.

Mary Riege Laner, *Journal of Homosexuality*, Volume 4, Number 3. © 1979 by The Haworth Press, Inc.

number of substantive areas (Hochschild, 1973). West's (1967) treatise on homosexuality offers a stereotypic view of male homosexual aging, but overlooks lesbian aging entirely. Rosen's (1974) monograph on lesbianism does not deal with any aspect of lesbian aging. Yet generalizations about homosexual women cannot be validly offered on the basis of information about homosexual men (Nyberg, 1976). Further, as Payne and Whittington (1976) caution, "just as older people are not a homogeneous group neither are older women" (p. 499).

Rosen (1974) asserts that "the only difference between the lesbian and other women is the choice of love object" (p. 65), and cites Simon and Gagnon's (1967) conclusion that "in most cases the female homosexual follows conventional female patterns." Given the failure of researchers to investigate lesbian aging processes or to compare lesbian with nonlesbian aging, these generalizations may not be warranted, even though homosexual women have been found in many other important areas to be virtually indistinguishable from heterosexual women in many other important areas (Armon, 1960; Freedman, 1968; Saghir & Robins, 1973; Thompson, McCandless, & Strickland, 1971).

The study reported here provides a beginning for the investigation of similarities and differences between lesbian and nonlesbian women as they age, using nonreactive data (Lewis, 1975) similar to those that have been utilized to investigate aging similarities and differences between heterosexual and homosexual men (Laner, in press).

OLDER WOMEN AS SICK, SEXLESS, AND SINGLE

Stereotypically, older women in general are pictured as "sick, sexless, uninvolved except for church work, and alone" (Payne & Whittington 1976, p. 488). They are held to have more health problems, both real and imaginary, than do men; to be either widowed or never married; to be sexually inactive and sexually uninterested; to be granny-types, rocking contentedly while knitting or sewing, with few outside interests or contacts beyond the church. Such images, Payne and Whittington contend, are negative, "patently false, and misleading" (p. 498). Yorburg (1974) notes that among heterosexuals reactions to aging vary along sex lines: "The decline in physical attractiveness that accompanies aging is, or at least has been, a greater source of conflict for females in our society. In our youth oriented culture, the obvious signs of aging . . . have been more negatively valued for the female than for the male" (pp. 46-47).

Among homosexuals, however, Bell (1971) describes a different picture: "It appears that aging is less traumatic for the lesbian [than for the gay male] because she doesn't operate in the same highly physical setting of competitiveness as does the male homosexual. There is some irony in a society where aging is generally more crucial and resisted more by women insofar as physical attractiveness is concerned, that the reverse may be true among homosexuals" (p. 298). Part of the reason for this, according to Bell, is that lesbians place more importance on interpersonal factors than do homosexual men (p. 298). However, this explanation does not account for the proposed differences in the experience of aging between hetero- and homosexual women.

ASSUMPTIONS AND HYPOTHESES

If, in fact, older women are not characteristically sick, sexless, or single, then it is reasonable to assume that among those who are not engaged in an exclusive relationship, the search for companions, dates, or potential mates continues into the later years through whatever socially appropriate avenues are available. One such avenue is the "Personals" column advertisement. Such advertisements have recently been used as a data base for studies of both heterosexual and homosexual men and women in other areas of concern (Cameron, Oskamp, & Sparks, 1977; Laner, 1978; Laner & Kamel, 1977).

Assuming that younger women or those more youthful in appearance, whether heterosexual or homosexual, might be more likely to seek companions, dates, or mates through face-to-face contacts, it is logical to expect that women between the ages of 49 and 62 (later middle age) and those between 63 and 80 (later maturity) would be overrepresented among newspaper Personals advertisers. Thus, the first hypothesis of this study predicts that *a higher proportion of older women than younger women will be found among Personals advertisers, whether hetero- or homosexual.*

Given purported differences in aging between heterosexual and homosexual women—namely, that aging has less negative impact on homo- than on heterosexual women—it is reasonable to expect that the "accelerated aging" said to occur among nonlesbians will be reflected in the age distribution of Personals advertisements. (Accelerated aging is the term used by Minnigerode, 1976, to indicate an earlier anticipation of middle or old age by members of one group when compared to members of another group.) Thus, without inconsistency with the first hypothesis, the second hypothesis predicts that *a higher proportion of heterosexual than homosexual women advertisers will be found in the early-middle-age range of the age distribution of Personals advertisements.*

A final hypothesis was developed regarding the desired age of respondents to advertisements. Gagnon and Simon (1973, p. 188) assert that older homosexual women are not typically interested in women considerably younger than themselves (as popular representations of the "older lesbian seductress" have argued). Among heterosexual women, the norm is to seek a male companion who is at least the same age as or, better still, a few years older than oneself. Thus, the third hypothesis is stated in the null form: *No statistically significant differences will be found between hetero- and homosexual women Personals advertisers with respect to age requirements for respondents to the advertisements.*

SIMILARITIES AND DIFFERENCES

Personals advertisements for heterosexual women were taken from a recent issue of the *National Singles Register,* a publication printed on the West Coast but distributed nationally. Lesbians' advertisements were taken from the *Wishing Well,* which also originates on the West Coast and is nationally circulated. One issue of the heterosexually oriented publication and two issues of the homosexually oriented publication yielded 229 heterosexual and 273 homosexual women's Personals advertisements.

Using an expanded version of Atchley's (1977) life-course categories, Table 1 displays the age distribution of lesbian and nonlesbian advertisers who stated their ages. The hypothesized overrepresentation of older advertisers was not found for either heterosexual or homosexual women, since 80% of the heterosexual and 89% of the homosexual women claimed ages within the young adulthood and early-middle-age categories. Apparently, women advertisers of neither sexual orientation see the Personals column as a marketplace limited to those who, because of their age, might be thought less successful in direct contact markets.

However, the second hypothesis, which predicted an overrepresentation of early-middle-age heterosexual advertisers, was supported and affirms the notion of accelerated aging, among heterosexual women.

Additionally, lesbian advertisers tended to be disproportionately frequent in the young adulthood category. This finding is similar to that reported by Laner (in press) for homosexual, as compared with heterosexual, men. As with gay men, the overrepresentation of young adult lesbians may be due to the stigma attached to homosexuality in American society and to the attendant fears of "coming out gay" among the young, coupled with a lack of knowledge as to where other lesbians might be contacted in person. With experience, lesbians are likely to become more familiar with a homosexual subculture within which they might find partners. Thus, the need to use an impersonal form of contact such as a newspaper advertise-

TABLE 1. Comparison of Heterosexual and Homosexual Women's Claimed
Ages in Personal Advertisements, Shown as Percentages

Age Groups	Heterosexual Women (*n* = 175)	Homosexual Women (*n* = 268)	*p*
Young adulthood (ages 18-34)	30	61	*p* < .01
Early middle age (ages 35-48)	50	28	*p* < .01
Later middle age (ages 49-62)	17	11	
Later maturity (ages 63-80)	3	--a	

Note: Heterosexual advertisers ranged in age from 21 to 72 years, and homosexual advertisers ranged from 18 to 63 years. Levels of significance in this and the following table were computed by Davies' (1962) method.
aLess than .5% of the homosexual advertisers were in this category.

ment in the search for a same-sex companion or potential mate would be reduced. Conversely, the overrepresentation of early-middle-age heterosexual women may be a product of the high divorce rate at early ages among heterosexuals (U.S. Bureau of the Census, 1976), coupled with the absence of a "field of eligibles" comparable to that which the lesbian community provides for homosexual women. Thus, the heterosexual woman of early middle age who is seeking a partner, and who is experiencing the stigmatization of age earlier than does her homosexual counterpart, might have greater need to turn to Personals columns to find friendship or other meaningful relationships.

An unpredicted difference was found in the proportions of hetero- and homosexual women who stated their age. Over 98% of the lesbian advertisers stated their age, as compared with about 76% of nonlesbians. This tendency to conceal chronological age (while not characteristic of the majority of heterosexual advertisers) may reflect the greater negative valence attached to aging by heterosexual women. Curiously, the opposite finding was reported by Laner (in press) for homosexual, as compared with heterosexual, men. Laner speculated that, on the one hand, perhaps age was simply less important to homosexual men, or, at the other extreme, that those homosexual men who did not state their age might all be in older age groups. However, further analysis of Laner's data led her to conclude against the "older, hence hiding age" explanation. In the present study of women, the data examined thus far appear to indicate that the tendency among some heterosexual women to avoid revealing chronological age is associated with a more powerful stigma among this group.

Table 2 shows the proportionate distribution of age claims and desires of both hetero- and homosexual women advertisers. Of all the possible age-claimed and age-desired combinations found in the advertisements, nonlesbian and lesbian women differed meaningfully on only two types: (a) almost twice as many lesbians as nonlesbians stated their own age but did not specify any desired age in a partner; and (b) four times as many heterosexual as homosexual women were seeking a stereotypically "same age or older" companion, date, or mate. Thus, as hypothesized, heterosexual and homosexual women did not differ significantly on five out of six combinations of age-claimed and age-desired categories. However, as noted above, in the seventh category (age specified for self but no age specified for the respondent to the advertisement), far fewer lesbians than nonlesbians restricted the age of the prospective ad respondent. This finding indicates that the respondent is not typically restricted to a "young or younger than self" category, and also suggests that the age of a partner is less important to lesbians than it is to heterosexually oriented women. A related finding is that a considerably higher proportion of heterosexual women (18%) than of homosexual women (.5%) specified an age desired in the respondent but did not specify their own age. Although the statistical significance of the difference could not be calculated due to the small numbers involved, it is clearly a meaningful one. This appears to be an

TABLE 2. Distribution of Age Claims and Desires of Female Heterosexual and Homosexual "Personals" Advertisers, Shown as Percentages

Age Claims and Desires	Heterosexual Women ($n = 229$)	Homosexual Women ($n = 273$)	p
Age claimed for self only	42	77	$p < .01$
Age specified for other only	18	.5	
Age specified for self and other:			
Other may be younger, same age, or older	17.5	13[a]	
Other must be young, or younger than self	--	1.2	
Other may be similar to self or younger	.8	3	
Other may be similar to self or older	16	4	$p < .01$
"Young" claimed for self only	.4	--	
"Young" claimed for self; other may be younger, same age, or older	.4	--	
"Young" claimed for self; other must be older	.4	--	
No age specified for self or for other	3	1.3	
Unclassifiable	1.5	--	

[a] This proportionate difference was not statistically significant. In all other cases, significance level of differences could not be calculated due to small numbers in these categories.

additional indication of the tendency of heterosexual women to hide their chronological age and, therefore, of the higher negative valence of age for heterosexual, as compared with homosexually oriented, women. These findings support the contention of Bell (1971) that heterosexual and homosexual "worlds" differ in their views of aging. Further, the low proportion of lesbian women seeking respondents as young as or younger than themselves–less than 5%–supports Gagnon and Simon's (1973) assertion that lesbians do not fit the stereotype of seductresses of the young.

Recent studies using similar data have reported that only about a third (37.2%) of heterosexual women's Personals ads seek either permanent or "meaningful" relationships (Cameron et al., 1977), whereas 57% of lesbians' Personals ads seek either permanent or meaningful relationships (Laner, 1978). Taken together with the findings of the present study, these data indicate that, unlike their male homosexual counterparts (who have been found to advertise mainly for sexual encounters), lesbians' ads seek long-term, stable relationships to an even greater extent than do those of their nonlesbian female counterparts. These findings support Gagnon and Simon's (1973) conclusion that "almost without exception, the lesbians we interviewed expressed a significant commitment to finding . . . an enduring love relationship" (p. 209).

DISCUSSION

Theoretical notions about what it means to be an older woman, either heterosexual or homosexual, led to the hypothesis that in Personals advertisements where a companion, date, or mate is sought, older women of both sexual orientations would be overrepresented. However, the highest proportions of advertisers, both hetero- and homosexual, were not found in the older age categories.

It was also hypothesized that heterosexual women, who are held to experience accelerated aging compared to their homosexual counterparts, would be overrepresented in the early-middle-age category. This prediction was supported.

Finally, no affirmation of the belief that homosexual women are potential seductresses of the young was found. The hypothesis of no difference between hetero- and homosexual women in terms of desired age of respondent was supported.

The findings of this study indicate that, insofar as aging is concerned, lesbians may have the advantage over nonlesbians. Lesbians do not experience the acceleration of aging as early, nor is the age of their partners as important, as in the heterosexual world. This means that the field of eligibles for lesbians, even though they are a minority among women in general, may be effectively larger than the experienced field of eligibles for heterosexual women who continue to seek the traditional "male older/female younger" age distribution in relationships. Finally, as traditionally oriented women frequently lose a community of friends (including potential companions, dates, or mates) upon breaking up with an opposite-sex partner (see Bohannan, 1971, p. 59), lesbians have the additional advantage of ongoing contact with a community of similarly oriented friends, even after a prior relationship has broken off.

Continued study of lesbian aging (vis-à-vis nonlesbian aging), especially using nonreactive data of other types, is clearly warranted. The present study was limited to a data base taken from only one of several lesbian publications containing Personals ads, and was limited further by the relatively low proportions of both hetero- and homosexual women found in the later maturity category. The implications suggested by the findings of this investigation should be tested by future studies using other methodological approaches.

REFERENCES

Armon, V. Some personality variables in overt female homosexuality. *Journal of Projective Techniques in Personality Assessment,* 1960, *24,* 292-309.

Atchley, R. C. *The social forces in later life* (2nd ed.). Belmont, Calif.: Wadsworth, 1977.

Bell, R. R. *Social deviance.* Homewood, Ill.: Dorsey Press, 1971.

Bohannan, P. The six stations of divorce. In P. Bohannan (Ed.), *Divorce and after.* Garden City, N.Y.: Anchor Books, 1971.

Cameron, C., Oskamp, S., & Sparks, W. Courtship American style: Newspaper ads. *Family Coordinator,* 1977, *26,* 27-30.

Davies, V. *A rapid method for determining the significance of differences between two percentages* (Rev. ed.). Pullman, Wash.: Institute of Agricultural Sciences, 1962.

Freedman, M. J. Homosexuality among women and psychological adjustment. *Ladder,* 1968, *12,* 2-3.

Gagnon, J. H., & Simon, W. *Sexual conduct: The social sources of human sexuality.* Chicago: Aldine, 1973.

Hochschild, A. R. A review of sex role research. *American Journal of Sociology,* 1973, *78,* 1011-1029.

Kelley, J. The aging male homosexual: Myth and reality. *Gerontologist,* 1977, *17,* 328-332.

Laner, M. R. Media mating II: "Personals" advertisements of lesbian women. *Journal of Homosexuality,* Fall 1978, *4*(1), 41-61.

Laner, M. R. Growing older male: Heterosexual and homosexual. *Gerontologist,* 1978, *18,* 496-501.b

Laner, M. R., & Kamel, G. W. L. Media mating I: Newspaper "personals" ads of homosexual men. *Journal of Homosexuality,* Winter 1977, *3*(2), 149-162.

Lewis, G. H. (Ed.), *Fist-fights in the kitchen: Manners and methods in social research.* Pacific Palisades, Calif.: Goodyear, 1975.

Minnigerode, F. A. Age-status labeling in homosexual men. *Journal of Homosexuality,* 1976, *1*(3), 273-276.

Nyberg, K. L. Sexual aspirations and sexual behaviors among homosexually behaving males and females: The impact of the gay community. *Journal of Homosexuality,* Fall 1976, *2*(1), 29-38.

Payne, B., & Whittington. F. Older women: An examination of popular stereotypes and research evidence. *Social Problems,* 1976, *23,* 488-504.

Rosen, D. H. *Lesbianism: A study of female homosexuality.* Springfield, Ill.: Charles C Thomas, 1974.

Saghir, M. R., & Robins, E. *Male and female homosexuality: A comprehensive investigation.* Baltimore: Williams & Wilkins, 1973.

Simon, W., & Gagnon, J. H. Femininity in the lesbian community. *Social Problems,* 1967, *14,* 212-221.

Thompson, N. D., McCandless, B. R., & Strickland, B. R. Personal adjustment of male and female homosexuals and heterosexuals. *Journal of Abnormal Psychology,* 1971, *78,* 237-240.

U.S. Bureau of the Census. Number, timing, and duration of marriages and divorces in the United States, June 1975. *Current population reports* (Series P-20, No. 297). Washington, D.C.: U.S. Government Printing Office, 1976.

West, D. J. *Homosexuality.* Chicago: Aldine, 1967.

Yorburg. B. *Sexual identity: Sex roles and social change.* New York: Wiley, 1974.

Lesbianism in Female and Coed Correctional Institutions

Alice M. Propper, PhD

SUMMARY. Questionnaire responses from 13- to 17-year-old girls in four all-female and three coed institutions were used to determine rates and causes of institutional homosexuality. Rates were as high in coed as in single-sexed institutions. The overall rates of homosexuality for all seven institutions were 14% for "going with or being married" to another girl, 10% for passionately kissing, 10% for writing love letters, and 7% for having sex, beyond hugging and kissing, with another girl. The data suggest that previous homosexuality, often experienced in other correctional programs, explains much of the variance in institutional homosexuality. *[Article copies available from The Haworth Document Delivery Service: 1-800-342-9678. E-mail address: getinfo@haworth.com]*

More has been written about homosexuality than any other aspect of inmate subculture, but the literature contains little good empirical data on

This research has been executed in conjunction with the National Assessment of Juvenile Corrections project supported by Grants N172-010-G and 73NI-99-0001G from the National Institute of Law Enforcement and Criminal Justice, Law Enforcement Assistance Administration, United States Department of Justice, under authorizing legislation of the Omnibus Crime Control and Safe Streets Act of 1968, and by Doctoral Fellowship Grant W70-5198 from the Canada Council. The author wishes to thank E. Douvan, M. Heirich, J. Gartrell, P. Isenstadt, R. Sarri, H. Schuman, E. Selo, R. Silverman, and D. Street for their advice and assistance with parts of the project.

Alice M. Propper, *Journal of Homosexuality*, Volume 3, Number 3. © 1978 by The Haworth Press, Inc.

its prevalence or causes. Estimates of the proportion of adult women who have had a homosexual experience in prison range from 14% (Tittle, 1972, p. 67) to 86% (Giallombardo, 1966, p. 151) and for girls in training schools from 2% (Selling, 1931, pp. 252-253) to 69% (Halleck & Hersko, 1962, p. 913). This wide variation results from lack of specific definitions, differences in definition, differences in sources and methods of obtaining estimates, and perhaps from actual differences in rates among institutions.

Among the limitations of the available estimates is investigators' failure to specify what they mean by terms, thus causing respondents to have differing interpretations of the terms employed. Because researchers have been either reluctant or unable to get permission to ask inmate respondents to report personal experiences, they generally relied on reports by staff and other inmates instead. Many of these respondents have little valid knowledge about all the inmates in an institution, and my experience is that their understanding of the concept of percentage is inadequate for accurate estimates based on this term. There are ways of overcoming all these problems, of course, and this research has attempted to do so.

Terms such as *lesbian, lesbianism, homosexual,* and *homosexuality* are variously defined by people in and out of institutions. As a consequence, estimates based on questions using these terms have limitations for comparative purposes. There may even be less consensus in prison than there is in the free world of what constitutes a homosexual experience because permissible free-world behavior is often regarded as deviant and problematic in institutions. Prison staffs have imputed homosexuality to female inmates who have asexual friendships, "masculine" or other specific styles of hair and dress, who touch another woman when combing her hair, who hold hands or put their arm around another's waist, who hug or lightly kiss, who speak too frequently with another inmate, who get high masculinity scores on masculinity-femininity tests, or who engage in "reckless eyeballing" or looking at another female too long.

There is evidence that incarcerated females almost always use a term other than lesbian or homosexual to describe romantic and sexual dyads in correctional institutions. Some of the argot terms reported by previous investigators are *girl-stuff, playing, being together, the doll racket, chick-vot relationships, having people, making it, tying in,* and *bull-dogging.* The terms probably function to distinguish some sort of special erotic relationship between females from a long-term commitment to homosexuality. Whether the argot terms refer to females having a close asexual friendship or make-believe family, an erotic emotional crush, limited physical contact such as light kissing, hand holding, or embracing, or overt sexual relations such as tongue kissing, fondling of breasts or genitals, tribadism, cunnilingus, or anilingus, is generally not clear.

Our lack of good empirical data about such basic information as rates of homosexuality has not prevented authors from explaining the *presumed* variations in rates in different kinds of prisons. One of the major theoretical perspectives used to explain the presumed variation in rates of homosexuality (and all other kinds of inmate behavior) is that it reflects varying intensities of actual and perceived deprivations in different kinds of prisons. This perspective (variously called the deprivation, functional, or situational model) assumes that homosexuality is most prevalent where inmates are exposed to the most severe hardships. Perhaps its least questioned assumption is that homosexuality is more prevalent in single-sexed than in coed institutions. The claim is accepted without empirical support partly because the "fact" seems so self-evident that researchers have not considered it a hypothesis worth testing. Proponents of the deprivation theory do not specify how one accounts for variations in individuals' homosexual experience within a particular institution; presumably one can infer that those experiencing the greatest severity of deprivation would be those most likely to have a homosexual experience.

A second theoretical perspective focuses on the role of previous socialization and social characteristics that inmates import or bring to prison. Proponents of this importation perspective claim that variations in homosexuality result from varying personal and social characteristics including offense history, race, socioeconomic status, age, and previous sex-role socialization. The relative importance of the numerous possible variables representing this perspective has not been established, nor has there been any emphasis on the role of imported homosexuality.

Recently, scholars have attempted to cover all bases by using both perspectives to explain prison homosexuality, but there is still no adequate specification or evidence on the relative importance of the numerous possible variables that could be selected to represent each perspective or of the nature of the interaction between the variables.

The present investigation was designed to determine the relative effectiveness of the importation and deprivation perspectives in determining individual and institutional variations in homosexuality, and to estimate the prevalence of homosexuality among young women in correctional institutions. A brief overview of some of the methods and nonobvious findings is presented in this report. Further details and documentation of the findings are available through Xerox microfilms (Propper, 1976).

METHOD

Data were collected by means of self-reports on questionnaires administered to 93% of the total female youth population (496 respondents) of a representative sample of four female and three coeducational institutions in the United States. All seven were residential institutions, with the majority of youths attending school and working on-grounds. The female populations ranged from 37 to 128 residents, aged from 13 to 17 years. The mean lengths of stay varied from 4.0 to 9.2 months. The three coed institutions varied in the ratio of male to female inmates (1:1.5, 1:2.9, and 1:3) and in the amount of interaction between the sexes (from separate campuses 1 mile apart and weekly dances, to daily cocducational classes and recreation).

To determine the extent of a respondent's homosexual experience during her current incarceration we asked questions about (a) "going with or being married" to another girl, (b) passionately kissing, (c) writing love letters, and (d) having sex beyond hugging and kissing with another girl. These terms were selected in an attempt to exclude asexual social and athletic contact, and include sexual or erotically tinged relationships that parallel heterosexual courting and going steady, as well as long, deep, tongue or French kisses, breast fondling, and genital contact between members of the same sex.

Local argot and vernacular terms for homosexuality were consciously avoided because sexual vernaculars differ across states, are not equally familiar to all respondents, and have different connotations and meanings even for people in the same region and institution. Terms such as homosexual and lesbian were also avoided because the numerous possible interpretations of these terms would have made it impossible to compare validly the rates of homosexuality across institutions.

The questions about the four different homosexual experiences were phrased to incorporate Kinsey, Pomeroy, and Martin's (1948, p. 53) advice to place the burden of denial on the respondent:

> The interviewer should not make it easy for a subject to deny his participation in any form of sexual activity. It is too easy to say no if he is simply asked whether he has ever engaged in a particular activity. We always assume that everyone has engaged in every type of activity. Consequently, we always begin by asking when they first engaged in such activity. This places a heavier burden on the individual who is inclined to deny his experience; and since it becomes apparent from the form of our question that we would not be surprised if he had had such experience, there seems to be less reason

for denying it. It might be thought that this approach would bias the answer, but there is no indication we get false admissions of participation in forms of sexual behavior in which the subject was not actually involved.

Rather than ask *if* the respondent ever had sex, beyond hugging and kissing, with another girl, we asked for the *number* of girls she had sex with. Asking about the different homosexual experiences in several contexts provided cross-checks on the respondents' self-reports. A respondent was classified as a self-reported participant or nonparticipant only if she gave consistent answers to all questions regarding a particular behavior.

Respondents also answered numerous other questions including some about actual and perceived deprivations of imprisonment (from which measures of 13 variables representing the deprivation perspective were constructed), and about preprison characteristics (from which measures of 15 variables representing the importation perspective were constructed).

FINDINGS

Rates and Patterns of Homosexual Experience

The overall rates of homosexuality (based on self-reports) for all seven institutions combined were 14% for "going with or being married" to another girl, 10% for passionately kissing, 10% for writing love letters, and 7% for having sex, beyond hugging and kissing. These are probably fairly accurate but slightly conservative estimates. If estimates on the three latter indicators were based on youths' estimates of the number of girls in their cottage or dorm having each experience, they are from 2% to 5% higher. Rates are from 4% to 9% higher when based on staffs' estimates of inmates' experiences.

Since no regular ranking of institutions emerged from the comparison of rates based on self-reports on the four indicators of homosexuality, individual use of the four indicators for determining institutional variations and causes of homosexuality was limited. An index, incorporating all four variables, was required for this purpose. When responses on each of the four indicators were coded (nonparticipation = 0, participation = 1) and then subjected to a Guttman scalogram analysis, a ranking of items emerged indicating a progression of experience from "going with or being married," to passionately kissing, to writing love letters, to having sex (coefficient of reproducibility = .91; coefficient of scalability = .70). That is, a respondent who reports one of the later experiences on the list also tends to report having experiences preceding it. Thus, when scores on the four indicators are summed to form a homosexuality index score, the score indicates both the number of different homosexual experiences reported and an approximation of the kinds of experience.

Girls having a score higher than zero reported at least one of the four homosexual experiences. The percentage of youths reporting at least one such experience in all seven institutions combined was 17%, with the rates varying from 6% to 30% depending on the institution. The highest rates were reported in one of the three coed institutions. This particular coed program also had the highest mean score on the homosexuality index. These results fail to support the widely held belief that homosexuality is less prevalent in coed institutions.

When scores on the homosexuality index were used to compute mean homosexuality scores for each institution, a one-way analysis of variance indicated that there were significant differences between institutions (eta^2 = .04, F = 2.55, p < .05), but these differences accounted for only 4% of the variance in the index. Since institutional differences accounted for such a small proportion of the variance, the analysis initially centered on trying to explain the 96% variance in levels of homosexual experience among individuals.

Testing the Deprivation and Importation Perspectives

To determine the relative effectiveness of each theoretical model in predicting homosexuality, regression analysis was used as a device for estimating the total amount of variance in the dependent variable (the homosexuality index scores) that the entire set of independent variables (representing each model) could account for as a set, and as a tool for evaluating the relative contribution of specific variables within each set.

Ideally, one would like to test the deprivation model by examining longitudinal data to determine if those who experienced and perceived the greatest deprivation would later get involved in homosexuality and have their feelings of deprivation reduced as a result of the homosexual experience. Since such data were not available, our approach was to determine whether those reporting the greatest deprivations at the time of the questionnaire administration would be those most likely to have participated in homosexuality. As with many cross-sectional designs, the labeling of the independent and dependent variables was determined by the theoretical perspectives.

If one assumes that punitive institutions are more depriving than are more humane institutions, one might want to compare rates of homosexuality in institutions varying along a continuum of punitiveness-humaneness to see if homosexuality is more pervasive in the environment where deprivations are assumed to be most severe. One problem with comparing institutions along this continuum is that people may feel as deprived in humane as in punitive institutions. The reasons could include feelings of injustice resulting from the philosophy of individual treatment, a heightened awareness of deprivation because of increased contact with the outside world to serve as a reference group, and anxiety created by the greater use of indeterminate sentences. In any case, this particular sample of institutions could not be ordered along such a continuum because all were relatively humane and treatment oriented.

To ensure that data used in this study measured deprivations experienced by the inmate (as opposed to deprivations assumed by the researcher), deprivation was measured directly by asking youths to describe experiences and perceptions on a variety of dimensions. Youths were asked about their length of stay in the institution, distance from family and friends, frequency of home visits, contact with parents, and heterosexual contact. Then, since perceived deprivations may be as important as actual deprivations, youths also reported their perceptions of the severity of deprivation of primary group contact, overemphasis on custody, inadequacy of staff efforts toward treatment, negative staff orientation toward youths, and negative relationships with peers.

When scores on the homosexuality index were regressed on the 13 deprivation variables, *none* of the "independent" variables showed a strong and statistically significant relationship to scores on the homosexuality index. The lack of support for hypotheses derived from the deprivation perspective was surprising in light of its dominance in the literature.

The results of a similar test of hypotheses suggested by the importation perspective were equally surprising. The preprison characteristics representing this perspective included age, social class, offense history, race, previous delinquency, previous correctional experience, and previous homosexual experience. When scores on the homosexuality index were regressed on the 15 importation variables, the results indicated that the best predictor of homosexuality during youths' current incarceration was previous homosexuality. It explained 29% of the variance in youths' homosexuality scores.

To see if the variables representing the importation and deprivation perspectives were any more effective in predicting homosexuality of the girls who reported no prior homosexual experience, we eliminated the 35 respondents who reported previous homosexuality and reran a regression analysis including the other 27 importation and deprivation variables. This analysis included only those who reported that their first homosexual experience occurred during their current incarceration ($n = 42$) as well as those who reported no homosexuality either prior to or during their current incarceration ($n = 312$). By controlling all the variation of previous homosexuality by eliminating respondents who reported it, all the other variables had another opportunity to predict current homosexuality. The result of the previous regression analysis which included both importation and deprivation variables was replicated. None of the variables had a strong and statistically significant relationship to scores on the homosexuality index even when previous homosexuality was eliminated.

Thus whether we focus on explaining homosexuality initiated at the sampled institutions or also include respondents whose homosexual behavior originated at another place, most of the variables that sociologists have previously used to explain homosexuality during incarceration are unimportant when subjected to empirical analysis. Only one variable representing the importation model had any practical significance, and that is previous homosexuality.

The Importance of Previous Homosexuality

Table 1 shows the relationship between current and previous homosexuality for the respondents in all seven institutions combined. The data show that previous homosexuality explains whether individuals will report a homosexual experience and the number of different homosexual experiences they report (i.e., their scores on the homosexuality index).

TABLE 1. Percentage with Various Homosexuality Scores by Previous Homosexuality

Score on Homosexuality Index	No Previous Homosexuality ($n = 354$)	Previous Homosexuality ($n = 35$)	Total ($n = 389$)
0	88.1%	28.6%	82.8%
1	5.9	8.6	6.2
2	2.3	11.4	3.1
3	2.0	25.7	4.0
4	1.7	25.7	3.9
Total Percent	100.0%	100.0%	100.0%

Note. $\chi^2 = 113.98$, $df = 4$, $p < .0001$. Indicator of previous homosexuality is, "The very first time, where did you write love letters, passionately kiss, or have sex with another girl?" Note that "going with or being married to another girl" is an indicator of homosexuality during current incarceration but not of previous homosexuality; thus, the definition of homosexuality for current incarceration is broader than that employed for previous homosexuality.

Most (88%, *n* = 312) of the 354 girls who reported no previous homosexual experience also reported no homosexual experience during their current incarceration. Those who reported their first homosexual experience during their current incarceration reported a lower level of involvement (8%, *n* = 29, with scores of 1 or 2 on the homosexuality index) than those who reported prior homosexual experience.

Most (71%, *n* = 25) of the 35 youths who reported prior homosexual experience also reported having at least one homosexual experience during their current incarceration. These girls report a higher level of institutional involvement (51%, *n* = 18, with scores of 3 or 4 on the homosexuality index) than those who reported no prior homosexual experience. Compared to the group of 42 youths who reported their first homosexual experience during their current incarceration, the 35 girls reporting both previous and current homosexual experiences reported having more varied kinds of homosexual experience during their current incarceration.

The role of previous homosexuality in explaining variations in homosexual experience extends to its importance in accounting for the small, but statistically significant, differences in homosexuality scores between institutions. The coed program with the highest rates of homosexuality also had the highest proportion of respondents reporting previous homosexuality. In this institution, 16 (30.3%) of the 53 respondents reported participation in at least one of the experiences incorporated into the homosexuality index. Of these, 14 (87.5%) reported previous homosexuality elsewhere, and only 2 (12.5%) reported their first homosexual experience during their current incarceration.

CONCLUSIONS

The results of this study give no support to explanations based on deprivation; thus, the theory is inadequate as a general explanation of the effects of confinement and as a satisfactory explanation of presumed variations in homosexuality. There is more empirical support for the importation perspective, but the nature of that support must be carefully qualified.

First, there is the possibility that some of the strong relationship between previous and current homosexual experience results from reporting bias. One interpretation is that those reporting homosexuality at one time of their life may simply be those more likely to report homosexuality at another time. However, the methodological bias hypothesis is inadequate as a *total* explanation of the strong relationship between past and current homosexuality because 52 youths reported homosexuality at one time but not at the other. Of the 354 youths with no prior experience, 42 reported current homosexual experience. Ten of the 35 youths reporting prior homosexuality reported none during their current incarceration. These data suggest that a more reasonable interpretation is that *most* of the relationship results from a real link between past and present behavior, although *some* of it may be due to the difficult methodological problem of reporting bias.

Previous homosexuality plays a far more important causal role than was previously recognized, but it would be wrong to conclude that most institutional homosexuality results from the importation of free-world homosexuality. The importation perspective may be relatively more effective than the deprivation perspective in explaining institutional homosexuality, but neither accounts for most of the homosexuality initiated in this sample. Two-thirds (63%) of the 67 respondents with homosexual experience during their current incarceration reported their first homosexual experience during their current incarceration. Among those with previous homosexual experience, about half reported that they first wrote love letters, kissed, or had sex in a correctional institution, detention center, or group home. Thus, even among this relatively young group of inmates, much prior homosexuality appears to be imported from other single-sexed and coed correctional programs. Although it is tempting to conclude that the institutional environment causes homosexuality because so many youths have their first homosexual experience in prison, we should recognize that there are youths with similar characteristics and backgrounds who would have had their first experience at home if they had never been sent to a correctional institution. Until we know more about the prevalence of similar forms of homosexuality, among a comparable population, we cannot adequately estimate the impact of the institutional environment.

The data may fail to support the widespread belief that homosexuality is more prevalent in single-sexed than in coed institutions because the belief is based on an inaccurate impression of the normality of a coed institution's environment. The opportunity for social and sexual interaction with those of the other sex is probably less than that for youths with the strictest of parents in the free world. In the three coed programs sampled here, and in most others I know of, there are strictly enforced rules against specified forms of body contact. All hetero*social* (as opposed to hetero*sexual* because of the nonphysical nature of the interaction) contact is conscientiously monitored to ensure that it is not sexual. Explicit rules proscribing bodily contact are more likely for opposite-sexed than for same-sexed interaction, partly because they function to prevent organizational problems resulting from the prevention and occurrence of unwanted pregnancies.

The lack of empirical support for the deprivation perspective suggests that future studies of homosexuality may benefit by expanding the former restrictive emphasis on depriving and negative aspects of personal and environmental characteristics and incorporating a serious evaluation of positive characteristics. For example, we may find homosexuality as pervasive in coed as in female institutions (of all kinds, including boarding schools, military programs, and camps) if all were to provide similar degrees of opportunity for interaction with nonfamilial same-sexed peers, similar sexual stimulation, and similar visibility of homosexual role models. The attractiveness of individuals, in both physical appearance and personality, may also determine if they are successful seducers and seducees. Attention should also be directed to determining the nature and role of first and early homosexual experience and of reinforcement in determining institutional homosexuality.

REFERENCES

Giallombardo, R. *Society of women: A study of a women's prison*. New York: Wiley, 1966.

Halleck, S. L., & Hersko, M. Homosexual behavior in a correctional institution for adolescent girls. *American Journal of Orthopsychiatry,* 1962, *32,* 911-917.

Kinsey, A. C., Pomeroy, W. B., & Martin, C. E. *Sexual behavior in the human male*. Philadelphia: W. B. Saunders, 1948.

Propper, A. M. Importation and deprivation perspectives on homosexuality in correctional institutions: An empirical test of their relative efficacy (Doctoral dissertation, University of Michigan, 1976). *Dissertation Abstracts International,* 1977, *37.* (University Microfilms No. 77-8280)

Selling, L. S. The pseudo family. *American Journal of Sociology,* 1931, *37,* 247-253.

Tittle, C. R. *Society of subordinates: Inmate organization in a narcotic hospital*. Bloomington: Indiana University Press, 1972.

Lesbian Women of Color:
Triple Jeopardy

Beverly Greene

The professional literature on mental health has in recent years significantly expanded its inquiry into the roles of culture, ethnicity, gender, and
sexual orientation in mental health, and the delivery of psychological
services to women. This inquiry has included closer scrutiny into the
impact of racism, sexism, heterocentric bias, and the factors associated
with them on the psychological development of women of color, and thus
on the process of assessment and treatment. The literature of professional
psychology in these areas has slowly begun to reflect the appropriate
exploration of the effects of membership in institutionally oppressed and
disparaged groups on the development of both psychological resilience
and psychological vulnerability, and has done so from a wide range of
perspectives (Greene, 1990a). Lesbian women of color, however, often
still find themselves and their concerns invisible in the scholarly research
of both women of color and of lesbians.

This chapter includes African American, Black American of Caribbean
descent, Latina, Asian American, Native American, and Indian women in
the designation "women of color." Those who consider that their primary
romantic/sexual attractions are to women are considered lesbian. Hence,
women from the aforementioned ethnic minority groups who consider
themselves lesbians will be the group referred to in this chapter as lesbian
women of color. Clearly, there are lesbians from other ethnic minority

In L. Comas-Díaz & B. Greene (Eds.), *Women of Color: Integrating Ethnic
and Gender Identities in Psychotherapy.* New York: Guilford, 1994. © 1994 by
The Guilford Press. Reprinted by permission.

[Haworth co-indexing entry note]: "Lesbian Women of Color: Triple Jeopardy." Greene, Beverly.
Co-published simultaneously in *Journal of Lesbian Studies* (The Haworth Press, Inc.) Vol. 1, No. 1,
1997, pp. 109-147; and: *Classics in Lesbian Studies* (ed: Esther D. Rothblum) The Haworth Press, Inc.,
1997, pp. 109-147; and: *Classics in Lesbian Studies* (ed: Esther D. Rothblum) Harrington Park Press, an
imprint of The Haworth Press, Inc., 1997, pp. 109-147.

groups who could also be considered lesbian women of color and to whom many of the statements made in this chapter could apply. The observations made here, however, are limited in their generalizability to the groups mentioned. The absence of specific mention of the others is not intended to suggest that their concerns are of lesser significance; rather, I have limited this discussion to those groups about whom there are clinical, empirical, or anecdotal studies available.

The vast majority of clinical and empirical research on or with lesbians is conducted with overwhelmingly White, middle-class respondents (Amaro, 1978; Chan, 1989, 1992; Gock, 1985, 1992; Greene, in press; Mays & Cochran, 1988; Mays, Cochran & Rhue, in press; Morales, 1989; Tremble, Schneider, & Appathurai, 1989; Wooden, Kawasaki, & Mayeda, 1983). Similarly, the scant research on women of color rarely if ever acknowledges that not all of the groups' members are heterosexual. Hence, there is no exploration of the complex interaction between sexual orientation and ethnic and gender identity development. Nor does the literature take into account the realistic social and psychological tasks and stressors that are a component of lesbian identity formation for women who are members of visible ethnic minority groups. An exploration of the vicissitudes of racism, sexism, homophobia, same-gender socialization, and their effects on the couple relationships of lesbians of color is another important but neglected area of scrutiny.

Empirical and clinical research on lesbians and on women of color rarely states that their generalizability is limited to heterosexual women of color and lesbians who are White. This practice can inadvertently lead readers of these studies to assume that findings that are applicable to women in these groups are equally applicable to lesbians of color, or that the concerns of lesbians of color do not warrant specific attention in the mental health literature. Such narrow clinical and research perspectives leave us with a limited understanding of the diversity of women of color and of lesbians as a group. Another more serious consequence of such omissions is that practitioners are left ill-equipped to address, in culturally sensitive and literate ways, the clinical needs of lesbians who are also stigmatized by their racial or ethnic identity.

A note of caution: broad descriptions of cultural practices or values in this chapter should not be applied with uniformity to all lesbian women of color or to all lesbians in any specific cultural or ethnic group. There are significant differences between the experiences and realities of lesbians of color and their White counterparts, but there is also great diversity within groups of lesbians from specific cultures and races. Clients should not be made to fit arbitrarily into preconceived notions of what all of the women of a group must be like. For example, lesbians who are Latina come from many different countries, with different languages and often many different cultural norms. Asian lesbians come from similarly diverse geographical regions and cultural backgrounds and speak different languages, as do their Indian and Native American counterparts. In these examples, the group's label conceals many different subgroups and distinct cultures. Furthermore, within each subgroup, distinctive differences may be found between lesbians from rural and urban environments as well as between lesbians from various socioeconomic and educational backgrounds within an ethnic culture.

Just as the experience of sexism is "colored" by the lens of race and ethnicity for women of color, so is the experience of heterosexism similarly filtered for lesbian women of color. This chapter provides practitioners with a framework from which to begin looking at lesbians and women of color from a more diverse perspective and at lesbians of color with greater cultural sensitivity. Its aim is to assist in sensitizing practitioners to cultural factors bearing significantly on the ways that lesbian women of color perceive the world, the unique tasks and stressors they must manage on a routine basis, and mental health and therapy issues. It is necessary, however, for practitioners to explore every client's plight with an understanding of the client's own unique perspective of her cultural heritage, sexual orientation, and the respective significance of these in her life.

THE CONDITIONS OF TRIPLE JEOPARDY

The underpinnings of traditional approaches to psychology are riddled with androcentric, heterocentric, and ethnocentric biases (Garnets & Kimmel, 1991; Glassgold, 1992; Greene, 1993a), thus reinforcing the triple discrimination lesbians of color face in the world at large. Heterocentric thinking often leads both professional and lay persons to make a range of inaccurate and unexamined but commonly held assumptions about lesbians. These assumptions are maintained to varying extents within ethnic minority groups as much as they are in the dominant culture. Among many commonly accepted and fallacious notions is that women who are lesbians either want to be men, are "mannish" in appearance (Taylor, 1983), are unattractive or less attractive than heterosexual women (Dew, 1985), are less extroverted (Kite, 1994), are unable to get a man, have had traumatic relationships with men which presumably "turned" them against men, or are defective females (Christian, 1985; Collins, 1990; Greene, 1994a; Kite, 1994). Members of ethnic minority groups, like their counterparts in the dominant culture, believe that sexual attraction to men is embedded in the definition of what it means to be a normal woman. Acceptance of this assumption often leads to a range of equally inaccurate conclusions. One is that reproductive sexuality is the only form of sexual expression that is psychologically normal and morally correct (Garnets & Kimmel, 1991; Glassgold, 1992). Another incorrect assumption is that there is a direct relationship between sexual orientation and a woman's conformity or lack thereof to traditional gender roles and physical appearance within the culture (Kite & Deaux, 1987; Newman, 1989; Whitley, 1987). The mistaken conclusions that follow are twofold. One is that women who do not conform to traditional gender-role stereotypes must be lesbian. The equally mistaken corollary to this is that those who do conform to such stereotypes must be heterosexual. These assumptions are used in many cultures to threaten women with the stigma of being labeled lesbian if they fail to adhere to traditional gender-role stereotypes in which males are dominant and females are submissive (Collins, 1990; Gomez & Smith, 1990; Smith, 1982).

The fear of being labeled a lesbian can be used to prevent women who fear it, whether they are lesbian or not, from seeking nontraditional roles or engaging in nontraditional behaviors. Shockley (1979) suggests that the fear of being labeled lesbian has been strong enough to have deterred Black women writers from examining lesbian themes in their writing. In an atmosphere of tenacious homophobia within ethnic minority groups as well as within the dominant culture, some scholars who are also women of color feel that simply writing about or acknowledging such themes will raise questions about their own sexual orientation (Clarke, 1991). In a patriarchal society, in which male dominance and female subordination has been viewed as normative, threats of being labeled lesbian, fears of that label, and its realistic negative social consequences may be used in the service of maintaining inequitable patterns in the distribution of power.

ASSESSMENT OF RELEVANT CULTURAL FACTORS

A range of factors should be considered in determining the impact of ethnic identity, gender, lesbian sexual orientation, and the ongoing dynamic interaction of these with one another in the course of a woman's development. An understanding of the meaning and the reality of being a woman of color who is lesbian requires a careful exploration and understanding of these factors. These factors include the nature and importance of the culture's traditional gender-role stereotypes and their relative fluidity or rigidity, the role and importance of family and community, and the role of religion/spirituality in the culture. Other important factors include the role of racial and ethnic stereotypes, the prevalence of sexism within their minority culture, racism and ethnic discrimination from the larger culture, and the contribution of these to the ethnosexual mythology applied to these women.

For members of some oppressed groups, specifically African Americans and Native Americans, reproductive sexuality is given even greater importance than it is given by other groups because it is the way of continuing the group's presence in the world, when that presence has been historically endangered by racist, genocidal practices. Hence, sexual practice that is not reproductive may be viewed by persons of color as yet another instrument of an oppressive system designed to limit the growth of these groups or to eliminate them altogether. Kanuha (1990) refers to such beliefs as "fears of extinction" (p. 176) and posits that they are used in the service of scapegoating lesbians of color as if they were responsible for threats to the group's survival. It is interesting to note that such fears do not attend to the reality that a lesbian sexual orientation is not synonymous with a disinclination toward having children, particularly among lesbians of color. This does not mean that fears of extinction among persons of color are unwarranted, rather that it is the institutional racism of the dominant culture that places the survival of persons of color at risk, not lesbians or heterosexual women of color who choose not to reproduce. Nonetheless, the internalization of this view can make it more difficult for a lesbian of color to accept affirmatively her sexual orientation. When this internalization occurs, addressing it must be considered a part of the therapeutic work.

In therapy with lesbian clients of color the family context, the role and expectations of parents in the lives of their children are important factors to consider. For example, the extent to which the parents or family of origin may continue to control or influence children, even when they are adults, and the importance of the family as a source of economic and emotional support warrants understanding (Mays & Cochran, 1988). Other factors to consider include the importance of procreation and the continuation of the family line, the importance of ties to the ethnic community, the degree of acculturation or assimilation of the individual client, significant differences between the degree of acculturation of family members and the individual, and the history of discrimination or oppression that the particular group has experienced from individuals and institutions of the dominant culture. When examining the history of discrimination of an ethnic group, it is imperative that group members' own understandings of their oppression and their strategies for coping with discrimination be incorporated into any analysis. A cursory review of only the dominant culture's perspectives on lesbians or women carries the danger of perpetuating ethnocentric, heterocentric, and androcentric biases.

Another important dimension that must be considered is that of sexuality. Sexuality and its meaning is contextual. Therefore what it means to be a lesbian will be related to the meaning assigned to both gender and sexuality in the individual's culture. Espín (1984) suggests that in most cultures a range of sexual behaviors is tolerated, and that that range varies from culture to culture. It is important for the clinician to determine where the client's behavior fits within the spectrum for her particular culture (Espín, 1984). The therapist must also explore the range of sexuality that is sanctioned, in what forms it may be expressed and by whom, as well as the consequences for those who deviate from or conform to such norms. In exploring the range of sexuality tolerated by the woman's culture it is helpful to determine if there are sexual practices that are formally forbidden but tolerated as long as they are not discussed and not labeled.

It is also important to determine the ethnosexual mythology that has been part of a woman of color's upbringing and its relationship to her understanding of a lesbian sexual orientation. This mythology may include the sexual myths the dominant culture has generated and holds about women of color. Such myths and stereotypes often represent a complex combination of racial and sexual stereotypes designed to objectify women of color, set them apart from their idealized White counterparts, and facilitate their sexual exploitation and control (Collins, 1990; Greene, 1993a; hooks, 1981). The symbolism of these stereotypes and its interaction with stereotypes held about lesbians are important areas of inquiry.

CULTURAL FACTORS IN THE LIVES
OF LESBIANS OF COLOR

Immigration and Acculturation

Espín (1987) suggests that the time of and reasons for immigration are important factors in the treatment of Latina lesbians in the United States. In my experience, these factors are also relevant for Black lesbians from the West Indies and Caribbean islands, as well as for other lesbians of color who are members of immigrant groups. In her discussion, Espín (1987) addresses the effect of separation from one's homeland. Such separation often involved leaving significant family members behind (or even perhaps having been left behind for a time) as well as other major changes in the family's lifestyle. A mourning process associated with this type of loss may be normative. Even when entire families immigrate, many persons of color continue to have intense attachment to their birthplace or homeland, often for many years after leaving. Lesbian women of color are no exception. Departures from the country they consider home may be painful in ways that a therapist who is born and raised in the United States, particularly if she or he is a member of the dominant culture, may have difficulty appreciating. Furthermore, just because immigration is voluntary–such as when the client is escaping an oppressive political regime, seeking a place where she may have greater freedom to be open as a lesbian, or seeking work that is unobtainable in her native country–this does not eradicate significant ties to the homeland itself.

If immigration is recent, the lesbian woman of color may have a significant dependence on her family members and members of her ethnic community for emotional and perhaps economic support. This may complicate issues involved in "coming out" or being open about a lesbian sexual orientation. It is particularly problematic if the family, community, and/or traditional cultural values are perceived or selectively interpreted as rejecting lesbian sexual orientation. New immigrants, if not acculturated, may not yet have contact with a broader lesbian community, or even with lesbians of their own communities. Chan (1989, 1992) writes that the latter tend to be invisible, if they exist at all in Asian and some other ethnic minority communities (Garnets & Kimmel, 1991; Pamela H., 1989). Some lesbians from the West Indies and other Caribbean islands have left their native lands because they believe that their sexual orientation will be easier to be open about in the heterogeneity of the United States than it is on small islands with smaller interconnected communities. In such a setting anonymity is nearly impossible and discovery is difficult to avoid. Silvera's (1991) essay effectively describes the shroud of secrecy around the existence of lesbians in her native home, Jamaica, as well as the contempt with which they are regarded.

Language

Espín (1984) writes that a bilingual woman's first language may be laden with affective meanings that are not captured in translating the words themselves. Since a language reflects a culture's values, it may contain few or no words for lesbian that are not negative, if the culture views lesbian sexual orientations negatively. Espín (1984) suggests that shifts between first (native) and second languages may represent attempts at distancing and estrangement around certain topics in therapy. Espín (1984) observes that a lesbian's second language may be used to express feelings or impulses that are culturally forbidden and that many women would not dare verbalize in their native tongue, which allows them to distance themselves from these feelings. Sexuality is considerably laden with cultural values and as such if a client shifts from speaking in one language to the other during discussions of this material it may be revealing. It is also worth noting that in cultures where English is spoken fluently by the majority of the population, such as India, some Caribbean islands, and for Native Americans, the second language is not always processed or understood similarly, nor do the same words necessarily have the meaning they do in mainstream America (Tafoya & Rowell, 1988).

Family and Gender Roles

Lesbian women of color (and their heterosexual counterparts) see the family as the primary social unit and as a major source of emotional and material support. The family and the ethnic community provide women of color with an additional and important support, functioning as a refuge and buffer against racism in the dominant culture. Lesbians feel separation and rejection by family and community keenly, and many women will not jeopardize their connections to their families and communities by forming alliances with the broader lesbian community or even by simply divulging the fact that they are lesbians. These observations are true for Latina, African American/Caribbean, Asian American, Indian, South Asian, and Native American lesbians (Allen, 1984, 1986; Amaro, 1978; Boyd-Franklin, 1990; Espín, 1984, 1987; Gock, 1992; Greene, 1986, 1993a; Hidalgo & Hidalgo-Christensen, 1976; Icard, 1986; Mays & Cochran, 1988; Morales, 1989, 1992; Moses & Hawkins, 1982; Vasquez, 1979). The boundaries of the family in many ethnic cultures go beyond that of the nuclear family in Western culture; they extend to persons who are not related by blood but are experienced as though they were. These persons are considered extended family. The complex networks of interdependence and support in these families that include lesbian members should not be seen as undifferentiated by a culturally naive therapist.

I will discuss characteristic features of negotiating a lesbian sexual orientation within the family and the ethnic community, complicated by the strong family ties that are common in most ethnic cultures. Lesbian women of color tend to perceive that their ethnic communities not only reject lesbian sexual orientations and are antagonistic to women who overtly label themselves as lesbian, but also that they are more tenaciously antagonistic than the dominant culture (Allen, 1984, 1986; Chan, 1987; Croom, 1993; Espín, 1987; Folayan, 1992; Greene, 1990b, 1993a, in press; Mays & Cochran, 1988; Morales, 1989; Namjoshi, 1992; Poussaint, 1990; Ratti, 1993; Weston, 1991). The perception that antagonism toward lesbians is greater in the ethnic than in the dominant culture is based only on anecdotal reports of lesbians of color about their respective communities. There are no empirical studies to date that systematically assess attitudes toward lesbian sexual orientation in any of these groups.

It is also important to distinguish same-gender sexual behavior that may be known and accepted within a culture from a lesbian identity. Chan (personal communication, November 1992), Espín (1984), Comas-Díaz (personal communication, January 1993) and Jayakar (1994) note that same-gender sexual behavior is known to occur in India, Asian, and Latin cultures between males, but that it is not accompanied by a self-identification as homosexual. It is noteworthy that in same-gender sexual behavior between Latino men, it is the role of the passive or female identified recipient that is devalued.

In many cultures same-gender sexual behavior between women may not be defined or adopted by those who engage in such behavior or relationships as lesbian sexual orientation. This may be particularly so in cultures where lesbians are not tolerated, but the behavior is tolerated as long as it is not accompanied by such a label. There may be a sense that the stigmatized identity would only result from adopting the label; such relationships or behavior can be engaged in in other ways. This type of strategy may also represent a culturally prescribed way of managing a potential conflict indirectly rather than in direct confrontation with it. This phenomenon can be problematic for the clinician in attempts to determine whether the avoidance of the label has its origins in culturally prescribed methods of managing potential conflicts, in culturally distinct or different concepts about what constitutes a lesbian identity, in a reflection of internalized homophobia, or in all of these elements. Attention to the client's personal history and a familiarity with her cultural norms will be crucial to making such determinations accurately. In many cultures, openly adopting the identity of lesbian or declaring a sexual preference for persons of the same gender is what is most problematic for and unacceptable to family members and heterosexual ethnic peers.

LESBIAN WOMEN OF COLOR: DISTINCT POPULATIONS

African American Lesbians

The legacy of sexual racism plays a role in the response of many African Americans to lesbians in their families and as visible members of their communities. Generally, the African American community is perceived by many of its lesbian members as extremely homophobic and rejecting of lesbians (Croom, 1993; Mays & Cochran, 1988). This rejection increases the pressure on lesbians to remain in the closet and hence invisible in their communities (Clarke, 1983; Collins, 1990; Croom, 1993; Gomez & Smith, 1990; Greene, 1993b, in press; Icard, 1986; Mays & Cochran, 1988; Mays, Cochran, & Rhue, in press; Poussaint, 1990; Smith, 1982).

Gender roles in African American families have been somewhat more flexible than in those of their White and many of their ethnic minority counterparts. This flexibility is explained in part as a derivative of the value of interdependence among group members and the more egalitarian nature of many precolonial African tribes. It is also a function of the need to adapt to racism in the United States. The question then is, how did this homophobia–and particularly that directed toward lesbian sexuality–develop?

African Americans are a diverse group of persons, whose cultural origins I have elaborated on in Greene (1994b). Their ancestors were unwilling participants in their immigration, as they were the primary objects of the U.S. slave trade (Greene, 1992, 1993a, 1993b, in press). The roles of African American women, as women, were as pieces of property; forced sexual relationships with African males and White slavemasters were the norm for them. African American women of Caribbean but not Latin descent come from diverse backgrounds in Caribbean islands that were colonized by Great Britain and France, their cultural values and practices may be significantly different from those of African Americans, reflecting the culture of the country responsible for their colonization.

Ethnosexual stereotypes about African American women have their roots in images created by a White society struggling to reconcile a range of contradictions. An elaboration of those contradictions is beyond the scope of this chapter (they are discussed in detail in Greene, 1994b). hooks (1981) proposes that the image of women as castrating was promulgated by psychoanalysis in the 1950s to stigmatize any woman who wanted to work outside the home or cross the gender-role barriers of a patriarchal culture. Because the history of racism had not conferred on African American women the feminine role of homemaker nearly to the degree White women held this role, these women were already working outside the home in greater proportion than White women. Popular images of these women as castrating, therefore, developed as part of an arrangement of social power in which African American men and women were subordinate to Whites, and women were subordinate to men. Hence, today's stereotypes are riddled with a legacy of ethnosexual myths that depict

African American women as not sufficiently subordinate to African American men, inherently sexually promiscuous, morally loose, independent, strong, assertive, matriarchal, and castrating masculinized females when compared to their White counterparts (Christian, 1985; Clarke, 1983; Collins, 1990; Greene, 1986, 1990a, 1990b, 1993a; hooks, 1981; Icard, 1989; Silvera, 1991). African American women clearly did not fit the traditional stereotypes of women as fragile, weak, and dependent, since they were never allowed to be that way. They came to be defined as all of the things that normal women were not supposed to be. Stereotypes that depict lesbians as masculinized women poignantly intersect with stereotypes of African American and African Caribbean women in this regard. They suggest that both lesbians and African American women are defective females who want to be or act like men and are sexually promiscuous. It is important to understand the history of institutional racism and the significant role it has had in the development of a legacy of myths and distortions regarding the sexuality of lesbians from these groups.

Additionally, racism and sexism come together in attempts to present African American women as the cause of failures in family functioning, suggesting that a lack of male dominance and female subordination has prevented African Americans from being truly emancipated. Males in the culture are encouraged to believe that strong women are responsible for their oppression, and not racist institutions. Many African American women, including those who are lesbians, have internalized these myths. When internalized, such distortions of the sexuality of African American women which is treated as if it were depraved, can intensify the negative psychological effects on African American lesbians and further compromise their ability to obtain support from the larger African American community (Clarke, 1983; Collins, 1990).

The African American family has functioned as a necessary and important protective barrier, a survival tool against and refuge from the racism of the dominant culture. Villarosa (quoted in Brownworth, 1993) observes that the status of the African American family and community as central tools for survival and a safe haven makes the process of "coming out" for African American lesbians significantly different from that of their White counterparts:

> It is harder for us to consider being rejected by our families . . . all we have is our families, our community. When the whole world is racist and against you, your family and your community are the only people who accept you and love you even though you are black. So you don't know what will happen if you lose them . . . and many black lesbians (and gay men) are afraid that's what will happen. (p. 18)

Because of the strength of family ties lesbian family members may not be automatically rejected, although there is an undisputed rejection of a lesbian sexual orientation. Villarosa observes that in African American families they do not throw a lesbian out because of the importance of family members to one another, rather, they "keep you around to talk you out of it" (Brownworth, 1993, p. 18).

A clinician should not infer from this "tolerance" that the family approves of its member being a lesbian (Acosta, 1979). Tolerance is usually contingent on silence about one's lesbian sexual orientation. Serious conflicts between family members may in fact erupt if a family member openly discloses, labels herself or discusses being a lesbian.

Homophobia among African Americans and many African Caribbeans can be explained as a function of many different determinants. One is the significant presence of Western Christian religiosity, which is often an exaggerated expression of the strong religion spiritual orientation of these cultures. In this context, selective interpretations of biblical scripture are used to reinforce homophobic attitudes (Claybourne, 1978; Greene, in press; Icard, 1986; Moses & Hawkins, 1982). Silvera (1991) writes that when she was 27 years old her grandmother discovered that she was a lesbian, sat her down with bible in hand, and explained that "this was a ting only people of mixed blood was involved in" (p. 16).

Clarke (1983), Silvera (1991), and Smith (1982) cite heterosexual privilege as another determinant of homophobia among African American women. Because of the rampant sexism in both the dominant and African American cultures, and racism in the dominant culture, African American women often find themselves at the bottom of the racial and gender hierarchies heap. Hence, being heterosexual is the only privileged status they may possess.

Internalized racism may be seen as another determinant of homophobia among African Americans and African Caribbeans. For those who have internalized negative stereotypes of people of African and Caribbean descent as they are constructed and held by the dominant culture, the notion that one mistake is a negative reflection on all African Americans is a common idea (Greene, in press; Poussaint, 1990).

Sexuality has always been an emotionally charged issue, intensified by pejorative ethnosexual myths and stereotypes about African American men and women (Wyatt, Strayer, & Lobitz, 1976). One reaction to negative stereotypes previously mentioned is that of avoiding any behavior that might conform to or resemble those stereotypes. Hence there may be an exaggerated need to demonstrate "normalcy" and fit into the dominant culture's depiction of what people are supposed to be (Clarke, 1983;

deMonteflores, 1986; Gomez, 1983; Greene, 1986, in press; Wyatt et al., 1976). As a result, acceptance of a lesbian sexual orientation can be thought of as contradicting the dominant culture's ideal. Hence lesbians may be experienced by persons who strongly identify with the dominant culture as an embarrassment to them (Poussaint, 1990). Indeed, the only names for lesbians in the African American community are derogatory: "funny women" or "bulldagger women" (Jeffries, 1992, p. 44; Omosupe, 1991). Silvera (1991) writes of her childhood in Jamaica,

> the words used to describe many of these women would be "Man royal" and/or "Sodomite." Dread words. So dread that women dare not use these words to name themselves. The act of loving someone from the same sex was sinful, abnormal—something to hide. (pp. 15-16)

She explains that the word "sodomite," derived from the Old Testament, is peculiar to Jamaica in its use to describe lesbians as well as any strong, independent woman. She continues, "Things are different now in Jamaica. Now all you have to do is not respond to a man's call to you and dem call you sodomite or lesbian" (p. 17).

Clarke (1983) and Jeffries (1992) observe that there was a period of quiet tolerance for gay men and lesbians in some poor African American communities in the 1940s, through the 1950s. Clark explains this as "seizing the opportunity to spite the White man" by tolerating members of a group that the dominant culture devalues. Jeffries attributes this "tolerance" to the empathy of African Americans as oppressed people for the plight of another oppressed group. The recent heightened visibility of lesbians in the dominant culture in general and the higher visibility of African American lesbians in African American communities may ultimately remove the denial of lesbian orientation that has heretofore been required for "tolerance."

Bell and Weinberg (1978), Bass-Hass (1968), Croom, (1993), Mays and Cochran (1988), and Mays et al. (in press) are among the few studies made up exclusively or that include significant numbers of African American lesbian respondents. Among the findings of these studies are that African American lesbians are more likely to maintain strong involvements with their families; more likely to have children; and to depend to a greater extent on family members or other African American lesbians for support than their White counterparts. The findings also indicate that they are likely to have more continued contact with men and with heterosexual peers than their White counterparts. The studies found a greater likelihood that African American lesbians will experience tension and loneliness but are less likely to seek professional help. This may contribute to a delay in the seeking of help during a crisis or a condition and may leave African American lesbians more vulnerable to negative psychological outcomes.

Despite the acknowledged homophobia in the African American community, African American lesbians claim a strong attachment to their cultural heritage and to their communities, and cite their identity as African Americans as primary (Acosta, 1979; Croom, 1993; Mays et al., in press). They also cite a sense of conflicting loyalties between the African American community and the mainstream lesbian community, particularly when confronted with homophobia in the African American community (Dyne, 1980; Greene, 1990b, in press; Icard, 1986; Mays & Cochran, 1988).

Native American Lesbians

Allen (1986) writes, "The lesbian is to the American Indian what the Indian is to the American–invisible" (p. 245). In her brilliant treatise on the role of women in American Native traditions, Allen explains that the written history of Native Americans is a selective one. Those portions of this written history that would establish (1) that the primary social order of native cultures were gynocentric prior to 1800, and (2) that in such systems women held important positions and had the authority to make decisions on all tribal levels–that essentially contradicted a Western, patriarchal worldview–were almost completely deleted. The existence and tolerance of Native American lesbians, who in fact played an integral part of tribal life, had to be obliterated to serve patriarchal interests, resulting in their contemporary invisibility (Allen, 1984, 1986; Tafoya, 1992).

Allen (1986) and Williams (1986) note that in precolonial Native American tribes, physical anatomy was not inextricably linked to gender roles and that mixed, third gender, or alternative gender roles were at one time accepted and integrated into tribal life. LaFromboise et al. (1994) examine important differences between Western and Native communities' understandings of the world, as well as important differences within the immense numbers of different tribes. Tafoya (1992) suggests that Native people may have a more "sophisticated taxonomy which addresses spirituality and function rather than appearance" (p. 254) and that these elements are understood as they appear situationally in relation to something else, not as absolute entities in and of themselves. Within such a paradigm, dichotomous or mutually exclusive categories such as male and female or lesbian and heterosexual may not accurately capture the Native person's understanding of sexuality and gender (Allen, 1984, 1986; Tafoya, 1992).

While there were divisions of roles by gender, they were divided in ways allowing men and women to assume them irrespective of their gender. For example, women who would be considered lesbians by today's standards would have assumed roles usually occupied by men and would have been considered men in some tribes (Allen, 1986). Persons whom we might consider androgynous or lesbian by today's standards were valued and in some tribes were accorded special respect and honor (Allen, 1986; Grahn, 1984; Weinrich & Williams, 1991). They were also often viewed as people who combined aspects of masculine and feminine styles in one person spiritually, reflected in the roles they assumed (Weinrich & Williams, 1991). Allen (1986) observes that in gynocratic systems, people assume roles within the social order by virtue of the realities of the human constitution, rather than on "denial based social fictions" (p. 3) that force people into arbitrary categories determined by powerful and privileged persons within that society.

Jacobs (cited in Grahn, 1984) found 88 tribes whose documented cultural characteristics mention gayness, and 22 of those include specific references to lesbians, with specific names for lesbians in each tribe (Allen, 1986). The 11 tribes who denied, to White anthropologists, the existence of lesbians were observed to come from territories where the most intense and severe puritanical influence from Whites was felt. Allen (1986), Tafoya (1992), and Williams (1986) observe that from the outset Native American people learned not to discuss matters of gender and sexuality with European settlers since the latter groups viewed tribal customs and rituals with contempt, quickly seeking to eradicate them.

It is important to understand the devastating effect of the colonization of Native Americans on tribal life, values, and practices and its role in current attitudes toward lesbians. The degree of acceptance of a gay or lesbian sexual orientation may also be a function of the religious group that was involved in colonizing a particular tribe (V. L. Sears, personal communication, May 1992). Allen (1986) asserts that colonization resulted in a shift from a gynocentric, egalitarian, ritual-based social system to a secular system that more closely resembles European patriarchy. In the course of this shift, women, lesbians, and leaders who observed tribal customs and rituals have suffered the most severe losses of power, status, and leadership (Allen, 1984, 1986; Tafoya, 1992). Colonizers who came from patriarchal cultures could not tolerate groups who allowed women to be powerful and sought to "discredit" the status of women, as well as the tolerance for lesbians and gay men by the deliberate destruction of both records and lives (Allen, 1986). Williams (1986) writes that the stark homophobia of White recorders of tribal life, reflected in their negative judgments of same-gender sexual relationships, stands in stark contrast to the recorded history of easy acceptance of lesbians and gay men among Native Americans themselves. The colonizers' ultimate goal was to present patriarchy as the best alternative (Allen, 1986). This trend is linked to the growth of homophobia, once a rare phenomenon in many tribes. Allen (1986) cites highly acculturated and Christianized Native Americans as those who are most likely to express "fear and loathing" for lesbians, as for any other aspects of traditional tribal life (p. 199).

Tafoya (1992) suggests that the concept of "two-spirited people" (p. 256) is more relevant to Native American people than English-defined categories of lesbian or heterosexual. A two-spirited person possesses a male and female spirit, regardless of his or her biological gender. In this paradigm, an individual's sexuality is viewed on a continuum, and a wide range of sexual behaviors are deemed acceptable. The dichotomous notions of heterosexuality and homosexuality are of little use in such a continuum model, where less stigma is attached to women whose behavior is "masculine" or to men whose behavior is "feminine" (Tafoya, 1992).

In Blumstein and Schwarz's (cited in Tafoya & Rowell, 1988) research with over 200 interracial same-sex couples, a higher rate of bisexual behavior was found among Native American respondents than among any other ethnic group in the United States. Additional findings reveal that self-identified Native American lesbians had higher reported rates of heterosexual experiences than their other ethnic counterparts (Tafoya, 1992). In this context, a Native American lesbian might assume more masculine or feminine behavior depending on her partner and the context (Tafoya & Rowell, 1988). This observation supports the assumption of a more fluid concept of gender relations and sexual expression among Native American people than in both their White and other ethnic counterparts.

Despite these findings, contemporary Native Americans, particularly those who reside on reservations, are less accepting of lesbian sexual orientation than their ancestors. This is explained as a function of colonization, genocide, internalized oppression, and a loss of contact with traditional values (Allen, 1986; V. L. Sears, personal communication, May 1992; Tafoya, 1992; Williams, 1986). Hence, Native American lesbians may experience more pressure to be closeted if they live on reservations than not, prompting many to move to larger, urban areas (V. L. Sears, personal communication, May 1992; Williams, 1986). Obliteration of Native American history and lingering fears about acknowledging practices that were once ridiculed and severely punished result in the continued invisibility of Native American lesbians on reservations. Tafoya (1992) notes that many younger lesbians may even assume that they must leave the reservation to find other lesbians.

Family and community assume as significant a level of importance to Native American lesbians as they do for their other ethnic counterparts, and for similar reasons. This country's legacy of pervasive, disparaging media depictions of Native Americans are often as deeply embedded in the psyche of lesbians in the mainstream as they are in that of the rest of the dominant culture. Hence, the mainstream lesbian community, while it provides a safer place to explore a nontraditional sexual orientation, is not free of the same racism that Native American lesbians experience in other parts of society. The move away from the reservation into the lesbian community may result in the experience of loss of culture and support from family and Native American community. This loss is significant and can precipitate feelings of isolation and depression (V. L. Sears, personal communication, May 1992). Tafoya and Rowell (1988) note that ethnic identity may be primary to Native American lesbians. They may be less likely to present themselves to Native American counseling agencies, out of fear that their sexual orientation will be viewed more negatively by other Native Americans (the same is often true of Asian lesbians, as discussed below).

Tafoya and Rowell (1988) suggest that family therapies are most useful in reintegrating a lesbian member back into the family, and thus they support the culturally syntonic value of reestablishing connectiveness. While there may not be great pressure to marry, the family is often most concerned that a lesbian sexual orientation is synonymous with being childless. Motherhood is an important role for Native American women, since children are seen as the future of the tribe. However, given the higher rates of heterosexual relations of Native American women, this may be less of a realistic concern for them than for their other lesbians of color (Tafoya & Rowell, 1988). Sears (personal communication, May 1992) reports that it is not uncommon for lesbians, including those on reservations, to have children.

Despite these findings, clinicians may encounter Native American lesbians who know nothing of these traditions or concepts and may believe, as do many lesbians on first acknowledging their sexual orientation, that there is no one else like them (Ratti, 1993; Tafoya, 1992).

Asian American Lesbians

Asian American lesbians come from a number of different ethnic groups, which makes any generalizations about them potentially inaccurate. For the purposes of this discussion, the category of Asian American lesbians will comprise lesbians of Japanese or Chinese ancestry only, because it is with these groups that most research has been done.

A salient feature of Asian American families is the expectation of obedience to one's parents and their demand for conformity. This is consistent with the respect accorded elders, and the sharp delineation of gender roles (Bradshaw, 1990, 1994; Chan, 1989, 1992; Garnets & Kimmel, 1991; Gock, 1985; H., 1989). Women are expected to derive status from their roles of dutiful daughter and ultimately wife and mother, passively deferring to men, to whom they are deemed inferior (Chan, 1992; H., 1989).

Pamela H. (1989) observes that for Asian women a problem in the development of an identity as a lesbian lies in their devalued identity as women in the culture. In her analysis, women are discouraged from developing any sense of basic self-worth or identity beyond their preordained roles in the family.

In the role of mother, they are responsible for socializing children appropriately, and are thus considered responsible by family and peers if children do not conform. Hence mothers, perhaps more than other family members, are apt to be blamed if a daughter strays from the predetermined path and declares that she is a lesbian (C. Chan, personal communication, November 1992).

Heterosexual marital relationships are seen as somewhat inevitable, not as something that occurs been two people, but rather between two families for the good of the families. It may be difficult in this context for family members to view a lesbian family member as anything but selfish, in that she has deliberately made her own sexual preference and therefore her own feelings the most important variable in selecting a mate and planning her life.

The development of any sexual identity is also complicated by the taboo against open discussions about sex, which is considered a shameful topic (Chan, 1992; H., 1989). Discussions about sexuality, when they occur, focus on its biological aspects and do not explore nontraditional sexual orientations (H., 1989). Chan (personal communication, November 1992) notes that sex is presumed to be unimportant to women. Asian women are depicted in stereotyped media images in the United States as "passive, quiet, servile" (H., 1989, p. 286) and either "exotically sexy or totally asexual" (p. 293). These images contribute to the ethnosexual mythology that members of the dominant culture hold about Asian women and that some Asian women internalize themselves. Racism in the mainstream lesbian community may be expressed in the expectations of other lesbians that Asian American lesbians actually fit those stereotypes. (Gock, 1992, has reported that this racism is also reflected in the practices of bars, dances, discos, and the like in the mainstream lesbian community, who require more types of identification from Asian American lesbians than from their White counterparts.)

Pamela H. (1989) appropriately reminds us that the media images of lesbians in American films are usually dominated by White women. The tendency for Asian parents to view lesbian sexual orientation as a "Western concept" (p. 284), a product of too much assimilation or a function of losing touch with Asian heritage, may have some of its origins in the invisibility of Asian lesbians in American media depictions of lesbians (Pamela H., 1989). Pamela H. further notes that many Asian parents may be quite "oblivious" to the existence of Asian lesbians and notes that there is no word for "lesbian" in most Asian languages. A declaration of a lesbian sexual orientation may be regarded as an act of open rebellion as well as a blatant rejection of Asian heritage. The declaration of the desire for same-gender relationships may also be regarded as a temporary disorder that the parents hope or just assume their daughter will outgrow. At the other extreme, a lesbian daughter may be thought of by parents as a source of shame to the entire family (Chan, 1992; Pamela H., 1989). Lesbian sexual orientation is viewed as volitional and is presumed to represent a conscious desire to tarnish the family honor. Parents may express the feeling that they can no longer face friends or community.

Because lesbians are incorrectly presumed to be disinterested in becoming parents, a daughter's open disclosure that she is lesbian may be interpreted as a rejection of the role of mother and therefore of her most important role culturally (Chan, 1992; Garnets & Kimmel, 1991; Wooden et al., 1983).

Openly adopting a lesbian sexual orientation will generally be met with disapproval, although individual reactions will of course vary (C. Chan, personal communication, November 1992). The maintenance of outward roles and conformity is an important and distinctive cultural expectation. The fear of negative reactions to disclosure contributes significantly to the pressure to remain closeted within the Asian American community or move away from it to avoid discovery. Chan (1989) noted that over 75% of Asian American lesbians (and gay men) surveyed expressed concerns about revealing their sexual orientation to other Asians because of what they perceived as the potential for rejection and stigmatization. This may have relevant implications for choice of therapist. More research is required to determine if Asian American or other lesbians of color deem sexual orientation or a familiarity with such issues a more important variable in therapist selection than the race or ethnicity of the therapist. If lesbians of color experience members of their own ethnic group as more homophobic than members of the dominant culture, this assumption may also apply to their perception of therapists who are members of the same ethnic group. Croom (1993) provides some support for this notion in her study on African American lesbians. Chan (1992) notes that invisibility leads to the absence of Asian American lesbians who might serve as role models for young women struggling with questions about their sexual identity.

Asian American lesbians, like their other ethnic counterparts, frequently report feeling a pressure to choose between these two communities and subsequently declare the aspect of their identity that is primary. In her 1989 study of Asian American gay men and lesbians, Chan found that most respondents saw their primary identification as a gay man or lesbian rather than Asian American. This study noted however that the primacy of sexual orientation and ethnicity shifts during development, depending on which stages of ethnic-identity development and sexual-orientation identity formation the individual fits at that time. Identification may also vary depending on the need at the time. Gock (1992) proposes a detailed descriptive analysis of the identity integration process of Asian Pacific American lesbians and gay men. Lee (1991) writes of her rejection of her cultural identity,

> For most of my life, I belonged to the "don't wanna be" tribe, being ashamed and embarrassed of my Asian back ground, rejecting it. . . . My father tried his best to jam "Chineseness" down my throat, . . . (he) warned, "If you marry a White we'll cut you out of our will." . . . With my father's wish for my awareness of cultural identity came his expectation that I grow up to be a "nice Chinese girl." This meant I should be a submissive . . . obedient, morally impeccable puppet who would spend the rest of her life deferring to and selflessly appeasing her husband. . . . He wanted me to become all that was against my nature, and so I rebelled with a fury, rejecting and denying everything remotely associated with Chinese culture. . . . Becoming a lesbian challenged everything in my upbringing and confirmed the fact that I was not a nice, ladylike pamperer of men. (pp. 116, 117)

Similar intricate and complex conflicts of loyalty are also observed in lesbians of color from other ethnic groups.

Unlike gay and lesbian members of other ethnic groups, who report feeling more discrimination for their race than sexual orientation, the Asian American gay male sample in this study reported experiencing more discrimination because they were gay than because they were Asian (Chan, 1989). This finding underscores the importance of exploring subtle gender differences in the experience and meaning of certain phenomena, even within the same culture.

Pamela H. (1989) writes that the persistent invisibility of lesbians within Asian American communities is slowly changing, with the development in the early 1980s of Asian American lesbian support and social groups within those communities. Such groups have developed in part in reaction to experiences of invisibility and racial discrimination in the broader lesbian communities, which are predominantly White and often offer little contact with other ethnic lesbians (Noda, Tsui, & Wong, 1979).

Indian and South Asian American Lesbians

Lesbians who identify with the cultures of Bhutan, Bangladesh, India, the Maldives, Nepal, Pakistan, and Sri Lanka are considered South Asian. Although they find themselves confronted with psychological tasks that are similar to other visibly ethnic lesbians (Ratti, 1993), they are virtually absent in the psychological literature. The lesbians of these cultures and countries are markedly heterogeneous. They do not necessarily identify with African American lesbians or other women of color, nor do they necessarily consider themselves persons of color at all. Vaid (cited in Meera, 1993) observes that many Indians view Great Britain as their mother country and for that reason may more closely identify with Whites. Hence clinicians must consider the psychological demands made of lesbians who may be viewed as women of color because of their skin color, but who do not experience themselves as ethnic minorities in the same way that lesbians of color who have been raised in the United States may. They must also consider the conundrum of identifications, alliances, and expectations lesbians of color often have of one another based on assumptions about the meaning of skin color as well as sexual orientation in different parts of the world (see Jayakar, 1994).

Bearing some similarity to broader Asian cultures, gender roles in Indian and South Asian societies are clearly delineated, in a patriarchal social organization. Strict obedience to parents, even among adult children, is expected, as is conformity to social expectations. Among those expectations is that of marriage, which is still frequently arranged by parents or families, and having children. The pressure to marry and have children is quite explicit and may be quite intense. As it is in most patriarchal societies, women are considered inferior and of less importance than men.

Ratti (1993) and Jayakar (1994) observe India and South Asia as lands of contradiction. Jayakar notes in particular that the open discussion or expression of sexuality is taboo, in the same land that produced the Kama Sutra, the world's first literary classic on sexual matters (AIDS Bhedbar

Virodhi Andolan [AIDS BVA], 1993; Ratti, 1993). This makes the discussion of lesbian sexual orientation even less likely and more difficult. Despite a history of sexual behavior between women, reflected in art, literature, sculpture, and painting, as well as sexual and emotional involvement that is self-identified as lesbian, contemporary mainstream Indians view lesbians in much the same way as their other ethnic counterparts, as a social or psychological aberration (AIDS BVA, 1993); as a Western phenomenon or disease that is alien to Indian culture (Bannerji, 1993; Heske, Khayal, & Utsa, 1986; Ratti, 1993).

Generally, the existence of lesbians is not acknowledged in these cultures, but this was not always the case. Heske et al. (1986) write that a history of tolerance of same-gender sexual behavior, particularly in India, was punished and then suppressed by British colonization. Utsa (in Heske et al., 1986) notes that despite (or because of) the patriarchal context of Indian society, there is significant emotional bonding and warmth between women. It would be natural, in a society that is segregated on the basis of gender in many arenas, that women who develop in great proximity to one another, and apart from men, would have more opportunities for close and intimate relationships among them.

The imposition of British morals and values influenced the creation of repressive Indian laws in 1861 (based on British law) that forbid homosexual behavior (Heske et al., 1986). As of 1986 homosexuality was still a legal offense under Section 377 of the Indian penal code, punishable with prison sentences ranging from 10 years to life (Heske et al., 1986). Kim (1993) observes that gay men and lesbians in India do not make themselves as visible as their White counterparts in the United States, out of a pragmatic fear of the backlash of homophobia that would accompany it.

Ratti (1993) notes that the intense pressure for women to marry—usually in arranged marriages—and raise a family makes it extremely difficult for women who are lesbians to build a life with another woman. This forces many into unhappy heterosexual marriages. Some of these women have secret liaisons with women lovers but maintain a heterosexual marriage. Another significant factor mitigating against such relationships is the economic dependence of women in India. Leaving the country and moving to the United States or Great Britain is often an alternative only for a well-educated or financially secure minority (Heske et al., 1986). Of course some women come to the United States to study, but they are usually not from the poorer classes or rural areas. Hence, many Indian lesbians encountered in treatment settings in the United States are from more economically or educationally privileged backgrounds.

Ratti (1993) estimates that there are 80 million gay men and lesbians in

India (based on an estimate of 10% of the general population). But these large numbers of lesbians in India are spread over a vast country. There are no organized, vocal lesbian movements or communities within the country, and few if any magazines or clubs similar to those in the United States. Heske et al. (1986) observes that with the exception of small isolated groups who meet individually and informally, it is difficult to know who is lesbian and who is not and thus even to meet other lesbians. Isolation is therefore a significant issue.

In the United States, Indian and South Asian lesbians report that while the broader lesbian community affords them the opportunity to meet other lesbians in a less stigmatized environment, there remains a significant sense of isolation and invisibility (Bannerji, 1993; Heske et al., 1986; Ratti, 1993). Ratti (1993) attributes this invisibility to scarcity and neglect of the concerns of Indian and South Asian lesbians in the lesbian movement in the United States as well as the expectation that lesbians fit a generic lesbian mold, one that is usually articulated from a majority perspective. This expectation overlooks important cultural differences, which Indian lesbians are left to negotiate. Heske et al. (1986) write that for some Indian lesbians, public displays of affection between lesbians in the United States and the transitory nature of some relationships is at variance with their culture's emphasis on public propriety and longstanding monogamy. Utsa (in Heske et al., 1986) states, "I come from a culture where people have very deep, longstanding bonds with each other. . . . For me to look at relationships and friendships in such a short-term fashion is very hard" (p. 143).

Jayakar (1994) notes that Indian women are socialized to deny directly both their sexuality and any sexual knowledge. The clinician may not assume that Indian lesbians would be any more comfortable with direct discussions of sexual matters than their heterosexual counterparts, even in the private context of therapy. Such discussions must be handled with particular sensitivity.

Another challenge confronting lesbians in these groups is that of racism and ethnocentrism in the broader lesbian community in the United States. Khayal (in Heske et al., 1986) characterizes White women as narrow minded in their concepts of lesbianism in other societies. Heske (in Heske et al., 1986) offers an example in reporting her own surprise in finding that an Indian woman dressed in traditional Indian clothing who she had recently met was a lesbian, and that there was a large population of Indian women who were lesbian as well. This phenomenon may also be a reflection of the invisibility of Indian lesbians in India and the absence of their images in the popular media depictions of lesbians in the United States. Each phenomenon may then circularly reinforce the other.

Like lesbians from other groups discussed here, Indian American lesbians are faced with marginalization and racism in the broader lesbian community (Bannerji, 1993; Heske et al., 1986; Khush, 1993; Ratti, 1993). Reports of being treated like strange, exotic creatures are not uncommon, nor are episodes of discrimination in bars, clubs, dances, meetings, and collectives (Bannerji, 1993; Heske et al., 1993). Bannerji (1993) writes:

> Much of the experience of racism is constructed through gender. As a child and adolescent, I not only yearned to be a White girl, . . . I also saw White femaleness through White men's eyes. . . . The first women to whom I was attracted reflected the White male gaze I had obediently eroticized. I found nothing sensual about my own body nor the bodies of black and Indian girls around me. (p. 61)

She continues and comments on the parallels between her invisibility as a woman in a patriarchal society and as an Indian lesbian in the broader U.S. lesbian community: "Just as men had silenced me in the solidarity committees and meetings of the left, so too I found White lesbians talking for me and about me as though I was not present" (Bannerji, 1993, p. 60).

Shah (1993) posits that South Asian lesbians have to define themselves because of the extreme lack of awareness of them in both South Asian patriarchal societies and in Western lesbian communities. In the absence of the word "lesbian" in their native languages, they have developed their own names for themselves. The Sanskrit word *"anamika"* (p. 114), which means "nameless" was taken by a lesbian collective in 1985 and was used to address the lack of names in South Asian languages for lesbian relationships (Shah, 1993). Other names have been developed out of various South Asian languages by lesbians of those cultures who wish to name themselves in affirmative ways.

Like their ethnic counterparts, the relationships between Indian and South Asian lesbians and their families is intense and complex. While there is a strong commitment to family, and family bonds may override the family's homophobia, Parmar (cited in Khush, 1993) notes that "coming out" carries the realistic risk of being rejected, to the extreme of being completely shunned.

Latina Lesbians

Espín (1984) and others (Amaro, 1978; Hidalgo & Hidalgo-Christensen, 1976; Morales, 1989; Vasquez, 1979) report that gender roles are well established within Latino families and culture. Women are generally expected to be overtly submissive, virtuous (virginal), respectful of elders, and willing to defer to men, who are considered superior to women (Espín, 1984; Morales, 1989). While women are encouraged to maintain emotional and physical closeness to other women, such behavior is not presumed to be lesbian (Amaro, 1978; Espín, 1984; Hidalgo & Hidalgo-Christensen, 1976). Closeness with female friends is encouraged, particularly during adolescence, and may serve as a way of protecting the virginity of young women by diminishing their contact with males. The open discussion of sex and sexuality between women is not culturally sanctioned, and women are expected to be sexually naive (Espín, 1984). Comas-Díaz (personal communication, January 1993) suggests that there is a known tolerance for same-gender sexual behavior among males, as long as it is not overtly labeled as the person's preferred behavior. This avoidance of adopting a stigmatized identity is explained as a function of the cultural importance of saving face, a key component of maintaining dignity and commanding respect. Being indirect is the culturally prescribed way of managing conflict, since in that way participants do not lose face. Espín (1987) contends that in labeling themselves lesbian, Latina women force a culture that denies the sexuality of women to confront it. Furthermore, it implies not only a woman's conscious participation in sexual behavior—behavior that is taboo and that is not performed out of duty to her husband but out of her own desire—but also a confrontation of others with the fact that she engages in forbidden behavior. This stance not only violates the taboo against engaging in such behavior but also challenges the cultural directive to be indirect or avoidant in the face of conflict.

According to Trujillo (1991), the majority of Chicano heterosexuals view Chicana lesbians as a threat to the established order of male dominance in Chicano communities. Their existence is viewed as having the potential of raising the consciousness of Chicana women, causing them to question the premises of male dominance and female subordination.

Espín (1984), Hidalgo and Hidalgo-Christensen (1976), and Morales (1992) suggest that disapproval in Latino communities is more intense than the homophobia in the dominant "Anglo" community. They further suggest that a powerful form of heterosexist oppression takes place within Latin cultures leaving many lesbian members feeling a pressure to remain closeted. Declaring a lesbian sexual orientation may be experienced as an act of treason against the culture and family. Espín (1984, 1987) and Hidalgo (1984) note that a lesbian family member may maintain a place in the family and be quietly tolerated, but this does not constitute acceptance of her lesbian sexual orientation. It is more likely that such tolerance reflects the family's denial. Generally, only masculine looking females ("butch") would be perceived as lesbian and challenged.

The extent to which Latina lesbians will present themselves as gender-role stereotyped in their own relationships, or the degree to which they will observe stereotypes learned in a culture where gender roles are somewhat rigid, will be a function of their level of acculturation, as well as of the extent to which their own families engage in traditional gender roles (Morales, 1989). Despite the anti-lesbian sentiment of their ethnic communities and families, Espín (1987) and Hidalgo (1984) found that there was a deep attachment among Latina lesbians to those communities. Gutierrez (1992) writes:

> It isn't easy to be part of a gay and lesbian culture whose rites and institutions too often consider us to be peripheral or an acquired taste. . . . Our families may reject us but we belong to them nonetheless. . . . The same is true for our friends, neighborhoods, etc. . . . We must not abandon them, . . . they are ours. . . . Even if it is impossible to stay, they remain ours for as long as we claim them. (p. 242)

MENTAL HEALTH ISSUES

Lesbian women of color exist within a tangle of multiply devalued identities, surrounded by the oppression and discrimination that accompany institutionalized racism, sexism, and heterosexism. Unlike their White counterparts, lesbians of color bear the additional task involved in integrating major features of their identity when they are conspicuously devalued. Unlike their ethnic identities, their sexual orientation and sometimes their gender may be devalued by those closest to them in their families.

Women of color usually receive positive cultural mirroring during development, generally but not exclusively through their families. This helps to buffer the demeaning messages and distorted, stereotyped images of themselves created and maintained by the dominant culture. Those who do not receive positive cultural mirroring are at risk for internalizing society's racism.

Lesbians of color also learn a range of negative stereotypes about lesbian sexual orientation long before they know that they are lesbian themselves. With the exception of Native Americans, other ethnic groups have either no words in their language for lesbian or only words and names that are degrading. The unquestioned internalization of pernicious attitudes about lesbians, gleaned from loved and trusted figures, complicates the process of lesbian identity development and self-acceptance for women of color in ways that are not as complex for their White counter-parts (Gock, 1992).

Regardless of the specific ethnic group to which they belong, lesbian women of color must manage the dominant culture's racism, sexism, and heterosexism, as well as that of their own ethnic group. Although most lesbians of color experience their ethnic communities as being of great practical and emotional significance, the homophobia in these communi-ties makes lesbian members more vulnerable, perhaps more inclined to remain closeted, and therefore invisible to them (Chan, 1992; Espín, 1984; Greene, 1993, in press; Mays & Cochran, 1988; Morales, 1989; Moses & Hawkins, 1982). This increases their psychological vulnerability. How important these ties may be to an individual client may vary depending on the degree of her attachment to her cultural background and the degree of acculturation (Falco, 1991). Appropriate, intense ties to ethnic community and family may complicate the "coming out" process for lesbians of color in ways that it may not for their White counterparts. Decisions about coming out to family members are already fraught with anxiety for most women who are lesbians, but for lesbians of color there is often more to lose. Lesbians of color cannot presume acceptance by the broader lesbian community if their families reject them, and they risk giving up an impor-tant source of support if this feared rejection occurs.

Just as the oppression created by heterosexism produces greater stress-ors for lesbians than for heterosexual women, the combined effects of racism, sexism, and heterosexism for lesbians of color intensify and com-plicate the stressors for them (Morgan & Eliason, 1992). While we may assume that the stress of coming out is intense for lesbians of color, because they must manage multiple oppressions, we must also assume that they may bring unique resources and resiliences to this task. Lesbians of color, unlike their White counterparts, have often been forced to learn useful coping mechanisms against racism and discrimination, long before they ever realized that they were lesbians. When confronted with manag-ing other devalued aspects of their identities they may call on the mecha-nisms used against racism to assist them. Psychotherapy can be useful in developing an awareness of these resources in the client and assisting her in their effective use. Problems occur when previously learned coping mechanisms are maladaptive or self-destructive, hence clients in this cate-gory are perhaps more vulnerable to the development of serious pathology. Other variables include not simply the mere presence of other stressors, but their intensity and the amount of attention they require on an ongoing basis. There is no empirical data with significant numbers of lesbians of color to justify more than clinical speculations in this area, but it might be safe to say that it is somewhat more difficult for lesbians of color to be out than for their White counterparts. Further research is needed.

The quiet toleration observed in many ethnic minority families for a lesbian member is generally marked by denial and the need to view lesbian sexual orientations as something whose origins exist outside the culture. Tremble et al. (1989) suggest that attributing lesbian sexual orientation to some outside source may in fact enable some families to accept a family member while removing themselves or that family member from any perceived sense of responsibility. Hence the ubiquitous notion that a lesbian sexual orientation is a Western or White man's disease that is "caught" or chosen. Thus a rationale for rejecting lesbian sexual orientation can be developed by presenting it as if it and ethnic identity were mutually exclusive (Chan, 1992; Espín, 1987; Greene, 1994a, in press; Hidalgo, 1984; Mays & Cochran, 1988; Morales, 1989, 1992; Tremble et al., 1989). The woman who is lesbian is then presented with the notion that if she were true to her ethnic heritage she would have no part in such a lifestyle.

Many people of color believe that only heterosexual orientation is natural or normal and, by correlation, that a woman of color who is lesbian has "chosen" her sexual orientation. Thus follows the assumption that she could choose to be heterosexual if she wanted to do so. Some family members may assert that the choice a lesbian family member makes to acknowledge this aspect of her identity is done deliberately to hurt them. When treating a family member of a lesbian of color it is important to be familiar with these stereotypes, to assist them in understanding that a lesbian relative does not consciously choose her sexual orientation any more than a heterosexual woman does, and to advise them that their support is important to her.

Members of ethnic minority communities as well as White lesbians often choose to view identity as if it were a singular entity. Strong identification with one's ethnic group and alternately sexual orientation are often perceived as if they were mutually exclusive of each other as well as other aspects of identity. Hence, being lesbian is often viewed by ethnic heterosexual peers as a repudiation of one's ethnicity. Similarly, lesbians from the dominant culture often lack an appreciation for the ongoing work required to cope adaptively with racism and, concomitantly the strength and importance of ethnic ties. This can leave lesbians of color feeling poorly understood, as well as guilt ridden about which community to devote their resources to.

Lesbians of color find themselves confronted with racial stereotypes and discrimination in the broader lesbian community. With the exception of large cities, most minority communities are not large enough to maintain a distinct or formal lesbian community of their own (Tremble et al., 1989). Hence, interactions with members of the mainstream lesbian community become important outlets for social support and for meeting others. However, lesbians of color commonly report discriminatory treatment in lesbian bars, clubs, and social and political gatherings and in individuals within the lesbian community (Chan, 1992; Dyne, 1980; Garnets & Kimmel, 1991; Greene, 1994a, in press; Gutierrez & Dworkin, 1992; Mays & Cochran, 1988; Morales, 1989). They describe feeling an intense sense of conflicting loyalties to two communities, in both of which they are marginalized by the requirement to conceal or minimize important aspects of their identities in order to be accepted.

Lesbians of color frequently experience a sense of never being part of any group completely, leaving them at greater risk for isolation, feelings of estrangement, and increased psychological vulnerability. When in the midst of groups like themselves there may be a tendency to idealize the group. What often follows is the expectation of a level of similarity, acceptance, being liked, and being understood in ways that never quite live up to the fantasy. Hence, a client may experience a disturbing sense of aloneness or disappointment, or a heightened sense of not fitting in any setting when idealized environments fail to meet all of their expectations, or when their expectations are unrealistic. While the variance within these groups may be as wide as the variance between them and other groups, that variance may be concealed by similarities. Similarities in experiences and characteristics between people are important, but they do not warrant the assumption that they will automatically result in a person's being perfectly understood on all levels.

Some clients with more serious preexisting psychopathology may tend to idealize people who are like them and devalue people who are not like them, rather than make judgments on a person-to-person basis. In some clients this may reflect a particular stage of lesbian-ethnic minority identity development. However, it may also represent the client's own deeply rooted sense of self-hate. In any case such a stance actually increases her difficulty getting support from the outside world by restricting the range of people from whom it may be obtained. This difficulty then fuels or confirms a self-fulfilling fear of being unable to get support or of being unworthy. More seriously disturbed clients may rapidly alternate between idealization and devaluation of the group, a particular aspect of themselves about which they feel conflicted, and, if known, that same aspect of the therapist. Ethnicity, gender, and sexual orientation are overdetermined characteristics for idealizing and devaluing stances; such behavior thus may be most acute during the early stages of coming out or at other times of crisis.

Relationship Issues for Lesbian Women of Color

Lesbian women of color find themselves in relationships that are largely unsupported outside of the lesbian community. Differences within the lesbian community on preferences for some relationship structures over others are pertinent, but beyond the scope of this chapter. What is clear, however, is that these women may encounter unique challenges in relationships with partners who have the same gender socialization, in a culture that has few open, healthy models of such relationships. That same environment conspicuously devalues their person and devalues their relationships on many levels as well. While lesbian women of color may be accustomed to obtaining family support for their struggles with racism and perhaps sexism they may not presume the appropriate support of family for their romantic relationships or for their appropriate distress if that relationship is troubled. On seeking professional assistance they may find few if any therapists who have training in addressing the many nuances of nontraditional relationships.

Lesbians of color are found in relationships with women who are not of their own ethnic group to a significantly greater degree than are their White counterparts (Croom, 1993; Mays & Cochran, 1988; Tafoya & Rowell, 1988), a phenomenon that has been attributed in part to the fact that there are larger numbers of White lesbians to choose from (Tafoya & Rowell, 1988). While heterosexual interracial relationships bring unique challenges and often lack support on both sides of families and communities, for lesbians of color, they provide yet another challenge in a process that is already fraught with difficulty.

An interracial lesbian couple may be more publicly visible, as a couple, than two women of the same ethnic group. This brings realities of racism that the White partner may have never encountered before. Clunis and Green (1988) observe that because women have tried to avoid racism does not mean that it disappears from their relationships. Lesbians of color have usually developed a variety of coping strategies in addressing racism, and often wear a protective psychological armor (Sears, 1987). Because it is a ubiquitous reality and stressor for them they learn to prioritize their responses to it. A White partner may never have had to do this and may be less prepared (Clunis & Green, 1988). The latter may either fail to notice slights that are racist in origin and experience her partner's anger as inappropriate, may overreact (experience her partner as underreactive), or may take on a protective role that her partner does not require or desire, and may even find patronizing.

A White partner may also feel guilty about racism and may be unaware of the distinction she must make between her personal behavior in the relationship and the racism in the outside world. In the latter case she may attempt to compensate her partner personally for the racism she faces in the world, a task that she cannot do successfully and that will ultimately leave her feeling angry and frustrated. In such relationships neither the lesbian of color nor her White partner can realistically assume that a White partner is free of racism because of her political beliefs or intentions (Clunis & Green, 1988; Garcia, Kennedy, Pearlman, & Perez, 1987). The lesbian of color in such relationships may also need to be aware of her own jealousy or resentment of her lover's privileged status in the dominant culture and in the lesbian community. Both partners may be perceived as lacking loyalty to their own cultures and may even feel ashamed of their involvement with a person who is not of the same race (Clunis & Green, 1988; Falco, 1991; Greene, in press). This complicates both the resolution of issues within the relationship and intensifies the complex web of loyalties and estrangements for lesbian women of color.

While racial issues and cultural differences may contribute to realistic challenges to lesbian relationships, they do not account for all of the problems within them. Racial and cultural differences are often scapegoated as the problem, allowing the couple to avoid looking at more threatening issues. Differences that are most visible lend themselves to be seen as the cause of problems, particularly when simple explanations are desired. At times racial differences may be the cause of significant difficulties, but other problems may be experienced as if they were about racial or ethnic differences when they have more complex origins within the relationship.

Choices of partners and feelings about those choices may reflect conflicts about intimacy and other interpersonal issues. They may also reflect conflicts about racial and ethnic identity. These conflicts may be expressed by lesbian women of color who choose or are attracted to White women exclusively, or who devalue lesbians of color as unsuitable partners.

Lesbians of color who experience themselves as racially or culturally deficient or ambiguous may presume that a partner who is a member of their own ethnic group will somehow compensate for their perceived deficiency or that such a choice will demonstrate their cultural loyalty. There may also be a tendency for a lesbian of color in a relationship with a lesbian from a different minority ethnic group to presume a level of similarity of experience or worldview that is not present. While many of their experiences in the dominant culture as oppressed women of color and

lesbians may be similar, their respective views on their roles in a relationship, maintaining a household, and the role of other family members in
their lives can be very different.

Some lesbians of color may be appropriately sensitive to what Sears
(personal communication, May 1992) refers to as "pony stealing" and
Clunis and Green (1988, p. 140) as "ethnic chasing," while Lee (1991,
p. 117) describes certain White lesbians as "Asianophiles." These terms
are used to identify White women who seek out lesbians of color as
partners to assuage their own guilt about being White, to compensate for
their lack of a strong ethnic identity, or to prove their liberal attitudes. The
ethnosexual stereotypes of lesbians of color as less sexually inhibited than
their White counterparts may serve as another determinant of this behavior. An ethnic chaser may seek, usually unconsciously, to gain from proximity to a lesbian of color whatever they perceive to be lacking in themselves. As these attempts at self-repair are doomed to fail, the partner who
is not a woman of color may respond by feeling angry, resentful, and
somehow betrayed by her partner. In treatment settings it is helpful to
assist women in such relationships to clarify their expectations about being
in any relationship. Beyond this general assessment, the kinds of assumptions held about ethnic or White women in an intimate relationship should
be explored.

Exclusive choices in this realm may also reflect a woman's tendency to
idealize people who are like her and devalue those who are not, or the
reverse. When this is the case, the reality often does not live up to the
fantasy, resulting in disappointment and self-denigration. It is important to
remember that many of these decisions are made without conscious
awareness of them and, most importantly, that they may have many different determinants.

A therapist should not presume that participation in an interracial lesbian relationship is an automatic expression of cultural or racial self-hate
in the woman of color. Nor should he or she presume that a relationship
between two lesbians of color is necessarily anchored in loyalty or respect
for that culture, or in any of the aforementioned problematic premises.
What is of significance is that the therapist be aware of a wide range of
clinical possibilities and explore them accordingly.

SUMMARY

Many lesbian women of color in the United States come from ethnic
groups who were at some point in history colonized or captured by invad-
ers from countries with patriarchal values. For all of these women, the

original values and practices of their cultures were altered by this contact; some were almost obliterated. As a result, many people took on the patriarchal values of their colonizers and others became more intensely patriarchal than they were prior to contact. In these systems, women who are not subordinate to men and who challenge or do not rigidly adhere to traditional gender roles must be discredited, making lesbian sexuality an affront. Men of color are expected to treat women in accordance with these values. Openly acknowledging or tolerating lesbians of color may be perceived as a failure to keep the women in their culture subordinate. Hence there are complex roots to homophobia in the groups discussed earlier, and in lesbians of color themselves.

In this context, there is the potential for negative effects on the health and psychological well-being of lesbian women of color. Mental health practitioners must make themselves aware of the distinct combinations of stressors and psychological demands impinging on lesbians of color, particularly the potential for isolation, anger, and frustration. Aside from being culturally literate, the practitioner must develop a sense of the unique experience of the client with respect to the importance of their ethnic identity, gender, and sexual orientation and their need to establish priorities in an often confusing and painful maze of loyalties and estrangements.

ACKNOWLEDGMENT

The author thanks Nancy Boyd-Franklin, Connie Chan, Lillian Comas-Díaz, Vickie Sears, and Judith White for their helpful comments and discussions during the preparation of this chapter. This work is dedicated to the memory of Dr. E. Kitch Childs (1937-1993) and Audre Lorde (1934-1992).

REFERENCES

Acosta, E. (1979, October). Affinity for Black heritage: Seeking lifestyle within a community. *The Blade, 11,* A-1, A-25.

AIDS Bhedbar Virodhi Andolan. (1993). Homosexuality in India: Culture and heritage. In R. Ratti (Ed.), *A lotus of another color* (pp. 21-33). Boston: Alyson.

Allen, P. G. (1984). Beloved women: The lesbian in American Indian culture. In T. Darty & S. Potter (Eds.), *Women identified women* (pp. 83-96). Palo Alto, CA: Mayfield.

Allen, P. G. (1986). *The sacred hoop: Recovering the feminine in American Indian traditions.* Boston: Beacon Press.

Amaro, H. (1978). *Coming out: Hispanic lesbians, their families and communities.* Paper presented at the National Coalition of Hispanic Mental Health and Human Services Organization, Austin, TX.

Bannerji, K. (1993). No apologies. In R. Ratti (Ed.), *A lotus of another color* (pp. 59-64). Boston: Alyson.

Bass-Hass, R. (1968). The lesbian dyad: Basic issues and value systems. *Journal of Sex Research, 4,* 126.

Bell, A., & Weinberg, M. (1978). *Homosexualities: A study of human diversity among men and women.* New York: Simon & Schuster.

Boyd-Franklin, N. (1990). *Black families in therapy: A multisystems approach.* New York: Guilford Press.

Bradshaw, C. (1990). A Japanese view of dependency: What can Amae psychology contribute to feminist theory and therapy? *Women & Therapy, 9,* 67-86.

Bradshaw, C. Asian and Asian American women: Historical and political considerations in psychotherapy. In L. Comas-Díaz and B. Greene (Eds.), *Women of color: Integrating ethnic and gender identities in psychotherapy* (pp. 72-113). NY: Guilford Press.

Brownworth, V. A. (1993, June). Linda Villarosa speaks out. *Deneuve, 3*(3), 16-19, 56.

Chan, C. (1987). Asian lesbians: Psychological issues in the "coming out" process. *Asian American Psychological Association Journal, 12,* 16-18.

Chan, C. (1989). Issues of identity development among Asian American lesbians and gay men. *Journal of Counseling and Development, 68*(1), 16-20.

Chan, C. (1992). Cultural considerations in counseling Asian American lesbians and gay men. In S. Dworkin & F. Gutierrez (Eds.), *Counseling gay men and lesbians* (pp. 115-124). Alexandria, VA: American Association for Counseling and Development.

Christian, B. (1985). *Black feminist criticism: Perspectives on Black women writers.* New York: Pergamon.

Clarke, C. (1983). The failure to transform: Homophobia in the Black community. In B. Smith (Ed.), *Home girls: A Black feminist anthology* (pp. 197-208). New York: Kitchen Table–Women of Color Press.

Clarke, C. (1991). Saying the least said, telling the least told: The voices of Black lesbian writers. In M. Silvera (Ed.), *Piece of my heart: A lesbian of color anthology* (pp. 171-179). Toronto, Ontario: Sister Vision Press.

Claybourne, J. (1978). Blacks and gay liberation. In K. Jay & A. Young (Eds.), *Lavender culture* (pp. 458-465). New York: Jove/Harcourt Brace Jovanovich.

Clunis, M., & Green, G. D. (1988). *Lesbian couples.* Seattle, WA: Seal Press.

Collins, P. H. (1990). Homophobia and Black lesbians. In *Black feminist thought: Knowledge, consciousness, and the politics of empowerment* (pp. 192-196). Boston: Unwin Hyman.

Croom, G. (1993). *The effects of a consolidated versus non-consolidated identity on expectations of African American lesbians selecting mates: A pilot study.* Unpublished doctoral dissertation, Illinois School of Professional Psychology, Chicago, IL.

deMonteflores, C. (1986). Notes on the management of difference. In T. Stein &

C. Cohen (Eds.), *Contemporary perspectives on psychotherapy with lesbians and gay men* (pp. 73-101). New York: Plenum.

Dew, M. A. (1985). The effects of attitudes on inferences of homosexuality and perceived physical attractiveness in women. *Sex Roles, 12,* 143-155.

Dyne, L. (1980, September). Is D.C. becoming the gay capitol of America? *Washingtonian,* pp. 96-101, 133-141.

Espín, O. (1984). Cultural and historical influences on sexuality in Hispanic/Latina women: Implications for psychotherapy. In C. Vance (Ed.), *Pleasure and danger: Exploring female sexuality* (pp. 149-163). London: Routledge & Kegan Paul.

Espín, O. (1987). Issues of identity in the psychology of Latina lesbians. In Boston Lesbian Psychologies Collective (Eds.), *Lesbian psychologies: Explorations and challenges* (pp. 35-51). Urbana, IL: University of Illinois Press.

Falco, K. L. (1991). *Psychotherapy with lesbian clients.* New York: Brunner/Mazel.

Folayan, A. (1992). African American issues: The soul of it. In B. Berzon (Ed.), *Positively gay* (pp. 235-239). Berkeley, CA: Celestial Arts.

Garcia, N., Kennedy, C., Pearlman, S. F., & Perez, J. (1987). The impact of race and culture differences: Challenges to intimacy in lesbian relationships. In Boston Lesbian Psychologies Collective (Eds.), *Lesbian psychologies: Explorations and challenges* (pp. 142-160). Urbana, IL: University of Illinois Press.

Garnets, L., & Kimmel, D. (1991). Lesbian and gay male dimensions in the psychological study of human diversity. In J. Goodchilds (Ed.), *Psychological perspectives on human diversity in America* (pp. 137-192). Washington, DC: American Psychological Association.

Gartrell, N. (1993). Boundaries in lesbian therapy relationships. *Women & Therapy, 12,* 29-50.

Glassgold, J. (1992). New directions in dynamic theories of lesbianism: From psychoanalysis to social constructionism. In J. Chrisler & D. Howard (Eds.), *New directions in feminist psychology: Practice, theory and research* (pp. 154-163). New York: Springer.

Gock, T. S. (1985, August). *Psychotherapy with Asian Pacific gay men: Psychological issues, treatment approach and therapeutic guidelines.* Paper presented at the meeting of the Asian American Psychological Association, Los Angeles, CA.

Gock, T. S. (1992). Asian-Pacific islander issues: Identity integration and pride. In B. Berzon (Ed.), *Positively gay* (pp. 247-252). Berkeley, CA: Celestial Arts.

Gomez, J. (1983). A cultural legacy denied and discovered: Black lesbians in fiction by women. In B. Smith (Ed.), *Home girls: A Black feminist anthology* (pp. 120-121). New York: Kitchen Table–Women of Color Press.

Gomez, J., & Smith, B. (1990). Taking the home out of homophobia: Black lesbian health. In E. C. White (Ed.), *The Black women's health book: Speaking for ourselves* (pp. 198-213). Seattle, WA: Seal Press.

Grahn, J. (1984). *Another mother tongue: Gay words, gay worlds.* Boston: Beacon Press.

Greene, B. (1986). When the therapist is White and the patient is Black: Considerations for psychotherapy in the feminist heterosexual and lesbian communities. *Women and Therapy, 5,* 41-66.

Greene, B. (1990a). Sturdy bridges: The role of African American mothers in the socialization of African American children. *Women and Therapy, 10*(1/2), 205-225.

Greene, B. (1990b). African American lesbians: The role of family, culture and racism. *BG Magazine,* pp. 6, 26.

Greene, B. (1993a). Psychotherapy with African-American women: Integrating feminist and psychodynamic models. *Journal of Training and Practice in Professional Psychology, 7*(1), 49-66.

Greene, B. (1993b). Stereotypes of African American sexuality: A commentary. In S. Rathus, J. Nevid, & L. Rathus-Fichner (Eds.), *Human sexuality in a world of diversity* (p. 257). Boston: Allyn & Bacon.

Greene, B. (in press). African American lesbians: Triple jeopardy. In A. Brown-Collins (Ed.), *The psychology of African American women.* New York: Guilford Press.

Greene, B. (1994a, April). Ethnic minority lesbians and gay men: Mental health and treatment issues. *Journal of Consulting and Clinical Psychology, 62*(2).

Greene, B. (1994b). African American women. In L. Comas-Díaz and B. Greene (Eds.), *Women of color: Integrating ethnic and gender identities in psychotherapy* (pp. 10-29). NY: Guilford Press.

Gutierrez, E. (1992). Latino issues: Gay and lesbian Latinos claiming La Raza. In B. Berzon (Ed.), *Positively gay* (pp. 240-246). Berkeley, CA: Celestial Arts.

Gutierrez, F., & Dworkin, S. (1992). Gay, lesbian, and African American: Managing the integration of identities. In S. Dworkin & F. Gutierrez (Eds.), *Counseling gay men and lesbians* (pp. 141-156). Alexandria, VA: American Association of Counseling and Development.

H., Pamela. (1989). Asian American lesbians: An emerging voice in the Asian American community. In Asian Women United of California (Eds.), *Making waves: An anthology of writings by and about Asian American women* (pp. 282-290). Boston: Beacon Press.

Heske, S., Khayal, & Utsa (1986). There are, always have been, always will be lesbians in India. *Conditions: 13. International focus,* 1, 135-146.

Hidalgo, H., & Hidalgo-Christensen, E. (1976). The Puerto-Rican lesbian and the Puerto-Rican community. *Journal of Homosexuality, 2,* 109-121.

Hidalgo, H. (1984). The Puerto Rican lesbian in the United States. In T. Darty & S. Potter (Eds.), *Woman identified women* (pp. 105-150). Palo Alto, CA: Mayfield.

hooks, b. (1981). *Ain't I a woman: Black women and feminism.* Boston: South End Press.

Icard, L. (1986). Black gay men and conflicting social identities: Sexual orientation versus racial identity. *Journal of Social Work and Human Sexuality, 4*(1/2), 83-93.

Jayakar, K. (1994). Women of the Indian subcontinent. In L. Comas-Díaz and B.

Greene (Eds.), *Women of color: Integrating ethnic and gender identities in psychotherapy* (pp. 161-184). NY: Guilford Press.

Jeffries, I. (1992, February 23). Strange fruits at the purple manor: Looking back on "the life" in Harlem. *NYQ, 17,* 40-45.

Kanuha, V. (1990). Compounding the triple jeopardy: Battering in lesbian of color relationships. *Women & Therapy, 9*(1/2), 169-183.

Khush. (1993). Fighting back: An interview with Pratibha Parmar. In R. Ratti (Ed.), *A lotus of another color* (pp. 34-40). Boston: Alyson.

Kim, (1993). They aren't that primitive back home. In R. Ratti (Ed.), *A lotus of another color* (pp. 92-97). Boston: Alyson.

Kite, M. (1994). When perceptions meet reality: Individual differences in reactions to lesbians and gay men. In B. Greene & G. Herek (Eds.), *Lesbian and gay psychology: Theory, research, and clinical applications*. Newbury Park, CA: Sage.

Kite, M., & Deaux, K. (1987). Gender belief systems: Homosexuality and the implicit inversion theory. *Psychology of Women Quarterly, 11,* 83-96.

LaFramboise, T.D., Berman, J.S., & Sohi, B.K. (1994). American Indian women. In L. Comas-Díaz and B. Greene (Eds.), *Women of color: Integrating ethnic and gender identities in psychotherapy* (pp. 30-71). NY: Guilford Press.

Lee, C. A. (1991). An Asian lesbian's struggle. In M. Silvera (Ed.), *Piece of my heart: A lesbian of color anthology* (pp. 115-118). Toronto, Ontario: Sister Vision Press.

Mays, V., & Cochran, S. (1988). The Black women's relationship project: A national survey of Black lesbians. In M. Shernoff & W. Scott (Eds.), *The sourcebook on lesbian/gay health care* (2nd ed., pp. 54-62). Washington, DC: National Lesbian and Gay Health Foundation.

Mays, V., Cochran, S., & Rhue, S. (in press). The impact of perceived discrimination on the intimate relationships of Black lesbians. *Journal of Homosexuality.*

Meera. (1993). Working together: An interview with Urvashi Vaid. In R. Ratti (Ed.), *A lotus of another color* (pp. 103-112). Boston: Alyson.

Morales, E. (1989). Ethnic minority families and minority gays and lesbians. *Marriage & Family Review, 14*(3/4), 217-239.

Morales, E. (1992). Latino gays and Latina lesbians. In S. Dworkin & F. Gutierrez (Eds.), *Counseling gay men and lesbians: Journey to the end of the rainbow* (pp. 125-139). Alexandria, VA: American Association for Counseling and Development.

Morgan, K., & Eliason, M. (1992). The role of psychotherapy in Caucasian lesbians' lives. *Women & Therapy, 13,* 27-52.

Moses, A. E., & Hawkins, R. (1982). *Counseling lesbian women and gay men: A life issues approach*. St. Louis, MO: C. V. Mosby.

Namjoshi, S. (1992, June 14). *Flesh and paper: An interview* [Television program]. New York: WNET.

Newman, B. S. (1989). The relative importance of gender role attitudes to male and female attitudes toward lesbians. *Sex Roles, 21,* 451-465.

Noda, B., Tsui, K., & Wong, Z. (1979, Spring). Coming out: We are here in the

Asian community: A dialogue with 3 Asian women. *Bridge: An Asian American perspective.*

Omosupe, K. (1991). Black/lesbian/bulldagger. *differences: A Journal of Feminist and Cultural Studies, 2*(2), 101-111.

Poussaint, A. (1990, September). An honest look at Black gays and lesbians. *Ebony,* pp. 124, 126, 130-131.

Ratti, R. (1993). Introduction. In R. Ratti (Ed.), *A lotus of another color: An unfolding of the South Asian gay and lesbian experience* (pp. 11-17). Boston: Alyson.

Sears, V. L. (1987). *Cross-cultural ethnic relationships.* Unpublished manuscript.

Shockley, A. (1979). The Black lesbian in American literature: An overview. In L. Bethel & B. Smith (Eds.), *Conditions: 5. The Black women's issue, 2*(2), 133-144.

Shah, N. (1993). Sexuality, identity, and the uses of history. In R. Ratti (Ed.), *A lotus of another color* (pp. 113-132). Boston: Alyson.

Silvera, M. (1991). Man royals and sodomites: Some thoughts on the invisibility of Afro-Caribbean lesbians. In M. Silvera (Ed.), *Piece of my heart: A lesbian of color anthology* (pp. 14-26). Toronto, Ontario: Sister Vision Press.

Smith, B. (1982). Toward a Black feminist criticism. In G. Hull, P. Scott, & B. Smith (Eds.), *All the women are white, all the blacks are men, but some of us are brave* (pp. 157-175). Old Westbury, NY: Feminist Press.

Smith, B., & Smith, B. (1981). Across the kitchen table: A sister to sister dialogue. In C. Moraga & G. Anzaldúa (Eds.), *This bridge called my back: Writings by radical women of color* (pp. 113-127). Watertown, MA: Persephone Press.

Tafoya, T. (1992). Native gay and lesbian issues: The two spirited. In B. Berzon (Ed.), *Positively gay* (pp. 253-260). Berkeley, CA: Celestial Arts.

Tafoya, T., & Rowell, R. (1988). Counseling Native American lesbians and gays. In M. Shernoff & W. A. Scott (Eds.), *The sourcebook on lesbian/gay health care* (pp. 63-67). Washington, DC: National Lesbian and Gay Health Foundation.

Taylor, A. T. (1983). Conceptions of masculinity and femininity as a basis for stereo types of male and female homosexuals. *Journal of Homosexuality, 9,* 37-53.

Tremble, B., Schneider, M., & Appathurai, C. (1989). Growing up gay or lesbian in a multicultural context. *Journal of Homosexuality, 17,* 253-267.

Trujillo, C. (Ed.). (1991). *Chicana lesbians: The girls our mothers warned us about.* Berkeley, CA: Third Woman Press.

Vasquez, E. (1979). Homosexuality in the context of the Mexican American culture. In D. Kukel (Ed.), *Sexual issues in social work: Emerging concerns in education and practice* (pp. 131-147). Honolulu: University of Hawaii School of Social Work.

Weinrich, J., & Williams, W. L. (1991). Strange customs, familiar lives: Homosexuality in other cultures. In J. Gonsiorek & J. Weinrich (Eds.), *Homosexuality: Research findings for public policy* (pp. 44-59). Newbury Park, CA: Sage.

Weston, K. (1991). *Families we choose: Lesbians, gays and kinship.* New York: Columbia University Press.

Whitley, B. E., Jr. (1987). The relation of sex role orientation to heterosexual attitudes toward homosexuality. *Sex Roles, 17,* 103-113.

Williams, W. L. (1986). *The spirit and the flesh: Sexual diversity in American Indian culture.* Boston: Beacon Press.

Wooden, W. S., Kawasaki, H., & Mayeda, R. (1983). Lifestyles and identity maintenance among gay Japanese-American males. *Alternative Lifestyles, 5,* 236-243.

Wyatt, G., Strayer, R., & Lobitz, W. C. (1976). Issues in the treatment of sexually dysfunctioning couples of African American descent. *Psychotherapy, 13,* 44-50.

HISTORY AND LITERATURE

Who Hid Lesbian History?

Lillian Faderman

Before the rise of the lesbian-feminist movement in the early 1970's, twentieth-century women writers were generally intimidated into silence about the lesbian experiences in their lives. In their literature, male personae took the voice of their most autobiographical characters, and they were thus permitted to love other women. Sometimes they disguised their homoerotic subject matter in code, which is at times all but unreadable. When they wrote of love most feelingly, and even laid down rules for loving well as Margaret Anderson did, they left out gender altogether. We cannot blame them for not providing us with a clear picture of what it was like for a woman to love other women in their day. If they had, they would have borne the brunt of the anti-lesbian prejudice which followed society's enlightenment by late nineteenth-century and early twentieth-century sexologists about love between women;[1] they knew that if they wished to be taken seriously, they had to hide their "arrested development" and

Lillian Faderman, *Frontiers* Volume IV, Number 3, copyright © 1979 FRONTIERS Editorial Collective. Reprinted by permission.

[Haworth co-indexing entry note]: "Who Hid Lesbian History?" Faderman, Lillian. Co-published simultaneously in *Journal of Lesbian Studies* (The Haworth Press, Inc.) Vol. 1, No. 2, 1997, pp. 149-154; and: *Classics in Lesbian Studies* (ed: Esther D. Rothblum) The Haworth Press, Inc., 1997, pp. 149-154; and: *Classics in Lesbian Studies* (ed: Esther D. Rothblum) Harrington Park Press, an imprint of The Haworth Press, Inc., 1997, pp. 149-154.

"neuropathic natures." But we might expect that before the twentieth century, before love between women was counted among the diseases, women would have had little reason to disguise their emotional attachments; therefore, they should have left a record of their love of other women. And they did. However, it is impossible to discover that record by reading what most of their twentieth-century biographers have had to say about their lives.

While pre-twentieth-century women would not have thought that their most intense feelings toward other women needed to be hidden, their twentieth-century biographers–brought up in a post-Krafft-Ebing, Havelock Ellis, Sigmund Freud world–did think that these feelings should be hidden, and they often altered their subjects' papers. Other twentieth-century biographers have refused to accept that their subjects "suffered from homosexuality," and have discounted the most intense expressions of love between their subjects and other women. And where it was impossible to ignore the fact that their subjects were despondent over some love relationship, many twentieth-century biographers frantically searched for the hidden man who must have been the object of their subject's affection, even though a beloved woman was in plain view. These techniques of bowdlerization, avoidance of the obvious, and *cherchez l'homme* appear in countless pre-1970's biographies about women of whom there is reason to suspect lesbian attachments.

In our heterocentric society, the latter technique is the most frequent. What can it mean when a woman expresses great affection for another woman? According to many of these biographies, it means that she is trying to get a man through her. What can it mean when a woman grieves for years over the marriage or death of a woman friend? It means that she is really unhappy because she had hoped to procure her friend's husband for herself, or she is unhappy because there must have been another man somewhere in the background who coincidentally jilted her at the same time–only all the concrete evidence has been lost. So why did Lady Mary Montagu write letters to Anne Wortley in 1709 which reveal a romantic passion?

> My dear, dear, adieu! I am entirely your's, and wish nothing more than it may be some time or other in my power to convince you that there is nobody dearer [to me] than yourself . . . [2]

> I cannot bear to be accused of coldness by one whom I shall love all my life. . . . You will think I forget you, who are never out of my thoughts. . . . I esteem you as I ought in esteeming you above the world.[3]

... your friendship is the only happiness of my life; and whenever I lose it, I have nothing to do but to take one of my garters and search for a convenient beam.[4]

Nobody ever was so entirely, so faithfully yours. . . . I put in your lovers, for I don't allow it possible for a man to be so sincere as I am.[5]

Lady Mary's biographer admits that Mary's letters to Anne carry "heart-burnings and reproaches and apologies" which might make us, the readers, "fancy ourselves in Lesbos,"[6] but, she assures us, Lady Mary knew that Anne's brother, Edward, would read what she wrote to Anne, "and she tried to shine in these letters for him."[7] Thus, Mary was not writing of her love for Anne; she was only showing Edward how smart, noble, and sensitive she was, so that he might be interested in her.

Why did Anna Seward, the eighteenth-century poet, grieve for thirty years over the marriage of Honora Sneyd? Why in a 1773 sonnet does she accuse Honora of killing "more than life,–e'en all that makes life dear"?[8] Why in another does she beg for merciful sleep which would "charm to rest the thoughts of whence, or how / Vanish'd that priz'd Affection"?(9] Why in still another poem does she weep because the "plighted love" of the woman she called "my life's adorner"[10] has now "changed to cold disdain"?[11] Well, speculates her 1930's biographer, it was probably because Anna Seward wished to marry the recently widowed Robert Edgeworth (whom Honora ensnared) herself. After all, "she was thirty years old–better suited to him in age and experience than Honora. Was she jealous of the easy success of [Honora]? Would she have snatched away, if she could have done so, the mature yet youthful bridegroom, so providentially released from his years of bondage?"[12]

Clearly, one of the worst examples of the *cherchez l'homme* technique concerns the letters of Emily Dickinson. Her biographers have filled tomes looking for the poet's elusive lover, and have come up with no fewer than ten candidates, generally with the vaguest bits of "evidence." Concrete evidence that the ruling passion of Dickinson's life may well have been a woman, Sue Gilbert, was eradicated from Dickinson's published letters, and has become available only within the last few decades through Thomas Johnson's complete edition of her correspondence.[13] The earlier publications of a sizable number of Dickinson's letters were the work of her niece, Martha Dickinson Bianchi, the author of *The Life and Letters of Emily Dickinson* (1924) and *Emily Dickinson Face to Face* (1932). Bianchi, a post-Freudian, felt compelled to hide what her aunt expressed without self-consciousness. Therefore Bianchi reproduced a February 6, 1852 (Johnson date) letter to Sue thus:

> Sometimes I shut my eyes and shut my heart towards you and try
> hard to forget you, but you'll never go away. Susie, forgive me,
> forget all that I say.[14]

What she did not reproduce of that letter tells a much more potent story:

> . . . sometimes I shut my eyes, and shut my heart towards you, and
> try hard to forget you because you grieve me so, but you'll never go
> away, Oh, you never will–say, Susie, promise me again, and I will
> smile faintly–and take up my little cross of sad–*sad* separation. How
> vain it seems to *write,* when one knows how to feel–how much more
> near and dear to sit beside you, talk with you, hear the tones of your
> voice; so hard to "deny thyself, and take up thy cross, and follow
> me"–give me strength, Susie, write me of hope and love, and of
> hearts that *endured,* and great was their reward of "Our Father who
> art in Heaven." I don't know how I shall bear it, when the gentle
> spring comes; if she should come and see me and talk to me of you,
> Oh it would surely kill me! While the frost clings to the windows,
> and the World is stern and drear; this absence is easier; the *Earth*
> mourns too, for all her little birds; but when they all come back
> again, and she sings and is so merry–pray, what will become of me?
> Susie, forgive me, forget all that I say. . . .

Sue Gilbert was later to marry Austin Dickinson, Emily's brother, and Martha
Dickinson Bianchi was the daughter of Sue and Austin. As anxious as she
was to prove that Sue played a great part in making Emily a poet and to show
that they were the closest friends, she was even more anxious to prove that
Emily and Sue were *only* friends. Thus she includes in *Face to Face* an
affectionate note that Emily sent Sue on June 27, 1852 (Johnson date):

> . . . Susie, will you indeed come home next Saturday? Shall I indeed
> behold you, not "darkly, but face to face"–or am I *fancying* so and
> dreaming blessed dreams from which the day will wake me? I hope
> for you so much and feel so eager for you–feel I cannot wait. Some-
> times I must have Saturday before tomorrow comes.[15]

But what Emily really said in that note places their relationship in quite a
different light:

> . . . Susie, will you indeed come home next Saturday, and be my own
> again, and kiss me as you used to? Shall I indeed behold you, not
> "darkly, but face to face" or am I *fancying* so, and dreaming blessed
> dreams from which the day will wake me? I hope for you so much,

and feel so eager for you, feel that I *cannot* wait, feel that *now* I must have you—that the expectation once more to see your face again, makes me feel hot and feverish, and my heart beats so fast—I go to sleep at night, and the first thing I know, I am sitting there wide awake, and clasping my hands tightly, and thinking of next Saturday, and "never a bit" of you.

Sometimes I must have Saturday before tomorrow comes.

Where biographers have been too scrupulous to bowdlerize, they have nevertheless managed to distort lesbian history by avoiding the obvious. Sometimes this has been done to "save" the reputations of their subjects (for example, Emma Stebbins, Alice B. Toklas, and Edith Lewis were the "companions" of Charlotte Cushman, Gertrude Stein, and Willa Cather) although illicit heterosexual affairs are seldom treated with such discretion by even the most sensitive biographers. Sometimes this has been done out of willful ignorance. For example, Amy Lowell so obviously made her "companion" Ada Russell the subject of her most erotic love poetry that even a casual acquaintance could observe it, and Lowell herself said, "How could so exact a portrait remain unrecognized?"[16] it did remain unrecognized by those who saw Lowell only as an overweight, unmarried woman whose "sources of inspiration are literary and secondary rather than primarily the expression of emotional experience,"[17] and whose characters thus never breathe, except for those "few frustrated persons such as the childless old women in 'The Doll,'" who share Lowell's "limited personal experiences."[18]

Although many biographies of the 1970's have been much more perceptive and honest with regard to their subjects' lesbian lovers (for example, Jean Gould's *Amy: The World of Amy Lowell and the Imagist Movement,* 1975 and Virginia Spencer Carr's *The Lonely Hunter: A Biography of Carson McCullers,* 1975), we cannot assume that lesbian history will never again be hidden by scholars who live in this heterocentric world. And, even where lesbian relationships are admitted in biographies of the 1970's, their importance is often discounted. A recent author of an Edna St. Vincent Millay biography squeezes Millay's lesbian relationships into a chapter entitled "Millay's Childhood and Youth," and organizes each of the subsequent chapters around a male with whom Millay had some contact, all of them ostensibly her lovers. Six who had relatively short contact with her are treated together in a chapter entitled "Millay's Other Men," although the author admits in that chapter that three of Millay's other men were homosexual.

This essay may read like a long complaint; it is. But it is also a warning and a hope. It is as difficult for heterocentric biographers to deal with love between women in their subjects' lives as it is for ethnocentric white scholars to deal with third world subject matter, and their products are generally not to be trusted. If we wish to know about the lives of women it is vital to go back to their diaries, letters (praying that they have not already been expurgated by some well-meaning heterosexist hand), and any original source material that is available. It is also vital to produce biographies divested of the heterocentric perspective. Women's lives need to be reinterpreted, and we need to do it ourselves.

NOTES

1. See my article, "The Morbidification of Love Between Women by Nineteenth-Century Sexologists," *Journal of Homosexuality,* 4, 1 (Fall 1978), 73-90.

2. *The Complete Letters of Lady Mary Wortley Montagu,* ed. Robert Halsband (Oxford: Clarendon Press, 1965), I, 4.

3. Ibid., I, 5.

4. Ibid., I, 12.

5. Ibid.

6. Iris Barry, *Portrait of Lady Mary Wortley Montagu* (Indianapolis: Bobbs-Merrill, 1928), p. 61.

7. Ibid., p. 54.

8. *The Poetical Works of Anna Seward with Extracts from her Literary Correspondence,* ed. Walter Scott (Edinburgh: John Ballantyne and Co., 1810), III, 135.

9. Ibid., III, 134.

10. Ibid., I, 76-77.

11. Ibid., III, 133.

12. Margaret Ashmun, *The Singing Swan: An Account of Anna Seward and her Acquaintance with Dr. Johnson, Boswell, and Others of their time* (New Haven: Yale Univ. Press, 1931), pp. 28-29.

13. *The Letters of Emily Dickinson,* ed. Thomas Johnson and Theodora Ward (Cambridge: Harvard Univ. Press, 1958). See also my article, "Emily Dickinson's Letters to Sue Gilbert," *The Massachusetts Review,* 18, 2 (Summer 1977), 197-225.

14. Martha Dickinson Bianchi, *Emily Dickinson Face to Face* (Boston: Houghton Mifflin, 1932), p. 184.

15. Ibid., p. 218.

16. Letter to John Livingston Lowes, February 13, 1918, in S. Foster Damon, *Amy Lowell: A Chronicle, With Extracts from her Correspondence* (Boston: Houghton Mifflin, 1935), p. 441.

17. Hervey Allen, "Amy Lowell as a Poet," *Saturday Review of Literature,* 3, 28 (February 5, 1927), 558. See also Horace Gregory, *Amy Lowell: Portrait of the Poet in Her Time* (New York: Thomas Nelson and Sons, 1958), p. 212 and Walter Lippmann, "Miss Lowell and Things," *New Republic,* 6 (March 18, 1916), 178-79.

18. Allen, 568.

"Imagine My Surprise":
Women's Relationships
in Historical Perspective*

Leila J. Rupp

When Carroll Smith-Rosenberg's article, "The Female World of Love and Ritual," appeared in the pages of *Signs* in 1975, it revolutionized the way in which women's historians look at nineteenth-century American society and even served notice on the historical profession at large that women's relationships would have to be taken into account in any consideration of Victorian society.[1] Since then we have learned more about relationships between women in the past, but we have not reached consensus on the issue of characterizing these relationships.[2] On the one hand, Smith-Rosenberg's work has increasingly been misused to deny the sexual aspect of relationships between prominent women in the past. On the other hand, feminist scholars have responded to such distortions by bestowing the label "lesbian" on women who would themselves not have used the term. The issue goes beyond labels, however, because the very nature of women's relationships is so complex. I would like to consider here the issue of women's relationships in historical perspective by reviewing the conflicting approaches, by presenting examples of different kinds of women's relationships from my own research on the American women's

The author wrote this essay "in a burst of anger" after reading *The Life of Lorena Hickok* and *The Making of a Feminist* while on fellowship at the Murray Research Center, and she is grateful to the Radcliffe Research Scholars Program for making possible her research at the Schlesinger Library.

Leila J. Rupp, *Frontiers* Volume V, Number 3, copyright © 1981 FRONTIERS Editorial Collective. Reprinted by permission.

[Haworth co-indexing entry note]: " 'Imagine My Surprise' ": Women's Relationships in Historical Perspective." Rupp, Leila J. Co-published simultaneously in *Journal of Lesbian Studies* (The Haworth Press, Inc.) Vol. 1, No. 2, 1997, pp. 155-176; and: *Classics in Lesbian Studies* (ed: Esther D. Rothblum) The Haworth Press, Inc., 1997, pp. 155-176; and: *Classics in Lesbian Studies* (ed: Esther D. Rothblum) Harrington Park Press, an imprint of The Haworth Press, Inc., 1997, pp. 155-176.

movement in the 1940's and 1950's, and finally, by suggesting a conceptual approach that recognizes the complexity of women's relationships without denying the common bond shared by all women who have committed their lives to other women in the past.

Looking first at what Blanche Cook proclaims "the historical denial of lesbianism," we find the most recent, most publicized, and most egregious example in Doris Faber's *The Life of Lorena Hickok: E.R.'s Friend,* the story of the relationship of Eleanor Roosevelt and reporter Lorena Hickok.[3]

The Hickok book would make fascinating material for a case study of homophobia. Author Doris Faber presents page after page of evidence that delineates the growth and development of a love affair between the two women, yet she steadfastly maintains that a woman of Eleanor Roosevelt's "stature" could not have *acted* on the love which she expressed for Hickok. This attitude forces Faber to go to great lengths with the evidence before her. For example, she quotes a letter Roosevelt wrote to Hickok and asserts that it is "particularly susceptible to misinterpretation." Roosevelt's wish to "lie down beside you tonight & take you in my arms," Faber claims represents maternal–"albeit rather extravagantly" maternal–solicitude. For Faber, "there can be little doubt that the final sentence of the above letter does not mean what it appears to mean."[4]

Faber's interpretation, unfortunately, is not an isolated one. She acknowledges an earlier "sensitive" and "fine" book, *Miss Marks and Miss Woolley,* for reinforcing her own views "regarding the unfairness of using contemporary standards to characterize the behavior of women brought up under almost inconceivably different standards."[5] Anna Mary Wells, the author of the Marks and Woolley book, set out originally to write a biography of Mary Woolley and almost abandoned the plan when she discovered the love letters of the two women. Ultimately Wells went ahead with a book about the relationship, but only after she decided, as she explains in the preface, that there was no physical relationship between them. Comforted by this conviction, Wells paints a detailed picture of the joys and sorrows of their life together, even acknowledging the role that hostility toward their relationship played in the careers of both women.

Another famous women's college president, M. Carey Thomas of Bryn Mawr, receives the same sort of treatment in a book that appeared at the same time as the Hickok book, but to less fanfare.[6] The discovery of the Woolley-Marks letters sparked a mild panic among Mount Holyoke alumnae and no doubt created apprehension about what might lurk in Thomas' papers, which were about to be microfilmed and opened to the public.[7] But Marjorie Dobkin, editor of *The Making of a Feminist: Early Journals and*

Letters of M. Carey Thomas, insists that there is nothing to worry about. Thomas admittedly fell for women throughout her life. At fifteen, she wrote: "I think I must feel towards Anna for instance like a boy would, for I admire her so. Not any particular thing but just an undefined sense of admiration and then I like to touch her and the other morning I woke up and she was asleep and I admired her hair so much that I kissed it. I never felt so much with anybody else." And at twenty: "One night we had stopped reading later than usual and obeying a sudden impulse I turned to her and asked, 'Do you love me?' She threw her arms around me and whispered, 'I love you passionately.' She did not go home that night and we talked and talked." At twenty-three, Thomas wrote to her mother: "If it were only possible for women to elect women as well as men for a 'life's love!' . . . It *is* possible but if families would only regard it in that light!"[8]

Thomas did in fact choose women for her "life's loves," but Dobkin, who finds it "hard to understand why anyone should very much care" about personal and private behavior and considers the question of lesbianism "a relatively inconsequential matter," assures us that "physical contact" unquestionably played a part in Thomas' relationships with women, but "sexuality" just as unquestionably did not.[9] Along with this labored distinction between "physical contact" and "sexuality," Dobkin presents a battery of reasons why Thomas was not a lesbian: she never expressed the desire to be a man; she expressed a strong aversion to heterosexual intercourse when she learned the "facts of life" from a book at the age of twenty-one, an aversion, Dobkin insists, that would have applied even more strongly to homosexual sex; she was conventional in everything but her feminism; she once loved a man–or was at least unable to stop thinking about him–and considered marrying him (Dobkin, with evident relief, devotes the middle section of the book to this relationship); Thomas established mother-daughter relationships with the two women with whom she lived (one moved in when the first eloped with a man); the women known at the time to be lesbians whom Thomas included among her friends traveled with her only after Thomas was already approaching old age; and, finally, Thomas expressed negative attitudes toward homosexuality, including the fear that public discussion of it would make it difficult for women who lived together. Dobkin's ignorance about lesbianism is staggering; on no other topic would a scholar so unfamiliar with the relevant literature forge ahead with the sort of assumptions she reveals.

The authors of these three books are determined to give us an "acceptable" version of women's relationships in the past, and they seize gratefully on Smith-Rosenberg's work to do it. But even Doris Faber's feverish denials could not eliminate public speculation about Eleanor Roosevelt's "sexual orientation." An article about the Hickok book was even carried in the *National Enquirer* which, for a change, probably presented the material more accurately, if more leeringly, than the respectable press.[10] Arthur Schlesinger, Jr., in *The New York Times Book Review,* for example, notes that the big question in "some people's minds" will be whether Hickok and Roosevelt were "lovers in the physical sense."[11] Schlesinger, like Dobkin, finds this an "issue of stunning inconsequence," but he "reluctantly" supposes that it must be discussed. After devoting the rest of his review to a subject he evidently finds distasteful, he cites Smith-Rosenberg's work and concludes that the two women were "children of the Victorian age" which accepted celibate love between women; they were "wounded women, doomed by chaotic childhoods to the unceasing quest for unattainable emotional security." Schlesinger is emphasizing here the incompatibility of our modern heterosexual-homosexual dichotomy with the sensibility of an earlier age. As Blanche Cook points out in her review of Faber's book, however, it is absurd to pretend that the years 1932 to 1962 now belong to the nineteenth century.[12] Although it is vitally important not to impose modern concepts and standards on the past, I believe that we have gone entirely too far with the notion of an idyllic Victorian age in which chaste love between people of the same sex was possible and acceptable. A recent review in *The New York Times Book Review,* for example, discusses a biography of J. M. Barrie, the creator of Peter Pan, and almost congratulates Barrie for his "innocent, asexual, natural and dignified" love for the five boys who were both subjects and recipients of his stories. Despite the fact that Barrie was fond of photographing the boys, as the reviewer says, "*tout nu,* often bottoms up," he insists that there was nothing sexual about this love.[13] I think that we are naive to believe this.

It is not surprising, in light of such denials of sexuality, that many feminist scholars choose to claim as lesbians all women who have loved women in the past. Blanche Cook concludes firmly that "women who love women, who choose women to nurture and support and to create a living environment in which to work creatively and independently, are lesbians."[14] Cook names as lesbians Jane Addams, the founder of Hull House, who lived for forty years with Mary Rozet Smith; Lillian Wald, also a settlement house pioneer, who left evidence of a series of intense relationships with women; and Jeannette Marks and Mary Woolley. All, Cook says, were lesbians, and in the homophobic society in which we live must be claimed as such.

As it now stands, we are faced with a choice between, on the one hand, labeling women lesbians who might violently reject the label, or, on the other hand, glossing over the significance of women's relationships by labeling them Victorian, and therefore innocent of our post-Freudian sexual awareness. Although I understand and share the political perspective that leads Cook to claim women like Jane Addams as lesbians, I feel we need to see more precision in the use of the term. I would like to illustrate the diversity of women's relationships in the past–and the complexity of those relationships–with evidence from the American women's movement in the late 1940's and 1950's.

I have found evidence of a variety of relationships in collections of women's papers and in the records of women's organizations from this period. I do not have enough information about many of these relationships to characterize them in any definitive way, nor can I even offer much information about some of the women. But we cannot afford to overlook whatever evidence women have left us, however fragmentary. I believe that it is important simply to present some of these relationships, because they illustrate the complexity of women's relationships in the past and the problems that confront us if we attempt any simple categorization. Since my research focuses on feminist activities, the women I discuss here are by no means a representative group of women. All of them are white, educated, and middle- or upper-class. The women's movement in the period after the Second World War was composed primarily of white, middle-class women, in part because of the racism and classism of the movement, and in part because black women and working-class women involved in social movement activity most often organized around issues of race and class, respectively, not gender.

Within the women's movement were two distinct phenomena–couple relationships and intense devotion to a charismatic leader–that help clarify the problems that face us if we attempt to define these relationships in any cut-and-dried fashion. None of the women who lived in couple relationships and belonged to the women's movement in the postwar period would, as far as can be determined, have identified themselves as lesbians. They did, however, often live together in long-term committed relationships, which were accepted in the movement, and they did sometimes build a community with other women like themselves. Descriptions of a few relationships that come down to us in the sources provide some insight into their nature.

Jeannette Marks and Mary Woolley, subjects of the biography mentioned earlier, met at Wellesley College in 1895 when Marks began her college education and Woolley arrived at the college as a history instructor. Less than five years later they made "a mutual declaration of ardent and exclusive love" and "exchanged tokens, a ring and a jeweled pin, with pledges of lifelong fidelity."[15] They spent the rest of their lives together, including the many years at Mount Holyoke where Woolley served as president and Marks taught English. Mary Woolley worked in the American Association of University Women and the Women's International League for Peace and Freedom. Jeannette Marks committed herself to suffrage and, later, through the National Woman's Party, to the Equal Rights Amendment. It is clear from Marks' correspondence with women in the movement that their relationship was accepted as a primary commitment. Few letters to Marks in the 1940's fail to inquire about Woolley, whose serious illness clouded Marks' life and work. One married woman, who found herself forced to withdraw from Woman's Party work because of her husband's health, acknowledged in a letter to Marks the centrality of Marks' and Woolley's commitment when she compared her own reasons for "pulling out" to "those that have bound you to Westport," the town in which the two women lived.[16] Mary Woolley died in 1947, and Jeannette Marks lived on until 1964, devoting herself to a biography of Woolley.

Lena Madesin Phillips, the founder of both the National and International Federations of Business and Professional Women's Clubs, lived for some thirty years with Marjory Lacey-Baker, an actress whom she first met in 1919. In an unpublished autobiography included in Phillips' papers, she straightforwardly wrote about her lack of interest in men and marriage. As a young girl, she wrote that she "cared little for boys," and at the age of seven she wrote a composition for school that explained: "There are so many little girls in the school and the thing i [sic] like about it there are no boys in school. i [sic] like that about it."[17] She noted that she had never taken seriously the idea of getting married. "Only the first of the half dozen proposals of marriage which came my way had any sense of reality to me. They made no impression because I was wholly without desire or even interest in the matter." Phillips seemed unperturbed by possible Freudian and/or homophobic explanations of her attitudes and behavior. She explained unabashedly that she wanted to be a boy and suffered severe disappointment when she learned that, contrary to her father's stories, there was no factory in Indiana that made girls into boys–and seemed impervious as well to the charges of lesbianism that her memories might provoke. She mentioned in her autobiography the "crushes" she had on girls at the Jessamine Female Institute–nothing out of the ordinary for a young woman of her generation, but perhaps a surprising piece of information chosen for inclusion in the autobiography of a woman who continued to devote her emotional energies to women.

In 1919, Phillips attended a pageant in which Lacey-Baker performed and she inquired about the identity of the woman who had "[t]he most beautiful voice I ever heard."[18] Phillips "lost her heart to the sound of that voice," and the two women moved in together in the 1920's. In 1924, according to notes that Lacey-Baker recorded for a biography of Phillips, the two women went different places for Easter; recording this caused Lacey-Baker to quote from *The Prophet*: "Love knows not its own depth until the hour of separation."[19] Phillips described Lacey-Baker in her voluminous correspondence as "my best friend," or noted that she "shares a home with me."[20] Phillips' friends and acquaintances regularly mentioned Lacey-Baker. One male correspondent, for example, commented that Phillips' "lady-friend" was "so lovely, and so devoted to you and cares for you."[21] Phillips happily described the tranquility of their life together to her many friends: "Marjory and I have had a lovely time, enjoying once more our home in summertime. . . . Marjory would join in the invitation of this letter and this loving greeting if she were around. Today she is busy with the cleaning woman, while I sit with the door closed working in my study."[22] "We have had a happy winter, with good health for both of us. We have a variety of interests and small obligations, but really enjoy most the quiet and comfort of Apple Acres."[23] "We read and talk and work."[24]

Madesin Phillips' papers suggest that she and Marjory Lacey-Baker lived in a world of politically active women friends. Phillips had devoted much of her energy to international work with women, and she kept in touch with European friends through her correspondence and through her regular trips to Europe accompanied by Lacey-Baker. Gordon Holmes, of the British Federation of Business and Professional Women, wrote regularly to "Madesin and Maggie." In a 1948 letter she teased Phillips by reporting that "two other of our oldest & closest Fed officers whom you know could get married but are refusing—as they are both more than middle-aged (never mind their looks) it suggests 50-60 is about the new dangerous age for women (look out for Maggie!)."[25] Phillips reported to Holmes on their social life: "With a new circle of friends around us here and a good many of our overseas members coming here for luncheon or tea with us the weeks slip by."[26] The integral relationship between Phillips' social life and her work in the movement is suggested by Lacey-Baker's analysis of Phillips' personal papers from the year 1924: "There is the usual crop of letters to LMP following the Convention [of the BPW] from newly-met members in hero-worshipping mood—most of whom went on to be her good friends over the years."[27] Lacey-Baker was a part of Phillips' movement world, and their relationship received acceptance and validation throughout the movement, both national and international.

The lifelong relationship between feminist biographer Alma Lutz and

Marguerite Smith began when they roomed together at Vassar in the early years of the twentieth century. From 1918 until Smith's death in 1959, they shared a Boston apartment and a summer home, Highmeadow, in the Berkshires. Lutz and Smith, a librarian at the Protestant Zion Research Library in Brookline, Massachusetts, worked together in the National Woman's Party. Like Madesin Phillips, Lutz wrote to friends in the movement of their lives together: "We are very happy here in the country—each busy with her work and digging in the garden."[28] They traveled together, visiting Europe several times in the 1950's. Letters to one of them about feminist work invariably sent greetings or love to the other. When Smith died in 1959, Lutz struggled with her grief. She wrote to her acquaintance Florence Kitchelt, in response to condolences: "I am at Highmeadow trying to get my bearings. . . . You will understand how hard it is. . . . It has been a very difficult anxious time for me."[29] She thanked another friend for her note and added: "It's a hard adjustment to make, but one we all have to face in one way or another and I am remembering that I have much to be grateful for."[30] In December she wrote to one of her regular correspondents that she was carrying on but it was very lonely for her.[31]

The fact that Lutz and Smith seemed to have many friends who lived in couple relationships with other women suggests that they had built a community of women within the women's movement. Every year Mabel Vernon, a suffragist and worker for peace, and her friend and companion Consuelo Reyes, whom Vernon had met through her work with the Inter-American Commission on Women, spent the summer at Highmeadow. Vernon, one of Alice Paul's closest associates during the suffrage struggle, had met Reyes two weeks after her arrival in the United States from Costa Rica in 1942. They began to work together in Vernon's organization, People's Mandate, in 1943, and they shared a Washington apartment from 1951 until Vernon's death in 1975.[32] Reyes received recognition in Vernon's obituaries as her "devoted companion" or "nurse-companion."[33] Two other women who also maintained a lifelong relationship, Alice Morgan Wright and Edith Goode, also kept in contact with Lutz, Smith, Vernon, and Reyes. Sometimes they visited Highmeadow in the summer.[34] Wright and Goode had met at Smith and were described as "always together" although they did not live together.[35] Like Lutz and Smith, they worked together in the National Woman's Party, traveled together and looked after each other as old age began to take its toll.[36]

These examples illustrate what the sources provide: the bare outlines of friendship networks made up of woman-committed women. Much of the evidence must be pieced together and it is even scantier when the women did not live together. Alma Lutz's papers, for example, do not include any personal correspondence from the postwar period, so what we know about her relationships with Marguerite Smith comes from the papers of her correspondents. Sometimes a relationship surfaces only upon the death of one of the women. For example, Agnes Wells, chairman of the National Woman's Party in the late 1940's, explained to an acquaintance in the Party that her "friend of forty-one years and house-companion for twenty-eight years" had just died.[37] When Mabel Griswold, executive secretary of the Woman's Party, died in 1955, a family member suggested that the Party send the telegram of sympathy to Elsie Wood, the woman with whom Griswold had lived.[38] This kind of reference tells us little about the nature of the relationship involved, but we do get a sense of the nature of couple relationships within the women's movement.

A second important phenomenon found in the women's movement—the charismatic leader who attracts intense devotion—also adds to our understanding of the complexity of women's relationships. Alice Paul, the founder and leading light of the National Woman's Party, inspired devotion that bordered on worship. One woman even addressed her as "My Beloved Deity."[39] But, contrary to both the ideal type of the charismatic leader and the portrait of Paul as it exists now in the historical scholarship, Paul maintained close relationships with a number of women she had first met in the suffrage struggle.[40] Paul's correspondence in the National Woman's Party papers does not reveal much about the nature of her relationships, but it does make it clear that her friendships provided love and support for her work.

It is true that many of the expressions of love, admiration, and devotion addressed to Paul seem to have been one-sided, from awe-struck followers, but this is not the only side of the story.

Paul maintained close friendships with a number of women discussed earlier who lived in couple relationships with other women. She had met Mabel Vernon when they attended Swarthmore College together, and they maintained contact throughout the years, despite Vernon's departure from the Woman's Party in the 1930's.[41] Of Alice Morgan Wright, she said that, when they first met, they ". . . just became sisters right away."[42] Jeannette Marks regularly sent her love to "dear Alice" until a conflict in the Woman's Party ruptured their relationship.[43] Other women, too, enjoyed a closer relationship than the formal work-related one for which Paul is so well known.

Paul obviously cared deeply, for example, for her old friend Nina Allender, the cartoonist of the suffrage movement. Allender, who lived alone in Chicago, wrote to Paul in 1947 of her memories of their long association: "No words can tell you what that [first] visit grew to mean to me & to my life. . . . I feel now as I did then–only more intensely–I have never changed or doubted–but have grown more inspired as the years have gone by. . . . There is no use going into words. I believe them to be unnecessary between us."[44] Paul wrote that she thought of Allender often and sent her "devoted love."[45] She worried about Allender's loneliness and gently encouraged her to come to Washington to live at Belmont House, the Woman's Party headquarters, where she would be surrounded by loving friends who appreciated the work she had done for the women's movement.[46] Paul failed to persuade her to move, however. Two years later Paul responded to a request from Allender's niece for help with the costs of a nursing home with a $100 check and a promise to contact others who might be able to help.[47] But Allender died, within a month, at the age of eighty-five.

Paul does not seem to have formed an intimate relationship with any one woman, but she did live and work within a close-knit female world. When in Washington, she lived, at least some of the time, at Belmont House; when away she lived either alone or with her sister, Helen Paul, in Vermont and later Connecticut. Helen Paul, through her relationship with Alice, often played a major role in Woman's Party work. It is clear that Alice Paul's ties–whether to her sister or to close friends or to admirers– served as a bond that knit the Woman's Party together. That Paul and her network could also tear the movement asunder is obvious from the stormy history of the Woman's Party.

Alice Paul is not the only example of a leader who inspired love and devotion among women in the movement. One senses from Marjory Lacey-Baker's comment, quoted above–that "newly-met members in hero-worshipping mood" wrote to Lena Madesin Phillips after every BPW convention–that Phillips too had a charismatic aura. But the best and most thoroughly documented example of a charismatic leader is Anna Lord Strauss of the League of Women Voters, an organization that opted out of the women's movement.

Strauss, the great-granddaughter of Lucretia Mott, came from an old and wealthy family; she was prominent and respected, a staunch liberal and an anti- or at best a nonfeminist. She never married and her papers leave no evidence of intimate relationships outside her family. Yet Strauss was the object of some very strong feelings on the part of the women with whom she worked. She, like Alice Paul and Madesin Phillips, received numerous hero-worshipping letters from awe-struck followers. But in her case we also have evidence that some of her coworkers fell deeply in love with her. It is hard to know how the following women would have interpreted their relationship with Strauss. The two women who expressed their feelings explicitly were both married women, and in one case Strauss obviously had a cordial relationship with the woman's husband and children. Yet there can be no question that this League officer fell in love with Strauss. She found Strauss "the finest human being I had ever known," and knowing her "the most beautiful and profound experience I have ever had."[48] Loving Strauss–she asked permission to say it–made the earth move and "the whole landscape of human affairs and nature" take on a new appearance.[49] Being with Strauss made "the tone and fiber" of her day different; although she could live without her, she could see no reason for having to prove it all the time.[50] She tried to "ration and control" her thoughts of Strauss, but it was small satisfaction.[51] When Strauss was recovering from an operation, this woman wrote: "I love you! I can't imagine the world without you. . . . I love you. I need you."[52]

Although our picture of this relationship is completely one-sided–for Strauss did not keep copies of most of her letters–it is clear that Strauss did not respond to such declarations of love. This woman urged Strauss to accept her and what she had to say without "the slightest sense of needing to be considerate of me because I feel as I do." She understood the "unilateral character" of her feelings, and insisted that she had more than she deserved by simply knowing Strauss at all.[53] But her hurt, and her growing suspicion that Strauss shunned intimacy, escaped on occasion. She asked: "And how would it hurt you to let someone tell you sometime how beautiful–how wonderful you are? Did you ever let anyone have a decent chance to try?"[54] She realized that loving someone did not always make things easier–that sometimes, in fact, it made life more of a struggle–but she believed that to withdraw from love was to withdraw from life. In what appears to have been a hastily written note, she expressed her understanding–an understanding that obviously gave her both pain and comfort–that Strauss was not perfect after all: "Way back there in the crow's nest (or at some such time) you decided not to become embroiled in any intimate human relationship, except those you were, by birth, committed to. I wonder. . . . There is something you haven't mastered. Something you've been afraid of after all."[55]

This woman's perception that Strauss avoided intimacy is confirmed elsewhere in Strauss' papers. One old friend was struck, in 1968, by Strauss' ability to "get your feelings out & down on paper!" She continued: "I know you so well that I consider this great progress in your own inner state of mental health. It is far from easy for you to express your feelings. . . ."[56] This aspect of Strauss' personality fits with the ideal type of the charismatic leader. The other case of a woman falling in love with Strauss that emerges clearly from her papers reinforces this picture. This woman, also a League officer, wrote in circuitous fashion of her intense pleasure at receiving Strauss' picture. In what was certainly a reference to lesbianism, she wrote that she hoped Strauss would not think that she was "one of those who had never outgrown the emotional extravaganzas of the adolescent." Before she got down to League business, she added:

> But, Darling, as I softly close the door on all this—as I should and as I want to—and as I must since all our meetings are likely to be formal ones in a group—as I go back in the office correspondence to "Dear Miss Strauss" and "Sincerely yours," . . . as I put myself as much as possible in the background at our March meeting in order to share you with the others who have not been with you as I have—as all these things happen, I want you to be very certain that what is merely under cover is still there—as it most surely will be—and that if all the hearts in the room could be exposed there'd be few, I'm certain, that would love you more than . . . [I].[57]

Apparently Strauss never responded to this letter, for a month later, this woman apologized for writing it: "I have had qualms, dear Anna, about that letter I wrote you. (You knew I would eventually of course!)." Continuing in a vein that reinforces the above quoted perception of Strauss' inability to be intimate, she wrote of imagining the "recoil . . . embarrassment, self-consciousness and general discomfort" her letter must have provoked in such a "reserved person." She admitted that the kind of admiration she had expressed, "at least in certain classes of relationships (of which mine to you is one)—becomes a bit of moral wrong-doing."[58] She felt ashamed and asked forgiveness. It is not at all clear what she meant by all of this, and I quote it here without speculating on the nature of their relationship.

What is clear is that this was a momentous and significant relationship to at least one of the parties. Almost twenty years later, this woman wrote of her deep disappointment in missing Strauss' visit to her city. She had allowed herself to dream that she could persuade Strauss to stay with her awhile, even though she knew that others would have prior claims on Strauss' time. She wrote:

> I have not seen you since that day in Atlantic City when you laid the gavel of the League of Women Voters down. . . . I do not look back on that moment of ending with any satisfaction for my own behavior, for I passed right by the platform on which you were still standing talking with one of the last persons left in the room and shyness at the thought of expressing my deep feeling about your going—*and* the

fact that you were talking with someone else led me to pass on without even a glance in your direction as I remember though you made some move to speak to me! . . . But if I gave you a hurt it is now a very old one and forgotten, I'm sure–as well as understood.[59]

Whatever the interpretation these two women would have devised to explain their feelings for Strauss, it is clear that the widely shared devotion to this woman leader could sometimes grow into something more intense. Strauss' reserve, and her inability to express her feelings may or may not have had anything to do with her own attitude toward intimate relationships between women. One tantalizing letter from a friend about to be married suggests that Strauss' decision not to marry had been made early: "I remember so well your answer when I pressed you, once, on why you had never married. . . . Well, it is very true, one does not marry unless one can see no other life."[60] A further fragment, consisting of entries in the diary of Doris Stevens–a leading suffragist who took a sharp swing to the right in the postwar period–suggests that at least some individuals suspected Strauss of lesbianism. Stevens, by this time a serious redbaiter and, from the evidence quoted here, a "queerbaiter" as well, apparently called a government official in 1953 to report that Strauss was "not a bit interested in men."[61] She seemed to be trying to discredit Strauss, far too liberal for her tastes, with a charge of "unorthodox morals."[62]

Stevens had her suspicions about other women in the movement as well. She recorded in her diary a conversation with a National Woman's Party member about Jeannette Marks and Mary Woolley, noting that the member, who had attended Wellesley with Marks, "Discreetly indicated there was 'talk.' "[63] At another point she reported a conversation with a different Woman's Party member who had grown disillusioned about Alice Paul. Stevens noted that her informant related "weird goings on at Wash. hedquts wherein it was clear she thought Paul a devotee of Lesbos & afflicted with Jeanne d'Arc identification."[64]

Stevens' charges suggest that the intensity of women's relationships and the existence of woman-committed women in women's organizations had the potential, particularly during the McCarthy years, to attract ridicule or denunciation. Stevens wrote to the viciously right-wing and anti-Semitic columnist, Westbrook Pegler, to "thank you for knowing I'm not a queerie."[65] This would suggest that, at least in certain circles, participation in the women's movement was highly suspect.

What exactly should we make of all this? In one way it is terribly frustrating to have such tantalizingly ambiguous glimpses into women's lives. In another way, it is exciting to find out so much about women's lives in the past. I think it is enormously important *not* to read into these letters what we want to find, or what we think we should find. At the same time, we cannot dismiss what little evidence we have as insufficient when it is all we have; nor can we continue to contribute to the conspiracy of silence that urges us to ignore what is not perfectly straightforward. Thus, although it is tempting to try to speculate about the relationships I have described here in order to impose some analysis on them, I would rather simply lay them out, fragmentary as they are, in order to suggest a conceptual approach that recognizes the complexities of the issue.

It is clear, I think, that none of these relationships can be easily categorized. There were women who lived their entire adult lives in couple relationships with other women, and married women who fell in love with other women. Were they lesbians? Probably they would be shocked to be identified in that way. Alice Paul, for example, spoke scornfully of *Ms.* magazine as "all about homosexuality and so on."[66] Another woman who lives in a couple relationship distinguished between the (respectable) women involved in the ERA struggle in the old days and the "lesbians and bra-burners" of the contemporary movement.[67] Sasha Lewis, in *Sunday's Women,* reports an incident we would do well to remember here. One of her informants, a lesbian, went to Florida to work against Anita Bryant and stayed with an older cousin who had lived for years in a marriage-like relationship with another woman. When Lewis' informant saw the way the two women lived–sharing everything, including a bedroom–she said something to them about the danger of Bryant's campaign for their lives. They were aghast that she would think them lesbians, since, they said, they did not do anything sexual together.[68] If even women who lived with or maintained close attachments to other women would reject the label "lesbian," what about the married women, or the women who avoided intimate relationships?

The fact that the three recent historical studies discussed here misuse the concept of women's culture to proclaim that their subjects did not have sexual relationships with other women makes it imperative that historians pull back the veil that has too often shrouded love between women in the past. But it is equally important that we not obscure the enormous significance, from both an individual and historical perspective, of the formation of a lesbian identity. Recent research on the history of homosexuality shows that the concept of a homosexual identity or role only emerged in relatively recent times.[69] Paradoxically, as Smith-Rosenberg points out, the nineteenth century permitted a great deal of freedom in moving along the sexual and emotional continuum that ranges from heterosexuality to homosexuality. The twentieth century has not. What is important here is that we can begin to speak of a "lesbian identity" in American society by the twentieth century.[70] Passionate love between women has always existed, but it has not always been named. Since it *has* been named in the twentieth century, we need to distinguish between women who identify as lesbians and/or who are part of a lesbian culture, where one exists, and a broader category of woman-committed women who would not identify as lesbians but whose primary commitment, in emotional and practical terms, was to other women. It is especially important, in considering twentieth-century women, that we not sloppily apply the label "Victorian." In the 1950's there *was* such a thing as a lesbian culture–in local communities, in the bars, in the military. There is an important difference between women who put themselves in such a culture on the very fringes of society and women like Eleanor Roosevelt and the women whose relationships I have described here. Similarly, there is an important difference today between a politically active lesbian feminist and a "maiden aunt" who has lived her entire life with another woman but would reject any suggestions of lesbianism.

Identity, and not sexual behavior, is the crucial factor in the discussion.[71] There are lesbians who have never had a sexual relationship with another woman and there are women who have had sexual experiences with women but do not identify as lesbians. This is not to suggest that there is no difference between women who loved each other and lived together but did not make love (although even that can be difficult to define, since sensuality and sexuality, "physical contact" and "sexual contact" have no distinct boundaries) and those who did. But sexual behavior–something about which we rarely have historical evidence anyway–is only one of a number of relevant factors in a relationship. Blanche Cook has said everything that needs to be said about the inevitable question of evidence: "Genital 'proofs' to confirm lesbianism are never required to confirm the heterosexuality of men and women who live together for 20, or 50, years." Cook reminds us of the recently publicized relationship of General Eisenhower and Kay Summersby during the Second World War: they "were passionately involved with each other. They looked ardently into each others' eyes. They held hands. They cantered swiftly across England's countryside. They played golf and bridge and laughed. They were inseparable. But they never 'consummated' their love in the acceptable, traditional, sexual manner. Now does that fact render Kay Summersby and Dwight David Eisenhower somehow less in love? Were they not heterosexual?"[72]

Of course, emphasizing identity rather than proof of genital contact does not make everything simple. At this point, I think, the best we can do is to describe carefully and sensitively what we do know about a woman's relationships, keeping in mind both the historical development of a lesbian identity (Did such a thing as a lesbian identity exist? Was there a lesbian culture?), and the individual process that we now identify as "coming out" (Did a woman feel attachment to another woman or women? Did she act on this feeling in some positive way? Did she recognize the existence of other women with the same commitment? Did she express solidarity with those women?).[73] Using this approach allows us to make distinctions among women's relationships in the past–intimate friendships, supportive relationships growing out of common political work, couple relationships–without denying their significance or drawing fixed boundaries. We can recognize the importance of friendships among a group of women who, like Alma Lutz, Marguerite Smith, Mabel Vernon, Consuelo Reyes, Alice Morgan Wright, and Edith Goode, built a community of women but did not identify it as a lesbian community. We can do justice to both the woman-committed woman who would angrily reject any suggestion of lesbianism and the self-identified lesbian without distorting their common experiences.

This approach does not solve all the problems of dealing with women's relationships in the past, but it is a beginning. The greatest problem remains the weakness of sources. Not only have women who loved women in the past been wisely reluctant to leave evidence of their relationships for the prying eyes of a homophobic society, but what evidence they did leave was often suppressed or destroyed.[74] Furthermore, as the three books discussed above show, even the evidence saved and brought to light can be savagely misinterpreted.

How do we know if a woman felt attachment, acted on it, recognized the existence of other women like her, or expressed solidarity? There is no easy answer to this, but it is revealing, I think, that both Doris Faber and Anna Mary Wells are fairly certain that Lorena Hickok and Jeannette Marks, respectively, *did* have "homosexual tendencies" (although Faber insists that even Hickok cannot fairly be placed in the "contemporary gay category"), even if the admirable figures in each book, Eleanor Roosevelt and Mary Woolley, certainly did not. That is, both of these authors, as hard as they try to deny lesbianism, find evidence that forces them to discuss it, and both cope by pinning the "blame" on the women they paint as unpleasant–fat, ugly, pathetic Lorena Hickok and nasty, tortured, arrogant Jeannette Marks.

And, of course, despite censorship, we do know about women in the past who acted on their feelings for other women and who created lesbian communities. Consider the French lesbian culture of the late nineteenth-early twentieth century, the world depicted in Radclyffe Hall's *The Well of*

Loneliness.[75] And we are beginning to learn more about working-class and middle-class lesbian communities in the 1950's as well—in the closet, in the bars, and in the military.[76]

Using this approach, then, allows us to make distinctions among different sorts of women's relationships in the past without denying their significance or assigning fixed categories. Returning to the relationships described in this paper, we can differentiate between the intimate and supportive friendships, the couple relationships with other women that some women formed, and the feelings of falling in love that others expressed. I think it is important to state here that these relationships, whatever their nature, are not simply a side issue for the history of feminism and the women's movement. Blanche Cook has argued that the existence of female support networks has been vital to women's political activism; Smith-Rosenberg and others have shown how nineteenth-century "women's culture" both led to, and ultimately limited, organizing and public activity among middle-class women.[77] I believe that women's relationships have been absolutely central to the success of feminist activity throughout history. Woman-committed women have had the emotional commitment, the support, and often the time to devote their lives to a cause, as did many of the women I have discussed.

It is important that nineteenth-century American women sought and found emotional support in a homosocial world. It is also important that throughout history there have been women who chose other women for the primary relationship in their lives. It is important that some of these women would have been shocked to be labeled lesbians, and it is important that some of them claimed their lesbianism and built a culture and community around it with other lesbians. It is imperative that we not deny the reality of any of these women's historical experiences by blurring the distinctions among them. At the same time, recognition of the common bond of commitment to women shared by diverse women throughout history strengthens our struggle against those who attempt to divide and defeat us.

NOTES

*Holly Near's song, "Imagine My Surprise," celebrates the discovery of women's relationships in the past. The song is recorded on the album, *Imagine My Surprise,* Redwood Records. I am grateful to Holly Near and Redwood Records for their permission to use the title here.

1. Carroll Smith-Rosenberg, "The Female World of Love and Ritual: Relations between Women in Nineteenth-Century America," *Signs,* 1, 1 (1975), 1-29.

2. Nancy F. Cott, *The Bonds of Womanhood* (New Haven: Yale Univ. Press, 1977), Ch. 5: Nancy Sahli, "Smashing: Women's Relationships Before the Fall," *Chrysalis*, No. 8 (1979), pp. 17-27; Blanche Wiesen Cook, "Female Support Networks and Political Activism: Lillian Wald, Crystal Eastman and Emma Goldman," *Chrysalis*, No. 3 (1977), pp. 43-61; and Blanche W. Cook, "The Historical Denial of Lesbianism," *Radical History Review*, 20 (1979), 60-65. See especially the Lesbian History issue of FRONTIERS, Vol. 4, No. 3 (Fall 1979); see also, Judith Schwarz, "*Yellow Clover*: Katharine Lee Bates and Katharine Coman," FRONTIERS, 4, 1 (Spring 1979), 59-67.

3. Doris Faber, *The Life of Lorena Hickok: E.R.'s Friend* (New York: William Morrow and Co., 1980).

4. Faber, p. 176.

5. Anna Mary Wells, *Miss Marks and Miss Woolley* (Boston: Houghton Mifflin, 1978); Faber, p. 354. Cook, "Historical Denial," is a review of the Wells book.

6. Marjorie Housepian Dobkin, *The Making of a Feminist: Early Journals and Letters of M. Carey Thomas* (Kent, Ohio: Kent State Univ. Press, 1980). See the review by Helen Vendler," Carey Thomas of Bryn Mawr," *The New York Times Book Review*, February 24, 1980, pp. 24-25. Vendler accuses Dobkin of psychological naivete in her portrait of Thomas.

7. *The New York Times*, August 21, 1976, p. 22.

8. Dobkin, p. 72; p. 118; p. 229.

9. Dobkin, pp. 79, 86.

10. Edward Sigall, "Eleanor Roosevelt's Secret Romance—the Untold Story," *National Enquirer*, November 13, 1979, pp. 20-21.

11. Arthur Schlesinger, Jr., "Interesting Women," *The New York Times Book Review*, February 17, 1980, p. 31.

12. Blanche Wiesen Cook, review of *The Life of Lorena Hickok*, *Feminist Studies*, 6 (1980), 511-16.

13. Morton N. Cohen, "Love Story, Victorian-Style" (review of Andrew Birkin's *J. M. Barrie and the Lost Boys*), *The New York Times Book Review*, January 13, 1980, p. 3.

14. Cook, "Female Support Networks," p. 48.

15. Wells, p. 56.

16. Caroline Babcock to Jeannette Marks, February 12, 1947, Babcock papers, box 8 (105), Schlesinger Library, Cambridge, Massachusetts. I am grateful to the Schlesinger Library for permission to use the material quoted here.

17. "The Unfinished Autobiography of Lena Madesin Phillips," Phillips papers, Schlesinger Library.

18. "Chronological Record of Events and Activities for the Biography of Lena Madesin Phillips, 1881-1955," Phillips papers, Schlesinger Library.

19. "Chronological Record of Events and Activities for the Biography of Lena Madesin Phillips, 1881-1955," Phillips papers, Schlesinger Library.

20. Lena Madesin Phillips to Audrey Turner, January 21, 1948, Phillips papers, Schlesinger Library; Lena Madesin Phillips to Olivia Rossetti Agresti, April 26, 1948, Phillips papers, Schlesinger Library.

21. Robert Heller to Lena Madesin Phillips, September 26, 1948, Phillips papers, Schlesinger Library.

22. Lena Madesin Phillips to Mary C. Kennedy, August 20, 1948, Phillips papers, Schlesinger Library.

23. Lena Madesin Phillips to Gordon Holmes, March 28, 1949, Phillips papers, Schlesinger Library.

24. Lena Madesin Phillips to [Ida Spitz], November 13, 1950, Phillips papers, Schlesinger Library.

25. Gordon Holmes to Madesin & Maggie, December 15, 1948, Phillips papers, Schlesinger Library.

26. Lena Madesin Phillips to Gordon Holmes, March 28, 1949, Phillips papers, Schlesinger Library.

27. "Chronological Record of Events and Activities for the Biography of Lena Madesin Phillips, 1881-1955," Phillips papers, Schlesinger Library.

28. Alma Lutz to Florence Kitchelt, July 1, 1948, Kitchelt papers, box 6 (177), Schlesinger Library.

29. Alma Lutz to Florence Kitchelt, July 29, 1959, Kitchelt papers, box 7 (178), Schlesinger Library.

30. Alma Lutz to Florence Armstrong, August 26, 1959, Armstrong papers, box 1 (17), Schlesinger Library.

31. Alma Lutz to Rose Arnold Powell, December 14, 1959, Powell papers, box 3 (43), Schlesinger Library.

32. Mabel Vernon, "Speaker for Suffrage and Petitioner for Peace." an oral history conducted in 1972 and 1973 by Amelia R. Fry, Regional Oral History Office, University of California, 1976.

33. Press release from Mabel Vernon Memorial Committee, Vernon, "Speaker for Suffrage"; obituary in the *Wilmington Morning News,* September 3, 1975, Vernon, "Speaker for Suffrage."

34. Alice Morgan Wright to Anita Pollitzer, July 9, 1946, National Woman's Party papers, reel 89. The National Woman's Party papers have been microfilmed and are distributed by the Microfilming Corporation of America. I am grateful to the National Woman's Party for permission to quote the material used here.

35. Alice Paul, "Conversations with Alice Paul: Woman Suffrage and the Equal Rights Amendment," an oral history conducted in 1972 and 1973 by Amelia R. Fry, Regional Oral History Office, University of California, 1976, p. 614. Courtesy, the Bancroft Library. Nora Stanton Barney to Alice Paul, n.d. (received May 10, 1945), National Woman's Party papers, reel 86.

36. Alice Morgan Wright to Caroline Babcock, June 28, 1945, National Woman's Party papers, reel 86; Edith Goode to Caroline Babcock, July 10, 1946, Babcock papers, box 7 (98), Schlesinger Library; Edith Goode to Emma Guffey Miller, December 23, 1963, National Woman's Party papers, reel 108; Edith

Goode to Jacques Sichel, March 22, 1967, National Woman's Party papers, reel 110; Paul. "Conversations," p. 614.

37. Agnes Wells to Anita Pollitzer, August 24, 1946, National Woman's Party papers, reel 89.

38. Alice Paul to Dorothy Griswold, February 2, 1955, National Woman's Party papers, reel 101.

39. Lavinia Dock to Alice Paul, May 9, 1945, National Woman's Party papers, reel 86.

40. See, for example, Susan D. Becker, "An Intellectual History of the National Woman's Party, 1920-1941," Diss. Case Western Reserve University 1975.

41. Vernon, "Speaker for Suffrage."

42. Paul. "Conversations," p. 197.

43. Jeannette Marks to Alice Paul, March 25, 1945, National Woman's Party papers, reel 85; Jeannette Marks to Alice Paul, March 30, 1945, National Woman's Party papers, reel 85; Jeannette Marks to Alice Paul, April 27, 1945, National Woman's Party papers, reel 85.

44. Nina Allender to Alice Paul, January 5, 1947, National Woman's Party papers, reel 90.

45. Alice Paul to Nina Allender, March 9, 1950, National Woman's Party papers, reel 96.

46. Alice Paul to Nina Allender, November 20, 1954, National Woman's Party papers, reel 100; Kay Boyle to Alice Paul, December 5, 1954, National Woman's Party papers, reel 100; Alice Paul to Nina Allender, December 6, 1954, National Woman's Party papers, reel 100.

47. Kay Boyle to Alice Paul, February 13, 1957, National Woman's Party papers, reel 103; Alice Paul to Kay Boyle, March 5, 1957, National Woman's Party papers, reel 103.

48. Letter to Anna Lord Strauss, December 22, 1945, Strauss papers, box 6 (118), Schlesinger Library. Because of the possibly sensitive nature of the material reported here, I am not using the names of the women involved.

49. Letter to Anna Lord Strauss, September 19, 1946, Strauss papers, box 6 (119), Schlesinger Library.

50. Letter to Anna Lord Strauss, May 9, 1947, Strauss papers, box 6 (121), Schlesinger Library.

51. Letter to Anna Lord Strauss, June 28, 1948, Strauss papers, box 6 (124), Schlesinger Library.

52. Letter to Anna Lord Strauss, February 26, 1951, Strauss papers, box 1 (15), Schlesinger Library.

53. Letter to Anna Lord Strauss, December 22, 1945, Strauss papers, box 6 (118), Schlesinger Library.

54. Letter to Anna Lord Strauss, May 9, 1947, Strauss papers, box 6 (121), Schlesinger Library.

55. "Stream of consciousness," March 10, 1948, Strauss papers, box 6 (124), Schlesinger Library.

56. Augusta Street to Anna Lord Strauss, n.d. [1968], Strauss papers, box 7 (135), Schlesinger Library.

57. Letter to Anna Lord Strauss, February 11, 1949, Strauss papers, box 6 (125), Schlesinger Library.

58. Letter to Anna Lord Strauss, March 3, 1949, Strauss papers, box 6 (125), Schlesinger Library.

59. Letter to Anna Lord Strauss, March 8, 1968, Strauss papers, box 7 (135), Schlesinger Library.

60. Lilian Lyndon to Anna Lord Strauss, April 23, 1950, Strauss papers, box 1 (14), Schlesinger Library.

61. Diary entries, August 30, 1953 and September 1, 1953, Doris Stevens papers, Schlesinger Library.

62. Diary entry, August 24, 1953, Doris Stevens papers, Schlesinger Library.

63. Diary entry, February 4, 1946, Doris Stevens papers, Schlesinger Library.

64. Diary entry, December 1, 1945, Doris Stevens papers, Schlesinger Library.

65. Doris Stevens to Westbrook Pegler, May 3, 1946, Stevens papers, Schlesinger Library.

66. Paul, "Conversations," pp. 195-96.

67. Interview conducted by Verta Taylor and Leila Rupp, December 10, 1979.

68. Sasha Gregory Lewis, *Sunday's Women: A Report on Lesbian Life Today* (Boston: Beacon Press, 1979), p. 94.

69. Mary McIntosh, "The Homosexual Role," *Social Problems,* 16, 2 (1968), 182-91; Jeffrey Weeks, *Coming Out: Homosexual Politics in Britain, from the Nineteenth Century to the Present* (London: Quartet Books, 1977); Bert Hansen, "The Historical Construction of Homosexuality," *Radical History Review,* 20 (1979), 66-73.

70. See Vern Bullough and Bonnie Bullough, "Lesbianism in the 1920s and 1930s: A Newfound Study." *Signs,* 2, 4 (1977), 895-904; Lewis; and Madeline Davis, Liz Kennedy, and Avra Michelson, "Aspects of the Buffalo Lesbian Community in the Fifties," Buffalo Women's Oral History Project, paper presented at the National Women's Studies Association Conference, Bloomington, Indiana, May 1980. Local research projects are beginning to explore the history of gay and lesbian culture in the pre-gay liberation and women's movement years in a number of cities in addition to Buffalo. Such projects currently exist in Boston, Chicago, New York, Philadelphia, and San Francisco.

71. Much of the recent literature on lesbianism emphasizes this crucial distinction between identity and experience. See, for example, Barbara Ponse, *Identities in the Lesbian World: The Social Construction of Self* (Westport, Conn.: Greenwood Press, 1978); and E. M. Ettore, *Lesbians, Women and Society* (London: Routledge & Kegan Paul, 1980).

72. Cook, "Historical Denial," p. 64.

73. On coming out as a process, see Ponse; Ettore; Julia Penelope Stanley and Susan J. Wolfe, *The Coming Out Stories* (Watertown, Mass.: Persephone Press, 1980); and Margaret Cruikshank, *The Lesbian Path* (Monterey, CA.: Angel Press, 1980).

74. The Mount Holyoke administration closed the Marks-Woolley papers when Wells discovered the love letters, and the papers are only open to researchers now because an American Historical Association committee, including Blanche Cook as one of its members, applied pressure to keep the papers open after Wells, to her credit, contacted them. Faber describes her unsuccessful attempts to persuade the archivists at the FDR Library to close the Lorena Hickok papers.

75. See Dolores Klaich, *Woman + Woman* (1974; rpt. New York: Morrow-Quill, 1979), pp. 129-215; and Barbara Grier and Coletta Reid, *Lesbian Lives: Biographies of Women from the Ladder* (Baltimore: Diana Press, 1976).

76. Lewis; Davis, Kennedy, and Michelson.

77. Cook, "Female Support Networks"; Smith-Rosenberg; Cott; Mary P. Ryan, "The Power of Women's Networks: A Case Study of Female Moral Reform in Antebellum America," *Feminist Studies*, 5 (1979), 66-85; Carroll Smith-Rosenberg, "Beauty, the Beast and the Militant Woman: A Case Study of Sex Roles and Social Stress in Jacksonian America," *American Quarterly*, 23, 4 (1971), 562-84. See Ellen DuBois et al., "Politics and Culture in Women's History," *Feminist Studies*, 6 (1980), 26-64.

Zero Degree Deviancy:
The Lesbian Novel in English

Catharine R. Stimpson

In her poem "Diving into the Wreck" (1972), Adrienne Rich imagined a descent into the sea of history that might see the damage that was done and the treasures that prevail. The poem has been a mandate for feminist critics as they measure the damage patriarchal cultures have inflicted and the treasures that a female tradition has nevertheless accumulated. We have yet to survey fully, however, the lesbian writers who worked under the double burden of a patriarchal culture and a strain in the female tradition that accepted and valued heterosexuality.[1] It is these writers whom I want to ground more securely in the domain of feminist criticism.[2]

My definition of the lesbian–as writer, as character, and as reader–will be conservative and severely literal. She is a woman who finds other women erotically attractive and gratifying. Of course a lesbian is more than her body, more than her flesh, but lesbianism partakes of the body, partakes of the flesh. That carnality distinguishes it from gestures of political sympathy with homosexuals and from affectionate friendships in which women enjoy each other, support each other, and commingle a sense of identity and well-being. Lesbianism represents a commitment of skin, blood, breast, and bone. If female and male gay writings have their differences, it is not only because one takes Sappho and the other Walt

Early versions of this paper were read at Brown University, Hampshire College, the Columbia University Seminar on Women in Society, and the Modern Language Association. I am grateful to Adrienne Rich, Elizabeth Wood, and Elizabeth Abel for their comments.

[Haworth co-indexing entry note]: "Zero Degree Deviancy: The Lesbian Novel in English." Stimpson, Catharine R. Co-published simultaneously in *Journal of Lesbian Studies* (The Haworth Press, Inc.) Vol. 1, No. 2, 1997, pp. 177-194; and: *Classics in Lesbian Studies* (ed: Esther D. Rothblum) The Haworth Press, Inc., 1997, pp. 177-194; and: *Classics in Lesbian Studies* (ed: Esther D. Rothblum) Harrington Park Press, an imprint of The Haworth Press, Inc., 1997, pp. 177-194.

Whitman as its great precursor. They simply do not spring from the same physical presence in the world.

To my lexicographical rigidity I will add an argument that is often grim. Because the violent yoking of homosexuality and deviancy has been so pervasive in the modern period, little or no writing about it can ignore that conjunction. A text may support it, leeringly or ruefully. It may reject it, fiercely or ebulliently. Moral or emotional indifference is improbable. Few, if any, homosexual texts can exemplify writing at the zero degree, that degree at which writing, according to Roland Barthes, is ". . . basically in the indicative mood, or . . . amodal . . . [a] new neutral writing . . . [that] takes its place in the midst of . . . ejaculation and judgements; without becoming involved in any of them; [that] . . . consists precisely in their absence."[3] Lesbian novels in English have responded judgmentally to the perversion that has made homosexuality perverse by developing two repetitive patterns: the dying fall, a narrative of damnation, of the lesbian's suffering as a lonely outcast attracted to a psychological lower caste; and the enabling escape, a narrative of the reversal of such descending trajectories, of the lesbian's rebellion against social stigma and self-contempt. Because the first has been dominant during the twentieth century, the second has had to flee from the imaginative grip of that tradition as well.

If the narratives of damnation reflect larger social attitudes about homosexuality, they can also extend an error of discourse about it: false universalizing, tyrannical univocalizing. Often ahistorical, as if pain erased the processes of time, they can fail to reveal the inseparability of the twentieth-century lesbian novel and the twentieth century: ". . . in the nineteenth century . . . homosexuality assumed its modern form," which the next century was to exhibit.[4] One symptom of modernization, of the refusal to exempt the lesbian from the lurching logic of change, was a new sexual vocabulary. Before the end of the nineteenth century, homosexuality might have been subsumed under such a term as "masturbation."[5] Then lesbians became "lesbians." The first citation for lesbianism as a female passion in *The Shorter Oxford English Dictionary* is 1908, for "sapphism" 1890.

The public used its new language with pity, hostility, and disdain.[6] The growing tolerance of an optionally nonprocreative heterosexuality failed to dilute the abhorrence of a necessarily nonprocreative homosexuality, especially if practicing it threatened to mean social as well as sexual self-sufficiency. In her study of birth control, Linda Gordon states: "We must notice that the sexual revolution was not a general loosening of sexual taboos but only of those on nonmarital heterosexual activity. Indeed, so specifically heterosexual was this change that it tended to intensify taboos on homosexual activity and did much to break patterns of emotional dependency and intensity among women."[7] Both female and male writers absorbed such strong cultural signals. If "guilt and anxiety rarely appear in homosexual literature until the late nineteenth century, . . . [they] become the major theme of *Angst* . . . after 1914."[8] Evidently, freedom in one place may serve as an inoculation against its permissible appearance elsewhere. The more autonomy women claim in one sphere, the more they may enter into an obscure balancing act that may lead to tighter restrictions upon them in another.

Such an environment nurtured external and internal censorship. During a century in which the woman writer as such became less of a freak, the lesbian writer had to inhibit her use of material she knew intimately but which her culture might hold to be, at best, freakish. She learned that being quiet, in literature and life, would enable her to "pass." Silence could be a passport into the territory of the dominant world. In a quick-witted recent novel, June Arnold's *Sister Gin,* an aging mother responds to her middle-aged daughter's attempt to talk to her about her lesbianism: "But she shouldn't say that word. It isn't a nice word. 'People don't care what you do as long as you don't tell them about it. I know that.'"[9] Such silence signifies a subterranean belief in the magical power of language. If the lesbian were to name herself, her utterance might carry a taint from speaker to listener, from mouth to ear. Silence is also a shrewd refusal to provoke punitive powers—be they of the family, workplace, law, or church. Obviously this survival tactic makes literature impossible. Culture, then, becomes the legatee of linguistic zeros, of blank pages encrypted in tombs critics will never excavate.

If the lesbian writer wished to name her experience but still feared plain speech, she could encrypt her text in another sense and use codes.[10] In the fallout of history, the words "code" and "zero" lie together. The Arabs translated the Hindu for "zero" as *sifr* ("empty space"), in English "cipher." As the Arabic grew in meanings, *sifr* came to represent a number system forbidden in several places but still secretly deployed, and cipher became "code." In some lesbian fiction, the encoding is allegorical, a straightforward shift from one set of terms to another, from a clitoris to a cow. Other acts are more resistant to any reading that might wholly reveal, or wholly deny, lesbian eroticism.

Take for example "the kiss," a staple of lesbian fiction. Because it has shared with women's writing in general a reticence about explicitly representing sexual activity, the kiss has had vast metonymic responsibilities. Simultaneously, its exact significance has been deliberately opaque. Look at three famous kiss scenes:

It was a very real oblivion. Adele was roused from it by a kiss that seemed to scale the very walls of chastity. She flung away on the instant filled with battle and revulsion. [Gertrude Stein, *Q. E. D.*]

Julia blazed. Julia kindled. Out of the night she burnt like a dead white star. Julia opened her arms. Julia kissed her on the lips. Julia possessed it. [Virginia Woolf, "Slater's Pins Nave No Points"]

Then came the most exquisite moment of her whole life passing a stone urn with flowers in it. Sally stopped; picked a flower; kissed her on the lips. The whole world might have turned upside down! . . . she felt that she had been given a present, wrapped up, and told just to keep it, not to look at it—a diamond, something infinitely precious, wrapped up . . . she uncovered, or the radiance burnt through the revelation, the religious feeling! [Woolf, *Mrs. Dalloway*]

Does the kiss encode transgression or permissibility? Singularity or repeatability? Impossibility or possibility? The same character, "O," can stand for both the zero of impossibility and for the possibilities of female sexuality.[11] Does the kiss predict the beginning of the end, or the end of the beginning, or a lesbian erotic enterprise? Or is it the event that literally embraces contradictions?

Still, the overt will out. As if making an implicit, perhaps unconscious pact with her culture, the lesbian writer who rejects both silence and excessive coding can claim the right to write for the public in exchange for adopting the narrative of damnation. The paradigm of this narrative is Radclyffe Hall's *The Well of Loneliness*—published, banned in England, and quickly issued elsewhere in 1928, by which time scorn for lesbianism had hardened into orthodoxy.[12] Novelist as well as novel have entered minor mythology. Hall represents the lesbian as scandal and the lesbian as woman-who-is-man, who proves "her" masculinity through taking a feminine woman-who-is-woman as "her" lover. In a baroque and savage satire published after *The Well of Loneliness,* Wyndham Lewis excoriates a den of dykes in which a woman artist in "a stiff Radcliffe-Hall collar, of antique masculine cut" torments a heterosexual fellow and dabbles with a voluptuous mate.[13] He is too jealous and enraged to recognize either the sadness of costume and role reversal (the stigmatized seeking to erase the mark through aping the stigmatizers) or the courage of the masquerade (the emblazoning of defiance and jaunty play).[14] Be it mimicry or bravery, the woman who would be man reaches for status and for freedom. The man who would be woman, because of the devaluation of the female and feminine, participates, in part, in a ritual of degradation.

Comparing *The Well of Loneliness* to Hall's life reveals a discrepancy between the pleasures she seems to have found with her lover, Una Taylor, Lady Troubridge, and the sorrows of her hero, Stephen Gordon. Hall offers a parallel to the phenomenon of the woman novelist who creates women characters less accomplished and successful than she. In addition, the novel is more pessimistic about the threat of homosexuality *as such* to happiness than Hall's earlier novel, *The Unlit Lamp* (1924). Set in roughly the same time period as *The Well of Loneliness, The Unlit Lamp* dramatizes a triangle of mother, daughter, and governess. The daughter and governess have a long, unconsummated, ultimately ruptured lesbian relationship. Their grief is less the result of a vile passion and the reactions to it than of the daughter's failure of nerve, her father's patriarchal crassness, her mother's possessive manipulations, and the constrictions provincial England places on the New Woman.

In brief, *The Well of Loneliness* tends to ignore the more benign possibilities of lesbianism. Hall projects homosexuality as a sickness. To deepen the horror, the abnormal illness is inescapable, preordained; an ascribed, not an achieved, status. For Stephen is a "congenital invert," the term John Addington Symonds probably coined around 1883 and Havelock Ellis later refined: "Sexual inversion, as here understood, means sexual instinct turned by inborn constitutional abnormality towards persons of the same sex. It is thus a narrower term than homosexuality, which includes all sexual attractions between persons of the same sex." The congenital female invert has male physical traits—narrow hips, wide shoulders—as "part of an organic instinct."[15] Stephen also has a livid scar on her cheek. Literally, it is a war wound; socially, a mark of the stigmatized individual who may blame the self for a lack of acceptability;[16] mythically, the mark of Cain. *The Well of Loneliness* stresses the morbidity of a stigma that the politics of heaven, not of earth, must first relieve.

Yet Hall planned an explicit protest against that morbidity. Indeed, having Stephen Gordon be a congenital invert who has no choice about her condition strengthens Hall's argument about the unfairness of equating homosexuality with punishable deviancy. The novel claims that God created homosexuals. If they are good enough for Him, they ought to be good enough for us. Hall cries out for sacred and social toleration, for an end to the cruelties of alienation. In the novel's famous last paragraph, Stephen gasps, "God . . . we believe; we have told You we believe. . . . We have not denied You, then rise up and defend us. Acknowledge us, oh God, before the whole world. Give us the right to our existence."[17] Ironically, the very explicitness of that cry in a climate increasingly harsh for lesbians, combined with the vividness of Hall's description of homosexual subworlds, propelled *The Well of Loneliness* into scandal while the far more subversive, if subtle, *Unlit Lamp* was a success. To double the irony, Hall's strategies of protest against damnation so entangle her in damnation that they intensify the sense of its inevitability and power. The novel's attack on homophobia becomes particularly self-defeating. The text is, then, like a Janus with one face looming larger than the other. It gives the heterosexual a voyeuristic tour and the vicarious comfort of reading about an enforced stigma–in greater measure than it provokes guilt. It gives the homosexual, particularly the lesbian, riddling images of pity, self-pity, and of terror–in greater measure than it consoles.

The Well of Loneliness lacks the intricacies of Djuna Barnes' *Nightwood*, another parable of damnation, published eight years later. Its lack of intricacy, plus its notoriety and the way in which it inscribes damnation, helped to transform its status from that of subject of an obscenity trial to that of an immensely influential, token lesbian text. As one historian writes, "most of us lesbians in the 1950s grew up knowing nothing about lesbianism except Stephen Gordon."[18] Despite, or perhaps because of, its reputation, critics have ignored its structural logic, an error I want to remedy now.

Each of the novel's five sections (or acts) ends unhappily, the parts replicating and reinforcing the movement of the whole. Book 1 begins with Stephen's birth to a loving, rich couple.[19] The happiness of their legitimate, heterosexual union is the positive term that opposes the woe lurking in wait for illegitimate, homosexual ones. Although Sir Philip Gordon had wanted a son, he loves his daughter. Wise, courageous, kind, honorable, attentive, athletic, he embodies a fantasy of the perfect father Hall never had, the perfect man she could never become. Lady Anna, however, who had simply wanted a baby, instinctively repudiates her "unnatural" daughter. Though mother and child are of the same sex, they share neither gender nor love. Hall's idealization of Sir Philip and her regrets about Lady Anna are early markers of a refusal to link a protest against homophobia with one against patriarchal values.

During her late adolescence, Stephen meets a visiting Canadian, Martin Hallam. They become the best of brotherly friends–until Martin falls in love with Stephen. His emotions shock her; her shock stuns him; he leaves the neighborhood. Stephen's introduction to heterosexual passion, to her a form of homosexual incest, confirms her inability to pass even the most benign of initiation rites for girls. The loss of her "brother," however, is far less painful than the accidental death of her father, which ends book 1: it deprives her of "companionship of mind, . . . a stalwart barrier between her and the world, . . . and above all of love" (p. 121).

So bereft, Stephen behaves blindly. She falls in love with Angela Crosby, fickle, shallow, and married. As Angela strings Stephen along with a few of those conventional kisses, she sets her up as a rival of two men: husband Ralph and lover Roger. The masculinized lesbian has few advantages in competition with natural males. To keep Ralph from finding out about Roger, Angela shows him a love letter from Stephen and claims to be the innocent victim of odd affections. Ralph takes the letter to Lady Anna, who gives Stephen the choice of leaving her beloved ancestral estate or watching Lady Anna leave it. Finding her "manhood," Stephen accepts exile. With a loyal governess, a favorite horse, and a private income, she abandons Eden for London. Hall concludes book 2 with the punishment of expulsion, proving that even the aristocratic homosexual must suffer.

In the city, Stephen completes the rites of maturity for inverts. She finds a home: Paris, the center of literary lesbianism in the first part of the twentieth century. She finds work: literature itself. She writes a wonderful and famous novel. As Cain's mark was from God, so both Ellis and Hall give their inverts some compensations: intelligence and talent. If the body is negatively deviant, the mind is positively so. Hall demands that the invert use that intelligence and talent. Hard work will be a weapon against the hostile world; cultural production an answer to the society that repudiates a Stephen because she has been forced to repudiate reproduction. Finally, serving a larger cause, Stephen becomes a valiant member of a World War I women's ambulance corps. (Hall here explores, if peripherally, that standard setting of the lesbian text: a community of women.) But despite the personal bravery of both female and male warriors, the war is a wasteland. Stephen's personal anguish and confusion over her sexuality, then, find a larger, historical correlative in the trenches, as Hall ends book 3 with a lament for the dead.

During the war, however, Stephen has met a poorer, younger, Welsh woman, Mary Llewellyn, whom she takes to a Mediterranean villa. For a while they suppress their physical longing. In Stephen's fears that sex will destroy love, ecstasy intimacy, Hall is suggesting that the stigma of homosexuality is tolerable as long as the erotic desire that distinguishes the lesbian remains repressed. The conclusion—that a released eros will provoke the destructive potential of the stigma—places Hall in that Western cultural tradition that links sex and death. In addition, she is attributing to lesbianism a conventional belief about female sexuality in general: that women prefer love and romance to physical consummation. Ultimately Mary's needs overwhelm Stephen's chivalrous hope to protect her from them. Though their bodies, like those of any homosexual couple, are anatomically similar, their relationship embodies a number of dyadic roles. Into their closed and exclusive world they structure multiple polarized differences, primarily that between female and male. Hall exults:

> Stephen as she held the girl in her arms, would feel that indeed she was all things to Mary; father, mother, friend and lover, all things; and Mary all things to her—the child, the friend, the beloved, all things. But Mary, because she was perfect woman, would rest without thought, without exultation, without question; finding no need to question since for her there was now only one thing—Stephen. [P. 134]

Seeking metaphors for their passion, Hall, like many lesbian novelists, turns to nature, both tamed and untamed: to vineyards, fruit trees, flowers, the four elements, the moon. Such standard tropes carry the implicit burden of dissolving the taint of "unnatural" actions through the cleansing power of natural language.[20]

Most idylls, even those of refound Edens, must end. Hall concludes book 4 with the ominous "And thus in a cloud of illusion and glory, sped the last enchanted days at Orotava" (p. 317). Stephen and Mary return to Paris. There, with their loving dog, they are happy—for a while; but Mary, restless, begins to seek diversion with other lesbians and in the homosexual underworld, particularly in the bars that modern cities nurture. Bars can serve as a source of warm, egalitarian *communitas* for the marginal homosexual who must also aspire to the far more prestigious heterosexual world that is a structural reference group.[21] But the fearful, puritanical Stephen despises them; like many fictive lesbians, she finds security in a sanctified domesticity. Though a friend reasonably tells Stephen that Mary has too little to do, especially when Stephen is obsessively writing, Hall just as reasonably locates the primary source of strain between the lovers in the tension between their little world and the larger world of society and family that fears them.

Whatever the cause, Mary mopes and hardens. Then, a secular *deus ex machina,* Martin Hallam returns. Stephen's alter ego, he, too, has been ounded in the war. He, too, falls in love with Mary. The two fight it out for her. Though Stephen wins, the price is too high: where she once had Mary's soul but feared possession of the body, she may now possess the body but not the soul. For God's scheme includes congenital heterosexuals as well as congenital inverts. Mary has, somewhat belatedly, realized that she is one of them. Martyring herself in the religion of love, Stephen pretends to be having an affair with a woman friend, Valerie Seymour. She stays out for two nights. When she returns, her mock confession of infidelity drives the distraught Mary into the night and the arms of the waiting Martin, whom Stephen has posted in the street below.

Throughout book 5, Hall's religiosity has become more and more omnipresent: her attraction to Catholic theology, architecture, and liturgy; her anxious queries about God's real allegiance in the war between Stephen's little world and that which would damn it. As Stephen renounces Mary, she has a compensatory vision, at once hallucination, inspiration, and conversion experience. She will become the voice of the voiceless stigmatized; she will help them break through to a new, sympathetic recognition. So willing, Stephen finds that "her barren womb became fruitful–it ached with its fearful and sterile burden" (p. 437).

That juxtaposition of fruitfulness and aching burdens is a final bit of information about the unevenly balanced duality of Hall's text. Yet she does create the figure of Valerie Seymour, a charismatic teetotaler who keeps a famous Parisian salon. Amidst the volatile gloom of Stephen's histrionics, she is serenely sunny. She, too, finds homosexuality congenital, but she lyrically interprets fate as a friendly boon: "Nature was trying to do her bit; inverts were being born in increasing numbers, and after a while their numbers would tell, even with the fools who still ignored Nature" (p. 406). Though Hall does little with Valerie, she signifies the presence of a second consciousness about lesbianism that *The Well of Loneliness* and the forces surrounding it helped to submerge, screen, and render secondary during the mid twentieth century. This consciousness, aware of the labelling of lesbianism as a pollutant, nevertheless chose to defy it.

The "Kinsey Report" suggests the existence of such a mentality. Of 142 women with much homosexual experience, 70 percent reported no regrets.[22] This consciousness has manifested itself in literature in two ways. First, in lesbian romanticism: fusions of life and death, happiness and woe, natural imagery and supernatural strivings, neoclassical paganism with a ritualistic cult of Sappho, and modern beliefs in evolutionary progress with a cult of the rebel. At its worst an inadvertent parody of *fin de siècle* decadence, at its best lesbian romanticism ruthlessly rejects a stifling dominant culture and asserts the value of psychological autonomy, women, art, and a European cultivation of the sensuous, sensual, and voluptuous. Woolf's *Orlando* is its most elegant and inventive text, but its symbol is probably the career of Natalie Barney, the cosmopolitan American who was the prototype of Valerie Seymour.[23]

The second mode is lesbian realism: the adaption of the conventions of the social and psychological novel to appraise bonds between women and demonstrate that such relationships are potentially of psychic and moral value. The slyest realistic text is Stein's *Autobiography of Alice B. Toklas,* but less tricky examples include *The Unlit Lamp* and another ignored novel, Helen R. Hull's *Labyrinth* (1923). There one sister marries an ambitious, egocentric man. A second sister lives with an ambitious, generous woman. The first sister is unhappy and confined; the second happy and productive.[24] What *Labyrinth* implies, other realistic texts state explicitly: even though the lesbian may have children whom she loves, she must reject the patriarchal family, which the stigma against her helps to maintain, if she is to reject repression as well. The tension between the role of mother, which the lesbian may desire, and the traditional family structure, in which women are subordinate, is obviously far more characteristic of lesbian than gay-male writing. A man may have both paternity and power, but a woman must too often choose between maternity and comparative powerlessness.

In 1963 Mary McCarthy's *The Group* brought that submerged, screened, secondary consciousness to public prominence. Second on the fiction best-seller list for its year, selling well over 3,000,000 copies by 1977, *The Group* showed that lesbianism could be an acceptable, even admirable, subject—particularly if a writer of unquestioned heterosexuality served as the gatekeeper. Moreover, McCarthy was tactfully judicious about the erotic details of lesbian sexuality. Cleverly, if perhaps inadvertently, McCarthy fused lesbian romanticism and lesbian realism. In characterization, setting, style, and some of its assumptions, *The Group* was realistic, but its heroine was wonderfully romantic. For Lakey is self-assured, intelligent, beautiful, charitable, and anti-Fascist; she wears violet suits; she has lived in Europe; she has an affair with a baroness. In brief, she personifies the most glamorous of enabling escapes from stigma and self-contempt. The members of The Group, all Vassar graduates, also prefigure the possible response of liberal readers of this novel to the claims of this secondary consciousness to primary status. Lakey, after she returns from Europe, cannot be damned; indeed, she must be respected. Yet The Group finds encounters with her awkwardly enigmatic and strange; strangely and enigmatically awkward.

Since *The Group,* a far less tormented lesbian has surfaced—to supplement, if not wholly supplant, the Stephens and the Marys. In some texts by nonlesbians, she is little more than a romp, a sexual interlude and caper. Like masturbation and the orgy, homosexuality has become a counter in the game of erotic writing. Trade fiction has claimed the provinces of pornography and sexology. Other texts, however, primarily by lesbians and sympathetic feminists, damn the lesbian's damnation. Their appearance in strength is the result of a confluence of forces. Certainly a material cause was the founding of several journals, magazines, and presses that

could publish the products of a more audacious sexual ideology and practice. Among the most substantial, for the lesbian novel, was the small trade
house, Daughters, Inc. Its subtitle, "Publishers of Books by Women,"
reflects its founders' theory that feminism would create new genres. Existing in that climate, which might have a certain early crudity, would be a
"freer lesbian novel, and Daughters would be a medium that lesbian
novelists could count on."[25] Among the social causes of the reappearance
of a submerged consciousness and its narrative of the enabling escape
have been the women's movement, more flexible attitudes toward marriage (so often contrasted favorably to the putative anarchy of homosexual
relations), the "modernization of sex," which encourages a rational, toler-
ant approach to the complexities of eros,[26] and the growing entrance of
more women into the public labor force, which gives a financial autonomy
inseparable from genuine sexual independence.

The new texts are hopeful about homosexuality and confident about the
lesbian's power to name her experience and experiment with literary
form.[27] These novels invert the application of the label of deviant: the
lesbian calls those who would call her sinful or sick themselves sinful or
sick; she claims for herself the language of respectability. In a sweet novel
of the 1960s, Elana Nachman's *Riverfinger Woman,* the protagonist fanta-
sizes about enlightening some benighted heterosexuals. She and her lover
will make a movie "so that people would see that lesbians are beautiful,
there is nothing, nothing at all unnatural about them, they too can have
weddings and be in the movies."[28] Mingling fiction, journalism, autobiography, and polemic, Jill Johnston declares in her book *Lesbian Nation* that
"that awful life of having to choose between being a criminal or going
straight was over. We were going to legitimatize ourselves as criminals."[29] Obviously these dreams and manifestos are still enmeshed in
older vocabularies of value. A few books approach indifference. Less
attracted to acts of reversal, they hint at a Barthian writing degree zero.[30]

Among the first of the more hopeful lesbian novels was *A Place for Us,*
which its author (using the name Isabel Miller) published privately in 1969
and which a commercial press reissued as *Patience and Sarah* in 1972.
That was the year of the Stonewall Resistance, the defense of a New York
gay bar against a police raid that symbolizes the beginning of the Gay
Liberation movement. The history of *A Place for Us*–the pseudonym, the
dual publication–shows both the presence and the dissolution of a fear of
lesbian material. Its author's comments about *The Well of Loneliness* reveal both the influence of and a resistance to Hall's earlier gesticulations:
"I think Radclyffe Hall was antihomosexual. . . . I first read *The Well of
Loneliness* when I was about seventeen. . . . I was very excited. But I

didn't like the characters, I didn't like the arrogance of the heroine."[31] Gentle, kindly, *A Place for Us* tells of two nineteenth-century women who run away together from patriarchal brutalities to build their farm in New York State. Almost immediately after *A Place for Us,* the most successful of the new texts appeared, Rita Mae Brown's *Rubyfruit Jungle* (1973), which during the 1970s replaced *The Well of Loneliness* as the one lesbian novel someone might have read. In *Rubyfruit Jungle* (the title alludes to the female genitals), Molly Bolt (a name that alludes to freedom and flight) escapes from a seedy provincial background to triumph over mean men, shallow women, bad schools, menial jobs, and lesbian-baiting.

If *A Place for Us* adapts the narrative of the enabling escape to the pastoral domestic idyll, *Rubyfruit Jungle* integrates it with the picaresque and the *Bildungsroman.* Together these novels dramatize two contradictory attitudes about sex and gender that pervade the contemporary lesbian novel. The first of these attitudes is a bristling contempt for sexual role playing (*A Place for Us* is an exception here). The protagonist in *Riverfinger Woman* asserts: "we were too modern already to believe that one of us was the man and the other . . . the woman. We felt like neither men nor women. We were females, we were queers. . . . We knew we had the right to love whomever we loved."[32] Under the influence of an existential ethic that praises the freely forged self and of a feminist ideology that negates patriarchal practices, such novels abandon the customs of a Radclyffe Hall. Yet they are simultaneously conscious of sex. Males, particularly traditional ones, are in disrepute. Some novels, such as Arnold's *Sister Gin,* articulate punitive fantasies—some violent, some playful—which they justify as catharsis or self-defense. The female and the female world are honorable, as structural reference and source of *communitas.* Women ask not only for equality but for self-celebration; less for the rehabilitation of men than for independence from them.

Lesbian novels thus map out the boundaries of female worlds.[33] Some of the bonds within these boundaries are erotic, a proud isosexuality that separates the lesbian novel from other, more guarded explorations, such as Charlotte Perkins Gilman's *Herland.* Characters also search, however, for alter egos, moral and psychological equivalents, which the term "sister" signifies. Poignantly, painfully, they seek the mother as well.[34] A mother waits at the heart of the labyrinth of some lesbian texts. There she unites past, present, and future. Finding her, in herself and through a surrogate, the lesbian reenacts a daughter's desire for the woman to whom she was once so linked, from whom she was then so severed. Because the mother was once a daughter, a woman approaching her can serve as the mother's mother even as she plays out the drama of a daughter. In such complex mother/daughter exchanges and interchanges, the women explore both narcissistic and anaclitic love. Of course lesbianism is far more than a matter of mother/daughter affairs, but the new texts suggest that one of its satisfactions is a return to primal origins, to primal loves, when female/female, not male/female, relationships structured the world. A lesbian's jealousy then, spurts like blood from the cut of terror at the possibility of losing again the intimacy that has at last been regained.

To focus on mothers and daughters–or on any personal bonds–is too narrow; psychology hardly defines the totality of our lives. In several texts the world of women is also a political center of solidarity and resistance. As such it can perform social experiments that the larger culture might regard attentively. To name such communities, the lesbian writer calls on myth: prehistorical matriarchies; the Amazons; Sappho and her school. The myths, also current in contemporary feminist ideology, were popular in stylish lesbian circles in the earlier part of the twentieth century. Part of their value is their ability to evoke atemporal resonances within narratives that are separate from such patriarchal religious structures as the Catholic church before which Hall knelt. When novelists grant myths the status of history (easier to do with Sappho than with Amazons and primeval matriarchs), their error, because it occurs in the freewheeling context of fiction, is more palatable than in the stricter context of programmatic ideology, political theory, and "herstory."

The most ambitious and the cleverest of the new novels in English is perhaps Bertha Harris' *Lover* (1976). The lesbian novel has tended to be, and remains, formally staid, a conventionality that has served both a homosexual and heterosexual audience. The lesbian, as she struggles against the hostilities of the larger world, can find comfort in the ease of reading. Between text and self she may also establish a sense of community. The heterosexual, as she or he nears unfamiliar and despised material, can find safety in the same ease of reading. The continued strength of literary form can stand for the continued strength of the larger community's norms. However, Harris, an American equivalent of Monique Wittig, experiments with narrative pattern as a possible coefficient of her vision of sexuality. A modernist, she fragments and collapses characters, settings, chronology, and states of mind. Her central presence appears as Veronica (also the name of the second wife of Veronica's bigamist grandfather); as Flynn; as Bertha; and as "I." In each guise the voice is both fiction and the author in the act of writing fiction. In brief, *Lover* is another book about becoming a book.

Harris is ingenious, sardonic, parodic–an economical comic intelligence. Another cultural consequence of the stigma against the lesbian is that it deforms comedy. Those who support the stigma, such as Wyndham Lewis, may freely assault the homosexual with hostile satire and burlesque. Those who internalize the stigma use the same weapons as a form of self-assault. Only when the stigma is simultaneously comprehended and despised can the comedy of a Harris, or of a Barnes before her, emerge.[35] It is a satire, often elaborate, even grotesque and baroque, that ultimately adorns rather than mutilates its subject. Barnes' enigmatic and rich prose has deeply influenced Harris, but more immediately, so has Nabokov's, his "tricking and fooling and punning and literary joking."

Some people in the feminist and lesbian press have criticized Harris and others for these adventures. Harris has been called inaccessible, as if modernism were itself an indecipherable code. She is, therefore, supposedly ideologically unsound, stopping that illusory creature, the average lesbian, from using literature to articulate her experience and urge rebellion against its nastier aspects. Harris has explanations for such prescriptive reviews. She believes that the feminist and lesbian press still lacks an informed criticism to mediate between texts and a large audience, and she finds too few "well-read reviewers, conscious of literary traditions." The press must learn to do what modern art has done: to create a self-explanatory body of criticism. Furthermore, "the lesbian readership" wants a "positive image" in its novels. Part of the huge popularity of *Rubyfruit Jungle* is due to its ebullient self-admiration. Such easy hedonism and heroism is, of course, didactically helpful and politically worthwhile, but it also "prevents a deeper look into the nature of things and the nature of lesbianism."

The baffled response to *Lover* is ironic, for few writers have given the lesbian a more lyrical identity. Harris explores the various roles women have played: grandmother, mother, daughter, sister, wife and second wife, businesswoman in man's clothing, prostitute, factory worker, movie star, muse and tutelary spirit, warrior, artist, fake saint, martyr. She codifies difference of role in order to assess similarities of the players and to find a common basis for a community of women. There the primary difference will be between lover and beloved—though lovers can be loved and the beloved lovers. The phallus may not be unwelcome, especially if necessary for breeding, but the nonphallic lesbian has a privileged status. In loving women she exalts both self and others. Harris also anoints this paradigm and paramour as an omnipotent cosmic spirit. Capable of anything and everything, she is polymorphic, amorphic, transmorphic, and orphic. She both pictures margins and escapes them. She is the principle of creativity, of a fertility of both mind and body. As such she incarnates the genesis of the world itself, once suppressed, which might be reappearing now. In an essay about Barnes and lesbian literature, Harris might be talking about *Lover* itself:

> There is not a literature that is not based on the pervasive sexuality of its time; and as that which is male disappears (sinks slowly in the west) and as the originally all-female world reasserts itself by making love to itself, the primary gesture toward the making at last of a decent literature out of the experience of a decent world might simply be a woman like myself following a woman like Djuna Barnes, and all she might represent down a single street on a particular afternoon.[36]

Not everyone will accept Harris' only partially ironic apocalyptic fantasy. Her picture of the damned does however, reverse that of *The Well of Loneliness.* The lesbian novel has offered up Hall's vision, hut it has also sheltered and released the rejection of that vision, offering an alternative process of affirmation of the lesbian body and transcendence of a culturally traced, scarring stigma. It has been a deviant voice that has both submitted to deviancy and yearned to nullify that judgment. Feminist critics, zeroing in on that voice, can serve as its acoustical engineers. We can listen for its variations, fluctuations, blurrings, coded signals, and lapses into mimicry or a void. As we do, we must also try to hear, in wonder and in rage, words and phrases that might explain what is now a mystery: why people wish to stigmatize, to dominate, to outlaw, and to erase a particular longing for passion and for love.

NOTES

1. The number of texts about lesbians, by lesbians and nonlesbians, is unclear. There are about twenty-three hundred entries in Gene Damon and Lee Stuart's *The Lesbian in Literature: A Bibliography* (San Francisco, 1967) and about nineteen hundred entries in the revised edition by Damon, Jan Watson, and Robin Jordan (Reno, Nev., 1975). While this second edition has more nonfiction entries and has been updated, the compilers have also cut over a thousand entries from the first edition because they referred to "trash" men had written for male readers (p. 26). The pioneering survey of the figure of the lesbian in Western literature remains Jeannette H. Foster's *Sex Variant Women in Literature: A Historical and Quantitative Survey* (London, 1958), but adding to it now is Lillian Faderman's valuable *Surpassing the Love of Men* (New York, 1981).

2. For a study of the French literary tradition, see Elaine Marks, "Lesbian Intertextuality," in *Homosexualities and French Literature,* ed. George Stambolian and Marks (Ithaca, N.Y., 1979), pp. 353-77. Several of the articles on female

sexuality which were collected in *Women–Sex and Sexuality,* ed. Stimpson and Ethel Spector Person (Chicago, 1980), have insights into modern lesbianism.

3. Roland Barthes, *Writing Degree Zero,* trans. Annette Lavers and Colin Smith (Boston, 1970) pp. 76-77. Barthes has claimed that a recent novel, Renaud Camus' *Tricks* (trans. Richard Howard [New York, 1981]), which I read in manuscript, exemplifies homosexual writing at the degree zero. In his preface, Barthes says that homosexuality is ". . . still at that stage of excitation where it provokes what might be called feats of discourse," but "Camus' narratives are neutral, they do not participate in the game of interpretation." I suggest that *Tricks* does interpret a pattern of male homosexual activity as a fascinating, intense, limited, and only apparently permissible form of experience.

4. Gayle Rubin, introduction to Renee Vivien's *A Woman Appeared to Me,* trans. Jeannette H. Foster (Reno, Nev., 1976), p. v.

5. See Vern L. Bullough and Martha Voght, "Homosexuality and Its Confusion with the 'Secret Sin' in Pre-Freudian America," *Journal of the History of Medicine and Allied Sciences* (Spring 1973): 143-55; rpt. in Bullough, *Sex, Society, and History* (New York, 1976), pp. 112-24. My thanks to Mari Jo Buhle for bringing this article to my attention.

6. See Bullough, *Sexual Variance in Society and History* (New York, 1976), p. 605.

7. Linda Gordon, *Woman's Body, Woman's Right: A Social History of Birth Control in America* (New York, 1976), p. 164.

8. Rictor Norton, "The Homosexual Literary Tradition," *College English* 35, no. 6 (March 1974): 677; see also *College English* 36, no. 3 (November 1974), "The Homosexual Imagination," ed. Norton and Louis Crew. For an enthusiastic survey of lesbian writing, see *Margins* 23 (August 1975), "Focus: Lesbian Feminist Writing and Publishing," ed. Beth Hodges, esp. Julia P. Stanley, "Uninhabited Angels: Metaphors for Love" (pp. 7-10), which makes several points similar to mine here. For critical studies of the literature about male homosexuals, see Roger Austen, *Playing the Game: The Homosexual Novel in America* (Indianapolis, 1977), and Robert K. Martin, *The Homosexual Tradition in American Poetry* (Austin, Tex., 1979).

9. June Arnold, *Sister Gin* (Plainfield, Vt., 1975), p. 82. For an account of a facade that a lesbian community kept up, see Vern and Bonnie Bullough, "Lesbianism in the 1920s and 1930s: A Newfound Study," *Signs* 2, no. 4 (Summer 1977): 895-904.

10. I have written about coding by those who consider themselves sexual anomalies in "The Mind, the Body, and Gertrude Stein," *Critical Inquiry* 3, no. 3 (Spring 1977): 489-506. Detailed work on Stein's codes includes: Richard Bridgman, *Gertrude Stein in Pieces* (New York, 1970); Linda Simon, *Biography of Alice B. Toklas* (Garden City, N.Y., 1977); William Gass, *World within the Word* (New York, 1978), pp. 63-123; and Elizabeth Fifer, "Is Flesh Advisable: The Interior Theater of Gertrude Stein," *Signs* 4, no. 3 (Spring 1979): 472-83.

11. See Nina Auerbach, *Communities of Women: An Idea in Fiction* (Cambridge, Mass., 1978), pp. 186-87., for more comment on the "O."

12. See Blanche Wiesen Cook,"'Women Alone Stir My Imagination': Lesbianism and the Cultural Tradition," *Signs* 4, no. 4 (Summer 1979): 718, and Lillian Faderman, "Love between Women in 1928" (paper delivered at the Berkshire Conference, Vassar College, Poughkeepsie, N.Y., 18 June 1981).

13. Wyndham Lewis, *The Apes of God* (New York, 1932), p. 222.

14. My comments footnote Sandra M. Gilbert's "Costumes of the Mind: Transvestism as Metaphor in Modern Literature," *Critical Inquiry* 7, no. 2 (Winter 1980): 391-417.

15. Havelock Ellis, "Sexual Inversion," *Studies in the Psychology of Sex*, 2 vols. (1901; New York, 1936), 1: 1, 122.

16. Erving Goffman's *Stigma: Notes on the Management of Spoiled Identity* (Englewood Cliffs, N.J., 1963), pp. 8-9, has influenced my analysis here.

17. Radclyffe Hall, *The Well of Loneliness* (1928; New York, 1950), p. 437; all further references to this work will be included in the text.

18. Cook, "'Women Alone,'" p. 719.

19. Though Hall's father deserted her mother around the time of Hall's birth, he left the child a generous inheritance. She was one of several aesthetic lesbians whose incomes permitted them to do more or less as they pleased. Class cannot abolish the stigma of homosexuality, but it can mitigate some of the more painful impressions.

20. As late as 1974, when the American Psychoanalytic Association voted to declassify homosexuality as a mental illness, lesbian writers were still dipping into the reservoir of such romantic tropes as in Kate Millett's *Flying* (New York, 1974): "Taste of salt. Catching it in my mouth. A thirst to suckle it. . . . Very small thing. Pain of tenderness. . . . Fire. The vulva a sun setting behind trees" (p. 536).

21. I am gratefully adapting these terms from Victor Turner's "Passages, Margins, and Poverty," *Dramas, Fields, and Metaphors: Symbolic Action in Human Society* (Ithaca, N.Y., 1974), p. 233.

22. Alfred C. Kinsey et al., *Sexual Behavior in the Human Female* (1953; New York, 1965) p. 477. I am sure that this secondary consciousness will appear in autobiographical texts that scholars have previously ignored or been ignorant of. See, e.g., Elsa Gidlow, "Memoirs," *Feminist Studies* 6, no. 1 (Spring 1980)): 103-27.

23. See Rubin, introduction to Vivien's *A Woman Appeared to Me*, and George Wickes, *The Amazon of Letters: The Life and Loves of Natalie Barney* (New York, 1976).

24. A more ironic and subtle English equivalent is Elizabeth Bowen's *The Hotel* (New York, 1928). Patricia Highsmith's ("Claire Morgan") *The Price of Salt* (New York, 1952), like *Labyrinth*, is about the family and the lesbian's need to leave it even if she is a mother.

25. Bertha Harris (personal interview, New York, 3 August 1977); unless otherwise indicated, all further quotations from Harris are from this interview. See also Lois Gould, "Creating a Women's World," *New York Times Magazine*, 2 January 1977, pp. 34, 36-38.

26. I am indebted for this concept to Paul Robinson's *The Modernization of Sex* (New York, 1976). I have written in more detail about the relationship of the

women's movement to American culture in "Women and American Culture," *Dissent* 27, no. 3 (Summer 1980): 299-307.

27. Ann Allen Shockley has suggested that the taboo on such a lesbian voice has been stronger in the black community than in the white, but even there the gags have loosened; see Shockley, "The Black Lesbian in American Literature: An Overview," in *Conditions Five, The Black Women's Issue,* ed. Lorraine Bethel and Barbara Smith (1979): 133-42. The entire issue is courageous and important. See also J. R. Roberts, *Black Lesbians: An Annotated Bibliography* (Tallahassee, 1981), with a foreword by Smith.

28. Elana Nachman, *Riverfinger Woman* (Plainfield, Vt., 1974), p. 13.

29. Jill Johnston, *Lesbian Nation: The Feminist Solution* (New York, 1973), p. 97.

30. For example, in Linda Crawford's *A Class by Herself* (New York, 1976), pills and booze compel a far greater renunciatory attention than does the stigma of lesbianism.

31. Alma Routsong ("Isabel Miller"), interview in Jonathan Katz, *Gay American History: Lesbians and Gay Men in the U.S.A.* (New York, 1976), p. 442. The career of one professional novelist replicates the historical shift from a stress on the stigmatized text to its rejection. As "Ann Aldrich," Marijane Meaker wrote widely read novels about the romances and difficulties of the lesbian subculture. Then under her own name she published *Shockproof Sydney Skate* (New York, 1972). Profitable, well received, it is about a triangle consisting of a woman, the younger woman with whom she has an affair, and her son, who is in love with the younger woman as well. The lesbian circles are little more absurd than any other subject of a comedy of manners.

32. Nachman, *Riverfinger Woman,* p. 13.

33. For a scrupulous exploration of lesbianism and women's worlds in the poetry of the 1960s and 1970s, see Mary Carruthers, "Imaging Women: Notes Towards a Feminist Poetic," *Massachusetts Review* 20, no. 2 (Summer 1979): 281-407.

34. See, e.g., Joan Winthrop, *Underwater* (New York, 1974), p. 256. Winthrop has her central character indulge in a good deal of masculine role playing, which occurs with a certain *esprit* but is only one aspect of personality, not a controlling force as it is in *The Well of Loneliness.* That the role playing takes place after a radical mastectomy is a point Winthrop does not explore. She does, however, say that her heroine's fantasies of being male were the product of years of her own "repression" (personal interview, Sag Harbor, N.Y., 28 July 1976).

35. A notable example is Barnes' *Ladies Almanack: Written and Illustrated by a Lady of Fashion* (1928; New York, 1972) A dazzling analysis of this work is Susan Sniader Lanser's "Speaking in Tongues: *Ladies Almanack* and the Language of Celebration," *Frontiers* 4, no. 3 (Fall 1979): 39-46. The issue devotes itself to lesbian history and culture.

36. Harris, "The More Profound Nationality of Their Lesbianism: Lesbian Society in Paris in the 1920s," in *Amazon Expedition: A Lesbian Feminist Anthology,* ed. Harris et al. (Washington, N.J., 1973), p. 88; see also "What We Mean to Say: Notes Toward defining the Nature of Lesbian Literature," *Heresies* 3 (Fall 1977): 5-8, an issue of exceptional interest.

Lesbian Ethics and Female Agency

Sarah Lucia Hoagland

INTRODUCTION

It is possible for us to engage in moral revolution and change the value we affirm by the choices we make. It is possible for lesbians to spin a revolution, for us to weave a transformation of consciousness.[1]

My focus is lesbian for several reasons. A central element of lesbian oppression has been and remains our erasure by the dominant society. If lesbians were truly perceptible, then the idea that women can survive without men might work its way into social reality. This suggests that lesbian existence is connected logically or formally in certain ways with female agency: the conceptual possibility of female agency not defined in terms of an other.

Besides a logical possibility, I find a more concrete possibility. By affirming our lesbianism, lesbians have questioned social knowledge at some level. In spite of our varied assimilation (including absorption of dominant, oppressive values), through lesbian existence comes a certain ability to resist and refocus, an ability which is crucial to the sort of moral change I think can occur. And because of this my focus is lesbian.

In naming my work 'lesbian' I invoke a lesbian context, and for this reason I choose not to define the term. To define 'lesbian' is to succumb to

Excerpted from *Lesbian Ethics,* Sarah Lucia Hoagland, Institute of Lesbian Studies, P.O. Box 25568, Chicago, IL 60625, and published in *Lesbian Philosophies and Cultures,* ed. Jeffner Allen, SUNY Press, 1990. © 1990 Sarah Lucia Hoagland. Reprinted by permission of the author.

[Haworth co-indexing entry note]: "Lesbian Ethics and Female Agency." Hoagland, Sarah Lucia. Co-published simultaneously in *Journal of Lesbian Studies* (The Haworth Press, Inc.) Vol. 1, No. 2, 1997, pp. 195-208; and: *Classics in Lesbian Studies* (ed: Esther D. Rothblum) The Haworth Press, Inc., 1997, pp. 195-208; and: *Classics in Lesbian Studies* (ed: Esther D. Rothblum) Harrington Park Press, an imprint of The Haworth Press, Inc., 1997, pp. 195-208.

a context of heterosexualism, to invoke a context in which lesbian is not the norm.

By 'heterosexualism,' I do not simply mean the matter of men having procreative sex with women. Heterosexualism is men dominating and de-skilling women in any of a number of forms, from outright attack to paternalistic care, and women devaluing (of necessity) female connection and engagement. Heterosexualism is a way of living (which actual practitioners exhibit to a greater or lesser degree) that normalizes the dominance of one person in a relationship and the subordination of another. As a result it undermines female agency.

I focus on 'lesbian' because I am interested in exploring lesbianism as a challenge to heterosexualism, as a challenge to the matter of men (or the masculine) dominating women (or the feminine), whether that be as protectors or predators, whether that domination be benevolent or malevolent. And I am interested in exploring ways to work the dominance and subordination out of lesbian choices.

I think of lesbian community as a ground of lesbian being, a ground of possibility. Once we thought it enough to just come out as a lesbian, now we know better; we know that at most it creates the possibility of a certain kind of female agency. And that involves the area of ethics.

My overall thesis is that the foundation of traditional anglo-european ethics (and I use "foundation" in the Wittgensteinian sense of an axis held in place by what surrounds it) is dominance and subordination, that its function is social control, and that as a result it serves to interrupt rather than promote lesbian connection and interaction. My focus is not a new standard of behavior, but rather concerns what it means to be a moral agent under oppression. In what follows I discuss the appeal to the feminine and the concept of self-sacrifice as a feminine virtue because I want to challenge these concepts and realize a different concept of female agency within a lesbian context.

THE FEMININE PRINCIPLE

We appeal to altruism, to self-sacrifice, and in general, to feminine virtuousness in a desperate attempt to find grace and goodness within a system marked by greed and fear. However, while these virtues may herald for us the possibility of ethics—the possibility of some goodness in an otherwise nasty world—nevertheless, as Mary Daly has pointed out, they are the virtues of subservience.[2]

Under modern phallocratic ethics, virtue is obedience and subservience,[3] and the virtuous are those who remain subordinate (accessible). The function of phallocratic ethics–the master/slave virtues–has been to insulate those on top and facilitate their access to the resources of those under them.

Despite this, and because of the effects of men's behavior, we can be tempted to regard the feminine as more valuable than the masculine. Many suffragists defended votes for women by appealing to women's "moral superiority."

Currently, some women are developing an ethics based on the feminine, noting values that pass between women and developing theories about these values, including an ethics of dependence. Without going this far, Carol Gilligan has argued that, in ethical matters, women tend to focus on interpersonal relations while men's ethical considerations involve principles.[4] In the process, she has attempted a vindication of what she perceives as women's morality.

Claudia Card has written a significant critique. Among other things, she argues that Carol Gilligan does not take into account women's oppression and, consequently, the damage to women of that oppression. And, she argues, the fact that women have developed necessary survival skills under oppression does not mean these skills contribute ultimately to women's good.

For example, while Carol Gilligan revalues women's concern for approval as actually a concern for maintaining relationships, Claudia Card reminds us that the approval women seek is usually male approval, which is granted for "obedience to conventions requiring affiliation with men, respect for their views, empathy for them, etc." Or again, while Carol Gilligan revalues the so-called weak ego boundaries of women as a capacity for affiliation, Claudia Card reminds us that only certain affiliations are pursued. Lesbian relations, for example, are more often than not a source of terror for women.[5]

In addition, it may be that women have a greater capacity for empathy. However, women tend to direct that empathy to men of their own race and class, not to women of other races and classes, or even women of their own race and class. (Early radical feminists called this male-identification.)

Further, Claudia Card points out that intimacy has not cured the violence in women's lives; instead, it "has given the violent greater access to their victims." She goes on: "Without validation of success in separating, we may learn to see our only decent option as trying to improve the quality of bad relationships." She adds:

> More likely to be mistaken for a caring virtue is a misplaced grati-
> tude women have felt toward men for taking less than full advantage
> of their power to abuse or for singling them out for the privilege of
> service in return for"protection."[6]

Claudia Card argues that misplaced gratitude is a form of moral damage
women have suffered; and she suggests there are others such as women's
skills at lying, being cunning, deceit, and manipulation.[7]

Actually, I go a step further and argue that, while men have designed
'the feminine' for their own purposes, women have refined these virtues in
defense and resistance, developing them as a means of obtaining some
control (individual and limited) in situations which *presume* female self-
sacrifice. Women have developed the "giving" expected of them into
survival skills, strategies for gaining some control in situations where their
energy and attention are focused on others.

That is, the power of control can be exercised from the subordinate
position, and under heterosexualism women have refined and developed
the feminine virtues for just that purpose. Under heterosexualism, female
agency involves manipulation and cunning—for example, a woman getting
what she needs for herself and her children by manipulating a man in such
a way that he thinks it was all his idea. And this power is the essence of
female agency under heterosexualism.

I will add here that manipulation, cunning, and deceit are not peculiar to
women. Men are also extremely manipulative and deceitful, and can exhibit considerable cunning, for example, in keeping their dominance over
their peers or subordinates from appearing overt, or in enlisting women to
support them. The difference, finally, between men and women under
heterosexualism may lie in who maintains dominance—though not, in every instance, in who maintains control.

Dominance is maintained by violence or the threat of violence—which,
in the long run, means by destruction or the threat of destruction.[8] If
nothing else works, men will disrupt or destroy what is going on. Thus, to
be different from men, women stress nonviolence. Under heterosexualism,
manipulation and control are not challenged; what is challenged is only the
threat of disruption or destruction. Women want men to "play fair" in the
game of manipulation and control by not resorting to the oneupmanship of
destruction.

While many claim that there is a feminine principle which must exert
itself to counterbalance masculinism pervading world cultures, what they
seem to ignore is that the feminine has its origin in masculinist ideology

and does not represent a break from it.* Further, the counterbalancing works both ways. Because of the non-discriminatory nature of feminine receptivity, that is, a lack of evaluating or judging what the feminine responds to, the feminine requires the masculine to protect it from foreign invasion.

Within lesbian community, many lesbians embrace a feminine principle and suggest that self-sacrifice and a romantic ideal of mothering and all-embracing nurturing, are desirable ethical norms in our relationships. I want to challenge this.

'SELFISHNESS', 'SELF-SACRIFICE', AND CHOICE

Consider, first, the use of the label 'selfish'. Those who are judged to be selfish are often those who do not respond to demands from others: the question of selfishness is a question of whether a person thinks only of herself. This consideration often develops into a complaint that the person deemed selfish does not act in ways that contribute to a social structure such as the nation, the family, the synagogue or church, the corporation, the sewing circle, or the collective. Significantly, when a person goes along with the group, even if she is only thinking of herself—being "selfish"—she may well be considered ethical for doing the "right" thing. Further, someone who is perceived as selflessly opposing the group nevertheless often is judged immoral and unethical. Thus someone can be "selfish" and yet "good"—as well as "unselfish" and yet "bad."

---

*This dualism is related to the manichean good/evil dualism and the taoist yin/yang dualism. The manichean approach holds the two opposites in constant conflict, each attempting to dominate and vanquish the other. The taoist approach embraces the conflict but strives for harmony and balance of the two opposites. And while the taoist ideal involves harmony and balance, the nature of the opposites is significant: yin/yang, female/male, dark/light, black/white, cold/heat, weakness/strength. The one is the opposite of the other because it is the absence of it. Thus, strength is the absence of weakness as weakness is the absence of strength. Further, one of the pair is the absence of the other because it is a void. While there are two opposites, in the long run, there is only one essence. The dualism is actually a monism.[9]

In discussing the new spiritualism, Susan Leigh Star argues that the new mystics have managed to mask male identity beneath the guise of androgyny. Further, she points out, "Amidst the escalation, it is vital for us to understand that the new mysticism has to do with the control of women: that it may be seen as a sexual as well as a spiritual phenomenon; that it represents a subtler form of oppression, not a form of liberation."[10]

Apparently, the relevant factor in judging a person to be selfish is, not whether she considers herself first, but whether or not she goes along with the group (or conforms to a higher order) in one of a number of prescribed ways. It seems that selfishness is not of prime concern; rather, the label is used as an excuse to manipulate our participation toward someone else's end.

Secondly, masculinist ideology suggests that true female nature affirms itself through self-sacrifice. Mary Daly defines 'self-sacrifice' as the handing over of our identity and energy to individuals or institutions.[11] This ethical value encourages a woman to give up pursuit of her needs and interests in order to dedicate her efforts to pursuing others' needs and interests, usually those of her husband and children.

Self-sacrifice appears to be a sacrifice of self-interest. Yet women face limited options: men limit women's options through conceptual, physical, and economic coercion. As a result, when a woman engages in self-denial, acquiesces to male authority, and apparently sacrifices her own interests to those of a man in conformity with the dictates of the feminine stereotype, she may actually be acting from self-interest, doing what she deems necessary to her own survival.[12]

One consequence is that, except perhaps in extreme cases of female sexual slavery, when a women is in a situation in which she is expected to shift her identity to that of a man or a child, the stage is set for her to work to control the arena wherein her identity is located. She has not sacrificed her self: by altruistically adopting another's interests, she has transferred that self, or rather it has been arrogated by the man.[13] And while she may have given up pursuit of her own unique interests and needs in favor of those of her husband (and to a lesser extent those of her children), she will pursue their interests and needs as her own.

This, in turn, gives rise to a double bind of heterosexualism: While she is expected to attend to everyone else's projects, she has no final say in how they are realized. She thus becomes the nagging wife or the fairy-tail stepmother. For example, mothers may "live vicariously" through their children and some wives may be "domineering." And those mothers who pursue their children's needs and interests too enthusiastically are criticized for not being passive enough.

Thirdly, the concepts of 'self-sacrifice', 'altruism', 'selfishness', and 'self-interest' may appear to be factual descriptions, but the implications we can draw from the sentences containing these words depend significantly on how we use them. Someone may "self-sacrifice" because it makes her feel good and so she is actually acting from "self-interest." "Self-sacrifice" may even be "selfish" if someone refuses to take her own risks or becomes a burden if she doesn't take care of herself as a result. We can play around with these concepts and come up with all sorts of interesting results; and through all this, acting in consideration of our own needs and limits does not exist as a moral consideration.

Fourthly, the selfish/selfless (or egoism/altruism) dichotomy does not accurately categorize our interactions. Often we do not consider our interests and the interests of others as being in conflict.[14] Concern for ourselves does not imply disregarding the needs of others.[15] In addition, doing good for others need not involve disregarding ourselves.

Now, fifthly, in challenging the concept of 'self-sacrifice', I do not mean to suggest that the sort of "selfish" behavior which self-sacrifice is supposed to counter does not exist among lesbians. For example, a lesbian may consistently act as if her feelings are the only ones, that she is warranted in interrupting anything else going on to demand attention (the strategies for this are many and varied). However, while the problem is real, the solution does not lie in advocating self-sacrifice. When a lesbian is acting this way, often it is because she hasn't a firm sense of herself in relation to others and is threatened; advocating self-sacrifice will only compound the problem.

Egocentrism is the perception that the world revolves around oneself. Now, it is important to have a healthy sense of oneself, centered and in relation to others. But egocentrism is our judgment that those around us have no other relationships, needs, commitments, or identity than that which they have with us. Egocentrism is perceiving and judging others only in relation to ourselves. Hence it is a confusion of our needs, reactions, and choices with those of others. Egocentrism is a form of "selfishness," for it entails a lack of consideration for others—it involves a lack of awareness that others are different and separate from us, and have needs distinct from our own.

In the community we tend to promote self-sacrifice as a virtue and a proper antidote for behavior resulting from egocentrism. However, self-sacrifice cannot solve the problem because egocentrism involves a confusion of needs similar in form to the confusion that occurs with self-sacrifice: my perception of my needs and concerns becomes so entwined with my perception of others that anything relating to the other must relate to me and vice versa.

The difference is that in the case of self-sacrifice we cease to have a distinct sense of ourselves. In the case of egocentrism we cease to have a distinct sense of the other. Thus, advocating self-sacrifice as a corrective measure to selfishness really feeds an underlying problem of ego boundary: the solution actually nurtures the problem.

And this brings me to my main point. We tend to regard choosing to do something as a sacrifice. I want to suggest, instead, that we regard choosing to do something as a creation. From heterosexualism we tend to believe that any time we help another, we are sacrificing something. Thus, we might regard helping a friend fix a carburetor, spending an evening listening to her when she's upset rather than going to a party, or helping her move, as a matter of self-sacrifice. But these acts do not necessarily involve self-sacrifice. Rather, they involve a choice between two or more things to do, and we will have reasons for any choice we make. Often we have choices to make. But that we have to make choices is not a matter of sacrifice.

There is another way of approaching this: we can regard our choosing to interact as part of how we engage in this living. Such choices are a matter of focus, not sacrifice. That I attend certain things and not others, that I focus here and not there, is part of how I create value. Far from sacrificing myself, or part of myself, I am creating; I am weaving lesbian value.

As I engage in lesbian living, I make choices—to start this relationship, to work on this project, to withdraw now, to dream now. I make daily choices; and at one time I may choose to help another, at another time not. But in choosing to help another, I am not thereby sacrificing myself. Instead, this is part of what I involve myself in. When we regard interacting with others as a sacrifice and not as an engagement, it is time to reassess the relationship.

Nor, when we make a choice to engage here rather than there, do we need to regard ourselves as sacrificing or compromising parts of our selves. When we interact, we pursue certain interests. We may have other interests, and we can choose which we want to develop, involving ourselves elsewhere for some. In any given engagement, what is possible exists only as a result of how those involved connect—as a result of what each brings to the engagement and of how it all works out. So when we decide to interact, we do not need to regard ourselves as compromising or losing anything, but rather as embarking on an adventure.

For example, a lesbian develops a friendship with another lesbian. They may have a common interest in the martial arts and work out together. In the process, they create possibilities that were not there, maybe eventually deciding over time to open a lesbian martial arts school. They may develop strategies specific to women and lesbians. And in the process they have created a connection between them, one that changes over the years. During this time, they are not opening a bookstore, writing a book, building a house—actually, they may take on another project, but there will be things they do not do. And they may create other possibilities with other lesbians, their lovers, for example. My point is that in making their choices, they have not sacrificed themselves or other projects. They have created something that did not exist.

There is an idea floating about to the effect that if we cannot do everything, if we have to choose some and let other things go, then we are sacrificing something. Given traditional anglo-european philosophy and u.s. imperialist ideology, u.s. lesbians, in particular, tend to think the whole world exists for us, that everything is potentially ours (or should be), so that when we have to choose between two or more options, we feel we are sacrificing something or that we have lost something. But everything is not ours; everything is not even potentially ours. In fact, nothing out there that exists is ours. Thus in acting, engaging, making choices–in choosing one thing rather than another–we are not losing anything. In acting, engaging, making choices, we are creating something. We create a relationship, we create value; as we focus on lesbian community and bring our backgrounds, interests, abilities, and desires to it, we create lesbian meaning.

What exists here as lesbian community is not some predetermined phenomenon which we opted for, but rather a result of what we've created. And the same is true of all our relationships. Thus, the choice to engage here rather than there is not a sacrifice of what's "out there"; to engage is to create something which did not exist before. I want to suggest that revaluing choice is central to Lesbian Ethics.

Now, if we decide to regard choice as a creation, not a sacrifice, situations requiring difficult decisions will still arise between us. However, we can regard our ability to make choices as a source of power, an enabling power, rather than a source of sacrifice or compromise. Thus by revaluing choice we begin to revalue female agency: female agency begins to be, not essentially a matter of sacrifice and manipulation, but rather a process of engagement and creation.

MOTHERING AND AMAZONING

Understanding choice as creation, not sacrifice, helps us better understand choices we make typically considered "altruistic." We often are drawn to helping others. That is one reason so many are drawn to healing, to teaching, to volunteering to work at shelters, to practicing therapy, to working at community centers or in political campaigns, to going to nicaragua–to all kinds of political work. In doing such work, we feel we are creating something, that we are participating in something; we engage and we make a difference.

However, there remains the danger that we treat choice and engagement as "handing our identity over to individuals or institutions," or even as "acting in, as though in, my own behalf, but in behalf of the other." In heteropatriarchy, engagement and creation for women amount to mothering. Mothering, perhaps, most clearly embodies the feminine virtues, is itself a feminine virtue. And appealing once again to the 'feminine', we tend to romanticize 'mothering' as women's function and regard it as unconditional loving, as a matter of selflessly protecting and nurturing all life.

In the first place, mothering is women's *function* only given the values of heterosexualism. What appears to be a factual statement about women's function is actually a disguised value statement in that men have picked one of the many things women do and decided to call *that* women's function.

If I were to pick one thing and claim it is women's function these days, I would suggest it is amazoning. Some women do it, and many women are capable of it. And, in my opinion, it is far more necessary than mothering. While some might focus on mothering, the vast majority might answer the call to amazon. Further, they would accomplish through amazoning what they keep trying to accomplish through mothering–appropriate atmosphere for children, self-esteem for girls, caring, room to grow and flourish.

The idea that mothering is women's function appears in women's spirituality, which is rushing to claim the 'feminine'. Women's spirituality embraces mothering as nurturing and as an ideal for all women.[16] Mothering, for many, is the paradigm of women's creativity and power, whether mothering takes the form of nurturing children (boys or girls or men) or saving the world and being the buttress of civilization.[17] The idea that all women are or should be mothers in one way or another is not only not challenged, it is pursued.

Mothering is one way of embracing and developing one ability to make a difference in this living; it is creating a quality of life through choice. As such, it does not always involve protecting living things, nor is the energy involved only nurturing energy. More significantly, we must challenge the concept of mothering as it is institutionalized in heteropatriarchy.[18]

As Jeffner Allen notes, mothering reproduces patriarchy and serves men.[19] And as Monique Wittig and Sande Zeig note, mothers are separate and distinct from the amazons:

> Then came a time when some daughters and some mothers did not like wandering anymore in the terrestrial garden. They began to stay in the cities and most often they watched their abdomens grow. . . .
> Things went so far in this direction that they refused to have any other interests.[20]

Thus some lesbians who have given up on the movement have turned to mothering as an alternative, presumably to work on the next generation. Further, as Baba Copper suggests, "heteromothering cannot break away from the heterosexualism of female socialization into subjugation." She argues that only "lesbian group-mothering can begin to rear daughters who will be capable of female bonding."[21] Perhaps then those who are called mothers will again ride with the amazons.

Baba Copper suggests that lesbians can develop a cosmology which can explain to a female child how she can learn to differentiate from and identify with others without dominance and subordination. She adds, "we will have to do all this without motherly domination of those same daughters in their infantile dependence, and without self-sacrifice on the part of the lesbian mothers and shareholders."[22] It may be that we come to deconstruct 'mother' as we do 'woman' and 'feminine'. In this respect, amazoning is more appropriate for girls and others to experience than mothering.

Secondly the ideal of 'mothering' appeals to 'unconditional love'. So we must ask whether we want an ideal of unconditional opening or giving. Perhaps the paradigm of unconditional loving lies in the stereotype of the mammy. Bell Hooks writes:

> Her greatest virtue was of course her love for white folk whom she willingly and passively served. The mammy image was portrayed with affection by whites because it epitomized the ultimate sexist-racist vision of ideal black womanhood—complete submission to the will of whites. In a sense whites created in the mammy figure a black woman who embodied solely those characteristics they as colonizers wished to exploit. They saw her as the embodiment of woman as passive nurturer, a mother figure who gave without expectation of return, who not only acknowledged her inferiority to whites but who loved them. The mammy as portrayed by whites poses no threat to the existing white patriarchal social order for she totally submits to the white racist regime. Contemporary television shows continue to present black mammy figures as prototypes of acceptable black womanhood.[23]

As Baba Copper argues, the unidirectional ideal of mothering undermines reciprocal interaction between mothers and daughters and so encourages incompetency and ageism among us.[24] In discussing Barbara Macdonald's thesis that children and husbands combine in exploiting mothers, helping to create ageist responses to older women,[25] Baba Copper describes her own experience:

> The children learned an assumption of privilege from their father, and he in turn became one of he children—legitimately passive, irresponsible. . . . [M]y older daughters never witnessed an exchange of nurturance. In their view of how the world worked, mothers gave, and men/daughters received. Ours was such an isolated nuclear family that they literally never had any opportunity to witness me being nourished, sustained, taken care of, or emotionally supported. . . . My own daughters, now in their thirties, are dutiful wives but still do not know how to extend nurturance to me, or to negotiate when we have a difference of interest. . . . As the children grow up, they continue to relate to older women with the clear expectations of service. By then they have laid claim to a place of privilege in the power hierarchy.[26]

In other words, the ideal of 'unconditional loving' as embodied by the stereotype of the mammy is not a distortion of unconditional loving but rather an accurate realization of it. To pursue the ideal of mothering as unconditional loving or total nurturing, to pursue this sense of female agency, is to pursue oppression. The masculine and the feminine are not significantly different in what they engender. Again, amazoning at this time is more appropriate and will provide a better atmosphere in which children can develop.

Thirdly, mothering as unconditional love is self-sacrifice. And in general I want to suggest that when we equate self-sacrifice with virtue—something we must exhibit to be considered ethical—and we act accordingly, control begins to enter our interactions as a logical and acceptable consequence. For if we do not perceive ourselves as both separate and related, we will be off-center and forced to control or try to control the arena and those in it in order to retain any sense of agency, of ability to act.

If my identity rests with another and her actions, then I am going to have to try to affect her choices and actions because, at the very least, they reflect back on me. For example, I may choose to help someone who is ill. Now, if I regard my choice as self-sacrifice, then who I am will be caught up in whether, how, and how soon she gets well. As a result I may well go beyond helping, to attempting to control her choices in certain key ways. And in exercising such control, I may not be allowing her time to heal in her own way, on her own terms, by her own means.

My goal in exploring the feminine virtues lies in uncovering the kind of interacting we enable—the sense of female agency we promote—when we believe that self-sacrifice, altruism, and unconditional loving are part of ethical behavior. The feminine virtues, virtues which accrue to the less powerful, are developed as strategies for manipulating and gaining control in a relationship of dominance and subordination. When self-sacrifice and altruism–rather than self-understanding–are regarded as prerequisites for ethical behavior, control–rather than integrity–permeates our interactions.

CONCLUSION

I am not simply saying that at times we don't behave as well as we might. I am saying, instead, that the *structure* of the feminine virtues will thwart even our best efforts because these virtues don't function to promote a female agency which stems from self-understanding and which is both related and separate. And far from facilitating our ethical interaction, the feminine virtues actually interrupt attempts among lesbians to connect and interact ethically by promoting control and distance and by erecting barriers. If we are to achieve a moral revolution, rather than possible moral reform or perhaps remain stuck in the status quo, it is important to understand the feminine as born of the masculine.

Finally, if we regard choice as creation, not sacrifice, we can regard our ability to make choices as a source of enabling power, rather than as a source of sacrifice or compromise. As a result, we can revalue female agency, developing it independently of the manipulation and control of the position of subordination of heterosexualism. Female agency becomes, not essentially a matter of sacrifice, but rather a process of engagement and creation.

NOTES

1. This paper is excerpted from a chapter of my book, *Lesbian Ethics: Toward New Value,* published by the Institute of Lesbian Studies, P.O. Box 25568, Chicago, IL 60625. A note on style: in the text I capitalize the phrase 'Lesbian Ethics', the word "i", names of books and journals, names of people, and first words of sentences only. I follow Marilyn Frye in using single quotation marks when referring to words or concepts. And I use double quotation marks around words or phrases I wish to stress as remarkable in one way or another, which remarkableness should be clear from the context.

2. Note *Beyond God the Father: Toward a Philosophy of Women's Liberation* (Boston: Beacon Press, 1973) and *Gyn/Ecology: The Metaethics of Radical Feminism* (Boston: Beacon Press, 1978).

3. Claudia Card, conversation.

4. Note, for example, Carol Gilligan, *In a Different Voice: Psychological Theory and Women's Development* (Cambridge, Mass.: Harvard University Press, 1982).

5. Claudia Card, *Virtues and Moral Luck,* Series 1, Institute for Legal Studies, Working Papers, University of Wisconsin-Madison, Law School, November 1985, pp. 14-15.

6. Claudia Card, *Virtues and Moral Luck,* pp. 16, 17.

7. Ibid., p. 23.

8. Conversations, Deidre D. McCalla, Anne Throop Leighton.

9. Conversation, Marilyn Frye.

10. [Susan] Leigh Star, "The Politics of Wholeness: Feminism and the New Spirituality," *Sinister Wisdom* 3 (Spring 1977): 39.

11. Mary Daly, *Gyn/Ecology,* pp. 374-75.

12. Marilyn Frye, "In and Out of Harm's Way: Arrogance and Love," in *The Politics of Reality: Essays in Feminist Theory* (Trumansburg, N.Y.: The Crossing Press, 1983, now in Freedom, Calif.), p. 73.

13. Ibid. pp. 66-72.

14. For further discussion, note Judith Tourmey, "Exploitation, Oppression, and Self-Sacrifice," in *Women and Philosophy,* ed. Carol C. Gould and Marx W. Wartofsky (New York: G.P. Putnam's Sons, 1976), pp. 206-21; and Larry Blum, Marcia Homiak, Judy Housman, and Naomi Schemen, "Altruism and Women's Oppression," in *Women and Philosophy,* pp. 222-47.

15. For further discussion, note James Rachels, "Morality and Self-Interest," in *Philosophical Issues: A Contemporary Introduction,* ed. James Rachels and Frank A. Tillman (New York: Harper & Row, 1972), pp. 120-1.

16. Note, for example, Z. Budapest, *The Feminist Book of Lights and Shadows*; and Billie Potts and River Lightwomoon, *Amazon Tarot* and *New Amazon Tarot* (Bearsville, N.Y.: Hecuba's Daughters, n.d.); for information, write Billie Potts, 18 Elm Street, Albany, NY 12202. Jean and Ruth Mountaingrove edited *Womanspirit* from 1974 to 1984.

17. Marilyn Frye, "A Note on Anger," in *The Politics of Reality,* p. 92.

18. Note for example, Adrienne Rich, *Of Woman Born: Motherhood as Experience and Institution* (New York: W.W. Norton & Co., Inc., 1976).

19. Jeffner Allen, "Motherhood: The Annihilation of Women," in *Mothering: Essays in Feminist Theory,* ed. Joyce Trebilcot (New Jersey: Rowman & Allanheld: 1984), pp. 315-330; republished in *Lesbian Philosophy: Explorations,* Jeffner Allen (Palo Alto, Calif.: Institute of Lesbian Studies, 1986), pp. 61-86.

20. Monique Wittig and Sande Zeig, *Lesbian Peoples: Material for a Dictionary* (New York: Avon, 1979), pp. 108-9.

21. Baba Copper, correspondence.

22. Ibid.

23. Bell Hooks, *Ain't I a Woman: Black Women and Feminism* (Boston: South End Press, 1981), pp. 84-85.

24. Baba Copper, "The View from Over the Hill: Notes on Ageism Between Lesbians," *Trivia: A Journal of Ideas* 7 (Summer 1985): 57, revised and reprinted in *Over the Hill: Reflections on Ageism Between Women* (Freedom, Calif., The Crossing Press, 1988).

25. Barbara Macdonald with Cynthia Rich, *Look Me in the Eye: On Women, Aging and Ageism* (San Francisco: Spinsters Ink, 1983, now Spinsters/Aunt Lute).

26. Baba Copper "View from Over the Hill," p. 57.

PHYSICAL AND SOCIAL SCIENCES

Toward a Laboratory of One's Own: Lesbians in Science

H. Patricia Hynes

In late spring of 1979, I submitted an entry to *Matrices*[1] announcing that four women, lesbians[2] in science, had formed a study group. We were students in geology, environmental engineering, forestry, and general science at the University of Massachusetts, Amherst. Science students are notoriously short on time for everything except labs, research reports, and unsolved problems. A unique, microscopic subset of women, lesbians in science is the only class of feminists I have known who will reject a women's studies course for yet another science course and who will pass up a once-a-year women's event to do problem no. 6, one of thirty assigned that semester. The intense preoccupation with itself which science fosters is double-edged. The workload and demands on time require al-

Reprinted, by permission, from H. Patricia Hynes, "Toward a Laboratory of One's Own: Lesbians in Science," in *Lesbian Studies: Present and Future*, ed., Margaret Cruikshank (New York: The Feminist Press at The City University of New York, 1982), pp. 174-178. © 1982 by The Feminist Press and Margaret Cruikshank.

[Haworth co-indexing entry note]: "Toward a Laboratory of One's Own: Lesbians in Science." Hynes, H. Patricia. Co-published simultaneously in *Journal of Lesbian Studies* (The Haworth Press, Inc.) Vol. 1, No. 2, 1997, pp. 209-215; and: *Classics in Lesbian Studies* (ed: Esther D. Rothblum) The Haworth Press, Inc., 1997, pp. 209-215; and: *Classics in Lesbian Studies* (ed: Esther D. Rothblum) Harrington Park Press, an imprint of The Haworth Press, Inc., 1997, pp. 209-215.

most a fealty of students, and we must jealously guard our time for feminist reading, lectures, and cultural events. On the other hand, science is a context of learning in which discipline and the ability to focus and organize our work is, of necessity, quickly learned.

Eager to bring feminist passion to science, we four immediately set about to plan papers and field trips on those ideas and investigations which had originally sparked our passion for science. Our agenda spanned an exciting spectrum of subjects:

- a voyage via slides through the Yucatan in search of gynocentric myth and solar architecture in Mayan culture, and a discussion of the natural resources of this Mexican province.
- the sources, effects, and chemistry of acid rain in New England.
- a portrait of Ellen Swallow, founder of the science of ecology.
- the basics of rock-climbing, slides of rock formation, caverns, and the results of an extensive field study of Karst geology and cavern development.
- fundamental electronic theory of computers.
- an overview of conventional energy sources in the United States and the potential for alternative energy.
- a geological history of the Connecticut River Valley told from the vantage point of Skinner Park, overlooking the Connecticut River Valley in South Hadley.
- a walk through a forest to demonstrate the principles of woodlot management.

The diversity of ideas was deliberate: to reopen chambers of curiosity and passionate reason which are sealed off by the prohibition of science against venturing outside of one's field. If one moves on or beyond the compartmental boundary, one is suspect of being restless, intellectually immature, undisciplined, generalist, and dilettantish. One is expected to stand still and bore ever deeper, urged on by the omnipresent imperative to specialize or perish.

Ellen Swallow's ultimate failure at the Massachusetts Institute of Technology is paradigmatic of this dilemma. Swallow, the first woman to receive a degree from MIT and to teach there, distinguished herself as a water and industrial chemist, a metallurgist, a mineralogist, an expert in food and nutrition, and an engineer. In the late nineteenth century, she devised and taught the first interdisciplinary curriculum and science methods of ecology, leading students to test air, soil, water, and food. Her science of ecology which integrated the chemistry of soil, air and water, biology, and the scientific study of the human environment, was ultimately rejected at

MIT. One biographer analyzes the failure of her new science accordingly: "It was, in spite of the validity of its parts, seen as an unpedigreed, mixed breed by the specialized science aristocracy."[3] He adds that "Swallow and most of her (ecology) friends were women and too few were scientists."

The idea of a lesbians in science study group came to me in my second year of graduate school. I had seen myself and other women in predominantly male sciences buffeted and demeaned in the scientific milieu:

- buffeted by the cruel rites of passage that characterize initiation into a male society: intense competition, always the threat of failure and expulsion, and willful obscuring of knowledge.
- demeaned by the sexual tension our anomalous presence catalyzed, by the invisibility of our talent and stamina, and by no recourse to women in power.

It was, though, the erosion of intellectual passion that I found to be the most appalling in science. I was and I remain confounded by the contradiction that the more advanced our study of science, the more remote becomes the subject of our intellectual passion: nature. It is absurd that field trips in botany courses for nonscience majors and lectures in "physics for poets" (so-called "pop-science") conjure up the dynamism, the variability, and the intelligence of nature, whereas fluid mechanics and advanced thermodynamics are arduous, mechanistic, and often spiritually dulling exercises in rote problem solving.

What, then, could be more appropriate for lesbians in science than to present to one another those ideas, those intellectual projects which had first fired our mental passion? With that one guide, we developed our agenda of presentations and field trips. Our meetings were thick with ideas and questions; they were always too brief. This unique collaboration created a background of pride and meaning altogether absent in science for woman-identified women.

Very simply I picture intellectual passion as a mind on fire: a fire whose metaphysical energy furiously gathers and creates ideas; a fire whose vital flames light the eyes; a fire whose heat warms the mind and expands the self. Patriarchal science has no passion. It has fractured passion into a chilling logic and pseudo-passion. Cold logic is all too familiar—it permits a nationally known toxicologist to stun his audience with larger-than-life pictures of thalidomide babies, drawing out clinical details of their deformities while bemoaning how difficult it was to do a valid statistical survey on the babies' mothers because the women were so suggestive that they could not be relied upon to know if they had taken thalidomide or not. "Furthermore," he added dryly, "women usually don't know when they get pregnant." Pseudo-passion has many guises. It is the tense excitement stirred up in students by pitting them against one another for grades, recommendations, and limited opportunities. Pseudo-passion is warmed by the prospect of inclusion in the high priesthood of science. It is the rush scientists have when doing research against time deadlines and budget constraints, in intense competition for grants, prizes, and publication. It is the bizarre fraternity and excitement men feel when they collaborate in a high-risk venture or in a climate of potential imminent tragedy. I heard one reserved chemist declare that the frenetic federal survey and cleanup operation of Love Canal in which he participated was "surprisingly exciting," one of the most exciting times in his life. In a commemorative article on Trinity Site at Los Alamos, New Mexico, where the first atomic bomb was exploded, *Time* magazine quoted two men who found the site and the event it conjured up "romantic."[4]

One wonders if the unique erasure of women in science–by erasure I mean both the cover-up of what women have done and the success of the lie that women cannot do science and mathematics–is really the erasure of passion from science. Nonetheless, it has imposed a silence so great that lesbian scientists have yet to imagine a history of lesbians in science. It does not occur to ask of the lone woman honored here and there in science: Was she a feminist? Were her mentors women? Did she dedicate her work to a woman? With whom did she live? It is so remarkable that she was honored in male history at all. All a woman need do is read the life of Ellen Swallow, Rachel Carson, or Rosalind Franklin to see the silencing and erasure of women by male "colleagues" for doing brilliant, passionate, and prodigious work. Their controversies unmask that face of patriarchy in which we read the disdain for, the envy of, and the hatred of women.

My mind still reels from the impact of H.J. Mozans's work, *Woman in Science.*[5] In one sweeping history of invention by women, Mozans unwittingly discloses the take-over of creative cultural work from women by men, the destruction of female power, and the effect of that violence on the character of male science. He cites the universal myths which record the creation by women of agriculture and agricultural implements, of dwellings which warm and cool naturally, of transport and sanitary storage of water, of the mechanical arts, in brief, of all vital systems. "Tradition in all parts of the world," he writes, "is unanimous in ascribing to woman the invention, in essentially their present form, of all the arts most conducive to the preservation and well-being of the human race." With great fervor, he then describes the brilliant work of hundreds of women scientists from classical Greece to the early twentieth century. The effect is like a great chain of lights being turned on, one by one, to illuminate female genius which, with the exception of one luminary, Mariè Curie,[6] has been systematically adumbrated by lies and silence.

None of us can measure or predict, I think, how it changes us to break the silence imposed by patriarchy. Presenting our ideas and projects to other women who welcome our intelligence and who know the woman-hatred in science, as in our study group, is much more than sharing ideas and gaining self-confidence. It is an act of rebellion against our own erasure. It is, too, exhilarating mental work which forges identity and meaning, identity and meaning which will never be given to a woman, no matter what degrees and prizes she achieves, by patriarchal science.

I have written this essay–as our study group proceeded–assuming that women who love science ought to study it. Why would a woman-identified woman study science when scarcely a grain of female genius is tolerated by male science, when the intention to preserve "the well-being of the human race" is only a fragile memory of the origins of science in prehistory, and when the petty passion of patriarchal science for splitting, splicing, and bombarding is so assaultive to nature? The scope of such a discussion goes beyond this short essay. I can only conclude with some open-ended remarks about women studying science.

The root of the word science is *scire,* to know, and *scientia,* knowledge. As I see it, the purpose of studying science for women is to know nature: because nature is fascinating, because we are part of nature and we depend on nature for our life, and because knowledge will guide our wise use of nature. Patriarchal science is no more what nature is about than the psychology of the female in Freud and the philosophy of female being in Jean-Paul Sartre is about women. As men assume that what they think about women is what women are, so they believe that what they theorize about nature is what nature is. I would suggest then that a woman who loves nature, who is intellectually curious and creative, would study science to identify precisely patriarchal science's definitions and construction of science. By studying and working in science, radical women can refuse to concede to men trained and degreed in science, the absolute power over nature that is assigned to and claimed by them. If since a child, a woman has loved the theory and inner logic of numbers, or if she wants to learn about soil, pH, bacteria and organic matter, out of some ill-defined fascination, out of a desire to grow food and flowers, or become soil, like her own body–is in dynamic chemical balance with air, water, plants, animals, and stone–then where is she to go but books, laboratories, and schools where, despite the pathology of science, she can learn some language and ideas which she can use for "the preservation and well-being of the human race" and the planet? There is another reason for studying science. Without implying that nature is female or female is nature, I see extraordinary parallels between woman-centered being and dimensions of nature. The ideas of energy, motion, and power in physics and mechanical engineering, the image of an expanding universe and moving center in astronomy, the theory of charge in chemistry, the golden mean, continuum, and infinite series in mathematics, the cycling of energy, nutrients, and water in hydrology and geology, the vital signs of ecosystems in ecology[7]–all of these intuitions of dynamism in nature have obvious, exciting parallels in feminist theory. They may clarify dimensions of oppression. They may offer new images and, ultimately, new pathways of woman-centered being.

NOTES

1. *Matrices* is a lesbian feminist research newsletter which publishes subscribers' profiles, notes, queries, calls for papers, reviews, statements, etc. For a subscription, write to Julia Penelope (Stanley) c/o Dept. of English, University of Nebraska, Lincoln, NE 68588.

2. I use the word lesbian interchangeably with woman-identified woman, woman-centered woman, and radical woman. All of these phrases have emerged from radical-feminist thinking. They imply a separation from patriarchal thinking and male parasitism. They describe the woman determined to search out the mystery of her own history and its connections with the lives of other women. In that same spirit, the lesbian in science searches out threads of connectedness between her own existence in this world and the subject of her intellectual passion, nature.

3. Robert Clarke, *Ellen Swallow, The Woman Who Founded Ecology* (Chicago: Follett Publishing Co., 1973), pp. 152-53. Judy Gold, a member of Lesbians in Science, has written an extremely comprehensive paper on Swallow's life and work, with a radical-feminist analysis of the reaction of male science to Swallow's precocious work

4. *Time,* November 3, 1980, p. 6, 10. One man "had been looking forward to this thing for a long time . . . The whole atomic thing during my lifetime, and this is kind of romantic." The other man had worked at Los Alamos more than thirty-five years. Speaking of the development and the testing of the atomic bomb, he said, "It's very difficult to convey the special spirit of that time and place. Working toward a common goal, people formed a strong bond and sensed they were part of something romantic–as indeed they were."

5. H.J. Mozans, *Woman in Science* (Cambridge: MIT Press, 1974; London: D. Appleton and Co., 1913).

6. In *Ideology in/of the Sciences,* Monique Couture-Cherki, a French physicist, exposes the method by which even such a memorable woman as Marie Curie is mediated to history as a second sex, in the following incident. Leprince-Ringuet, a distinguished French physicist, when questioned by the French media about Marie Curie, replied: "Between Pierre and Marie Curie, Pierre Curie was a creator

whose very genius established new laws of physics. Marie radiated other qualities: her character, her exceptional tenacity, her precision, and her patience." Leprince-Ringuet characterized Marie Curie as a superb laboratory technician. He cast her as a model of "feminine" research skills and denied her her genius. By polarizing her and Pierre Curie's abilities, he insinuated that she, on her own, was not an exceptional scientist, but that she was, however, a most desirable life partner for an eminent male theoretician.

7. One example of drawing ideas from science for feminist analysis is the subject of a paper I wrote which was published in the *Heresies* issue on Feminism and Ecology, number 13. I have taken four principles of natural ecosystems and shown the parallels between the conditions of women under patriarchy and that of natural ecosystems under the stress of extreme pollution.

National Lesbian Health Care Survey: Implications for Mental Health Care

Judith Bradford
Caitlin Ryan
Esther D. Rothblum

SUMMARY. This article presents demographic, lifestyle, and mental health information about 1,925 lesbians from all 50 states who participated as respondents in the National Lesbian Health Care Survey (1984-1985), the most comprehensive study on U.S. lesbians to date. Over half the sample had had thoughts about suicide at some time, and 18% had attempted suicide. Thirty-seven percent had been physically abused as a child or adult, 32% had been raped or sexually attacked, and 19% had been involved in incestuous relationships while growing up. Almost one third used tobacco on a daily basis, and about 30% drank alcohol more than once a week, 6% daily. About three fourths had received counseling at some time, and half had done so for reasons of sadness and depression. Lesbians in the survey also were socially connected and had a variety of social sup-

Preparation of this article was supported in part by the MS Foundation, the Chicago Resource Center, the Sophia Fund, the Fund for Human Dignity, and the National Institute of Mental Health (data analysis), awarded to Judith Bradford and Caitlin Ryan.

[Haworth co-indexing entry note]: "National Lesbian Health Care Survey: Implications for Mental Health Care." Bradford, Judith, Caitlin Ryan, and Esther D. Rothblum. Co-published simultaneously in *Journal of Lesbian Studies* (The Haworth Press, Inc.) Vol. 1, No. 2, 1997, pp. 217-249; and: *Classics in Lesbian Studies* (ed: Esther D. Rothblum) The Haworth Press, Inc., 1997, pp. 217-249; and: *Classics in Lesbian Studies* (ed: Esther D. Rothblum) Harrington Park Press, an imprint of The Haworth Press, Inc., 1997, pp. 217-249.

ports, mostly within the lesbian community. However, few had come out to all family members and coworkers. Level of openness about lesbianism was associated with less fear of exposure and with more choices about mental health counseling.

Until very recently, homosexuality in itself was considered to be a form of mental illness, and although mental health professionals no longer consider this to be true, research on the mental health of lesbians is limited. Most of the literature on lesbian mental health has been theoretical in nature, and research studies have been small in scale. For example, several authors have written about societal factors that may place lesbians and gay men at risk for suicide (e.g., Saunders & Valente, 1987), particularly lesbian and gay adolescents (Kourany, 1987). Using a sample of 27 men and 142 women with anorexia and bulimia, Herzog, Norman, Gordon, and Pepose (1984) found gay men (but not lesbians) to predominate among those with eating disorders. There has been some research on battering within lesbian relationships (e.g., Lobel, 1986), but virtually none on other forms of violence against women, such as physical abuse, rape, and incest.

One exception to the paucity of research on lesbian mental health has been alcohol abuse. In the 1970s, Fifield (1975) studied alcohol use among people who frequented gay bars. The lesbians and gay men in her survey consumed an average of six drinks per bar visit and went to bars an average of 19 times a month. Furthermore, Fifield found her sample of bar users to be relatively isolated from most other lesbian and gay community events, so that the gay bar took on an important social function. Studies such as this one resulted in several theoretical articles (e.g., Glaus, 1988) that discussed reasons why lesbians were at risk for alcohol abuse. Recently, McKirnan and Peterson (1989a, 1989b) surveyed 748 lesbians and 2,652 gay men, and compared the data on their alcohol and drug use with data from the general population (Clark & Midanik, 1982). The results indicated that a higher percentage of lesbians and gay men used alcohol, marijuana, and cocaine than did the general population. Lesbians and gay men did not have higher rates of heavy use of alcohol than the general population, but they did have more alcohol-related problems. In the general population, alcohol use declines with age, and this was not the case for lesbians and gay men (McKirnan & Peterson, 1989a).

Recognition of the need for normative information about the health and mental health care needs of lesbians served as the primary purpose of the National Lesbian Health Care Survey. Although it was assumed that lesbians must have health and mental health care needs, it was not known whether or not these needs were different from those of heterosexual women. The study was designed to explore the community and social life of lesbians, including their mental health and mental health needs. No previous research has been large enough in scale and comprehensive enough in scope to permit development of a broad definition of lesbian mental health which is not reactive to the concept of lesbians as deviant. As a result, information which could provide a basis for the development of sensitive and effective services to lesbians has not been widely available.

Furthermore, the present study wanted to examine the prevalence of social supports for lesbians. Public attitudes about lesbians are still negative, and lesbians are openly barred from participation in the community institutions (e.g., organized religion) that sustain heterosexuals. Finally, "outness" is a critical concept for understanding lesbians, as it refers to an aspect of daily reality that has no counterpart in the lives of heterosexuals. It is within this dimension of lesbian life that social marginality can best be understood, for although some people see lesbians as another minority group, many more still view lesbians as profoundly different and disgusting. Thus, lesbians risk rejection whenever they disclose their sexual orientation ("come out") to heterosexuals. To live a two-world existence requires a great deal of psychic energy and is thereby inherently stressful. A number of researchers have documented the psychological benefits which accompany being out (e.g., Lewis, 1984). Although being out may offer an opportunity for personal integration, coming out presents lesbians with difficult challenges. Other studies of lesbians have documented the anticipated and actual experiences of discrimination which have happened to many lesbians who have either come out or been found out (e.g., Gartrell, 1981). In addition, lesbians who are members of ethnic minority groups may experience racism to an even greater degree than heterosexism (Mays & Cochran, 1986).

The importance of disclosure of lesbian sexual orientation to health and mental health professionals has been emphasized (Dardick & Grady, 1980), and a linkage has been presumed between being out and access to needed health and mental health information, as well as increased emotional and psychological health (Bradford, 1986). Clearly, understanding the role of outness in the lives of lesbians has important implications for mental health, and so, in this study, we measured outness to correlate it with measures of mental health.

We focused on six mental health components (for the results of physical health and health care measures, see Ryan & Bradford, 1988, 1993): (a) current stressors, (b) depression and anxiety, (c) suicide ideation and attempts, (d) physical and sexual abuse, (e) alcohol and drug abuse, and (f) eating disorders. We examined community and social supports and outness to assess the role of these variables in the lives of lesbians and their impact on mental health. Finally, we assessed use of professional mental health services.

METHOD

Subjects

Four thousand and six hundred surveys were distributed and completed surveys were received from 1,925 lesbians from all 50 U.S. states; this represents a response rate of 42%. Because the survey was titled National Lesbian Health Care Survey, only two participants were exclusively heterosexual (7 on the item about sexual orientation); the majority were lesbian (94.5% circled 1-3 on this item). Table 1 displays demographic data of respondents and also compares demographic characteristics of the sample with the 1980 U.S. census data for women (U.S. Department of Commerce, 1984). Eighty-eight percent of the sample were White, 6% were African American, and 4% were Latina. Very small numbers of Asian Americans and Native Americans were also included. The age range of the sample was 17-80 years; 80% were between the ages of 25 and 44. A high percentage (69%) had graduated from college. Most respondents worked full-time, in professional or managerial positions. Nevertheless, all but 12% earned less than $30,000 per year, and 64% earned less than $20,000. In comparison with 1980 U.S. census data, the lesbian sample was younger, more educated, and employed in more professional and managerial occupations than the general female population. The percentage of White, Asian-American, Latina, and Native-American lesbians was roughly similar to that in the census data, but the lesbian sample had only half the percentage of African Americans, compared with those in the census data.

Sixty percent of the sample were involved in a primary relationship with another woman. Less than 20% were single and uninvolved. Two percent were legally married to men at the time of the survey. Since marriage between lesbians is not legal in any U.S. state, direct comparisons between marital status could not be made. However, the percentage of lesbians in primary relationships was similar to the percentage of married women in the census data.

Sixty-six percent of the sample reported no current religious affiliation, although all but 8% had been raised in connection to a religious community (75% had been raised Catholic or Protestant). Eight percent of the sample was Catholic, 11.6% Protestant, 7.4% Jewish, 2.5% participated in

TABLE 1. Demographic Characteristics of Lesbian Sample Compared with U.S. Census Data for Women

Characteristic	Unweighted percentage of total (N = 1,917)	Weighted percentage of total (N = 1,917)	U.S. Census data on the adult female in 1980[a]
Age			
17-24	8.8	8.9	12.5
25-34	48.0	48.4	16.6
35-44	32.2	32.5	12.0
45-54	7.0	7.1	9.7
55 or older	3.1	3.1	23.4
Education			
Less than high school	2.4	2.5	29.1
High school	9.5	9.5	37.9
Vocational training	2.5	2.5	-
Some college	16.3	16.4	15.3
College	26.0	26.2	-
Advanced studies	11.6	11.6	17.7
Advanced degree	31.2	31.3	-
Type of work			
Professional	39.5	53.3	25.2
Manager/official	14.8	19.9	-
Clerical	6.9	9.3	42.5
Craftsperson	3.8	5.1	2.3
Operative/unskilled worker	2.9	4.1	9.7
Farmer	0.1	0.1	-
Service worker	5.2	7.0	16.8
Private household worker	0.8	1.1	2.1
Worker status			
Employed full time	66.6	-	-
Employed part time	18.5	-	-
Student	21.6	-	-
Unemployed	9.0	-	-
Personal income			
$9,999 or less	27.6	27.9	-
$10,000-$19,999	35.8	36.2	-
$20,000-$29,999	23.5	23.8	-
$30,000-$39,999	7.9	8.0	-
$40,000 or more	4.1	4.2	-
Marital status			
Married	-	-	61.9
Single and never married	-	-	17.6
Divorced	-	-	-
Separated	-	-	8.0
Widowed	-	-	12.5

Note. From *The National Lesbian Health Care Survey: Final Report* (pp. 11-13) by J. Bradford and C. Ryan, 1988, Washington, DC: National Lesbian and Gay Health Foundation. Copyright 1988 by J. Bradford and C. Ryan. Reprinted by permission. Dashes indicate that comparable data were not available.
[a]Data in this column were taken from the *1984 Statistical Abstract of the United States* (104th edition), published by the U.S. Department of Commerce.

TABLE 1 (continued)

Characteristic	Unweighted percentage of total (N = 1,917)	Weighted percentage of total (N = 1,917)	U.S. Census data on the adult female in 1980[a]
Relationship status			
Primary relationship with a woman	59.9	-	-
Single, somewhat involved with a woman	17.5	-	-
Single and uninvolved	19.1	-	-
Living with a male lover	0.4	-	-
Legally married to a man	2.2	-	-
Number of people in household			
1	20.9	22.7	23.2
2	45.7	49.7	31.7
3	13.0	14.0	17.5
4-5	8.7	9.4	22.7
6 or more	3.7	4.0	4.9
Race/ethnicity			
Asian/Pacific Islander	0.8	0.8	1.2
Aleut, Eskimo, or American Indian	0.6	0.6	0.6
Latina	4.2	4.2	6.4
African American (non-Hispanic)	5.6	5.6	11.7
White (non-Hispanic)	88.2	88.5	83.1
Other	0.3	0.3	3.0
Religious affiliation			
None	64.5	66.2	-
Protestant	11.2	11.5	-
Catholic	7.8	8.0	-
Islamic	0.2	0.2	-
Jewish	7.3	7.4	-
Pagan, witch	0.8	0.8	-
Unitarian	1.0	1.0	-
Buddhist	0.5	0.5	-
Gay church	2.4	2.5	-
Christian Science	0.2	0.2	-
Quaker	0.5	0.5	-
Mormon	0.2	0.2	-
Unity	0.3	0.3	-
Mennonite	0.2	0.2	-
Other Christian	0.6	0.6	-

gay churches, and 1% or less participated in other religions (Islamic, pagan/ witch, Unitarian, Buddhist, Christian Science, Quaker, Unity, Mennonite, or other). Only a few participants lived in the same town or city where they had been born, and most lived in metropolitan areas. Overall, there had been a migration from the Northeast, where 31% were born and 25% lived at the time of the study, to the Pacific states, where 10% had been born and 19% lived at the time of the study. The remainder of participants were living in the North Central states (21%), South (28%), and Mountain states (7%). At the time of the survey, nine respondents were in prison, 19 were living in a shelter, and two on an Indian reservation.

Measures

Questions for the survey were formulated from the existing knowledge, experience, and perceptions of health and mental health care workers who had direct contact with lesbians, as well as informed consumers. The survey was constructed from a different conceptual framework than had traditionally been applied to the discussion of lesbianism. Within this framework is a core assumption of normalcy, of difference rather than deviance, of diversity rather than social conformity. The connection between living on the margins of society and the impact of this upon daily life and an adequate sense of psychosocial security warrants exploration, and the survey was designed to examine how lesbians live in relationship to this tension. Because of its broad agenda, incorporating both social and personal information about lesbians, the survey could provide implications for mental health treatment and planning.

Preliminary versions of the survey were pretested in locations throughout the United States. In addition to mailing early versions to contacts in various cities, the second author travelled to several major cities to conduct focus group meetings related to survey design and distribution. One focus was to keep the language free from jargon and understandable to people of diverse educational levels. Efforts were made to use language that would reflect the terminology of lesbians, including subgroups of lesbians in different regions of the country. Strategies were suggested for distributing surveys to women in prisons and shelters, in the military, in rural areas, and to those who were so closeted as to be practically unreachable through organizational contacts. About 100 people participated in constructing the survey, through direct participation or written feedback.

The resulting survey was a 10-page measure consisting of the following categories: (1) demographic information; (2) participation in community activities and social life; (3) outness; (4) current concerns and worries; (5) depression, anxiety, and general mental health; (6) suicide; (7) physical and sexual abuse; (8) anti-gay discrimination; (9) impact of AIDS; (10) substance use; (11) eating disorders; and (12) counseling. For exact wording of items and a copy of the questionnaire, see Bradford and Ryan (1987, 1988), or contact the authors directly.

Procedure

Initially, the survey was targeted for distribution in 10 major cities, but as requests for copies increased, surveys were sent to contacts all over the United States. Copies were distributed during 1984-1985 to lesbian and gay health and mental health organizations and practitioners across the country. A number of professional organizations publicized the study. For example, the National Coalition of Black Gays and Lesbians sponsored a mailing to its entire membership, endorsing the study and recommending that members participate. Some local agencies and government agencies provided staff support for distribution of surveys.

The survey was also distributed by means of personal networks, with specific instructions to reach as diverse a group as possible. Volunteer distributors described the project and handed out questionnaires to lesbians through social and organizational contacts. Special outreach efforts through bookstores, women's organizations, prisons, and gay newspapers were used to reach lesbians who may not participate in lesbian and gay community events. Since it was impossible to devise a strategy for reaching a random sample of a hidden population, survey respondents included lesbians who could be reached and who were willing to participate in the project. Results of the survey, therefore, cannot be generalized to represent all lesbians in the United States.

RESULTS

Current Concerns and Worries

Current concerns. Participants were asked if any of 12 items were currently bothering them. The most common concern was money, identified by over half the sample (57%).[1] Concerns listed by at least one fifth of respondents included job or school worries (31%), problems with lover

---

[1]All results, unless otherwise specified, refer to frequencies and percentages. Thus, statements such as "most" or "the highest percentage" should not be interpreted to mean statistically significant differences.

(27%), too much work responsibility (23%), and problems with family (21%). Only 12% of respondents indicated that they were concerned about people knowing that they were lesbian. However, few were out to all family members or coworkers. Other concerns were job dissatisfaction (18%), worry about illness or death (16%), legal problems (9%), not being able to find a job (7%), problems with children (7%), feeling unsafe (7%), problems with friends (2%), loneliness (2%), basic needs (1%), stress (1%), and worry about the future (1%).

Table 2 displays data for the seven most common concerns separately by age, and race or ethnicity. Money was the most common concern for lesbians in all age groups, except for those aged 55 or older, who were most concerned about problems with their lovers. More African-American lesbians were concerned with money than were White or Latina lesbians. A much smaller percentage of Latina women (1%) were concerned about illness than were African-American (21%) or White (16%) women.

Inability to accomplish ordinary tasks because of worry. In response to the question "In the past year, how often were you so worried or nervous that you could not do necessary things?" more than half the sample reported that during the past year they "often" (18%) or "sometimes" (38%) couldn't get things done because of nervousness or worry. Only 12% of the sample reported that they had "never" been too nervous to accomplish the things they had to do during the past year. Older women reported more frequent worrying. Forty-five percent of those aged 55 or older reported frequent worrying, compared with 13% of those aged 17-24 and 23% of those aged 45-55.

TABLE 2. Percentages of Participation with Current Mental Health Concerns

Demographic	Money	Family	Job	Illness	Responsibility	Lover
Age (years)						
17-24	69	40	24	12	2	28
25-34	62	24	29	14	23	28
35-44	52	20	29	18	23	25
45-54	50	14	28	24	24	29
55+	15	5	7	14	8	19
Race/ethnicity						
Latina	57	20	28	1	21	35
African American	79	16	28	21	19	32
White	56	23	27	16	23	26

Note. From *The National Lesbian Health Care Survey: Final Report* (p. 47) by J. Bradford and C. Ryan, 1988, Washington, DC: National Lesbian and Gay Health Foundation. Copyright 1988 by J. Bradford and C. Ryan. Adapted by permission.

Depression and Anxiety

Over one third of the sample reported that they had experienced a "long depression or sadness" at some point in the past, 11% were experiencing depression currently, and 11% were currently receiving treatment for depression. Similar percentages for "constant anxiety or fear" were 11%, 7%, and 7%, respectively. Table 3 contains percentages of depression, anxiety, and "other mental health problems" by age and race or ethnicity. Depression and anxiety were least likely to be reported by the oldest group of lesbians.

Suicide

Data on the presence of suicidal thoughts and suicide attempts are presented in Table 4. Less than half the sample (43%) indicated that they "never" had thoughts about suicide. Thirty-five percent had such thoughts only rarely, 19% had them sometimes, and 2% often. Women aged 55 or older were most likely to report never having thoughts about suicide (60%).

Eighteen percent of the sample had attempted suicide. Older women were less likely to have attempted suicide. African-American (27%) and Latina (28%) women were more likely to have attempted suicide than were White women (16%).

TABLE 3. Percentages of Participants with Depression, Anxiety, and Other Mental Health Problems

Demographic	In the past			At present			Current Treatment		
	Dep	Anx	Other	Dep	Anx	Other	Dep	Anx	Other
Age (years)									
17-24	31	17	10	14	9	6	12	7	6
25-34	38	20	13	11	7	7	10	7	7
35-44	40	19	12	13	7	8	13	8	8
45-54	33	17	11	10	4	8	11	4	5
55+	24	8	8	4	1	7	3	3	8
Race/ethnicity									
Latina	36	23	10	14	9	6	11	6	5
African American	35	18	9	11	10	7	14	12	4
White	37	18	12	11	7	8	11	7	8
Total	37	19	12	11	7	8	11	7	7

Note. From *The National Lesbian Helath Care Survey: Final Report* (pp. 20-22) by J. Bradford and C. Ryan, 1988, Washington, DC: National Lesbian and Gay Health Foundation. Copyright 1988 by J. Bradford and C. Ryan. Adapted by permission. Dep = depression; Anx = anxiety.

TABLE 4. Number and Percentage of Participants Who Had Suicidal Thoughts and Attempts

Demographic		Frequency of thoughts about suicide				Responses to the question, "Have you ever tried to kill yourself?"		
	Never	Rarely	Sometimes	Often	n	Yes	No	n
Age (years)								
17-24	41	32	25	2	167	24	76	167
25-34	42	37	10	2	913	17	83	908
35-44	44	37	17	3	613	18	82	614
45-54	47	32	19	1	134	13	87	135
55 or older	60	19	19	2	58	3	97	59
Race/ethnicity								
Latina	43	37	19	1	79	28	72	79
African American	39	36	22	3	102	27	73	106
White	44	35	19	2	1,681	16	84	1,677
Total	43	35	19	2	1,900	18	82	1,898

Note. From *The National Lesbian Helath Care Survey: Final Report* (p. 50) by J. Bradford and C. Ryan, 1988, Washington, DC: National Lesbian and Gay Health Foundation. Copyright 1988 by J. Bradford and C. Ryan. Adapted by permission.

The most common means of attempted suicide was drugs, which represented 63% of all attempts. Ten percent of suicide attempts involved the use of a razor blade, 4% alcohol, 3% a gun, 3% a knife, 2% gas, 4% a car, and 10% involved other means.

Physical and Sexual Abuse

Physical abuse. Table 5 displays the frequency of physical abuse by age and race or ethnicity. Thirty-seven percent of the sample had been harshly beaten or physically abused at least once. Twenty-four percent had been physically abused while growing up, 16% as adults, and 6% as both children and adults. In all, 701 of the 1,925 women stated that they had been harshly beaten or physically abused. White women were the least often abused, both as children and adults. Half of Latina and African-American women had been abused at some time in their lives, compared with one third of White women. One third of Latina and African-American women had been abused as children, compared with one fifth of White women.

Perpetrators of physical abuse. Seventy percent of those who experienced being physically abused while growing up reported that the perpe-

TABLE 5. Experiences with Physical and Sexual Abuse

Demographic	Ever		As child		As adult		Both		N
	n	%	n	%.	n	%	n	%	
Physical abuse									
Age (years)									
17-24	49	29	38	23	15	9	7	4	169
25-34	337	36	220	24	133	14	56	6	921
35-44	235	38	160	26	113	18	51	8	618
45-54	54	40	27	20	28	21	5	4	135
55+	26	35	8	11	13	18	1	1	74
Race/ethnicity									
Latina	39	48	29	36	15	19	9	11	80
African American	52	48	38	36	22	21	11	10	107
White	595	35	372	22	261	15	97	6	1,691
Total	701	37	453	24	302	16	120	6	1,917
Rape and sexual abuse									
Age (years)									
17-24	83	50	54	32	16	10	4	2	169
25-34	377	41	195	21	151	16	43	5	921
35-44	255	41	108	18	105	17	25	4	618
45-54	53	39	30	22	18	13	4	3	135
55+	26	35	11	15	5	7	1	1	74
Race/ethnicity									
Latina	37	46	20	25	11	14	3	4	80
African American	55	51	35	33	18	17	4	4	107
White	681	40	331	20	260	15	68	4	1,691
Total	794	41	398	21	295	15	77	4	1,917

Note: From *The National Lesbian Health Care Survey: Final Report* (pp. 77, 80) by J. Bradford and C. Ryan, 1988, Washington, DC: National Lesbian and Gay Health Foundation. Copyright 1988 by J. Bradford and C. Ryan. Adapted by permission. All percentages were calculated using row *n*s.

trator was a male relative, and 45% mentioned a female relative. Seventeen percent were physically abused by a known man who was not a relative, 9% by a male stranger, 4% by a known woman, and 1% by a female stranger. More than half of women who had been abused as adults were abused by their lover (53%; gender unspecified) and 27% had been abused by their husbands. Other perpetrators of adult physical abuse were male relative (9%), female relative (3%), known male (14%), male stranger (26%), known female (13%), and female stranger (3%).

Sources of help after physical abuse. Respondents were asked where they had tried to get help after being physically abused. The largest number (29%) had contacted friends; smaller numbers had sought some assistance from police (17%) or from a counselor (16%). Approximately half of those who contacted a friend or counselor stated that they definitely received help, whereas only 11% of those who contacted the police reported being definitely helped. The most dissatisfaction was reported for contacts with members of the clergy, the police, and private physicians. Although the small number of women who reported contacting a women's health center or women's healing circle may have produced a sampling bias, women who sought help from these groups overwhelmingly reported having received beneficial assistance.

Rape and sexual attack. Table 5 also indicates the frequency of rape and sexual attack by age and race or ethnicity. Forty-one percent of the sample (*n* = 794) reported that they had been raped or sexually attacked at least once in their lives, with more reporting that this had happened while they were growing up (21%) than during adulthood (15%). Four percent had been raped or sexually attacked both as children and as adults. A smaller percentage of White women (40%) than Latinas (46%) and African-American women (51%) reported having been raped or sexually abused, and this difference was particularly apparent during childhood. One third of African-American lesbians had been sexually abused as children, compared with one fifth of White and one fourth of Latina lesbians.

Perpetrators of sexual abuse. The overwhelming majority of lesbians reported that the perpetrator of sexual abuse was a man. For lesbians sexually abused as children, the perpetrators were male relatives (31%), other known men (45%), and male strangers (33%). Only 1% of lesbians indicated that perpetrators were either female relatives, known women, or female strangers, respectively. For lesbians sexually abused as adults, the perpetrators were lovers (10%; gender unspecified), husbands (8%), male relatives (5%), other known men (42%), and male strangers (47%), with no more than 1% of lesbians sexually abused by female relatives, strangers, or known women, respectively.

Sources of help after rape or sexual attack. Although 794 women reported having been raped or sexually attacked at some point in their lives, only 35% stated that they had sought assistance afterward. Friends were sought most often (19%), followed by police (12%) and counselors (10%). The highest rates of satisfaction were reported by those who sought help from special groups organized to help women (women's healing circles, 75%; women's health centers, 56%; and rape crisis centers, 57%), from friends (63%), and from counselors (59%). Respondents were most dissatisfied with assistance offered by members of the clergy, private doctors, emergency rooms, and the police.

Incest. Of the 1,779 in the sample who responded to the question about having sex with one or more relatives while growing up, 19% (*n* = 336) reported that this had happened to them. White lesbians had lower rates of incest (16%) than did Latina (29%) or Black (31%) lesbians. The frequency of incest did not vary much across age groups; 18% of lesbians aged 17-24 and 25-34, 17% of lesbians aged 35-44, 18% of lesbians aged 45-54, and 14% of lesbians aged 55 or older reported incestuous experiences while growing up.

Perpetrators of incest. The most common perpetrator of incest were brothers (34%), followed by fathers (28%), uncles (27%), cousins (18%), stepfathers (9%), grandfathers (8%), mothers (3%), sisters (3%), and aunts (1%). About one half of lesbians who had experienced incest had told someone about it. The percentages of lesbians who had told someone about the incest were 44% when the perpetrator was their father; 48% when the perpetrator was their mother; 45%, grandfather; 32%, uncle; 60%, aunt; 41%, brother; 40%, sister; 48%, stepfather; and 30%, cousin.

Experiences with Discrimination

Respondents were asked if specific discrimination had happened to them because they were lesbians. Over half the sample (52%) had been verbally attacked for being lesbian, and another 4% thought that this might have happened. Eight percent had lost their jobs (another 5% weren't sure), 6% had been physically attacked (another 2% weren't sure), 4% had their health affected (another 4% weren't sure), and 1% had been discharged from the military, for being lesbian.

Impact of AIDS

Although these data were collected in 1984-1985, before AIDS was perceived to have a significant impact on the lesbian and gay communities, six out of ten lesbians in the sample reported that AIDS had affected their lives. Forty percent were worried about gay male friends while others reported increased awareness of the political implications of the epidemic and concern for those affected, expressing a range of emotions from anger to sadness.

One lesbian in the sample had AIDS. She and her lover lived in a Midwestern city at the time of the survey. She reported feelings of isolation from the community, lack of support for lesbians with AIDS, and fear of infecting her lover and son.

Alcohol and Drug Use

Respondents were asked to report on both the frequency of their alcohol and drug use and whether they were worried about their use of these substances. Data are presented in Table 6.

TABLE 6. Frequency of Substance Abuse

Substance, age and race/ethnicity	% Subjects who abuse substances					% Worried about their substance abuse
	Daily	>1/week	>1/month	<1/month	Never	
Substance use						
Tobacco	30	3	3	5	58	26
Alcohol	6	25	30	23	17	14
Marijuana	5	9	8	25	53	7
Cocaine	-	1	2	16	81	2
Tranquilizers	1	1	2	8	89	1
Stimulants	-	-	2	6	92	-
Heroin	0	0	-	-	99	-
Use of tobacco (n = 1,791)						
Total	30	3	3	5	58	
Age (years)						
17-24	32	4	4	5	54	
25-34	28	3	3	6	59	
35-44	30	4	2	5	59	
45-54	36	1	2	2	60	
55 or older	38	0	0	2	60	
Race/ethnicity						
Latina	31	8	1	8	51	
African American	49	4	3	4	39	
White	29	3	3	5	60	
Use of alcohol (n = 1,852)						
Total	6	25	30	23	17	
Age (years)						
17-24	3	29	40	17	11	
25-34	3	25	31	24	16	
35-44	7	24	26	24	18	
45-54	10	24	24	25	17	
55 or older	21	19	19	23	18	
Race/ethnicity						
Latina	5	33	28	20	13	
African American	3	25	30	19	23	
White	6	25	29	24	16	

Note. From *The National Lesbian Health Care Survey: Final Report* (pp. 86, 89) by J. Bradford and C. Ryan, 1988, Washington, DC: National Lesbian and Gay Health Foundation. Copyright 1988 by J. Bradford and C. Ryan. Adapted by permission. Dashes indicate that comparable data were not available.

Tobacco. Thirty percent of the sample smoked cigarettes daily, and another 11% were occasional smokers; just over half (58%) reported that they never used tobacco. Twenty-six percent of the sample were worried about their use of tobacco. Middle-aged (36%) and older (38%) lesbians were more frequent daily smokers than younger lesbians. Higher percentages of African-American lesbians (49%) reported regular use of tobacco.

Alcohol. Almost one third of the sample reported regular use of alcohol: 6% drank every day and another 25% drank more than once a week. Eighty-three percent drank alcohol at least occasionally; 14% were worried about their use of alcohol. The percentages of those who drank daily were higher for older women (10% for those aged 45-54 and 21% among those 55 and older).

Other drugs. Nearly half the sample reported at least occasional use of marijuana; 53% stated that they never used this drug. Seven percent of the sample was worried about their marijuana use. Younger lesbians smoked marijuana more often than did older lesbians (e.g., 29% of lesbians aged 17-24 used marijuana less than once a month, compared with 13% of lesbians in the oldest age group), and higher percentages of African-American lesbians reported daily (11%) or more than weekly use (14%).

Nineteen percent of the sample had tried cocaine. One percent used it more than once a week, and another 2% more than once a month. Two percent were worried about their use of this drug. Eleven percent of the sample had used tranquilizers; only 1% reported daily use, and another 1% reported tranquilizer use more than once a week. One percent was worried about their use of tranquilizers. Among the very small number who used tranquilizers daily, most were 45 years old or older.

Almost no one in the sample reported regular use of amphetamines; of the few who did, most were between 17-24 years old. Higher percentages of younger women used amphetamines on occasion; only 78% of those aged 17-24 had never used this type of drug, compared with 90-98% of those in other age groups. No one in the sample reported regular use of heroin. However, a small number reported occasional use, typically less than once a month. Those who did use heroin were either Native American, Latina, or African American; no Whites in the sample reported use of heroin.

Eating Disorders

Within the sample, overeating was reported by a much larger percentage than was undereating or overeating and vomiting. Results are portrayed in Table 7. Two thirds of the sample indicated that they sometimes or often overate, and one third indicated that they sometimes or often

TABLE 7. Frequency of Eating Disorders

	% Subjects who:					
	Overeat (n = 1,841)		Undereat (n = 1,517)		Overeat then vomit (n = 1,383)	
Demographic	Never/ rarely	Sometimes/ often	Never/ rarely	Sometimes/ often	Never/ rarely	Sometimes/ often
Age (years)						
17-24	36	64	61	39	96	4
25-34	31	69	63	37	96	4
35-44	33	67	72	28	97	3
45-54	30	70	76	24	99	1
55 or older	34	66	76	24	97	3
Race/ethnicity						
Latina	29	71	63	38	94	6
African American	36	64	52	47	90	10
White	32	68	68	32	97	3
Total	32	68	67	33	96	4

Note. From *The National Lesbian Health Care Survey: Final Report* (p. 94) by J. Bradford and C. Ryan, 1988, Washington, DC: National Lesbian and Gay Health Foundation. Copyright 1988 by J. Bradford and C. Ryan. Adapted by permission.

underate, but only 4% indicated that they overate and then vomited. Undereating was most prevalent among younger and low-income women and least prevalent among older lesbians. Overeating followed by vomiting was low for all groups, but highest among African-American lesbians (10%).

Counseling

Sources of counseling. Nearly three fourths of the sample (73%) were in counseling or had received some form of mental health support from a professional mental health counselor at some time in the past. Included as professional mental health counselors were private counselors (63%), school counselors (14%), clinics (14%), hospitals (7%), and employee counselors (1%). In addition, 36% of the sample had received help with mental health problems from nonprofessionals, such as friends, support groups, and peer counselors. One third of the sample had sought help from both professionals and nonprofessionals in attempting to deal with mental health problems.

Demographics of lesbians who sought counseling. Table 8 presents information about counseling by demographic category. Age, education,

TABLE 8. Percentage of Subjects Who Make Use of Counseling

Demographic	Professional		Non-professional		Both		No. of cases
	No	Yes	No	Yes	No	yes	
Total	27	73	64	36	67	33	1,917
Age (years)							
17-24	38	62	69	31	72	28	169
25-34	27	73	61	39	65	35	921
35-44	24	76	64	36	67	33	618
45-54	25	75	69	31	73	27	135
55 or older	36	64	72	28	72	28	74
Race/ethnicity							
Latina	30	70	72	27	75	25	80
African American	39	61	72	28	77	23	107
White	26	74	63	37	66	34	1,691
Education							
Less than high school	33	67	72	28	74	26	46
High school	37	63	69	31	72	28	182
Vocational training	27	73	54	46	56	44	48
Some college	29	71	59	41	64	36	313
College	31	69	63	37	67	33	499
Advanced studies	28	72	63	37	68	32	222
Advanced degree	20	80	67	33	68	32	598
Religion							
Catholic	41	59	72	28	75	25	149
Jewish	15	85	59	41	60	40	139
Protestant	40	60	71	29	76	24	214
None	25	75	63	37	66	34	1,236
Pagan, witch	13	87	47	53	53	47	15
Unitarian	16	84	42	58	47	53	19
Gay church	28	72	59	41	65	35	46
Personal income							
$9,999 or less	28	72	57	43	61	39	529
$10,000-$19,999	29	71	62	38	66	34	687
$20,000-$29,999	27	73	71	29	74	26	451
$30,000-$39,999	23	77	66	34	68	32	151
$40,000 or more	18	82	78	22	78	22	79

Note. From The National Lesbian Health Care Survey: Final Report (p. 53) by J. Bradford and C. Ryan, 1988, Washington, DC: National Lesbian and Gay Health Foundation. Copyright 1988 by J. Bradford and C. Ryan. Adapted by permission.

income, religious affiliation, and race or ethnicity all seemed to have an effect on the likelihood of receiving mental health counseling. Women in the youngest (62%) and oldest (64%) age groups saw counselors less frequently than did women aged 25-34 (73%), 35-44 (76%), and 45-54 (75%). Eighty percent of women with advanced degrees saw counselors, compared with 67% of women with less than a high school degree, but this trend was not apparent with regard to nonprofessional counseling. Higher percentages of Jewish women (85%) and those who identified themselves as Unitarian (84%) or pagan or witch (87%) had received professional counseling than had those of other religious groups, and the same was true of nonprofessional counseling (40%, 53%, and 47% for these three religious groups, respectively). Higher percentages of White (74%) and Latina (61%) lesbians had received professional counseling than African-American lesbians (61%), and White lesbians had used more nonprofessional help (37%) than had African-American (28%) or Latina (27%) lesbians.

Reasons for counseling. Among those who had sought counseling (*n* = 1,442), half the sample (50%) reported that the most common reason for seeking counseling was feeling sad or depressed. Lesbians had also sought help for other emotional problems: 31% for feeling anxious or scared and 21% for loneliness. Many lesbians sought counseling because of problems in personal relationships: 44% because of problems with lovers, 34% for problems with family, and 10% for problems with friends. Other reasons mentioned were personal growth issues (30%), being gay (21%), alcohol and drugs (16%), upset at work (11%), problems due to racism (3%), and loss of significant other (1%).

Length and frequency of counseling. Most lesbians who had sought counseling had done so for 1 year or less (49%), 18% for 1-2 years, 11% for 2-3 years, 7% for 3-4 years, and 14% for over 4 years. Thirty-seven percent of lesbians who had sought counseling had seen one counselor, 26% had seen two counselors, 18% had seen three, and 22% four or more.

Reasons for not seeking counseling. Respondents were also asked to indicate their reasons for not seeking counseling, if they had thought about it but decided not to go. Twenty-one percent of the sample (*n* = 402) responded to this question. The most frequently cited reason was believing there was no need (30%); another 23% had been putting off seeking help. Other reasons for not seeking counseling were not knowing where to go (11%), finances (9%), counselors can't help (8%), don't like the idea of counseling (6%), fear of coming out (3%), and other (8%).

Demographic characteristics of counselors. Respondents were asked about their preferences about the gender, race, and sexual orientation of counselors. Respondents were most concerned about the gender of counselors; 89% preferred to see a woman, and less than 1% preferred to see a man. Only 10% did not care about the gender of their counselor. Gender mattered least to younger women. Sexual orientation was less important. Sixty-six preferred to see a counselor who was lesbian or gay, 33% didn't care, and only 1% preferred to see a heterosexual counselor. Older lesbians, White lesbians, and those with higher incomes were least concerned about the sexual orientation of the counselor. Ethnicity mattered least of all. Seventy-three percent of lesbians indicated no preference for a counselor of the same or a different ethnic background, and 27% preferred a counselor of their ethnic background. Thirty-three percent of Latina lesbians, 31% of African-American lesbians, and 27% of White lesbians preferred a counselor of their ethnic background.

Community and Social Life

Living arrangements. Forty-nine percent of lesbians were living with a lover at the time of the survey, 24% were living alone, and 20% were living with a roommate or friend. Small percentages of lesbians were living with their children (9%), other people's children (5%), their parents (3%), their husband (1%), or with other relatives (2%).

Community and neighborhood activities. Lesbians were most likely to participate in lesbian and gay rights groups (38%), women's support groups (34%), social groups (33%), and women's rights groups (30%). Lesbians also belonged to union, trade, or professional groups (26%), health centers or clubs (24%), other political groups (23%), women's spirituality groups (18%), religious organizations (16%), and other support groups (14%). Smaller numbers of lesbians belonged to neighborhood associations (11%), other minority rights groups (10%), groups for their children (7%), women's martial arts groups (4%), and self-help groups (4%).

Availability of lesbian activities. Seventy-six percent of lesbians lived in a community where there was a lesbian counselor or therapist. Lesbians were also likely to state that their community had lesbian support groups (70%), lesbian cultural events (70%), lesbian sports teams (68%), a lesbian bar or nightclub (67%), lesbian or gay religious groups (66%), lesbian or feminist bookstores (60%), lesbian hotline or information center (55%), and lesbian social clubs (51%). Less than half of lesbians had access to lesbian health care centers (39%) or lesbian healing circles (25%) in their community. Only 18% of lesbians lived in communities in which there were no available lesbian activities. Of those who lived in communities without lesbian activities, 50% lived within 50 miles and 22% lived within 100 miles of communities with lesbian activities.

Frequency of attendance at lesbian-only events. Most of the sample attended lesbian-only events at least several times a year; only 2% never did and only 5% attended such events less than once a year. Nearly two thirds attended lesbian events once or twice a month (38%) or at least once a week (23%). Older lesbians attended these events less frequently than did younger lesbians; 8% of those aged 55 or older never went to lesbian-only events. More highly educated lesbians attended these events more often; only 1-2% of those who had been to college never attended and most of them (61%) did so at least once or twice a month. Only 43% of lesbians who had not graduated from high school attended lesbian-only events; 9% never do.

Sexual orientation and ethnicity of close friends. Most of the sample had female friends who were also lesbians. Sixty-four percent had only or mostly lesbian friends. Thirty percent of the sample had half lesbian and half heterosexual friends; 5% had mostly heterosexual female friends, and 1% had no friends at all. For those who had male friends (78% of the sample did), 31% had mostly gay friends, 19% had both gay and heterosexual male friends, and 22% had mostly heterosexual male friends. Sixty-one percent of the sample had friends who were only or mostly of the same ethnicity, 23% had friends of both the same and other ethnic backgrounds, and 13% had friends who were mostly of a different ethnic background.

Outness

"Outness" was assessed by asking participants to indicate what percentage of (a) family, (b) gay and lesbian friends, (c) heterosexual friends, and (d) coworkers knew that they were lesbian. Choices ranged from 0-100%. Responses to the outness question were scaled from 0 (*out to 0%*) to 6 (*out to 100%*), and the outness score for the four groups was summed for a total score that ranged from 0-24.

The results on degree of outness are displayed in Table 9. Although 88% of the sample was openly lesbian to all gay and lesbian people they knew, much smaller percentages were out to all family members (27%), heterosexual friends (28%), and coworkers (17%). Furthermore, 19% were out to no family members and 29% were out to no coworkers. Table 10 also displays the mean outness scores for each category.

The lowest total outness score was achieved by lesbians aged 55 or older. Lesbians aged 25-34 were most out in all areas of their lives. This also represents an age cohort that would have benefitted most from the organizations and resources developed out of the lesbian and gay civil

TABLE 9. Outness: Disclosing Sexual Orientation to Others

People aware of subject's sexual orientation	0 (None)	1 (10% or less)	2 (11%-25%)	3 (26%-50%)	4 (51%-75%)	5 (76%-99%)	6 (100%)
Family members	19	5	16	11	18	5	27
Gay friends	1	0	1	2	4	4	88
Straight friends	7	3	18	18	20	5	28
Coworkers	29	7	20	13	11	3	17

Note. From The National Lesbian Health Care Survey: Final Report (pp. 102-103) by J. Bradford and C. Ryan, 1988, Washington, DC: National Lesbian and Gay Health Foundation. Copyright 1988 by J. Bradford and C. Ryan. Adapted by permission.

TABLE 10. Outness: Demographics of Subjects Who Have Disclosed Their Sexual Orientation to Others

Demographic	Total outness score	Mean score for coming out to:			
		Family	Gay friends	Straight friends	Coworkers
Age (years)					
17-24	12.06	2.80	5.63	3.47	2.13
25-34	13.52	3.38	5.76	3.81	2.54
35-44	13.18	3.26	5.68	3.73	2.46
45-54	12.27	2.82	5.65	3.37	2.39
55 or older	11.59	3.07	5.50	2.89	2.04
Race/ethnicity					
Latina	12.56	3.23	5.67	3.34	2.30
African American	12.41	3.35	5.38	3.50	2.10
White	13.16	3.22	5.73	3.71	2.47
Education					
Less than high school	12.34	3.72	5.07	3.20	2.20
High school	12.14	3.04	5.53	3.27	2.24
Vocational training	14.83	3.98	5.73	4.21	2.88
Some college	13.67	3.45	5.72	3.74	2.73
College	12.91	3.20	5.73	3.69	2.26
Advanced studies	13.16	3.27	5.73	3.67	2.46
Advanced degree	13.14	3.08	5.77	3.78	2.49
Type of work					
Professional	13.00	3.18	5.76	3.67	2.36
Manager/official	13.27	3.16	5.75	3.65	2.69
Clerical	12.88	3.20	5.67	3.67	2.31
Craftsperson	14.68	3.74	5.67	4.01	3.19
Operative	12.62	3.31	5.69	3.69	1.91
Laborer	14.64	3.73	6.00	4.14	2.77
Farmer	6.00	0.00	6.00	2.00	0.00
Service worker	13.88	3.66	5.54	3.81	2.81
Personal income					
$9,999 or less	13.45	3.42	5.60	3.81	2.57
$10,000-$19,999	13.31	3.24	5.72	3.77	2.55
$20,000-$29,999	12.53	2.98	5.82	3.51	2.23
$30,000-$39,999	12.56	3.21	5.74	3.40	2.19
$40,000 or more	13.87	3.62	5.67	3.84	2.68

Note. From *The National Lesbian Health Care Survey: Final Report* (pp. 102-103) by J. Bradford and C. Ryan, 1988, Washington, DC: National Lesbian and Gay Health Foundation. Copyright 1988 by J. Bradford and C. Ryan. Adapted by permission.

TABLE 11. Correlations Among Outness and Counseling Variables

Variable	Family	Gay friends	Straight friends	Coworkers	Total outness
Fear of exposure	−.16	−.09	−.23	−.21	−.25
Received counseling	.18	.09	.23	.14	.23
Sources of counseling					
Private	.17	.09	.19	.11	.20
Support	.07	.02	.12	.08	.11
Friends	.09	.04	.16	.12	.15
Psychic	.10	.05	.14	.11	.15
Reasons for counseling					
Problems with lover	.15	.08	.16	.14	.19
Problems with family	.11	.02	.11	.07	.12
Sadness/depression	.09	.03	.14	.06	.12
Growth issues	.11	.08	.19	.13	.17

Note. From *The National Lesbian Health Care Survey: Final Report* (pp. 116-118) by J. Bradford and C. Ryan, 1988, Washington, DC: National Lesbian and Gay Health Foundation. Copyright 1988 by J. Bradford and C. Ryan. Adapted by permission.

rights movement. Women with vocational training were more out than those with any other type of educational background. Women with at least some college education were most out. Interestingly, women in the lowest and the highest income groups were most out. White lesbians had higher scores of outness than did Latina or African-American lesbians. Most lesbians were out to heterosexual friends before they were out to family or coworkers.

Pearson product-moment correlation coefficients were calculated among the four groups (family, lesbian and gay friends, heterosexual friends, and coworkers) and also with attendance at lesbian events. All five measures were significantly intercorrelated ($p < .002$ or less). Highest correlation coefficients were .562 (out to coworkers and heterosexual friends), .499 (out to family and heterosexual friends), and .342 (out to family and coworkers).

All measures of outness and total outness were correlated with the individual items of Current Concerns and Worries. Correlations that were significant at $p < .002$ or less are reported in Table 11. The only item of this scale that was significantly correlated with outness was fear of exposure as a lesbian. This item was negatively correlated with all measures of outness, particularly the total score of outness ($r = -.25$), outness to heterosexual friends ($r = -.23$) and outness to coworkers ($r = -.21$). It seems evident that lesbians who are out to people in the workplace and also to heterosexuals are those who have the least fear of exposure.

All measures of outness were also correlated with three measures of counseling: (a) whether participants had ever received counseling, (b) source of counseling, and (c) reason for counseling. These results are also displayed in Table 11. All measures of outness were positively correlated with whether lesbians had received counseling, with the highest correlations for total outness and outness to heterosexual friends (both *r*s = .23). Four types of counseling were also significantly and positively correlated with measures of outness. Being out was associated with receiving help from the following sources: private counselors, support groups, friends, and psychic or spiritual healers. Other potential sources of help (e.g., from clinics or schools) were not significantly correlated with any of the outness measures. A similar pattern of correlations was also the case between outness and reasons for seeking counseling. Statistically significant correlations were found between all outness measures and the following reasons for seeking help: problems with lovers, with family, feeling sad or depressed, and personal growth issues.

DISCUSSION

The lesbians who participated in the National Lesbian Health Care Survey were mostly between the ages of 25 and 44, mostly well-educated and professionally employed, though significantly underpaid relative to educational status. There had been a dramatic shift from traditional religious upbringing to more lesbian-affirmative religions. All but a few lived in or near metropolitan areas and had access to a variety of lesbian community activities. The sample was thus limited to a more privileged group, in every sense other than its minority status, and may represent the "best scenario" for lesbians in the U.S. In its demographics, the sample is similar to most other studies of lesbians. Albro and Tully (1979) described the typical lesbian in their study as White, young, single, living on the East Coast, college educated, professionally employed, and unaffiliated with an organized religion. The response rate of 46% for this stigmatized group compares favorably with the response rate of 16% achieved by McKirnan and Peterson (1989a) in their large-scale community survey of lesbians and gay men in Chicago. Lesbians who were not represented in the current study are more likely to be cut off from a sympathetic community and therefore to be at greater risk for distress and need for supportive help. A major limitation of the current study, then, is that we still know little about the mental health of lesbians in rural and isolated settings.

Among the sample as a whole, there was a distressingly high prevalence of life events and behaviors related to mental health problems.

Thirty-seven percent had been physically abused and 32% had been raped or sexually attacked. Nineteen percent had been involved in incestuous relationships while growing up. Almost one third used tobacco on a daily basis, and about 30% drank alcohol more than once a week; 6% drank daily. One in five smoked marijuana more than once a month. Twenty-one percent of the sample had thoughts about suicide sometimes or often, and 18% had actually tried to kill themselves. Half of those who had received counseling had done so for feelings of sadness or depression. More than half had felt too nervous to accomplish ordinary activities at some time during the past year, and over one third had been depressed. Almost everyone in the sample was concerned about money, relationships, and work. Although most were well-educated, their incomes were not commensurate with the amount of training they had received. In general, lesbians who were older, who earned less money, and who were not White reported higher levels of abuse, mental distress, and reliance upon professional help.

Lesbians as Similar to Heterosexual Women

How do these data compare with mental health statistics on heterosexual women, who are also at risk for a number of mental health problems when compared with men? It must be kept in mind that this lesbian sample is demographically different (e.g., younger, more educated) than women in the general population, and also that it is more difficult to find adequate control groups for lesbians (e.g., should lesbian couples be compared with married heterosexual women, cohabiting heterosexual women, or even single heterosexual women because lesbians are often viewed as "single" by society?).

Depression. A large number of community studies and studies of people in treatment have examined gender ratios of depression, and found that in the United States and Europe, women are twice as likely as men to experience depression (see McGrath, Keita, Strickland, & Russo, 1990, for a review). Field trials conducted for the third edition of the Diagnostic and Statistical Manual of Mental Disorders (*DSM-III*; American Psychiatric Association, 1980) found 18%-23% of women and 8%-11% of men to have once had a major depressive episode, using the *DSM-III* criteria for depression. Studies that use broader definitions of depression (as in the current survey), as well as symptom scales, find rates of depression to be even higher. The current study is the first to have examined depression among lesbians in a community survey, and the high rate of depression among lesbians is similar to heterosexual women.

Suicide. Research among heterosexual women has found that the rate of reported suicide attempts is very high among professional women such as physicians, perhaps somewhat comparable to the large percentage of lesbians in professional occupations in the current study. For example, Pitts, Schuller, Rich, and Pitts (1979) found the suicide rate for female physicians to be higher than that of male physicians, and four times higher than White U.S. women of the same age.

The present study did not assess lesbian adolescents, and this group has been viewed as at particularly high risk for suicide (e.g., Kourany, 1987; Saunders & Valente, 1987). The results of the present study do indicate higher percentages of suicidal thoughts and attempts among the youngest age group, which would indicate that more research on suicide and its prevention among adolescent lesbians is necessary.

Sexual abuse. Several people have speculated that lesbianism is somehow related to the experience of incest during childhood (e.g., Herman & Hirschman, 1981) and a not-uncommon stereotype has held that lesbianism is a reaction to this experience. However, the results of the current study indicate that the rate of incest among lesbians (18.7% overall) is quite similar to that among the general female population (16%; Russell, 1984). The percentage of lesbians who reported having been raped or sexually attacked was the same in the current study as it was in Russell's (1984) sample of the general female population (34% in both studies for women under age 25). However, percentages follow different patterns for older lesbians. In Russell's sample, percentages of those who experienced rape or sexual attack increase with age, while for lesbians in the current study, percentages decrease with age. It is possible that lesbians have fewer social contacts with men as they become more involved in the lesbian community, and this may protect lesbians from sexual abuse by men.

Eating disorders. Lesbians in the current study reported similar percentages of eating disorders as did women surveyed in the general population (Ettore, 1980). The range of women in the general population who reported overeating was from 41%-69%, compared with 45% in the current study. One to five percent of Ettore's study reported overeating and then vomiting, compared with 2% in the current study. Eating disorders have been discussed within the context of female socialization, and research has indicated that lesbians are similar to heterosexual women along some dimensions of weight (e.g., dieting) but dissimilar on others (e.g., preoccupation with weight; Brand, Rothblum, & Solomon, 1992). In fact, some authors have speculated that a large component of concern with weight is the need to be sexually attractive to men (e.g., Brown, 1987). This would imply that heterosexual women and gay men would be at greater risk for eating disorders than would lesbians and heterosexual men, and further research is needed to examine the effect of both gender and sexual orientation on eating disorders.

Lesbians as Different from Heterosexual Women

Alcohol and drug use. The results of the current study concur with the other large-scale survey on substance use by McKirnan and Peterson (1989a). Both studies found high rates of alcohol use among lesbians, and both studies also found that rates of alcohol use do not decline with age as they do among heterosexual women. The use of bars for lesbians as a social resource was widely available to lesbians in the current study (67%). McKirnan and Peterson (1989a) have discussed alcohol and drug use among older lesbians as reflecting the independence lesbians may have from age-related social role changes that may affect heterosexual women. In the current study, however, less frequent involvement among older lesbians with the lesbian and gay community and decreased openness about their sexual orientation may lead to increased reliance on alcohol to mitigate the long-term effects of isolation, lack of adequate support, and compartmentalization of their identity.

Use of counseling. About three fourths of the sample reported a history of having used professional mental health services. This high use of counseling by lesbians has been born out by recent research (Morgan, 1992; Morgan & Eliason, 1992). Morgan (1992) compared 100 lesbian and 309 heterosexual women on their use of therapy, and found that 77.5% of lesbians and 28.9% of heterosexual women had been in therapy. Morgan and Eliason (1992) asked lesbians who had and those who had never been in therapy for reasons why so many lesbians seek therapy. Themes mentioned by at least half the sample included the fact that societal oppression causes stress for lesbians, therapy and personal growth are modelled and accepted by the lesbian community, and lesbians are introspective and have practice facing hard issues. Given the results of these studies, it is understandable why lesbians in the current study who were more out were also more likely to have used counseling. Lesbians who were more out also were more likely to have sought counseling for reasons related to being lesbian, such as difficulties with lovers or family, than were more closeted lesbians.

Furthermore, the present study found over one third of the lesbian sample to report using supportive resources, such as friends and women's groups, for help with mental health concerns. Research by Kurdek and Schmidt (1987) found lesbians three times more likely to list their friends rather than their family as the most frequent providers of social support. In contrast, heterosexuals tended to rate friends and family about equally as sources of support.

Minority status of lesbians. Lesbians who participated in the survey reported on the effects of their minority status in a number of ways. Over half had been verbally attacked for being lesbian, and 13% had lost jobs as the result of antigay discrimination. A small number expressed concern about seeking mental health services in the past because of being discriminated against or stereotyped by counselors. Others were simply afraid to disclose their lesbianism, even to professionals whose help they needed.

Nevertheless, lesbians who participated in the survey appeared to be socially connected and to have enough people to rely on for support with basic needs. Their connections were primarily with lesbian friends and lesbian community activities, however. Many had left traditional religious institutions and now belonged to nontraditional denominations or gay churches. Many had learned how to take care of their own mental health needs. It appeared that this group of mostly young, well-educated, professionally employed, urban lesbians lived in a way that is typical for people who occupy a minority status and who are socially marginal. They had two lives: one in which they earned the money needed for self-sufficiency and another in which they were socially connected to lesbians and lesbian-affirmative people.

Being out had positive aspects. It was associated with less fear of exposure; it was also associated with receiving mental health services and having more choices about where to seek help. Survey findings such as these lead to an enhanced understanding of the relationship between "rational outness" and various aspects of mental health. This concept includes both a personal dimension, in which lesbians come out to themselves and other lesbians in a more or less continuous process over time, and a social dimension, in which lesbians make deliberate decisions about who can be trusted to know without harming them, among all the people they encounter on an ongoing basis. Positive mental health requires that human beings function adequately in both their personal and social lives and that they achieve a workable integration of the two. For some lesbians, behavior within these two dimensions may be very similar, but for others it may be very divergent. Few have the luxury to be completely out to everyone, even though such behavior would be psychologically beneficial if it were safe. These survey data begin to illuminate the complexities of psychosocial decision-making, development of positive coping skills, and survival within a homophobic society, that are inherent in living as a lesbian.

Implications for Treatment

In assessing treatment needs of lesbians, data from this survey suggest several issues to explore. Relationships are a major treatment focus for all lesbians. A large percentage of lesbians had sought treatment because of problems with lovers (44%), family (34%), and friends (10%), as well as loneliness (21%). Depression was a precipitating factor for one out of two lesbians seeking treatment. Among midlife lesbians, higher percentages sought treatment for depression, problems with their lovers, and problems with their sexual orientation, than did younger lesbians (see Bradford & Ryan, 1991, for a review of data on midlife lesbians from this survey). While personal growth was the major treatment issue for nearly one out of three lesbians overall, significantly fewer African-American and Latina lesbians had sought professional help for personal growth issues than had White lesbians.

Sixteen percent of the sample had sought counseling for substance abuse problems. Use of alcohol increased with age, with highest rates of use reported by lesbians aged 55 or older. Not surprisingly, these lesbians were least open about their sexual orientation and were the least connected to the organized lesbian community. Lack of support and fear of exposure as a lesbian may lead to increased reliance on alcohol. Inclusion of a substance abuse history during intake and sensitivity to the unreported use of alcohol and drugs to self-medicate for depression are recommended, particularly for practitioners working with midlife and older lesbians.

Although nearly three fourths of the sample had sought mental health services at some time and a majority found these services to be helpful, the low income level of lesbians in the sample presents an inherent barrier to receiving quality mental health care. This represents both a treatment and a policy issue in meeting the mental health needs of lesbians. Worry about money was the primary concern for lesbians in the survey (57%) and was greatest for African-American lesbians and those aged 54 and younger. Although most lesbians preferred a private practitioner than lower-cost options, nearly 9 out of 10 earned less than $30,000 annually, and only 65% had health insurance (see Bradford & Ryan, 1988; Ryan & Bradford, 1988, for results of physical health). Lack of third-party payments and insufficient personal resources may prevent many lesbians from receiving services.

More than 68% of lesbians reported having had a range of mental health problems in the past, including long-term depression and sadness, constant anxiety and fear, and other mental health concerns. At the time of the survey, however, only 23% reported having such problems and they were receiving treatment for these problems. Given the high rate of mental health problems in the past, it is noteworthy that nearly half of lesbians receiving counseling (49%) had been in therapy for one year or less. This suggests the development of coping and survival skills, in addition to reliance on friends and alternative social supports to manage these concerns. The survival strengths of lesbians, while not measured specifically in this survey, warrant further consideration. In view of their low socioeconomic status and experiences with discrimination and stigma, the capacity of lesbians in this survey to maintain interpersonal and primary relationships, educate themselves, hold responsible jobs and participate in the social, political, and professional activities of their communities should be perceived as adaptive and resilient. Assessing the psychological resources and adaptability of lesbians to survive in a hostile and stressful environment is an area of future research with applicability to the larger society.

REFERENCES

Albro, J. C., & Tully, C. (1979). A study of lesbian lifestyle in the homosexual micro-culture and the heterosexual macro-culture. *Journal of Homosexuality, 4*, 331-344.

American Psychiatric Association. (1980). *Diagnostic and statistical manual of mental disorders* (3rd ed.) Washington, DC: Author.

Bradford J. B. (1986). *Reactions of gay men to AIDS: A survey of self-reported change.* Unpublished doctoral dissertation, Virginia Commonwealth University, Department of Social Policy and Social Work.

Bradford, J. B., & Ryan, C. (1987). *National Lesbian Health Care Survey: Mental health implications for lesbians.* (Report No. PB88-201496/AS). Bethesda, MD: National Institute of Mental Health.

Bradford, J. B., & Ryan, C. (1988). *The National Lesbian Health Care Survey: Final Report.* Washington, DC: National Lesbian and Gay Health Foundation.

Bradford, J. B., & Ryan, C. (1991). Who we are: Health concerns of middle-aged lesbians. In B. Sang, J. Warshow, & A. J. Smith (Eds.) *Lesbians at midlife: The creative transition* (pp. 147-163). San Francisco, CA: Spinsters Book Company.

Brand, P. A., Rothblum, E. D., & Solomon, L. J. (1992). A comparison of lesbians, gay men, and heterosexuals on weight and restrained eating. *International Journal of Eating Disorders, 11*, 253-259.

Brown, L. S. (1987). Lesbians, weight, and eating: New analyses and perspectives. In Boston Lesbian Psychologies Collective (Eds.), *Lesbian psychologies: Explorations and challenges* (pp. 294-309). Urbana, IL: University of Illinois Press.

Clark, W. B., & Midanik, L. (1982). Alcohol use and alcohol problems among U.S. adults: Results of the 1979 national survey. In National Institute of Alcohol Abuse and Alcoholism, *Alcohol and health: Alcohol consumption and related problems* (Monograph No. 1).

Dardick, L., & Grady, K. E. (1980). Openness between gay persons and health professionals. *Annals of Internal Medicine, 93*(Part 1), 115-119.

Ettore, E. M. (1980). *Lesbians, women and society.* London: Routledge and Kegan Paul.

Fifield, L. (1975). *On my way to nowhere: Alienated, isolated, drunk.* Unpublished report of the Gay Community Services Center, Los Angeles, CA.

Gartrell, N. (1981). The lesbian as a "single" woman. *American Journal of Psychiatry, 35,* 502-510.

Glaus, K. (1988). Alcoholism, chemical dependency and the lesbian client. *Women and Therapy, 8,* 131-144.

Herman, J. L., & Hirschman, L. (1981). *Father-daughter incest.* Cambridge, MA: Harvard University Press.

Herzog, D. B., Norman, D. K., Gordon, C., & Pepose, M. (1984). Sexual conflict and eating disorders in 27 males. *American Journal of Psychiatry, 141,* 989-990.

Kourany, R. F. C. (1987). Suicide among homosexual adolescents. *Journal of Homosexuality, 13,* 111-117.

Kurdek, L. A., & Schmidt, J. P. (1987). Perceived emotional support from family and friends in members of homosexual, married, and heterosexual cohabiting couples. *Journal of Homosexuality, 14,* 57-68.

Lewis, L. A. (1984). The coming-out process for lesbians: Integrating a stable identity. *Social Work, 29,* 464-469.

Lobel, K. (1986). (Ed.). *Naming the violence: Speaking out about lesbian battering.* Seattle, WA: Seal Press.

Mays, V. M., & Cochran, S. D. (August, 1986). *Relationship experiences and the perception of discrimination by Black lesbians.* Paper presented at the 94th Annual Convention of the American Psychological Association, Washington, DC.

McGrath, E., Keita, G. P., Strickland, B. R., & Russo, N. F. (1990). *Women and depression: Risk factors and treatment issues.* Washington, DC: American Psychological Association.

McKirnan, D. J., & Peterson, P. L. (1989a). Alcohol and drug use among homosexual men and women: Epidemiology and population characteristics. *Addictive Behaviors, 14,* 545-553.

McKirnan, D. J., & Peterson, P. L. (1989b). Psychosocial and cultural factors in alcohol and drug abuse: An analysis of a homosexual community. *Addictive Behaviors, 14,* 555-563.

Morgan, K. S. (1992). Caucasian lesbians' use of psychotherapy: A matter of attitude? *Psychology of Women Quarterly, 16,* 127-130.

Morgan, K. S., & Eliason, M. J. (1992). The role of psychotherapy in Caucasian lesbians' lives. *Women and Therapy, 13,* 27-52.

Pitts, F. N., Schuller, B., Rich, C. L., & Pitts, A. F. (1979). Suicide among U.S. women physicians, 1967-1972. *American Journal of Psychiatry, 136,* 694-696.

Russell, D. E. H. (1984). *Sexual exploitation: Rape, child sexual abuse, and workplace harassment.* Beverly Hills, CA: Sage.

Ryan, C., & Bradford, J. (1988). The National Lesbian Health Care Survey: An overview. In M. Shernoff & W. Scott (Eds.), *Sourcebook on lesbian and gay health care* (pp. 30-40). Washington, DC: National Lesbian and Gay Health Foundation.

Ryan, C., & Bradford, J. (1993). The National Lesbian Health Care Survey: An overview. In D. Garnets & D. C. Kimmel (Eds.), *Psychological perspectives on lesbian and gay male experiences* (pp. 541-556). New York: Columbia University Press.

Saunders, J. M., & Valente, S. M. (1987). Suicide risk among gay men and lesbians: A review. *Death Studies, 11,* 1-23.

U.S. Department of Commerce (1984). *1984 statistical abstract of the United States, 104th edition.* Washington, DC: Author.

Negative Sexual Experiences with Men Among Heterosexual Women and Lesbians

JoAnn C. Brannock, PhD
Beata E. Chapman, MA

SUMMARY. Survey responses on traumatic experiences with men were compared from 50 matched pairs of heterosexual women and lesbians. Prior research has implied that lesbians have had more traumatic experiences with men than heterosexual women. The purpose of this study was to test the hypothesis that lesbians would report more negative sexual experiences with men than heterosexual women. The findings of the present study did not support this hypothesis. The only significant difference found between the two groups was that heterosexual women were more likely to report multiple categories of traumatic experiences and lesbians were more likely to report experiences in only one category of trauma. Contrary to prior studies, these results indicate that previous traumatic experiences with men may not be a significant factor in the development of sexual orientation. *[Article copies available from The Haworth Document Delivery Service: 1-800-342-9678. E-mail address: getinfo@haworth.com]*

Several researchers have hypothesized that a relationship exists between traumatic experiences with men and lesbian behavior (Belcastro,

JoAnn C. Brannock and Beata E. Chapman, *Journal of Homosexuality,* Volume 19, Number 1. © 1990 by The Haworth Press, Inc.

[Haworth co-indexing entry note]: "Negative Sexual Experiences with Men Among Heterosexual Women and Lesbians." Brannock, JoAnn C., and Beata E. Chapman. Co-published simultaneously in *Journal of Lesbian Studies* (The Haworth Press, Inc.) Vol. 1, No. 2, 1997, pp. 251-255; and: *Classics in Lesbian Studies* (ed: Esther D. Rothblum) The Haworth Press, Inc., 1997, pp. 251-255; and: *Classics in Lesbian Studies* (ed: Esther D. Rothblum) Harrington Park Press, an imprint of The Haworth Press, Inc., 1997, pp. 251-255. Single or multiple copies of this article are available from The Haworth Document Delivery Service [1-800-342-9678, 9:00 a.m. - 5:00 p.m. (EST). E-mail address: getinfo@haworth.com].

1982; Robertiello, 1973; Simari and Baskin, 1984; and Swanson, Loomis, Lukesh, Cronin, and Smith, 1972). Swanson et al. studied 40 lesbians who were in therapy and compared them with a control group of 40 heterosexual female psychiatric patients. They found that the lesbians differed significantly from the heterosexuals in that they reported greater paternal abusiveness. This study, however, is limited in that the sample consisted of therapeutic groups who may not represent the lesbian and heterosexual community at large.

Simari and Baskin (1984) compared lesbians and male homosexuals on experiences with incest. They found that heterosexual incest was the only form of incest reported by females (38% of the total sample) and that homosexual incest was the only form reported by males (46% of the total sample). The authors imply a relationship between homosexuality and prior incestuous experiences. Their conclusions, however, are inconsistent in that males would become homosexual due to homosexual incestual experiences, while females would become homosexual due to heterosexual incestuous experiences. Before such conclusions can be drawn, a comparative sample of heterosexual respondents on the same variables is needed.

In a comparative study of 397 female undergraduates who had not been raped and 40 female undergraduates who had been raped, Belcastro (1982) found that raped women reported having significantly more heterosexual partners than women who had never been raped, were significantly younger at their first pregnancy than nonvictims, and reported significantly more lesbian experiences than nonvictims. The author infers that a relationship exists between rape and lesbian behavior, yet the results indicate that rape is related to promiscuity, whether heterosexual or otherwise.

The purposes of the present study were twofold. The first objective was to compare the incidence of past trauma among lesbians and heterosexual women by asking participants directly about their past traumatic experiences. Our second objective was to assess a sample of women who were not limited to those in a therapeutic situation, thus correcting some of the methodological deficiencies noted in prior research efforts. The hypothesis that lesbians would report more negative sexual experiences with men than heterosexual women was tested.

One hundred forty-eight female students, all of whom reported that they were heterosexual, were surveyed. Lesbian respondents were drawn from the data collected in a prior study of 190 lesbians, part of which inquired about negative sexual experiences with men (Chapman and Brannock, 1987). These women were drawn from various social and educational groups in the gay and lesbian community.

Fifty women from each group were then matched with each other on their age at the time of the survey. The average age was 28.89 years, with a range of 19-57 years and a mode of 23 years.

The heterosexual women and lesbians were asked identical questions regarding their negative sexual or traumatic experiences with men on a survey instrument. Specifically, the women were requested to indicate, by placing a check mark on a list, whether they had experienced incest, molestation, rape, physical abuse, and other negative sexual experiences with men. They were also asked their age at the time of their first negative sexual experience with a man and at the time of the survey. The total questionnaire was comprised of those three items. All those given questionnaires were informed that participation in the study was voluntary and that the data would be used for research purposes. They were assured anonymity and confidentiality.

As shown in Table 1, both groups of women reported the same number of categories of traumatic experiences with men. No significant differences were found using the chi-square statistic between the heterosexual women and lesbians on reported experiences of incest, molestation, rape, physical or "other" negative experiences with men.

The median age at the time of first experiences for the heterosexual women was 10 years, with a range of three to 24 years. The median age for lesbians was 7 years, with a range from two to 28 years. As shown in Table 2, heterosexual women were twice as likely to report multiple negative experiences with men than were lesbians.

Chi-square analyses were performed on the total number of categories reported by the respondents within each group. In order to achieve cell frequencies greater than five on total number of categories of negative experiences reported, responses were combined for those women reporting three to five categories of such experiences. Women reporting two categories of experiences were then compared to those reporting three to five categories of experiences. The chi-square with Yates Correction was significant, $\chi^2 (1, N\ 18) = 7.61, p < .01$. Heterosexual women were significantly more likely to report multiple negative experiences with men. One

TABLE 1. Number of Heterosexual Women and Lesbians Reporting Traumatic Experiences

	Incest	Molestation	Rape	Physical Abuse	Other	Total
Heterosexuals	3	10	7	12	6	38
Lesbians	7	11	7	6	7	38

could hypothesize that heterosexual women are at higher risk for traumatic experiences with men over a more extended period of time than are lesbians.

Our hypothesis that lesbians would report more negative sexual experiences with men than heterosexual women was not supported in that the total number of traumatic experiences reported by the two groups were equal. There were no significant differences between the two groups on each of the categories of negative experiences with men. The only significant finding was that heterosexual women were more likely to have had multiple categories of traumatic experiences with men, while lesbians were more likely to have experienced one category of trauma.

In light of previous findings cited, it is interesting to note that the two groups in the study reported equal numbers of traumatic experiences with men. The pattern of experiences were different which creates the impression that heterosexual women and lesbians differ significantly, as was reported by Swanson et al. This impression is not borne out when the data are examined on a case-by-case basis by category of trauma.

Several previous studies have utilized women in therapeutic treatment situations as the subjects of their study. It is difficult to determine whether such subjects are representative of the general population of heterosexual women and lesbians. According to Maggio and Mead (1983) surveys have indicated that "as many as 33 percent of adult females were sexually assaulted in their youth" (p. 32). Our study yielded findings very similar to these, and therefore we conclude that our respondents were typical of the general population of women.

TABLE 2. Number of Heterosexual Women and Lesbians Reporting Multiple Categories of Traumatic Experiences with Men

	Two	Three	Four	Five	Total
Heterosexuals	7	3	1	1	12
Lesbians	3	2	1	0	6

REFERENCES

Belcastro, P.A. (1982). A comparison of latent sexual behavior patterns between raped and never raped females. *Victimology, 7,* 224-230.

Chapman, B.E. & Brannock, J.C. (1987). Proposed model of lesbian identity development: An empirical examination. *Journal of Homosexuality, 14,* p. 69-80.

Maggio, E. & Mead, J.J. (1983). *Child abuse and neglect.* Brea, CA: For Kids Sake Press.

Robertiello, R.C. (1973). One psychiatrist's view of female homosexuality. *Journal of Sex Research, 9,* 30-33.

Simari, C. & Baskin, D. (1984). Incestuous experiences within lesbian and male homosexual populations: A preliminary study. *Child Psychiatry Quarterly, 17,* 21-40.

Swanson, D.W., Loomis, S.D., Lukesh, R., Cronin, R., & Smith, J.A. (1972). Clinical features of the female homosexual patient: A comparison with the heterosexual patient. *Journal of Nervous and Mental Disease, 155,* 119-124.

Therapy for Lesbians?:
The Case Against

Rachel Perkins

SUMMARY. From a lesbian feminist perspective the problematic nature of developments in 'lesbian' and 'feminist' psychological therapies is considered. It is argued that such therapies are, despite their expressed aims, essentially anti-lesbian and anti-feminist.

The last 25 years have seen a general move away from attempts by clinical psychologists to cure lesbians by reorientating us to become heterosexual. Instead, as Rothblum (1989) describes, there is a 'cautious acceptance' of lesbianism as a 'positive lifestyle choice for women' by mainstream mental health professionals. In line with this change, the last decade has seen an increasing literature concerning 'affirmative' therapy with lesbian clients, both in academic psychology journals and in lesbian and feminist publications. From a position of hostility towards therapy there has been a development of lesbian and feminist therapies and therapists that have gained widespread popularity and acceptance amongst lesbians and many have undoubtedly experienced such therapy as beneficial. Lesbians seek therapy for a variety of problems, the most common being distress, worry and misery arising from relationship difficulties and lesbian identity problems, and psychological adjustment more generally (Sang, 1989). Many lesbians seek help from specifically lesbian or feminist therapists and agencies, others see lesbian and feminist psychologists and therapists working within mainstream statutory agencies like the National Health Service in the UK.

Rachel Perkins, *Feminism & Psychology* © 1991 SAGE (London, Newbury Park and New Delhi), Vol. 1(3): 325-338. Reprinted by permission.

[Haworth co-indexing entry note]: "Therapy for Lesbians?: The Case Against." Perkins, Rachel. Co-published simultaneously in *Journal of Lesbian Studies* (The Haworth Press, Inc.) Vol. 1, No. 2, 1997, pp. 257-271; and: *Classics in Lesbian Studies* (ed: Esther D. Rothblum) The Haworth Press, Inc., 1997, pp. 257-271; and: *Classics in Lesbian Studies* (ed: Esther D. Rothblum) Harrington Park Press, an imprint of The Haworth Press, Inc., 1997, pp. 257-271.

However, as a lesbian and a feminist, as well as a clinical psychologist, I am concerned about these developments. The purpose of this paper is not to consider psychology as a whole, but more particularly to explore some of my concerns about psychological therapies with lesbians. I argue that lesbian feminists should exercise extreme caution in accepting the incursion of such therapies, albeit of a purportedly lesbian or feminist variety, into our lesbian communities. Likewise, I would urge clinical psychologists and therapists to consider carefully the consequences and implications of their undoubtedly well-intentioned endeavours before embarking upon helping lesbians with the distress that our oppression in an anti-lesbian society often brings.

Lesbian and feminist psychological therapy is not a unitary concept. A variety of psychological models and approaches have been invoked, from feminist psychoanalytic perspectives (e.g., Margolies et al., 1987; Mitchell, 1989), through versions of object relations theory (e.g., Ryan, 1983; Starzecpyzel, 1987) to cognitive-behavioural approaches (e.g., Sophie, 1982, 1987; Smalley, 1987; Padesky, 1989). Discussions amongst both feminists and psychologists often centre around which model is best. Psychology is a broad church and this serves to enhance its pervasiveness and impenetrability: in criticizing one model, another is almost invariably proffered as an alternative, and the number of different therapeutic approaches within and outside mainstream psychology is large and growing. A focus of debate on the relative merits of one model/therapy versus another can, however, be diversionary in drawing attention away from the features that they all share, and that are of concern from a lesbian feminist perspective.

DEPOLITICIZATION:
OPPRESSION AS INDIVIDUAL PATHOLOGY

The range of lesbian and feminist therapies available to address lesbians' problems share a common theme: they are designed to help us overcome the problems we experience as lesbians in an anti-lesbian and patriarchal society.

Within these psychological models, however, a subtle sleight of hand occurs. Oppression becomes psychologized as a pathological entity in the form of homophobia, a term first coined not by lesbians or feminists but by a psychoanalyst, Weinberg (1973). Homophobia is defined by psychologists as an irrational fear, hatred and intolerance of, and negative attitudes towards, homosexuals. From a political issue requiring social change, anti-lesbianism becomes a province of psychology: a form of individual dysfunction requiring therapy and individual change. The literature contains many reports of investigations into, and therapeutic efforts to reduce, homophobia in heterosexual therapists, counsellors and others (e.g., Seigel, 1987; Schmitz, 1988; Jones, 1988; Poverny and Finch, 1988; Newman, 1989; Randell, 1989; Rudolph, 1989). Further, to define fear of lesbians as irrational–a phobia–is, from a feminist perspective, paradoxical. By failing both to define ourselves in terms of men, and to service men in the required manner, lesbians represent a threat to heteropatriarchal social organization. Like my fear of being run over if I stand in the middle of a busy road, fear of a real threat cannot be phobic or irrational. (For a more thorough consideration of the politically reactionary implications of the concept of 'homophobia' see Kitzinger, 1987, 1989.)

Such a redefinition of realistic fear as pathological phobia is, however, functional in that it serves to defuse and incorporate the potential threat. Within this depoliticized, psychologized, version, anti-lesbianism becomes the individual pathology of homophobia, and lesbianism becomes a harmless lifestyle choice: '. . . an affirmative model of non-traditional lifestyle' (Rothblum, 1989). This conceptualization permits the psychologization of the problems and distress that lesbians experience in the face of this homophobia (oppression) as poor psychological adjustment and self-identity/self-esteem difficulties. These are seen as resulting from internalized homophobia–the internalization of the fear, hatred and negative attitudes of homophobia. Such a translation of our oppression into individual pathological terms means that the change process becomes a therapeutic one: reducing/eliminating the individual lesbian's irrational fear, self-hatred, and negative attitudes to achieve better 'psychological adjustment' and a 'positive self-identity' (e.g., Sophie, 1982; Margolies et al., 1987; Miranda and Storms, 1989; Padesky, 1989). For example, Sophie (1987: 53), while acknowledging the '. . . strength and pervasiveness of anti-homosexual attitudes in our society', argues that '. . . the major source of distress is usually the individual's internalised homophobia'.

This implies pathology or at least that the lesbian is functioning suboptimally. It implies that the individual lesbian or her relationships could in some way be better and that changes in individuals or couple/group dynamics are required. While paying lip-service to the need for broader social/political change, therapy with lesbians, whether it be 'feminist' or otherwise, aims to change the individual and her interactions with others to alleviate the problems that she/they experience. This is none other than victim-blaming. It once again pathologizes lesbians. The cause of distress resulting from oppression is seen as lying squarely within the individual and, however conceptualized (in terms of intrapsychic conflicts, dysfunctional assumptions and beliefs, etc.), the solution becomes cure: 'Identifying and treating the oppressor within' (Margolies et al., 1987: 229).

Lesbians also seek therapy for help with more general 'human' problems, such as death of a loved one. It is probably true to say that many lesbians have felt better as a result of therapy when they have experienced such distressing events. However, there are problems. If therapy is used to resolve the distress consequent upon unpleasant events that many lesbians experience this has important political implications for us and our lesbian communities. The privatization of distress in a therapeutic setting means that issues of shared concern become marginalized and excluded from everyday discourse. The more this happens the greater the need for therapy. Ordinary, understandable unhappiness is rendered personal, private and pathological. The individual lesbian is rendered isolated and alone in her distress. Something has gone wrong with her and she has nowhere to turn for help and support other than to her therapist. Unhappiness becomes an individual problem that the individual must resolve rather than a shared event that our communities must address, accept and accommodate. Nasty things happen to us all. We all become distressed. Lesbian culture and politics will he an arid place if it cannot incorporate this distress rather than consigning it to the private realm of therapy.

According to Gilbert (1980) a basic principle of feminist therapy is that 'the personal is political'. To pathologize this axiom of feminism in the form of therapy, of whatever genre, is to torture it beyond recognition. The use of psychological constructs such as those of homophobia and internalized homophobia that underpin feminist approaches to helping lesbians attain a positive self-identity and resolve difficulties we experience essentially renders the political personal, individual and pathological. This cannot be construed as feminism.

'PSYCHOLOGICAL PROCESSES'
AND THE NEED FOR AN 'EXPERT'

Having defined the distress experienced by lesbians in terms of our own individual pathology or suboptimal functioning, and therapy as the means of reducing this distress, an expert, in the form of a therapist, is required to sort out what has gone wrong. Before the development of feminist and lesbian therapy, these experts were treated with scepticism in lesbian feminist writing. With the extension of the psychological therapy to lesbian communities the position has changed.

It has become something of a given that lesbian therapists occupy a special position in the social structure of lesbian communities . . . .

We are leaders, teachers, oracles. In much the same way that the clergy, who healed the wounds in the black community, are leaders there, so we, the perceived healers of the wounds of sexism, misogyny, and homophobia, have become leaders among white lesbians. The power available to any therapist is potentially magnified for lesbian therapists because of this special position in our culture. (Brown, 1989: 15)

In understanding distress, both psychologists and feminists have long eschewed the 'medical model'. However, psychological models represent only a marginal departure from traditional disease concepts. Having defined problems in individual terms, the need for individual remedy is implied and, in order to effect this, a framework for understanding what has gone wrong with the person is required. Instead of invoking physical disease labels and processes, the various psychological models have proceeded to invent their own psychological processes that have malfunctioned. Within behavioural models we have 'faulty learning'; within cognitive models we have 'dysfunctional beliefs, assumptions, and thinking errors'; and within psychoanalytic models we have a battle-ground of 'intrapsychic processes': a super-ego and an id–and an ego with the awesome task of trying to balance the demands of the two, and all too often employing dysfunctional defence mechanisms such as internalized homophobia in its efforts.

These processes are not immediately obvious to the person experiencing them, or to anyone other than the therapist. They are the inventions of psychological experts for understanding experience. As such they require experts, in the form of therapists, to interpret them, understand what is going on, and help us to put the problems right. The therapist's initial task is, of course, to teach her client to understand her experience in psychologized terms and to recognize what the 'real' cause of her problems is.

For example, as Padesky (1989) describes, the lesbian client who tells her therapist that she is '. . . concerned with what others may think' has to be made aware, by her therapist, that her 'real' difficulties lie not in others, but in her own negative beliefs about what it means to be a lesbian. She must learn that it is only by confronting and modifying these that her distress can be alleviated. Margolies et al. (1987: 234) similarly point out that 'Clients rarely seek therapy to deal with self-identified internalised homophobia'–they must be helped to realize that this is the 'true' underlying cause of their problems.

The professional expert–the therapist–is not any kind of 'expert in lesbianism'. Rather she is an expert in interpreting the experience of others within a framework the profession has invented. To accord such a therapist expertise over one's beliefs, thoughts and opinions–to accord this expert the power to understand, reframe and reinterpret what we 'really' mean–is not an apolitical exercise and may be dangerous. According to psychological models, if a woman says something, expresses a belief, or opinion, it cannot be taken as her way of understanding her experience and discussed or debated as such–it must be analysed for its 'true' meaning.

Clearly it is possible for a lesbian to reconstruct her experience in the terms of the various psychological models available, but this is essentially a political exercise not a therapeutic one. 'Women's experience' is not some 'given' it '. . . is never prior to the particular social occasions, the discourses, and other practices through which experience becomes articulated . . . . Experience may also be reconstructed, remembered, rearticulated' (Haraway, 1990: 243). Therapy may be construed as one lesbian persuading another that her perspective is correct. However, this is not an open political debate of different values, perspectives and ways of construing experience. Therapy and political debate are quite different enterprises. The therapeutic relationship is a special, privileged one in which one lesbian (the therapist) subtly encourages another (the client) to understand her experience in personal, private, psychological terms. The aim of the enterprise is to improve psychological adjustment and well-being but neither of these occur in a vacuum: adjustment within heteropatriarchal culture means adjustment to heteropatriarchal values. Whilst politics debates and considers issues of morality, right and wrong, social change, therapy nudges, interprets, seeks 'true' meaning in terms of its own framework, seeks individual change and aims to enhance adjustment: adjustment to an anti-lesbian and patriarchal world.

This is anti-feminist and anti-lesbian. Political debate is stifled as such debate is impossible if every belief, opinion or perspective must be interpreted in terms of 'psychological processes': was it 'really' an 'ego defence mechanism' at work, or a 'negative automatic thought' predicated on a 'dysfunctional belief' resulting from 'internalized homophobia'? In this way all political debate has the potential to be psychologized and the psychological expert becomes not only an expert in understanding our experience for us, but also defines our politics, our relationships and our lives.

'EQUALITY' IN THE 'THERAPEUTIC RELATIONSHIP'

Having accorded expert status to the therapist who will help us to interpret our experience, issues then arise about the relationship between ourselves and this expert: the therapist-client or therapeutic relationship.

Feminist commitment to collective, rather than hierarchical, structures is supposedly reflected in a principle of feminist therapy outlined by

Gilbert (1980) and echoed by many others (e.g., Israel, 1985; Penfold and Walker, 1984; Padesky, 1989): there should be an 'egalitarian' client-therapist relationship. However, the feminist principle of collectivity, like that of the 'personal is political', is mutilated to fit into an individualized psychological therapy framework.

The relationship between therapist and client is not an ordinary, everyday relationship, it is a 'special', 'therapeutic' relationship and the concept of equality takes on an alien meaning within its frame. In the psychologized version of the term, equality means encouraging a woman to be self-directed, autonomous and self-nurturant, therapist and client working collaboratively.

This is not my understanding of the term equality. Equality means 'having identical privileges, rights, status', 'evenly balanced' and so forth (*Collins Concise English Dictionary*, 1985)—and a therapist-client relationship can never have these properties. The client goes to the therapist for help, not vice versa; the therapist is the expert ('leader', 'teacher', 'oracle': Brown, 1989); the client tells the therapist about her problems, not vice versa (or only in limited therapeutically desirable amounts in the form of 'self-disclosures'); the client aims to resolve her difficulties via the therapeutic situation, the therapist does not. While the client is '. . . grappling with the issue of lesbian identity' the therapist must remain neutral: 'The goal of therapy, then, is not to achieve a particular identity, but the reduction in internalised homophobia which enables the woman to accept her own desires and experiences and choose her own identity' (Sophie, 1987: 54).

In feminist therapy, therapist and client may work collaboratively, but this does not imply collectivity or the equality of which Gilbert (1980) and others speak: 'collaborate . . . 1. to work with another or others on a joint project. 2. to cooperate as a traitor, esp. with an enemy occupying one's own country' (*Collins Concise English Dictionary*, 1985).

SELF-HELP:
AN EXTENSION OF THE PSYCHOLOGIZATION PROCESS

Recent years have seen an expansion of the therapy industry in the form of a range of 'self-help' approaches. These approaches have been developed within a variety of therapeutic models and are essentially extensions of the psychologization process already described.

Margolies et al. (1987: 234) argue that meeting together as lesbians in 'consciousness raising' or 'political action groups' is of limited value because 'the more deeply internalized forms of homophobia, those without clear political sources, are rarely reached by these' and 'when feelings are not afforded room for conscious expression they are acted out instead . . . the internal forms become more subtle and insidious'–very dangerous, be warned!

Instead, they argue that it is important that lesbians attend one of the many therapy training workshops available, or read one of the various self-help books on the market such as that by Ernst and Goodison (1981) (and judging by the seven reprints of this book, many have). Such texts teach us '. . . a way to understand the use of the therapy process by listing the most basic assumptions which underlie almost all therapy approaches and which make group therapy so different from a consciousness raising group' (Ernst and Goodison, 1981). They outline the various psychological models that we should use to understand our experience; give tortuous detail about how we can be our own expert therapists (what to say, what not to say, how to say it, how not to say it, how not to be judgemental . . .); and tell us how to organize our relationships in the group to ensure that they are therapeutically beneficial. It seems incredible that we ever managed to communicate with each other without them!

The self-help movement, then, shares with lesbian and feminist therapy the majority of the dangers already outlined. However, in extending the psychology empire beyond the availability of trained therapists, it has the potential for a more widespread (and more destructive) influence on lesbian communities.

These, then are some of my general concerns about the role of clinical psychologists, therapists, and the therapy they practise in relation to the problems and distress experienced by lesbians. These concerns apply to all therapeutic approaches. No matter how feminist a therapy purports to be, it essentially transforms the political into personal, individual and pathological terms. Therapy implies that something is wrong with the individual or that she is in some way functioning less well than she might. By offering therapy to lesbians experiencing distress and difficulties, whether these be a direct consequence of anti-lesbianism or not, clinical psychologists and therapists locate the cause of problems, and their solution, firmly within the individual concerned. Attention is thus deflected from a political understanding of the nature and effects of oppression and centres instead upon changing the individual to fit in to an oppressive world. This is not neutral or non-judgemental (as therapists purport to be) but actively supportive of heteropatriarchy and thus anti-lesbian and anti-feminist.

I now move on to illustrate some of these general concerns with reference to a specific set of approaches to helping lesbians–cognitive-behavioural perspectives. These are important because they are probably the most widely used by clinical psychologists working within the Health Service in Britain; they are taught on all clinical psychology training courses; and are currently enjoying an expansionist phase: their use is being extended to a wide range of problems and client groups (Scott et al., 1989). One of these applications has been to work with lesbian clients where a cognitive approach has been hailed as a feminist perspective for helping lesbians to overcome their internalized homophobia and achieve a positive self-identity and better psychological adjustment (Sophie, 1982, 1987; Padesky, 1989).

In part the popularity of such approaches may lie in the fact that they seem to be compatible with, and therapeutic extensions of, the social constructionist/postmodernist theoretical approaches currently favoured in feminist academic circles. It is my contention that this apparent compatibility is illusory and that cognitive therapy shares with other lesbian and feminist therapies all the dangers already outlined.

LESBIANS AND COGNITIVE THERAPY

Cognitive therapy models might best be understood as a development of behavioural models in which it is postulated that a woman's perception of environmental events, rather than the events themselves, determines her behaviour. The meaning a woman imposes on an event determines both her feelings and behaviour. Within a cognitive model it is assumed that these 'cognitive factors' (the ways a woman thinks, the things she thinks, her models of the world) produce distress (depression, anxiety, anger, etc.) and determine what she does. Consequently, therapy to reduce distress and/or change behaviour is directed towards modifying cognitions–changing the way we think and the interpretations we place on events–by challenging our underlying ('dysfunctional') assumptions, beliefs and attitudes.

Within the framework and jargon of a cognitive therapy model 'dysfunctional cognitive structures' (underlying beliefs, assumptions and attitudes) lie dormant, but render a woman vulnerable to distress and disturbance in the face of stress. The combination of stress and dysfunctional cognitive structures causes 'negative cognitive events' (specific thoughts, interpretations of events, ideas of loss) to increase in frequency and intensity, and it is these that lead to distress, disturbance and 'maladaptive' behaviour. These same cognitive factors serve to maintain the distress and disturbance in a kind of negative feedback loop (see, for example, Beck, 1976; Beck et al., 1979; Beck and Emery, 1985; Scott et al., 1989).

Internalized homophobia, within this model, is understood as a set of dysfunctional cognitive structures or cognitive schemata–attitudes, beliefs and assumptions about lesbians that render the lesbian vulnerable to distress when faced with external stresses (e.g., Padesky, 1989; Sophie, 1987). Cognitive restructuring is the name given to the therapeutic process of changing these dysfunctional underlying assumptions, beliefs and attitudes: 'Cognitive restructuring is the basic process which underlies the elimination or reduction of internalised homophobia and its replacement with a positive view of homosexuality' (Sophie, 1987).

Within a cognitive framework, the political is rendered personal and individual through invoking a set of pathological homophobic cognitive structures (beliefs, attitudes and assumptions) that are defined as dysfunctional because they detract from good psychological adjustment in an oppressive world. The task then becomes one of helping the individual to modify her beliefs, attitudes and assumptions, to change what and how she thinks, via therapy.

To change lesbians' minds (homophobic cognitive schemata), cognitive restructuring employs methods of collaborative, so-called, guided discovery: 'the client is assisted in the process of learning to evaluate her experience and draw her own conclusions' (Padesky, 1989). This does not involve the application of a unitary set of techniques in cookbook fashion. Instead, it is characterized by a perspective that aims to bring about changes in underlying dysfunctional attitudes, beliefs and assumptions via a variety of means. Williams and Moorey (1989) have categorized these into a hierarchy of three 'levels of complexity': behavioural techniques, cognitive coping strategies (both designed to facilitate cognitive restructuring); and direct attention to the cognitive events and underlying assumptions and beliefs themselves.

In employing a cognitive therapy framework to reduce internalized homophobia, behavioural techniques include such 'therapeutic interventions' as meeting other lesbians' and 'habituation to lesbianism', 'reading positive lesbian and gay literature can [also] be helpful . . .' (Sophie, 1987: 62-3). Within a cognitive therapy framework, these are seen as facilitating cognitive restructuring by providing the evidence necessary for contradicting negative stereotypes and providing positive role models. Engagement with the lesbian community, with its politics and culture, is thus transformed into a therapeutic exercise.

Amongst the cognitive coping strategies most frequently discussed in relation to therapy with lesbians, self-labelling and self-disclosure are generally considered to be of central importance in the development and maintenance of a positive self-identity and healthy psychological adjustment (e.g., de Monteflores and Schultz, 1978; Beane, 1981; Coleman,

1982; Sophie, 1982, 1987; Miranda and Storms, 1989). Indeed, Sophie (1987) argues that one of the indicators of the success of therapy (whether internalized homophobia has been reduced) is positive self-disclosures.

'Through presenting these *political* strategies in the individualized terms of mental health, psychology again seeks to depoliticize lesbianism' (Kitzinger, 1987: 151). A politically desirable lesbian visibility in challenging anti-lesbianism is transformed into individual, psychologized terms: 'self-labelling may be an important intrapersonal strategy and self-disclosure may be an important interpersonal strategy related to positive lesbian and gay identity' (Miranda and Storms, 1989: 41). This psychologization of a political decision (to be visible or not) serves to deny political reality: discrimination exists and many lesbians, including a large number of lesbians who are psychologists and therapists, consider it politically inexpedient to be open about their lesbianism. From a feminist perspective this is a political decision based on political reality—not some reflection of individual pathology indicating poor psychological adjustment.

In addition to these behavioural and cognitive coping strategies, cognitive therapy addresses cognitive structures and cognitive events directly. In an attempt to achieve the desired cognitive restructuring lesbians are encouraged to make explicit, challenge and modify our homophobic beliefs and attitudes. 'Negative stereotypes of lesbians are similar to other irrational ideas and can be uncovered and challenged in the same way in therapy' (Sophie, 1987: 57). However, the form of this challenge is not open debate of different perspectives. No, this is therapy. 'When people relate facts, they are asked about their interpretations, their thoughts, their feelings. When they make a statement about themselves, the statement is reflected back but only after having been gently placed within a cognitive framework. The therapist's style thus acts as a model . . .' (Williams and Moorey, 1989: 229); 'new learning has much greater impact if it comes from Socratic nudging . . .' (Padesky, 1989: 150). Via use of subtle questions 'which implicitly reflect the cognitive framework' (Williams and Moorey, 1989: 230), the therapist elicits the lesbian's thoughts and interpretations of events; infers/identifies from these her underlying homophobic cognitive schemata; and helps her to recognize these, and to realize that her beliefs may be 'dysfunctional', that there are other ways of looking at things. Padesky (1989) further argues that such cognitive restructuring approaches are a means by which lesbians themselves can reduce the homophobia of others. Thus social change, the elimination of lesbian oppression, is transformed into an individual therapeutic exercise of cognitive restructuring to eliminate homophobia!

Although cognitive therapy talks about 'dysfunctional cognitive structures' as underlying assumptions, beliefs and attitudes, these cannot be separated from less neutral terms like politics, morals, ethics and values. Within a cognitive framework, these are transformed into personalized, and potentially dysfunctional, homophobic cognitive schemata. When dysfunctional they require individual solutions in the form of cognitive restructuring (usually with the assistance of a therapist because finding underlying cognitive structures and modifying them can be a tricky business!).

Within this framework, our oppression, the problems it produces, and the ways in which we deal with these, cease to be the province of rational political debate, consciousness raising and collective political action. Instead, the locus of problems and change is placed squarely within the pathological beliefs of the individual lesbian, and change becomes a therapeutic exercise: defining and modifying what we think and believe via a process of 'guided discovery'. This process is designed to increase our personal well-being–psychological adjustment–and may be achieved by group or individual therapy or via various self-help approaches. The guide is the expert–the therapist–either in person or via the books and courses she produces so that we can be our own psychologists.

Claims that this constitutes a feminist approach to therapy (Sophie, 1987; Padesky, 1989) should be treated with caution. A belief is dysfunctional if it leads to distress and behaviour deemed inappropriate in the context in which it occurs. Beliefs most likely to lead to 'adaptive' behaviour and the absence of anxiety, anger, depression and so forth are those consonant with prevailing societal norms and values: anti-lesbian and patriarchal values and ideas which see lesbianism as either remediable deviance or harmless lifestyle choice. To hold an alternative perspective, to believe something other than the accepted wisdom of an anti-lesbian world may at times exacerbate distress and result in behaviour construed as dysfunctional.

I, for example, hold a set of lesbian feminist beliefs and assumptions, and these no doubt guide my behaviour. The things I do may not always be considered 'functional': expressing views such as those in this paper is unlikely to be 'functional' in furthering my career either as a clinical psychologist, or as a 'lesbian feminist' therapist. By holding, and expressing such views I encounter anger and hostility from others and this can, and has, caused me distress. I have frequently questioned my beliefs, actions and feelings–debated, discussed them with others whose opinions I value. I am sure that a cognitive therapist would agree that I should challenge such beliefs, feelings and behaviours, but within a psychologized framework the nature of this process would be changed. Cognitive therapy would encourage me to question the underlying assumptions and beliefs about the oppressive nature of the world in which we live that give rise to the views I have expressed about the anti-lesbian nature of purportedly lesbian and feminist therapies. I should look at the consequences of these upon my well-being. If I find that, in expressing views such as those in this paper I encounter anger and 'hostility and that these reactions from others cause me personal distress (as they do), then I should conclude that my lesbian feminist beliefs are dysfunctional to my adjustment and well-being–I should test out alternative, more adaptive assumptions and beliefs. Maybe I should think that lesbianism is a harmless lifestyle choice, that I represent no threat to heteropatriarchal order and that those who think otherwise suffer homophobia and lesbophobia–problems for which they can be helped through therapy. I could then gain the acceptance of psychologists and therapists and practise without qualms the therapies in which I have been trained: I would then be better adjusted to the world in which I live.

The terms functional and dysfunctional have a scientific, value-free ring about them, consonant with therapy's claims, and therapists' desire, to be neutral and non-judgemental. This neutrality is illusory: 'functional' and 'dysfunctional' are no different from terms like 'good/bad', 'right/wrong' and the question is: 'functional/dysfunctional' for what, on whose terms . . . ? These are political questions–or as clinical psychologists would prefer 'value judgements'.

Within a therapeutic framework issues of right and wrong, good and bad, can only be considered in terms of individual adjustment and well-being: that which makes me feel good and allows me to function in a heteropatriarchal world is by definition right and good, that which does not is wrong. This is not feminism. These are political questions and as feminists we must treat them as such. There are morals and values–lesbian feminist politics–beyond personal adjustment and well-being: the broader social and political context must not be lost. To consign judgements about right and wrong, good and bad, to the therapeutic preserve is extremely dangerous.

Our beliefs, attitudes and assumptions, our feelings and behaviour–the targets of 'therapeutic' change in cognitive as in all therapies–have been formed and exist within a social and political context: '. . . our "inner selves"–the way we think and feel about and how we define ourselves–are connected in an active and reciprocal way with larger social and political structures and processes in the context of which they are construed' (Kitzinger, 1987: 62). The personal is political.

ACKNOWLEDGEMENTS

Many thanks to Celia Kitzinger for her encouragement and helpful comments on earlier drafts of this paper, and to Sue Wilkinson for assistance with the title.

REFERENCES

Beane, J. (1981) '"I'd Rather Be Dead Than Gay": Counseling with Gay Men Who Are Coming Out', *The Personnel and Guidance Journal* 60: 222-6.

Beck, A.T. (1976) *Cognitive Therapy and the Emotional Disorders.* New York: International Universities Press.

Beck, A.T. and Emery, G.D. (1985) *Anxiety Disorders and Phobias: A Cognitive Perspective.* New York: Basic Books.

Beck, A.T., Rush, A.J., Shaw, B.F. and Emery, G. (1979) *Cognitive Therapy of Depression.* New York: The Guilford Press.

Brown, L.S. (1989) 'Beyond Thou Shalt Not: Thinking about Ethics in the Lesbian Therapy Community', *Women & Therapy* 8(1-2): 13-25.

Coleman, E. (1982) 'Developmental Stages in the Coming-out Process', in W. Paul, J.D. Weinrich, J.C. Gonsiorek and M.E. Hotvedt (eds) *Homosexuality: Social, Psychological and Biological Issues.* Newbury Park, CA: Sage.

Collins Concise English Dictionary (1985) London: Guild Publishing.

de Monteflores, C. and Schultz, S.J. (1978) 'Coming Out; Similarities and Differences for Lesbians and Gay Men', *Journal of Social Issues* 34: 180-97.

Ernst, S. and Goodison, L. (1981) *In Our Own Hands. A Book of Self-help Therapy.* London: Women's Press.

Gilbert, L.A. (1980) 'Feminist Therapy', in A.M. Brodsky and R. Hare-Mustin (eds) *Women and Psychotherapy: An Assessment of Research and Practice.* New York: Guilford Press.

Haraway, D. (1990) 'Reading Buchi Emecheta: Contests for Women's Experience in Women's Studies', *Women: A Cultural Review* 1(3): 240-55.

Israel, J. (1985) 'Feminist Therapy', in C.T. Mowbray, S. Lanir and M. Hulce (eds) *Women and Mental Health.* New York: Harrington Park Press.

Jones, R. (1988) 'With Respect to Lesbians', *Nursing Times* 18(20): 48-9.

Kitzinger, C. (1987) *The Social Construction of Lesbianism.* London: Sage.

Kitzinger, C. (1989) 'Heteropatriarchal Language: The Case Against Homophobia', *Gossip: A Journal of Lesbian Feminist Ethics* 5: 15-20.

Margolies, L., Becker, M. and Jackson-Brewer, K. (1987) 'Internalised Homophobia: Identifying and Treating the Oppressor Within', in Boston Lesbian Psychologies Collective (ed.) *Lesbian Psychologies.* Chicago: University of Illinois Press.

Miranda, J. and Storms, M. (1989) 'Psychological Adjustment of Lesbians and Gay Men', *Journal of Counseling and Development* 68: 41-5.

Mitchell, V. (1989) 'Using Kohut's Self Psychology in Work with Lesbian Couples', *Women & Therapy* 8(1-2): 157-66.

Newman, B.S. (1989) 'The Relative Importance of Gender Role Attitudes to Male and Female Attitudes toward Lesbians', *Sex Roles* 21(7-8): 451-65.

Padesky, C.A. (1989) 'Attaining and Maintaining Positive Self-identity: A Cognitive Therapy Approach', *Women & Therapy* 8(1-2): 145-56.

Penfold, P.S. and Walker, G.A. (1984) *Women and the Psychiatric Paradox.* Milton Keynes: Open University Press.

Poverny, L.M. and Finch, W.A. (1988) 'Integrating Work-related Issues on Gay and Lesbian Employees into Occupational Social Work Practice', *Employers' Assistance Quarterly* 4(2): 15-29.

Randell, C.E. (1989) 'Lesbian Phobia among BSN Educators: A Survey', *Journal of Nurse Education* 28(7): 302-6.

Rothblum, E.D. (1989) 'Introduction: Lesbianism as a Model of a Positive Lifestyle for Women', *Women & Therapy* 8(1-2): 1-12.

Rudolph, J. (1989) 'Effects of a Workshop on Mental Health Practitioners' Attitudes toward Homosexuality and Counseling Effectiveness', *Journal of Counseling and Development* 68: 81-5.

Ryan, J. (1983) 'Psychoanalysis and Women Loving Women', in S. Cartledge and J. Ryan (eds) *Sex and Love. New Thoughts on Old Contradictions.* London: Women's Press.

Sang, B.E. (1989) 'New Directions in Lesbian Research, Theory, and Education', *Journal of Counseling and Development* 68: 92-6.

Schmitz, T.J. (1988) 'Career Counseling Implications with the Gay and Lesbian Population', *Journal of Employment Counselling* 25(2): 51-6.

Scott, J., Williams, J.M.G. and Beck, A.T., eds (1989) *Cognitive Therapy in Clinical Practice.* London: Routledge.

Seigel, R.J. (1987) 'Beyond Homophobia: Learning to Work with Lesbian Clients', *Women and Therapy* 6(1-2): 125-33.

Smalley, S. (1987) 'Dependency Issues in Lesbian Relationships', *Journal of Homosexuality* 14(1-2): 125-35.

Sophie, J. (1982) 'Counseling Lesbians', *The Personnel and Guidance Journal* 6: 341-5.

Sophie, J. (1987) 'Internalised Homophobia and Lesbian Identity', *Journal of Homosexuality* 14(1-2): 53-65.

Starzecpyzel, E. (1987) 'The Persephone Complex: Incest Dynamics and the Lesbian Preference', in Boston Lesbian Psychologies Collective (ed.) *Lesbian Psychologies.* Chicago: University of Illinois Press.

Weinberg, G. (1973) *Society and the Healthy Homosexual.* New York: St Martins Press.

Williams, J.M.G. and Moorey, S. (1989) 'The Wider Application of Cognitive Therapy: The End of the Beginning', in J. Scott, J.M.G. Williams and A.T. Beck (eds) *Cognitive Therapy in Clinical Practice.* London: Routledge.

Putting the Politics Back into Lesbianism

Janice G. Raymond

SUMMARY. This article contrasts lesbianism as a political move-ment to lesbianism as a lifestyle. It addresses the current emphasis in lesbian circles on "sex as salvation," and maintains that this empha-sis re-sexualizes women and de-politicizes lesbianism. The liberal-ism of lesbian lifestylism makes the male-power modes of sexuality, such as s & m, butch-femme, and bondage and domination, sexy for women. In the name of tolerance, difference, and lesbian communi-ty, many lesbians are dissuaded from making judgments and oppos-ing such acts. Finally, the article describes the values of a lesbian feminism that has principles, politics, and passion. It proposes a con-text for what lesbian sexuality might look like rooted in lesbian imagination—not lesbian fantasies.

This article was originally a talk given to the Lesbian Summer School at Wesley House in London, July, 1988.

Janice G. Raymond, *Women's Studies International Forum* Volume 12, Num-ber 2, "Putting the Politics Back into Lesbianism," © 1989 Elsevier Science Limited, Oxford, England. Reprinted with permission.

[Haworth co-indexing entry note]: "Putting the Politics Back into Lesbianism." Raymond, Janice G. Co-published simultaneously in *Journal of Lesbian Studies* (The Haworth Press, Inc.) Vol. 1, No. 2, 1997, pp. 273-286; and: *Classics in Lesbian Studies* (ed: Esther D. Rothblum) The Haworth Press, Inc., 1997, pp. 273-286; and: *Classics in Lesbian Studies* (ed: Esther D. Rothblum) Harrington Park Press, an imprint of The Haworth Press, Inc., 1997, pp. 273-286.

We used to talk a lot about lesbianism as a political movement—back in the old days when lesbianism and feminism went together, and one heard the phrase, lesbian feminism. Today, we hear more about lesbian sadomasochism, lesbians having babies, and everything lesbians need to know about sex—what has fashionably come to be called the "politics of desire." In this article, I want to talk about *lesbianism as a political movement,* but before doing that it is necessary to address *lesbianism as a lifestyle*—what has for many come to be a sexual preference without a feminist politics.

For one thing, this lesbian lifestyle is preoccupied with sex. Not lesbian sexuality as a political statement, that is, as a challenge to hetero-reality, but lesbian sex as fucking—how to do it, when to do it, what makes it work—in short how to liberate lesbian libido. Lesbian lifestylers and hetero-conservatives agree on one thing—that for women sex is salvation—something that will get us into the promised land, the afterlife, that amazing grace. For example, Marabel Morgan in *The Total Woman* teaches right-wing Christian women how to act out the fantasies of their husbands complete with all the accoutrements and sexual postures that would rival the lesbian libertarian warehouse. For the Marabel Morgans of this world, inside marriage, anything goes. A wife should act like a mistress. Samois, an American lesbian sadomasochist group, embraces whips and chains, "pain is pleasure, enslavement by consent, freedom-through-bondage, reality-as-game, [and] equality-through-role-play" (Meredith, 1982, p. 97). Outside marriage, in fact outside heterosexuality, anything goes. Lesbian liberation has become lesbian libertarianism.

In comparing Marabel Morgan to Samois, are we talking about the *difference* between a lullaby and heavy metal? Or are we talking about the *similarities* between those bumper stickers that read "sea divers do it deeper," "sky divers do it higher," "conservatives do it with conscience," "lesbians do it with lust?" There seems to be little difference between a conservative world view which locates women in this world sexually for men and a lesbian libertarian lifestyle that is increasingly preoccupied with fucking as the apogée of lesbian existence. For all the perpetual talk about sex, libertarian lesbian discourse is speechless about its connection to the rest of a woman's life and, therefore, it is speechless about sex itself.

In *The Sexuality Papers,* Margaret Jackson points out that historically, female sexuality has been defined, paradoxically, as both different from and the same as male sexuality. As different, female sexuality has been portrayed as difficult to arouse, more emotional, and less localized; as similar, it has been depicted as originating in the same biological drive. Traditionally, the *differentness* of female sexuality has been used to show how it complements male sexuality and thus legitimates heterosexuality as the natural and normative condition of sexual existence for women; its sameness to male sexuality has been used to legitimate the forms that male sexuality has taken and to proclaim those forms as transcending gender. "To put it another way, female sexuality has been remoulded on the model of male sexuality, so that [women] are now held to equal or even surpass men in terms of our sexual capacity" (Jackson, 1984, p. 81).

The emphasis in the most recent lesbian lifestyle and libertarian theories of sexuality has tended to confirm the *sameness* of female sexuality to male sexuality—evidenced by the supposed "fact" that women act, or want to act, or should be free to act, in the same ways that men have been able to act sexually. Lesbian lifestylers argue that female-female sexuality must be "freed up" to take on the forms of the male-power model of male sexuality, that is, the forms that have endowed males with the power of uninhibited sexuality in a patriarchal society. The various forms that male-power sex has taken—s & m, pornography, butch-femme role playing, pederasty, etc.—will supposedly release the so-called "repressed power" of female sexuality.

The libertarians and lesbian lifestylers might protest that male sexuality has no corner on these forms. Many would maintain that these forms of sexuality have existed repressed in the very being of women, only waiting to be called forth by a different social context in which women are encouraged to express themselves with the sexual latitude that men have enjoyed. Several years ago, in the United States, a group called FACT (Feminist Anti-Censorship Taskforce)—composed of academics, lawyers, artists, literati, and many big-name feminists—joined forces with the pornography industry to do battle against feminist civil rights legislation that makes pornography legally actionable. FACT defends pornography specifically citing the need that lesbians have for it, and calling it "enjoyable sexually arousing material" which women must have the freedom to choose. "The range of feminist imagination and expression in the realm of sexuality has barely begun to find voice. Women need the socially recognized space to appropriate for themselves the robustness of what traditionally has been male language," that is, pornography (FACT, 1985, p. 31).

What is wrong here is not the assertion that women need more sexual latitude, but its confinement to the forms that male sexuality has taken. The sexual libertarians and lesbian lifestylers, for all their emphasis on sexual fantasy, lack real sexual imagination. There is a lot of sexy talk in the libertarian literature about the necessity for women to he freed from the chains of the "goody-goody" concept of eroticism, from femininity posing as feminism, and from sentimental, spiritualized, and soft sex. Yet nowhere do we see the forms that this vital, vigorous, and robust female sexuality would take articulated as anything different than the forms of the male-power sexuality model.

The modes and manifestations of sexuality that the libertarians and lesbian lifestylers hold up as liberating range from the innocuous to the injurious. The melange of forms that have been given equal status, and represented as rebellious sex for women, deserves analysis on these grounds alone. For example, Ellen Willis states, "It is precisely sex as an aggressive, unladylike activity, an expression of violent and unpretty emotion, an exercise of erotic power, and a specifically genital experience that has been taboo for women" (Willis, 1983, p. 85). Side by side, we see Willis equating "sex as aggressive" and as "violent emotion," with sex as the "exercise of erotic power" and "genital experience." All are represented as mere taboo. No slippery slope here; just slippery prose for slippery goals.

Judith Walkowitz has termed the libertarian perspective on sexuality the "advanced position" (Diary, 1981, p. 72). It is difficult to see what is so advanced or progressive about a position that locates "desire," and that imprisons female sexual dynamism, vitality, and vigor, in old forms of sexual objectification, subordination, and violence, this time initiated by women and done with women's consent. The libertarians offer a supposed sexuality stripped naked of feminine taboo, but only able to dress itself in masculine garb. It is a male-constructed sexuality in drag.

But more appears in this drag show than the male-power sexual actors and activities. De-politicizing is also in drag, disguised as the social construction of sexuality. When the social construction of sexuality entered the center stage of feminist discourse, the politics of sexuality and sexual domination were forced to exit—and so too were the politics of lesbianism. For example, the editors of *Desire: The Politics of Sexuality* argue that lesbianism has been *unsexed*—by a sexual consensus between lesbians and heterosexual feminists that "theoretically accepted each other's moderated, healthy sexual proclivities . . . in somewhat the same spirit that St. Paul accepted the inevitability of marriage for those weak of flesh and soul" (Snitow, Stansell, & Thompson, 1983, p. 27). The "advanced position" does not talk about political lesbianism and compulsive heterosexuality anymore. They have been relegated to a bit part in feminist discourse. And it's those extremist, anti-sex, repressed, puritanical radical feminists who insist on giving them even that much of a role!

There is the arrogant and patronizing assumption in libertarian arguments that those who make problematic the concept of sexual pleasure are themselves deprived of its more vital and vigorous delights. Sexual wimps! Problematizing the concept of sexual pleasure means talking about male power. So the "advanced position" hardly talks about male power anymore–that's simplistic and grim. And as the FACT brief so facilely phrased it, that only portrays men as vicious "attack dogs" and women as victims (FACT, 1985, p. 39). Instead, the libertarian position talks a lot about social conditioning to sexuality or the role of socialization in achieving a sexuality. So that when men act in certain ways, they are mere products of their socialization, as are women. These theories lack a concept of power that highlights that male sexuality is bound up with power–that there are positive advantages in status, ego, and authority for men in the ways they have exercised their sexuality. Women cannot uncritically bracket this analysis in order to revel in the joy of sex.

The scenario of sexual forms that mimic the male-power mode of sexuality is only one focus. Another, as Susanne Kappeler has pointed out with respect to pornography, is the *structure of representation* that must be taken into consideration. This means that somebody is making those representations, and somebody is looking at them, "through a complex array of means and conventions" (Kappeler, 1986, p. 3). The libertarians and lesbian lifestylers tell us that the sexual actors who act out certain roles, such as butch/femme and master/slave, are women who can be both subjects and objects in the sexual event. In other words, when lesbians, for example, take on butch/femme or master/slave roles, because they are two women–two lesbians–engaged in such sex "play," no one is objectified, hurt, or violated. Libertarianism and lesbian lifestylism purport to level the cultural inequality of male subject and female object. Let's look more closely at this claim.

Many libertarians and lesbian lifestylers, when they engage in various sexual acts, claim that they and their acts are resolutely sequestered from anything these acts might represent "out there." The privacy of the bedroom and what goes on there is separated, they say, from reality, in a "room of one's own"–the libertarian and lesbian lifestyle sphere of *fantasy*. In sado-masochism, for example, the whips, the chains, the swastikas, the military paraphernalia, the handcuffs, the dog collars, the masters, the slaves have no dimension in the real world. The master or slave roles for example, are treated in a world apart, in a sanctuary of sexual activity, where the game is played according to other rules, valid in that fantasy world. The artist insulates the aesthetic, often claiming it as a reality-free zone. The libertarian in the same insular fashion attempts to shelter the sexual sphere making her activities here independent of reality, independent of critique. The sexual actors and activities exist in a rarefied atmosphere. It's like playing in the sandbox, or more accurately in the kitty litter box.

The libertarians and lesbian lifestylers would have it that until women "deal with" the whole issue of sexuality, no true liberation will ensue. What this focus has achieved is the re-sexualization of women, this time in the name of women's liberation. The sexualization of women, of course, is an old theme that is common to both old and "new" sex reformers and sexologists, as is the theme that women need to be freed up sexually in order to be liberated. Havelock Ellis said it, as did Kinsey, and most recently Masters and Johnson. But this time the "new" sex reformers are women, and the theme is that the female sexual urge is enormously powerful, more so than it has been given credit for in the flaccid feminist literature that preceded this particular libertarian "sexual revolution."

The hidden dogmatism here is that sex is the source of power. Sex is central—not creativity, not thinking, not anything else but sex. Following a kind of Freudian line, the libertarians exert a re-conservatizing influence on feminism and lesbianism essentializing some vaguely defined "power of desire."

Sexuality seems to be at the base of everything in the libertarian and lesbian lifestyle literature. Here, the primacy of sex is reasserted, this time not necessarily as a biological drive, but as a propelling social force—a force that has not only influence but deterministic power. Sexuality takes on the tone of a new natural law theory in libertarian discourse, reversing the "anatomy is destiny" theory of sexuality into a theory of social determinism. Sex as a primary biological drive reappears in sex as a primary social motor, driving itself to fulfillment by utilizing all of the male-power modes of sexual objectification, subordination, and oppression. Like any motor, sex requires the assistance of tinkering and technique. The mechanistic model once more prevails.

Can we so readily believe that sex is our salvation? Haven't we heard this line before—that what really counts is the quality of our sex lives, our orgasms?

Our most recent wave of feminism has spent much of its time de-sexualizing the images of women in the media, the marketplace, and the cosmos in general. What the libertarian position has succeeded in doing is re-sexualizing women, using feminist and lesbian liberation rhetoric to assert that sexuality is a radical impulse. But sexuality is no more radical than anything else. There are certain forms of it that may be radical and there are certain forms of it that are not. It is ironic that the libertarians want to reassert the male-power forms of sexuality to empower women.

This was not always the case, however. There was a time when this movement called lesbian feminism had a passion, principles, and politics.

Without romanticizing that period as the golden age of lesbian feminism, I would like to recall for us what that movement was and what it stood for.

This movement was the strongest challenge to hetero-reality that feminism embodied. It challenged the worldview that women exist for men and primarily in relation to them. It challenged the history of women as primarily revealed in the family—a history that often in the best of accounts, rendered women only in relation to men and male-defined events. It challenged that seemingly eternal truth that "Thou as a woman must bond with a man," forever seeking our lost halves in the complementarity of hetero-relations. It even challenged the definition of feminism itself as the equality of women with men. Instead, it made real a vision of the equality of women with our Selves. It defined equality as being equal to those women who have been for women, those who have lived for women's freedom and those who have died for it; those who have fought for women and survived by women's strength; those who have loved women and who have realized that without the consciousness and conviction that women are primary in each other's lives, nothing else is in perspective.

This movement worked on behalf of all women. It wasn't afraid to define rape as sex—not just violence but sex. It criticized prostitution and pornography as sexually hip for women and wasn't afraid to speak out against the male sexual revolutionaries who wanted to liberate all the women they could get access to in the name of this fake freedom. It established centers for battered women and led the feminist campaign against violence against women.

But then something happened. Women—often other lesbians—began to define things differently. Pornography came to be called erotica and enlisted in the service of lesbian speech and self-expression. Violence against women came to be called lesbian sadomasochism and enlisted in the service of lesbian sex, that is, fucking. Prostitution came to be called necessary women's work and enlisted in the service of female economic reality. What had changed was that instead of men, women—including women who called themselves lesbians—were endorsing these activities for other women. And other women, other lesbians, were reluctant to criticize in the name of some pseudo-feminist and lesbian unity.

Certainly many lesbians resisted these debasements of women's lives. Certainly, many lesbians are still in the forefront of the anti-pornography movement. Many lesbians are fighting worldwide against international prostitution and sex slavery. And many lesbians have spoken out against lesbian sadomasochism. But whereas formerly, you could count on a political movement of lesbian feminism to fight against these antifeminist activities, the politics of lesbian feminism has diminished.

Lesbian feminism was a movement based on the power of a "we," not on an individual woman's fantasy or self-expression. This was a movement that had a politics—that realized that prostitution, pornography, and sexual violence could not be redefined as therapeutic, economic, or sexy to fit any individual woman's whim in the name of free choice. It was a movement that recognized the complexities of choice and how so-called choices for women are politically constructed.

Now I want to tell you a story—about choice, because every time radical feminists point out the political construction of women's choices, we are accused of being condescending to women and of making women into victims. Thus, my story.

Once upon a time, in the beginnings of this wave of feminism, there was a feminist consensus that women's choices were constructed, burdened, framed, impaired, constrained, limited, coerced, shaped, etc. by patriarchy. No one proposed that this meant women's choices were *determined,* or that women were passive or helpless victims of the patriarchy. That was because many women believed in the power of feminism to change women's lives and obviously, women could not change if they were socially determined in their roles or pliant putty in the hands of the patriarchs. We even talked about compulsory motherhood and yes, compulsory heterosexuality! We talked about the ways in which women and young girls were seasoned into prostitution, accommodated themselves to male battering, and were channeled into low paying and dead-ended jobs. And the more moderate among us talked about sex roles socialization. The more radical wrote manifestos detailing the patriarchal construction of women's oppression. But most of us agreed, that call it what you will, women were not free just to be "you and me."

Time passed, and along came a more "nuanced" view of feminism. It told us to watch our language of women as victims. More women went to graduate and professional schools, grew "smarter," were received at the bar, went into the academy, and became experts in all sorts of fields. They partook of the power that the male gods had created and "saw that it was good." They perceived the plethora of options available to them, and thus they projected to all women, and voilà the gospel of unadulterated choice. They started saying things like " . . . great care needs to be taken not to portray women as incapable of responsible decisions" (Andrews, 1987, p. 46).

Some women thought these words were familiar, that they had heard them before, but the feminist discourse analysts didn't seem particularly interested in tracing this back to what "old-fashioned" feminists labelled liberal patriarchal discourse. They said this was boring and outmoded, and besides women had already heard enough of this, and it was depressing. Let's not be simplistic and blame men, they said, since this analysis "offers so few leverage points for action, so few imaginative entry points for visions of change" (Snitow et al., 1983. p. 30). Instead they began to talk about the "Happy Breeders," and the "Happy Hookers" and the "women who loved it" and those who would love it if they could only have "the freedom and the socially recognized space to appropriate for themselves the robustness of what traditionally has been male language" (read pornography).

This was familiar too, but then something strange happened. Those women who had noted the thread of continuity between liberal patriarchal men and FACT feminism, for example, began to notice that instead of women mimicking male speech, men began to mimic women. In the United States, along came a phenomenon called surrogate motherhood. A New Jersey court decision upheld the right of men to buy women—paid breeders—to have their babies for them (Superior Court of New Jersey, 1987). But one of these so-called surrogates decided to fight for herself and her child, recognizing that surrogacy exploits women. This was popularly known as the case of Mary Beth Whitehead versus Bill Stern. Gary Skoloff, the lawyer for Bill Stern in the New Jersey surrogacy case, summed up his court argument by saying: "If you prevent women from becoming surrogate mothers and deny them the freedom to decide . . . you are saying that they do not have the ability to make their own decisions . . . It's being unfairly paternalistic and it's an insult to the female population of this nation." Some women felt that "Imitation is the sincerest of flattery." They began to testify in favor of things like pornography and surrogacy so that they could imitate all the men who imitated them. It became difficult to tell who was imitating whom.

And then American legislators began to submit bills advocating surrogate contracts, with proper regulations of course, that mostly protected the sperm donor and the brokerage agencies, because feminism was in the best interests of men, and finally men had realized this. It was as the feminist humanists had always said, that feminism is good for men too.

Before this decision was reversed by a higher court, the judge, Harvey Sorkow, proclaimed that Bill Stern was overwhelmed with the "intense desire" to procreate and even said it was "within the soul." He said the feminist argument that an "elite upper economic group of people will use the lower economic group of women to 'make their babies'" was "insensitive and offensive" to the Bill Sterns of this world. A man of feeling himself, he said that Mary Beth Whitehead was a "woman without empathy." He was very concerned that Mr. Stern experience his "fulfillment" as a father, and so he gave him Baby Sara whom Mr. Stern called Baby Melissa.

Shortly before this, the Attorney General convened a Commission on Pornography which heard testimony from women who had been brought into pornography. Howard Kurtz of the *Washington Post,* another man of feeling, questioned the veracity of these women by caricaturing their feelings. ". . . a parade of *self-described victims* who tell their *sad stories* from behind an opaque screen . . . Many experts on both sides of the question say such *anecdotal tales of woe* prove nothing about the effect of sexually explicit materials" (Kurtz, 1985, A4, emphasis mine). Not to be outdone in feeling, Carol Vance poured scorn on the testimony of these same women by quoting with approval a male reporter who would nudge her during the hearings and say "phoney witness" (Coveney & Kaye, 1987, p. 12).

To make a long story short, the men got this language of disbelief from feminists who are now telling us that victims of pornography choose their own beds to lie in. Mary Beth Whitehead chose to sign her contract. All men and women of feeling understand this. It's our right to choose, after all, which is at stake. Pornography and surrogacy protect that right of choice. This kind of freedom of choice, this kind of liberty is liberalism. And unfortunately, lifestyle lesbianism is also liberalism.

The liberalism of lifestyle lesbianism means that *we*–that is, lesbians– can't say *we* anymore. Instead, women say: "in my opinion," or "for me," or "as I see it" or 'I have the right to what turns me on." So what are we left with? Certainly not political lesbianism which cannot even frame a sentence in the first person plural at this point in lesbian history. No, rather–an extremely self-centered lesbian worldview. And we are left with a tyranny of tolerance that passes for difference.

It is as if every individual desire has become a personal or cultural difference that other women must not only tolerate but also promote. So one woman's *desire,* rationalized as a *need* to free up her sexuality by engaging in s & m for example, must be tolerated by other women and/or lesbians in the name of promoting lesbian differences and fostering lesbian unity by making room for all such differences. In the name of some amorphously defined feminist and/or lesbian community, value judgments cannot be made because that's being divisive. What kind of unity can be built on an unwillingness to make judgments?

For example, many women vaguely "feel" that so-called lesbian sadomasochism is wrong but hold themselves back from translating that feeling into words and action. Other women tell them that no one has the right to judge the behavior of others or enforce one's own values. This is what I mean by a tyranny of tolerance–"doing your own thing." The tyranny of tolerance dissuades women from tough-minded thinking, from responsibility for disagreeing with others, and from the will to act. This puts us in an extremely passive position. What is defined as value freedom, that is, not making judgments, may appear sensitive to and respectful of other women but in reality it makes women passive and uncritical since it stops both judgments and action. And active social and political life stem from values, choices, and activities that are defined with clarity and exercised with commitment.

Mary Daly has outlined several elements of radical feminism (Daly, 1984, pp. 397-398; Daly, 1987, p. 75). In a similar fashion I would highlight several commonly-held values of Lesbian feminism that allow us to say *we* again. If we are lesbian feminists, we have clear and present knowledge that the boys, and some of the girls, are not going to like us and that we just might run into trouble along the way.

If we are lesbian feminists, we are radically different from what the hetero-society wants us to be. It not a fake difference, but a real difference. For example, lesbian sexuality is *different,* rooted in the lesbian imagination. It is not the same old sexuality that women must submit to in hetero-reality. It is not pornography, it is not butch and femme, and it is not bondage and domination. It is for one thing, a sexuality that is imagination rooted in reality. As Andrea Dworkin has written, "Imagination is not a synonym for sexual fantasy . . ." Fantasy can only conjure up a scripted bag of tricks that are an endless repetition of heterosexual conformist practices. "Imagination finds new meanings, new forms; values and acts. The person with imagination is pushed forward by it into a world of possibility and risk, a distinct world of meaning and choice" (Dworkin, 1987, p. 48); not into the heterosexual junkyard of lesbian libertarian and lifestyle activities that get recycled to women as fantastic goods. Lesbian lifestylism puts fantasy in place of imagination. Have you ever noticed how everyone talks about their fantasies. and not about imagination?

If we are lesbian feminists, we feel and act on behalf of women as women. Lesbian feminism is not a one issue movement. It makes connections between all issues that affect women—not only what affects this particular group, class, nationality, and not only what affects lesbians. We feel and act for all women because we are women, and even if we were the last ones to profess this, we would still be there for women.

If we are lesbian feminists, we keep going. Even when it's not popular. Even when it's not rewarded. Not just yesterday. Not just today. Not just a couple of hours on the weekend. Lesbian feminism is a way of life, a way of living for our deepest Selves and for other women.

And those who think that the objectification, subordination and violation of women is acceptable just as long as you call it lesbian erotica or lesbian sadomasochism–they're not lesbian feminists. And those who think that it's acceptable in the privacy of their own bedrooms, where they enjoy it, where they get off on it–especially sexually–they're not lesbian feminists either. As Mary Daly has said, they're lesbians "from the waist down."

And to those who say, how dare we define what feminism means, I say–if we don't define what feminism means, what does feminism mean?

For years, we fought against the depiction of lesbians in hetero-pornography. We said, "that's not us in those poses of butch and femme role-playing. That's not the way we make love. That's not us treating each other as sadists or as masochists. That's not us bound by those chains, with those whips, and in those male fantasies of what women do with other women. That's a male wet dream of what a lesbian is and what lesbians do," we said. And we didn't only say it. We fought it. So now what happens. We have lesbian pornography appearing in U.S. "women's" porn mags such as "Bad Attitude" and "On Our Backs." And we have the FACT Brief. And all of this "feminist and lesbian literature" tells us that straight pornography, that heteropornography, is right. We are butches and femmes, we are sadists and masochists, and we do get off on doing violence to each other. We've come full circle–unfortunately back to the same negative starting point.

So I want to end by talking about a vision and a context for lesbian sexuality. For those who want how-to-do-it guidelines, this ending will be a great disappointment. I want to suggest what sexuality might look like rooted in lesbian imagination, not in the hetero-fantasies of lesbian pornography. This is a vision, a context, an endnote that is really a beginning.

This vision of sexuality includes the "ability to touch and be touched." But more, a touch that makes contact, as James Baldwin has phrased it. Andrea Dworkin, building on these words of Baldwin, writes about sexuality as the act, the point of connection, where touch makes contact if self-knowledge is present. It is also the act, the point of connection, where the inability of touch to make contact is revealed and where the results may be devastating. In sexuality, intimacy is always possible, as much as we say that sex is sex–that is, simple pleasure. In sexuality, a range of emotions about life get expressed, however casual or impersonal the intercourse–feelings of betrayal, rage, isolation, and bitterness as well as hope, joy, tenderness, love, and communion (Dworkin, 1987, pp. 47-61). All, although not all together, reside in this passion we call sexuality. Sexuality is where these emotions become accessible or anesthetized. A whole human life does not stand still in sex.

Libertarian and lesbian lifestylism simplifies the complexity of that whole human life that is present in the sex act. Abandoning that totality—that history, those feelings, those thoughts–allows for wildfire but not for passion. "All touch but no contact . . ." (Baldwin, 1962, p. 82).

Passion, of course, allows for love. Its possibility, not its inevitability. Passion is a passage between two people. Love is an extension of that passage. Passion can become love, but not without the openness to it. Sex as passion, and perhaps as love, not merely as wildfire is a radical experience of being and becoming, of excavating possibilities within the self surely, and within another perhaps, that have been unknown.

I began this talk by stating that, although the lesbian lifestylers talk about sex constantly, they are speechless about its connection to a whole human life, and, therefore, they are speechless about sex itself. The presence of a whole human life in the act of sexuality negates any reductionistic view of sex as good or bad, sheer pleasure or sheer perversion. Dworkin reminds us that when sex is getting even, when sex is hatred, when sex is utility, when sex is indifferent, then sex is the destroying of a human being, another person perhaps, assuredly one's self. Sex is a whole human life rooted in passion, in flesh. This whole human life is at stake always.

REFERENCES

Andrews, Lori. (1988). Feminist perspectives on reproductive technologies. In *Reproductive laws for the 1990's,* Briefing Handbook. Newark, NJ: Women's Rights Litigation Clinic, Rutgers Law School.

Baldwin, James. (1962). *Giovanni's room.* New York: The Dial Press.

Coveney, Lal, & Kaye, Leslie. (1987). A symposium of feminism, sexuality, and power. *Off our backs.* January.

Daly, Mary. (1984). *Pure lust: Elemental feminist philosophy.* Boston: Beacon Press.

Daly, Mary in cahoots with Jane Caputi. (1987). *Webster's First New Intergalactic Wickedary.* Boston: Beacon Press.

Diary of a Conference on Sexuality. (1981). Unpublished Notes of Original Diary Circulated Among Conference Planners for the 1982 Barnard Conference on The Scholar and the Feminist: Toward a Politics of Sexuality.

Dworkin, Andrea. (1987). *Intercourse.* New York: The Free Press.

FACT (Feminist Anti-Censorship Taskforce et al.). (1985). *Brief Amici Curiae,* No. 84-3147. In the U.S. Court of Appeals, 7th Circuit, Southern District of Indiana.

Jackson, Margaret. (1984). Sexology and the Universalization of Male Sexuality (from Ellis to Kinsey, and Masters and Johnson). In L. Coveney et al. (Eds.), *The sexuality papers.* London: Hutchinson & Co.

Kappeler, Susanne. (1986). *The pornography of representation.* Minneapolis: University of Minnesota Press.

Kurtz, Howard. (1985). Pornography Panel's Objectivity Disputed. *Washington Post.* October 15.

Meredith, Jesse. (1982). A response to Samois. In Robin Ruth Linden et al. (Eds.), *Against sadomasochism*. East Palo Alto, CA: Frog in the Well Press.

Snitow, Ann, Stansell, Christine, & Thompson, Sharon. (Eds.). (1983). Introduction. *Desire: The politics of sexuality*. London: Virago Press.

Superior Court of New Jersey. 1987. "In the Matter of Baby 'M'." Opinion. March 31: 1-121.

Willis, Ellen. (1983). Feminism, moralism, and pornography. In Ann Snitow, Christine Stansell, & Sharon Thompson (Eds.), *Desire: The politics of sexuality*. London: Virago Press.

*For Product Safety Concerns and Information please contact
our EU representative GPSR@taylorandfrancis.com Taylor & Francis
Verlag GmbH, Kaufingerstraße 24, 80331 München, Germany*

T - #0095 - 270225 - C0 - 212/152/16 - PB - 9781560230939 - Gloss Lamination